Winterfall

Lauren Rivers

Published by Iridescence Studios

Galveston, TX

Printed in the United States of America

First trade paperback edition

First Printing, July 2025

Cover by Red-Izak

ISBN:
ISBN-13: 978-0-9996170-2-1

DEDICATION

This book is dedicated to absent friends. Though you are no longer with us, you are never far from our hearts. Rabbitfangs and JBadger, we miss you.

CONTENTS

ACKNOWLEDGMENTS

This book would not be possible without the support of my partner, Shrag. Thanks for always being there when I need you. Appreciation also to Khaki, whose sage advice helped me find the balance that had eluded me for so long, as well as bringing me into a community where I could at last feel confident about developing my talents. Without that push to submit to the Voice of Dog, who knows if I would have ever found my way. Thanks also go to Solomon Harries, who provided much needed encouragement during the writing process, and Utunu who made this book better.

PROLOGUE

USS ABRAHAM LINCOLN
SOMEWHERE IN THE ATLANTIC OCEAN

Shivering in his survival jacket, a hyena sat huddled before his console on the bridge of the large Navy destroyer on which he served. The glow from the screen was about the only source of light besides his small lantern, which faded in the face of such brutal temperatures. With some effort he pulled a blanket around himself, steeled his body for what might very well be his final act, and spoke into the camera feed.

"This is Commander Alan Tucker of the USS Abraham Lincoln. I'm going to try to explain what happened so that there's some sort of record of the fate of my ship and crew. I don't know how much time I have left, but someone has to know.

"It's been six days since the ship became trapped here by the sudden formation of ice. It began as a sudden drop in temperature, enough that it almost seemed unnatural, as if someone had turned off the heat around us like a switch. Before I knew it the ship was freezing as hell. Turning the heat up helped for a little while but less than twenty four hours later the system was overwhelmed by the drop in temperature. We all bundled up as best we could, with the crew trying to stay warm while we searched for a way to escape the mysterious effect.

"We don't know what caused the incident, only that it came upon us suddenly and without warning. Some of the crew thought it was some government experiment. Others thought maybe the climate scientists just had it backwards. Whoever was right, it doesn't matter at this point.

"My captain attempted to return us to Norfolk but the rapidly decreasing temperature soon rendered that impossible. Before long every potential route back home was blocked by an increasing number of icebergs, and for four days the ship has been trapped in position from the frozen seawater. Despite our best efforts to maintain the ships systems the engines failed not long after and we have done everything possible to maintain life on board long enough to come up with a better option.

"By the third day of being stuck in the ice half the crew started suffering from hypothermia, and before long people started dying. The temperature all around us has fallen to critical levels. The oceans themselves have begun to ice over.

"Most of the crew is gone, frozen to death after we lost the primary reactor. I'm probably not far behind. My lungs are burning with every breath, and it's getting harder to move. The air itself feels like ice even through my layers. I've kept myself alive burning whatever I can find to buy myself a little more time hoping there's still someone out there that can find me.

"Just in case anyone discovers this log, know that my commanding officer Captain Joshua Clark did everything possible to safeguard the ship and its crew. He fought to his last breath to get us home, sacrificing himself in an attempt to keep his ship moving just a little longer. Know that if there is fault to be had it lies with us for failing him, not the captain himself.

"As far as attempts to contact home, the communications array went offline five days ago. Whether our distress call got out or not, I don't know. Even if it did, no one would be able to get to us in time. I've tried to contact the rest of the ship but my only answer so far has been silence. I'm beginning to wonder if anyone else on board survived at all.

"By the sixth day I was the only officer left. I'm honestly surprised I made it through the night. The temperature keeps dropping and unless a miracle happens I don't know what chance I have. If this is the end, my only regret is that I didn't get a chance to talk to my girl before I left port. I just wish I'd told her that I love her. I'm having a hard time staying awake. Maybe a little nap. Just a little one." He curled up into the blanket and closed his eyes.

CHAPTER ONE
STORM FRONT

46 YEARS LATER

Mornings always came too early for Joe's liking. With every sunrise it seemed to get harder to haul his bones out of bed, or maybe it was just the fact that it was the only time of the day he didn't feel the cold. With a grunt of protest, he unwillingly removed the covers feeling the chill that always pierced his fur every day when the morning bell went off. Searching for his robe, he wrapped it around himself before making his way down what could barely be called a hallway.

The Kennedy home was a small makeshift structure made mostly of metal welded onto a frame that blocked the wind but did little else. The only heat was primarily generated by the coal burning oven in the kitchen which radiated heat to the sleeping area when not cooking. The majority of the time it made the home just barely livable enough to sustain the family of four.

Rubbing his arms, he entered the combined kitchen and living room where his wife stood over the stove cooking a hearty breakfast. It was not much, especially for a full-grown polar bear, but such things were at a premium, as was just about everything else here in Coldhaven. Supplies were limited and nowhere was this more the case than with the daily rations. Few lower species had survived The Freeze, and what livestock they had managed to save was carefully overseen by the food production facility. Every morning each family would be required to send one member to pick up the prescribed allotment for the entire day, no exceptions. Failure to do so would result in your allocation being given out late at night to those seeking extra rations so as not to let it go to waste. As a result, Laura was always up in time to receive their share.

"Good morning," she said, kissing him as he came close. Her light blonde hair fell to her shoulders, covering the straps of her white apron. Wearing a heavy red sweater and thick pants, it suited her muscular frame well.

"That smells delicious," he replied, leaning in for a careful sniff. The smell filled the entire room with the tantalizing aroma of bacon and eggs. "You're spoiling us, Laura."

"I know, but it was our turn in the rotation for the good stuff and I wanted to cook them when we were all together. It's not often we get something more than the standard rations and I felt we should enjoy them, especially considering how hard you work." Laura smiled and flipped the eggs, being certain not to overcook anything.

The way the food ration system worked was that everyone got a turn with the premium items, but most of the time you got whatever they had. The law was very specific about what happened if you attempted to steal food, either from someone else or the food production facility. In general people obeyed the rules, if only so that when it was their turn, they could enjoy a little bit of the good life. Those who could not wait were often cut out of the premium items entirely with no mechanism to work their way back into the rotation. It was remarkably effective.

Stepping back to allow her to focus on the meal, he spotted his daughter sitting on the couch underneath a heavy blanket. Dressed in an olive shirt, dark pants, and a purple hat she pulled the covers around her to conserve heat. Thin for her age, Emily was young enough that she was not yet required to sign up for a work detail and was allowed to spend the day at home with her mother. Holding a small stuffed toy resembling a furless mammal save for the tiny bit at the top of its head, she brightened at the sight of her father. "Papa!" she shouted, her arms reaching out to embrace him.

He held her close for several moments, wrapping his large arms around her enough to encircle her entire body. "Good Morning, sweetheart!"

"Daddy, you're holding me too tight!" she cried, giggling all the while.

"Oh, am I? Perhaps you're just getting bigger." He smiled, taking a seat beside her.

"Momma says I'm an inch taller than I was last year," she proudly declared, her ears perking up higher.

"She does, does she?"

Laura turned her attention away from the cooking for a moment. "Yes indeed. I measured her yesterday. Go see for yourself."

He rose and walked towards the front door of their home to see the marks in the frame. The latest was just a little bit taller than the last with 'Emily' etched in the metal. "My little girl is getting so big now. Pretty soon she'll be big enough to take on her older brother! Where is Lucas, anyway?"

Laura shrugged. "He's out with his friends."

"This early?" he asked.

"He's a teenager. Who can predict their routines? He has a few hours before he needs to be in class. Let him enjoy himself. At least he's not loafing in bed like some husbands I know," Laura said.

"Oh really? Well, a certain wife doesn't seem to complain when I…," he began.

"Ah!" she said, interrupting.

Catching himself, he smiled at his daughter. "When I show mommy how much I love her."

"You guys are weird," Emily said.

"Weird, are we? Well, I'll have you know young lady that weirdness is the reason you and your brother exist. Did he say how long he'd be gone?" he asked, shaking his head.

Laura shrugged. "Who knows. He'll be back when he's back."

"He should be here, looking after his little sister and eating this wonderful bacon and eggs you've prepared," he said, gesturing at her work.

His wife could only throw up her paws in mock surrender as she sat at the small table. For any other species it would probably be considered standard, but for a family of polar bears it was downright insufficient. With just enough room for their plates it barely fulfilled the task of being a table. There was no room for serving dishes. If you wanted anything it had to sit on the counter. With some effort Emily slid off of the couch and walked unsteadily towards the table. Taking her seat, her eyes widened at the feast.

"It looks so wonderful!" she shouted.

"Inside voices, little one," Laura replied.

"I'm sorry, Mama," the young polar bear girl responded.

"We'll let it go, this time." She placed two eggs and two strips of bacon on her plate. "Be sure to eat it all. We don't know when we'll get more." Doing the same to the other two plates she put her son's portion in the oven to keep it warm. "Now eat up, both of you. I won't have my cooking going to waste. You understand?"

Joe held up his paws, taking the fork and purposely making a show of separating part of the egg whites and putting it in his mouth. He savored the taste, and partly out of pleasure and part out of a desire to tease his wife he moaned and took an exceptionally long time to chew his first bite of egg.

When she had clearly had enough, she smacked him on the chest with the back of her paw. "Don't play with your food."

"Sorry, love," he said, locking eyes with Emily as they both chuckled.

"And don't you two be ganging up on me. I know you're Daddy's little girl, but I can still spank you both." She menaced her husband with a fork. "Now eat."

Putting another forkful of egg into his mouth he recalled his mother telling him about her youth when there were shelves of these things everywhere. When she was a little cub, her father would take her to the market and they would buy all sorts of delicious foods to fill their bellies with and take them home to her mother. One would take pieces of paper which were not actually paper to places lined as far as the eye could see with so much food you could not eat it if you tried.

Being one of the first generations to be born after The Freeze, Joe had always had a hard time picturing the things his mother described in her stories. Motorized vehicles that ran on liquid dinosaur bones, buildings tall enough to pierce the sky, and flying machines capable of crossing the planet in hours all seemed like mere fantasy. Yet enough of the older folks told similar stories so he knew it was true.

The world he had grown up in was one of harsh survival. A cold wasteland where there was nothing else beyond the city's borders other than long abandoned ruins. The world had become a frozen graveyard, save for Coldhaven, the last functioning city on Earth. It was here that the previous generation had built the generator, which provided the bulk of their heat and power. It was by far the most dangerous place to work, but necessary for survival in this harsh climate. Running twenty-four hours a day, the massive machine burned coal sourced from the vast underground deposits beneath and around the city, which had been the reason this location had been chosen.

Taking a bite of his bacon, it was no exaggeration when he savored the flavor of his first muzzleful for a full minute before swallowing it. Fresh meat was rare in Coldhaven and so much of it was even more uncommon. Such luxuries were to be treasured. Emily had already eaten most of her breakfast, with only a small bite of egg left. Joe could not help but be glad to see she had regained her appetite enough to be so voracious. Smiling warmly, he indicated her plate with his fork. "Had enough, sweetie?" he asked.

"It was so good, I wish I had more," Emily said.

Her mother held up her fork. "Now, now, don't be greedy, you know there isn't any more."

"She's a growing girl, Laura." He moved a piece of bacon from his plate to his daughter's. The young polar bear lit up with joy as her father continued to eat his egg. Emily looked at her mother for permission as she shot a mild reproving glare at her husband. When he ignored her and continued to eat his egg, she nodded and Emily gleefully bit into the bacon.

Once he finished his breakfast, he rose to place his plate in the sink. As his wife walked past he felt a gentle brush on his arm fur, which he knew meant 'we need to talk'. It was a conversation he knew was coming but one he had hoped to delay as long as possible. He took his daughter's plate and deposited it in the basin while she herself walked slowly back over to the sofa to resume her previous position. Certain she was all right he followed his wife into their bedroom.

The space was just large enough to contain their bed and room for each to stand, and nothing else. Once he had entered, he had to turn in place to close the door behind him. With a deep breath he placed his back against the door and looked her in the eyes.

"I really wish you wouldn't do that," she said.

"It's just a piece of bacon, Laura."

"No, it isn't! You know they don't give us enough as it is." She frowned and sat on the bed. "Every time you give some more to Emily there's that much less for you and you still have to work a full day in the workshop."

"I know, but every time I see her smile it makes me forget about all this for a few minutes." He gestured around himself to the city as a whole. "I start to feel like how my mother must have felt before The Freeze, when every day wasn't a struggle to survive to the next. If I can give her a little more food in the process, then to me it's worth it." Joe reached out to hold his wife, joining her on the bed.

Laura looked away from him. "They're cutting the rations again."

"What?" he asked. "When?"

"Starting this Friday. They haven't announced it yet, but I've heard rumors from the other ladies. The scouting teams haven't found as much wildlife out there and the livestock we have aren't enough to support everyone by themselves. They just don't have enough land to raise them properly. What little they have barely sustains them enough to use them as food animals." She sighed. "And that's not all." Laura rose and walked to the small nightstand on the side of the table. Opening the drawer, she removed a small glass bottle with a medical label on it. "We're almost out of her medicine."

Joe sat up straight. "How much do we have left?"

"Maybe a few weeks' worth at the most. I've been stretching it out, giving her smaller doses where I can, but I can only stretch it so far. We need more," she said, placing it in his palm.

He held the small glass bottle in his paw, staring down at it and the precious clear liquid within. Most would not comprehend its value, to them it would be little more than something to be traded for booze or something else to make the days here a little easier, but to Joe and Laura Kennedy, it was the only thing keeping their youngest child alive.

As a young girl, Emily had caught an illness no one even remembered the name for. Before the cataclysm, treating it would have been simple, but in Coldhaven medicines were rare and their value immeasurable. Drugs capable of treating the sicknesses that infected the people here were worth more than practically any other resource. It had been a minor miracle that one of the scouting teams had returned with a fairly good supply of assorted drugs. Through his friendship with the local doctor, he had gotten enough to find one that treated his daughter's condition. After a few days, she had gotten better, strong enough to walk on her own.

But it would not last, it never did. After a few days of not taking it she would begin to weaken again, and her symptoms would return. With no cure, their only option was to continue to provide her with doses of the drug for as long as possible. To pay for this last bottle he had given the physician his wedding ring, a gift from his father when he married Laura. The bottle had lasted for several months, but with barely any of it left it would not hold out much longer.

"I'll talk to the doc after my shift," he promised. "Maybe I can get him to give me another supply."

"You have to get it, as much as you can," she begged. "Whatever it takes." Reaching around her neck, she removed her locket, containing pictures of her children and the only item of value the Kennedy family had left.

Unable to stand it any longer, he took her paws in his and pushed it gently back towards her. "No, I won't hear of it. I'll find a way."

"How?" she asked.

"I don't know," he replied, taking her into his arms. "But I can't stand the thought of you without that locket. Promise me you'll keep it right where it belongs."

Laura held it between her paws for a moment, cracking it open with the gentle placement of a claw. Looking at the smiling faces of her children she began to cry, tears soaking into her fur as she smiled at their joyful expressions. After a moment, she regained her composure and nodded. "Okay."

"Now give it to me and turn around." He took it from her and waited until she faced away from him with her hair held up by her paw. With a practiced skill he returned the locket to its proper place adorning her neck and smiled. "Beautiful as the day I married you." Wrapping his arms around her he planted a kiss on her cheek.

"You honey tongued teddy bear," she said, blushing at the compliment. "You should get ready for work or they'll reassign you to waste extraction."

Joe let out a deep sigh and released his wife from his embrace but not before planting one more kiss on her nose. He smiled and allowed her to slide past him to open the door. "Yes, dear." He pulled out his work clothes. Well-worn and deeply used, they did not insulate him from the cold as well as they once did, but they were comfortable and easy to move around in as well as fitting perfectly to his ursine frame. Pulling on his thick pants and warm shirt he tossed on a jacket and a black wool cap before emerging once more into the kitchen.

"All right, my love. I trust you can keep things running until I come back?" he asked.

"I'll do my best," she said. "Now say goodbye to Emily before you go."

Joe looked towards his daughter, and as soon as he saw her grin his face lit up with a bright smile. "It is going to be so hard focusing on work knowing I have these two beautiful women at home to look forward to. I'm counting on you to help your mother around the house. She's got a lot to take care of and she needs a smart helper to get everything done. Can you do that for me?" he asked.

"I promise I'll do my best, Papa." She held her doll super tight.

Looking at it, he made a funny face. "You sure you don't want a better toy? It looks like a hairless monkey."

Squeezing it even tighter she opened her muzzle in offense. "Papa! You'll hurt his feelings. Apologize right now."

"You're right, you're right, I'm sorry. He's very handsome. Whatever his name is," the elder bear said.

"His name is Andre, and he's an actuary. He helps people find deductions in their insurance plans," she declared proudly.

Standing up, he looked at his wife. "Who's been

teaching her words like that? I think she's reading too much of those fantasy books you have."

Putting her left fist on her hip she waggled a wooden spoon at him with the other. "They're history books, and I have to teach her something other than how to work at the factory. Now get to work before you're demoted."

"I love you too, dear," he said, saluting them both before pushing the door open. No matter what the temperature read, Coldhaven was always chilly. Perhaps that was to be expected in the world after The Freeze, but it always took him by surprise in those first few moments after leaving the house. Standing outside the small metal shack that was the Kennedy home, Joe turned to make certain the door was closed. Heat was a precious resource and not to be wasted, especially with his young daughter at home.

So focused was he on the task he almost did not notice his teenage son standing next to the door until he took his paw off the knob. "Lucas!" he shouted. Touching his paw to his chest he shook his head. "You're going to give me a heart attack." Taking stock of his presence he waited for his heart to slow to normal. "What are you doing standing around out here?" he asked.

The young polar bear offered a shrug. "I just needed some fresh air," he said. He tossed his wheat-colored hair in the wind, his thick jacket covering his sturdy torso.

"Fresh air is cold air. You should go inside where it's warmer." He gestured towards the door. When his son did not move, the elder polar bear tilted his head. "Your mother has bacon and eggs. You should eat them before they're overcooked." The mention of food preceded a growl from his young son's stomach, at which his father smiled. "Look, I have to go to work. Just promise me you won't stay out here too long?" he asked.

No sooner had he turned to leave than he felt his

son's paw on his arm. "Dad, can I ask you something?"

"Yes, but quickly, son. I only have a few moments." He turned to face him. "What's on your mind?"

"My birthday is in a few days." He said nothing more, but Joe already knew what was on his mind.

"I see," Joe replied. "You're worried about what assignment you might receive."

The younger polar bear nodded. "I don't want to leave school, Papa." He sighed. "I want to stay and learn and make my way into the engineering program, like you."

Every person in Coldhaven above the age of thirteen was required to perform some sort of function for the benefit of the city. If there were enough people to handle all of the essential tasks then the children were allowed to continue their schooling, but if not any openings would be filled with the eldest children. Given how many of the city's systems relied on people to keep them running, it was not uncommon to see more than a few teenagers pulled from their schooling to serve the greater needs of the population. This past season had been particularly hard with more than a dozen people succumbing to frostbite and other various injuries.

Hardest hit had been the furnace, which burned nonstop throughout the day. Holding a central location in the city, it kept the buildings warm and made life in the frozen wasteland possible in the first place. Without it, there would be no final surviving city and no chance for sentient life in general. Even those species acclimated to the cold would not be able to continue to exist without the refuge of the warmth of the city.

In an effort to reassure his son, he squeezed his shoulder gently. "Hey, don't worry, okay? Even if they assign you a work detail which there is no guarantee they will, you can still study. I will help you with your classes either way. We will get you into that program, I promise. Fair enough?"

His son nodded. "I trust you."

"Good. Now get inside before your bacon turns to charcoal." He nudged him towards the door. "And close the door quick, we don't want your sister getting sick."

"Okay, okay, I'm going." Lucas squeezed him for one more hug before disappearing inside the house. With a warmth that temporarily made him forget about the frozen wasteland beyond the city, he smiled and made his way to work.

*   *   *

The Workshop was the nickname for the maintenance and repair facility responsible for the city's continued operation. A fairly large building close to the central furnace, it was here where the most mechanically minded members of the population were typically assigned. One of the few areas with practically universal access, its mechanics were regularly tasked with jobs all over the city ranging from repairing heaters to keeping the city's primary systems operational.

Dispatched in teams of two they would receive their assignments at the beginning of the day from the foreman before moving on to their various tasks. Those not assigned to external functions worked on the service floor repairing any malfunctioning equipment brought in by the general population.

So important was this service that all of the engineers and mechanics were highly paid, being given a home and larger rations than the general population as a reward for their perpetual hard work.

Arriving just a few minutes early for his scheduled

shift, Joe entered through the main door into the lobby where his partner was already waiting for him. "Morning, Mike," he said with as much cheer as he could muster.

"Morning to you too," he replied, with a smile on his face. A king penguin, he was a few inches shorter than Joe. Wearing a matching coat and pants he completed the look with mitten style gloves to cover his avian hands. "I've already got our work assignments for the day. All you need to do is get your stuff and meet me out back."

"Sounds good. Just give me a minute to get my tools." He walked into the locker room where several mechanics were already dressed in their standard work clothes, getting ready to go out and do their part to keep the city running. Nodding to a few of them as he passed, he made his way to the back where his locker waited. Written on a piece of tape was his name, Joe Kennedy, affixed to the metal at eye level. Pulling it open, he removed his tool kit from the locker and laid it on the bench, inspecting his equipment before declaring it satisfactory and closing the door with his elbow.

Carrying them in his right paw he made his way out of the back of the Workshop where his partner waited with his hard hat under his arm. Handing Joe his own he tapped the headgear with his knuckles. "Safety first," his friend said.

He accepted it with a grateful smile. "I don't know what I'd do without you, Mike."

"Probably freeze to death trying to figure out which end of the wrench to hold," the penguin joked.

"Hey. I'm a better mechanic than you are, and don't you forget it." He pointed a finger at him for emphasis. "So, what have we got today?"

Looking at the clipboard, Mike cleared his throat. "To start, we've got a few faulty valves that need replacing, one heating unit in residence twenty-three that the residents can't bring in for service, and steam hub fourteen is malfunctioning again."

"You're kidding," he replied.

"Fraid not." He sighed. "See for yourself."

"I thought we fixed that thing two weeks ago," he said, taking the clipboard into his paws.

Mike shrugged. "We did, and the week before that, and two weeks before that. The problem is they're not willing to shut the equipment down any longer than absolutely necessary."

Joe rolled his eyes. "Don't they realize that if you don't shut the equipment down for regular maintenance and repairs, they're going to keep having problems like this?" he asked to no one in particular. "You need to shut these things down every week for at least a few hours to give them time to rest. This equipment was never designed to operate continuously like this."

"I know, but you try and tell three hundred people they're going to have to go without heat for a while. Instead of dealing with the complaints they'd rather just have us fix it every time it breaks," Mike said.

"Which is becoming more and more often, lately," Joe remarked. Handing the clipboard back he shook his head. "If they don't figure out something, they're going to have a bigger problem on their hands than a faulty steam hub."

Taking the clipboard back Mike nodded his agreement as the two walked out of the back area into the city at large. Designed and built around a single point, the massive furnace known in Coldhaven as The Candle burned coal twenty-four hours a day, putting out massive amounts of heat to combat the freezing temperatures that swept the planet's surface just outside the perimeter. Positioned in the middle of the central core, it allowed the heat to radiate equally in all directions keeping the center of the city as close to the world that was as they could get.

Most of the city's essential functions were placed here, closest to the heat source. Food, engineering functions, and government were all located within the nexus of the circular city. Roads extended outward from there like spokes in a wheel traveling all the way to the rim where a ring of lights marked the outer edge of the habitable area.

Just outside of the central core was the residential section, where most of the city's population lived, Joe included. The houses here were of modest construction, functional, if not spacious, and more than enough to house a family. Shops and what little businesses remained shared this ring both for the comparatively sufficient heat level as well as proximity to the general population.

Outside the residential area was the industrial ring, where most of the resource gathering and storage of essential materials was held. It was here where the massive machines that provided the city with coal were positioned, working daily to extract the precious material from the ground below to be processed and delivered to The Candle to keep the city's population alive another day. Those not fortunate enough to be housed in the residential area lived here in tents, with barrels burning whatever they could to supplement the minimal heat that made it out that far.

The last area was only habitable due to the supplemental steam hubs that were positioned throughout the city. Extending The Candle's reach to the edge of the crater, they allowed the heat to elevate the temperature of the outermost section to a survivable level. Most of the time they functioned with little need for maintenance but when problems did occur, they needed to be dealt with while they were still relatively minor. Since the task was the highest priority on their list, they made their way towards the outer ring.

Jobs out towards the edge of the city always made Joe grateful he was a polar bear. His thick fur added an extra layer of insulation some of the other species lacked. While the majority of those living in Coldhaven tended to be of species naturally inclined towards the cold, almost forty percent of them were species from other temperature zones. While he doubted there was anyone in the city who would call it comfortable, he did not know what he would do without the extra insulation.

Upon arrival it was immediately clear what the problem was. One of the components had broken causing an immediate shutdown. The temperature regulation system had burned out causing the steam hub to immediately route its load to other units in the system until it could be repaired. It was a common problem but one that despite its simple solution was getting harder and harder to implement. "It's the temperature control unit again," he said, indicating the damaged piece of equipment.

Mike frowned and wrote it down on the clipboard. "We can't keep replacing these things. We're going to run out of them pretty soon if this keeps happening." The penguin tapped his foot in frustration. "These units run half the systems in the city."

Joe frowned as he removed the faulty component. Holding it in his paw it did not seem like that much, but it represented perhaps the most valuable thing in Coldhaven. Heat. Without it the steam hubs could not warm the city, nor would The Candle continue to provide its life sustaining warmth. They lasted forever, provided they were run at their expected level of use. Given the harsh environment the engineers regularly pushed their equipment at far higher levels than the specs recommended. "At least it wasn't something more serious."

"Still, sooner or later this won't be a problem we can fix." Mike pulled a replacement from his tool kit and the steam hub once again thrummed to life, suddenly making the area around it that much warmer. Stepping away, Mike nodded his approval. "That's probably the only time of the day I feel too hot."

"I thought only ladies got hot flashes," Joe said, earning himself a smack from his partner. "Hey, Mike, have you heard anything from central?" he asked.

"Like what?" The penguin tilted his head curiously.

Joe looked around to be certain no one was near before he continued. "Laura heard a rumor that they're cutting the rations."

"I haven't heard anything about that," Mike said.

"You're sure?" he asked.

"As far as I know. Central doesn't share everything with us but they usually keep the engineers in the loop and to my knowledge I haven't heard anything about a reduction in rations." He shrugged.

"Maybe it's nothing," Joe said.

Mike picked up his tool kit. "Do you know where she heard it?" he asked.

"Not really, she just mentioned it when I was leaving the house this morning," he said. "I suppose it might just be people making the usual complaints but she's usually right about these sorts of things."

"Well, I'm not aware of anything along those lines but I tell you what, if I hear anything I promise I will let you know, okay?" he asked.

"Thanks, Mike," Joe replied. He looked at the display board. "Damn it."

"What?"

Joe pointed at the gauges. "Look for yourself." One

of the indicators had not gone up as it should have. Examining the readout, Joe shook his head. "One of the valves didn't open properly. It's still trying to route steam through the wrong junction. Hold on." Pulling out his maintenance manual, he traced the pipe on the schematic to its current output. "It's putting it out in an empty warehouse. This will just take a second."

Mike took the schematic and frowned. "It's underground. Let me do that, I'm smaller."

"Sorry, my friend, but this job requires muscle, and I've just got more of it." He flexed his arm and pulled the grate off the street level, looking up at the buildings the steam hub serviced, one of which was a tall foreboding rectangle holding Coldhaven's most problematic citizens. Dropping down into the tunnel, he tugged at his red scarf and made his way down to the nearest junction box.

Recalling the schematic, he gripped the wheel on the stubborn valve and turned it, redirecting the steam once more to the proper location. Satisfied, he climbed back out, replacing the grate with a grunt and a nod. "That ought to do it."

"Showoff." Mike smirked.

The rest of the day passed without much fanfare. Once their tasks were completed and the day was done, he bid Mike farewell before making his way to his next stop on his way home to see his family.

Doctor Reed's office was one of the few operating in the residential ring close to the border between it and the Nexus. It was just close enough to the primary heat zone that it still derived some benefit from the general proximity to The Candle. Most days the waiting area was about half full but today it seemed a little more crowded than usual. Consisting of a small rectangular area with a front desk and several chairs, he made his way up to the counter. "I need to see the doc."

"Do you have an appointment?" she asked.

"It's not for me, it's about my daughter," he replied.

"If you don't have an appointment you'll have to wait." She gestured towards the chairs.

"Please, I just need to speak to him for a moment," he said.

The blond koala shook her head. "I understand that, but as you can see the doctor has a lot of patients to see today and they were here first. Now if you'd like you can leave him a message, or I can put you in as a consultation and you can wait your turn."

Thinking of Emily, he nodded. "Okay." With a quiet sigh he turned around and scanned the waiting room for a place to sit. Examining the mismatched chairs, he found an empty one and sat down.

It was forty-five minutes before he was called back into the treatment area to speak with the red panda. Dressed in his white coat and beige shirt, the handsome physician had neatly arranged dark brown hair and glasses that sat upon his muzzle. The frames were thin and metal, a perk of his position as one of the skilled physicians in Coldhaven. "Chris," the polar bear said.

"Joe! How are you? I haven't seen you in a few weeks. Everything okay with Emily?" he asked.

"That's why I'm here," he said.

Holding his finger up for silence, he walked over to the door and closed it with his paw. The red panda turned around and looked at his ursine visitor. "Is everything okay? Has her condition worsened?" he asked.

Joe kept his gaze on the floor. "No, doc, but we're running out of medicine. She's only got a little left and we've been doing all we can to make it last, but she needs it or she's going to die," he said.

"I know, and I've given you all I can. You know that resources are limited, and I have to make sure there's enough of what we have for everyone," he said.

"They don't need it. I do." He gestured towards the shelves. "I know you have more. I don't have a lot to offer, but I'll give you what I can." He pulled out his toolkit and held it out for him to take.

"That's not the point," he said, holding up his paws. "You know that I take my job very seriously, and I have a responsibility of making sure that the next Joe Kennedy that comes in here can get the medicine he needs to keep his daughter alive." He looked into his eyes. "Do you think I enjoy telling people no?" he asked. "I have to make choices every day to save as many as possible, all the while answering to the government for every resource I use. If I give you what you're asking for then they'll demand answers."

"So we don't tell them," he said. "Chris, look, I know I'm asking a lot, but this is my little girl here. If we don't do something she's going to get sicker and she won't make it through the year." The polar bear leaned against one of the cabinets. "I'm sorry. I know it's not fair. But I don't care about some hypothetical case that may or may not happen. My daughter is sick and she needs this medicine now." He threw up his paws in frustration. "There's got to be something you can do."

Doctor Reed stared at him for a few moments and then cursed. Getting up, he opened one of the cabinets and removed two small glass bottles. One of which was empty and the other containing the lifesaving medication that kept Emily alive a little while longer. He removed a syringe from the drawer and used it to fill the second with the same level of water. Handing him the first bottle he held his paw in his own. "Joe, I'm putting both of our lives on the line with this. If anyone finds out that that stuff is missing, I can't help you anymore."

"Thank you, Chris," he replied.

The red panda picked up the second bottle. "This will keep them from asking questions for a little while, but it's going to have to be replaced eventually. And as you know it's not exactly easy to come by." He replaced it in the cabinet and closed the door. "With any luck no one will come in needing any but if they do...," he started.

"If they do I promise I'll take full responsibility," Joe said.

"I appreciate the thought but if they find out I gave that to you I doubt it'll matter. You know the rules, and you know what'll happen if we get caught," he said.

Joe looked at the precious bottle, gripping it carefully in his paw. "Then why give it to me in the first place?"

"Because I'm a doctor, and if I can keep one more person from dying for another few days then it's worth it. It may not matter in the long run but if I have to go to my grave for something like this, I'd rather it be because I chose to help rather than the alternative." Joe embraced the red panda gratefully before placing the bottle in his pocket and making his way out of the office.

He walked the short distance towards his home in the light of the city's streetlamps. Examining the bottle in his paw he frowned. There was practically nothing there, just enough to buy him a few days, even with his wife rationing out the supply. For this he had convinced the doctor to leverage his entire career against the hope that he could find more before the subterfuge was discovered. It was a temporary solution at best, but it bought him precious time needed to figure out a way to keep Emily alive, and for that he would do anything, including give his life to keep her warm and safe a few days longer.

Returning home, his wife and daughter were eating

dinner in the kitchen while his son could be seen in their bedroom studying for his classes. Standing in the doorway, he made every effort to burn the image into his memory, fearful that it would not last for long.

His wife looked up and gestured for him to come inside. "Close the door before all the heat gets out."

He obliged, quickly entering and shutting the door behind him, removing his jacket and hanging it on the hook. "Sorry I'm late," he said, exchanging a knowing glance with Laura.

"I kept some soup warm for you, it's there on the stove," she said, a bowl already waiting for him at his spot on the table. Walking around the table, he squeezed her shoulder as he passed, picking up his bowl and pouring the soup into it. It was warm and delicious tomato basil soup, one of the more popular varieties given its comparative simplicity to produce due to the limited ingredients. He inhaled the aroma letting it fill his nostrils with the wonderful smell while the warmth suffused through his paws. Carrying it to the table, he ate a few spoonfuls, feeling the pleasant sensation of the soup heating him gradually from the inside.

"How was work today, Papa?" Emily asked, bright and cheerful.

"Work was good, sweetheart. Daddy and Uncle Mike went all over the city fixing anything that needed fixing." He looked at her doll. "And how was Andre, did he find lots of deductions for his clients?"

"Daddy, he can't tell you that. He's subject to confident... Confident...," she began.

"Confidentiality," he finished for her.

"That's right," she said. "He can't discuss his clients, it'd be unprofessional."

After sharing a look with his wife, she smirked. "Eat your soup."

Joe finished the small bowl far faster than he would have liked. Even taking his time the rations were barely enough to fill his stomach. It kept him and his family fed but they were never quite sufficient to make him forget about the constant struggle to keep the city running. Every day they would fight to survive and every day they would stave off freezing for one more sunrise.

For forty-six years Coldhaven had waged this constant battle against the harsh and unforgiving environment just outside the perimeter of the city, and in all of that time the city had never suffered a catastrophic systems failure. According to the powers that be there were multiple redundancies built into all the critical systems to prevent any such occurrence, but a part of Joe wondered just how close to constant frozen Armageddon they truly were.

Maybe nothing he did mattered, but as long as he had Emily, Lucas, and Laura, he would fight like hell to buy them every second he could. Smiling at his precious little girl he felt his wife's paw on his shoulder as she took his empty bowl. Always her subtle signal she wanted to talk, he knew it must have taken every ounce of her self-control to keep from pouncing on him the moment he got home for news of his daughter's medicine. Even though the entire family knew she was ill, Joe and Laura did all they could to shield their children from the worst of it. Such things were for adults to worry about, not for a teenage boy and a young girl.

Rising, he gave Emily a kiss on the cheek and squeezed his son's shoulder with a muscular paw before holding a digit in front of his muzzle for silence. Following his wife into the bedroom he closed the door behind him.

Moving close to him, she pressed up into his arms. "Please tell me you got it."

"I got some. Not much, but he gave me all he could spare." He reached into his pocket and presented the small bottle.

Three quarters empty, she shook the clear liquid as if that would somehow produce more within the tiny container. "This isn't enough," she said. "Not nearly enough."

"It's all I could get," he said. "The doc switched it with another bottle, but I have to replace it eventually or we'll both be brought up on charges."

Laura pressed her head against his chest. "What are we going to do? This won't last more than a few days. Maybe a week if I stretch it. Then we'll be right back where we started."

"I don't know. It was risky even getting us that much. But it does buy us time," he said.

"To do what?" she asked. "What can we do in a week?" she asked.

"I'm working on that." He sighed, squeezing her free paw gently as she held the precious bottle. "In the meantime, you give her that and don't tell her anything's wrong. I'll figure something out. I've got no idea where I'm going to find more of that stuff, but I swear to you I will not let our daughter die."

Laura nodded, taking the bottle and holding it close to her chest. Turning around, she placed it inside the nightstand where she kept the rest of the medicine and composed herself. Once she was calm once more, she kissed him. "We'd better go back before the kids start to worry."

Joe gave her one last squeeze before opening the door and coming back out. "I don't want you kids staying up too late tonight, okay? You need your rest, and so do I."

"Yes, Daddy." Emily smiled, hugging her plush toy. Seeing his wistful smile, she looked at him with those pure innocent eyes. "Is everything okay, Papa?"

Shaking his head to hide the fear resting just beneath

the surface, he smiled. "Everything's fine, kiddo."

CHAPTER TWO
THANK YOU FOR YOUR LOYALTY

Announcements were rare in Coldhaven. News was typically relayed through word of mouth with information gradually making its way through the population in bits and pieces. The only time mass gatherings were assembled was when it was something significant. Whispers had spread for several days as to the purpose of this meeting, with attendance being mandatory for everyone regardless of their position.

This meant a significant amount of coordination, as most of the city's systems had to be put on automatic, and those that could not be set to run by themselves required their operators to listen on the few functional radios that still existed for the city's use. Rarely did the entire population gather together in one place for anything.

While most days the bitter cold kept people from gathering outside in any significant amount, the large number of furred bodies warmed the air enough that it was tolerable. Clustered around The Candle, it was the one open space large enough to accommodate this many people.

Joe made his way towards the massive heat source with his family in tow. Keeping Emily in his arms both reassured him that he would not lose her in the crowd as well as allowing them to share their warmth for the time she was outside. Holding her close he looked at his wife as they found a spot out of the way of the ever increasing collection of the city's inhabitants.

"This should do, don't you think?" he asked Laura, his breath visible in the frigid air.

With a bit of a frown she said, "It's going to be bad news, I just know it." Wrapping her scarf around her neck a little tighter she looked back at her husband before checking to make sure their son was still beside them. Satisfied, she rubbed her paws together to warm them up.

"Maybe the scouting teams have found something," he said. "There were rumors of other survivors out there. Maybe even another settlement."

"After all this time?" Her ears flattened. "There's nothing out there. We're the last city on Earth. None of the scout teams have ever found anything other than ruins and remnants of the old world."

Giving her a lick on the cheek he chuckled. "You'd better be careful, or the kids are going to think you're a pessimist."

"Hey, I consider myself to be realistic. You show me the scouting team that comes back with something other than leftovers from the world before The Freeze and then we can talk. Until then I don't see the point in idle speculation." Laura gave her husband a smirk before turning her head towards the raised catwalk extending around The Candle, often used as a makeshift podium.

Joe chuckled to himself and nodded his surrender. "Fair enough." Even though she had a point, he could not bring himself to consider the possibility that nothing survived beyond the confines of Coldhaven. Despite the fact that all evidence tended to side with Laura's assessment, somewhere out there had to be something that survived the deadly cataclysm that covered the surface of the planet in a thick sheet of permanent ice.

Being the first generation to grow up in the frozen city, Joe and Laura had never seen the world before the cold. All they had were pictures and stories from those who had experienced it, and his children would have even less than that. In a few generations, people might not even remember there had been a world before all this.

Giving his daughter another squeeze he looked up as his coworker emerged from the latest group of arrivals. "Mike!"

"Joe!" The king penguin waved as he approached, his webbed feet making distinctive marks in the snow. "Have you been here long?" he asked.

"Not long." Joe embraced his friend in a bear hug. "Just got here with the family a few minutes ago. Lisa's not coming?"

Mike shook his head. "She couldn't get away. Being one of the few people in the main kitchen who knows how to make something edible they thought they should keep her on duty. They gave her a radio so she'll be listening along with the rest of us."

"Too bad, I was hoping to say hello to her." Laura blew into her cupped hands to heat them up.

"I'll be sure to pass it along," Mike replied.

Joe looked up at the still empty catwalk. "Do you have any idea what this is about?"

"Not a clue," he replied. "No one seems to know a

thing." Mike rubbed his webbed hands together to generate warmth.

"I hope it's not another extended shift. I'd hate to have to work a double again," Joe said, not really expecting a response.

Mike smirked. "Well, you know what they say if you have issues with your schedule."

"Shut up and get back to work?" he asked.

"Exactly."

The two coworkers enjoyed the momentary amusement at their mutual expense before Laura touched him on the shoulder. "Hey, it's starting."

The crowd continued to murmur as the procession of government officials began to make its way through the raised passage on the upper level to the catwalk. Led by Governor Natalie Cole, they walked towards the section usually reserved for public addresses. Along with a few lights for whenever this was done during the night, they had also installed a microphone so she could be heard evenly throughout the central nexus.

A tall vixen with well-kept fur, she was dressed in a heavy coat with thick lining along with a matching set of gloves. The picture of dignity and poise, her tail waved back and forth in slow loping rhythms as she walked. Silver haired, it was more a trait of her particular breed of vulpine rather than an indicator of age as with most such members of her species.

Taking her place at the head of the assembly, the arctic fox vixen waited a moment before raising her arms to gather the attention of the crowd. Every single creature in attendance fell silent as she prepared to speak. Lowering her paws to her sides, she began. "My fellow citizens, it is good to see you all today. As I stand here before you, I am pleased to see you all in such high spirits."

A fairly generic opening, Joe looked up at the woman who held control over most of the major resources in Coldhaven. Though she was generally considered to be a strong and reasonable leader, she was capable of making life very difficult for people like Joe. Able to set work limits, resource allocation, and even potentially population control, she along with everyone else that had held the position previously had been given broad discretion to ensure the survival of the city.

Considered to be a top priority, it was not unheard of for governors to make unpopular decisions to preserve the collective well-being of the city's inhabitants. While it had never come close to outright insurrection, from time to time there had been riots when it was believed the government had gone too far. Fortunately for all concerned these were few and far between, but it was not beyond the realm of possibility. As Joe continued to listen, he held his wife and daughter that much tighter.

"For forty-six years we have fought back the cold. The Candle continues to burn, providing life giving warmth to you and your families. Every day we work to make sure that your homes are heated and your bellies are full," she said.

Here it comes.

"That is why I regret to inform you that for the next few weeks rations will be reduced by ten percent." She waited as the inevitable unhappy reaction rippled through the crowd. Most were accepting of the reduction if not enthusiastic, but a few could not keep themselves from voicing their anger.

"How am I supposed to feed my family on that? You don't give us enough as it is!" a German shepherd shouted.

"There haven't been enough eggs lately!" another added.

After a few more shouted comments, Governor Cole

gave a gracious nod. "And this is why we must reduce rations for the short term. Although we continue to work on ways to increase the food supply, in order to do that we must ease the demands on our resources in order to give us the time to stockpile essential foodstuffs. I assure you that these reductions are temporary and full rations will be restored as soon as possible. In addition, I have authorized the creation of two additional scouting teams as soon as they can be staffed. Our expeditions have discovered a few potential locations of untapped resources we may be able to reach within the next few weeks." Taking a deep breath, she waited for the crowd to calm. "Rest assured every step is being taken to make sure this lasts as briefly as possible. That is all. Thank you for your loyalty." With a bow, she turned and left as quickly as she had come.

"Well, doesn't that just freeze my fire," Mike said, kicking the snow at his feet.

"Mike," Joe began, attempting to calm his friend.

"No, Joe, I can't afford a reduction in rations. Lisa and I barely get enough to keep us fed as it is, and unlike you I don't get a little extra because of the family bonus." Distraught, he stared angrily at the empty catwalk. "What do they expect us to do?"

Joe reached into his pocket and handed him a small loaf of corn bread. "Here. It's not much, but they gave it to me at this morning's rations and I want you to have it. It was probably to placate us for the upcoming reductions."

Mike, suddenly looking very guilty over his outburst, attempted to push it back towards him. "No, I couldn't do that."

"Mike, please. We've been friends for years. We'll be fine without it, but you and Lisa need it. Take it and share it with your wife." He smiled and once again offered the small wrapped cornbread.

Taking it in his webbed hands the penguin slipped it in his pocket. "Thank you."

"You'd do the same," he replied.

Laura leaned in and kissed him. "You're a good animal, Joe Kennedy." She smiled, pressing close to her husband and nuzzling his cheek.

Emily giggled. "You guys, everyone will see!"

Joe laughed and kissed her on the nose. "Then everyone will also see how much I love my baby girl."

"Papa!" she protested, and with an exaggerated smile he handed her to his wife.

"Okay, sweetie, Daddy will stop." He held her paw.

"Are we going to be okay?" she asked.

After looking at each other, Joe nodded. "We'll be okay, sweetheart. We've been through things like this plenty of times before. We'll find a way around it. We always have. Isn't that right, Lucas?" He turned just in time to see his son was nowhere to be found. "Lucas?"

"Where did he go?" Laura asked. "Mike, do you see him anywhere?"

The king penguin shook his head. "In this crowd?" He looked at Joe and shrugged helplessly. "I can't see anything."

Joe frowned. "Laura, you take Emily home. I'll find Lucas, okay?"

"I…." She hesitated, holding their daughter tight as she looked around desperately for her son.

"He's probably just upset and needed to blow off some steam. He can't have gone far. Now I need you to look after Emily while I do that, so go straight home in case he goes there. One of us should be at the house and our little girl shouldn't be out in this cold any longer than necessary," he said, holding her and looking into her eyes.

Nodding, Laura started to walk in the direction of

their house. After a few steps, she stopped and spoke over her shoulder. "You bring our son home."

"I will," Joe replied. "I promise."

Mike waited until she was gone, then turned to Joe and asked, "You need any help?"

"No, I should be all right. I think I know where he's going. You go home to your wife," he replied, bidding his friend farewell. Following the flow of traffic as the city's population dispersed he began to trace his son's likely path. It would be some time before everyone got where they were supposed to be, but knowing his son would want to be alone he would try to find someplace out of the way. Most likely he'd hide some distance from the central nexus, far from all the people.

Once he had gotten to the residential ring and the population was more spread out, he stepped off to the side and looked around. There were no maps or signage in Coldhaven, just numbers indicating zones which after you lived here long enough you knew how to read. Joe scanned the intersection he had just reached and paused.

Lucas would have used the first exit out of the nexus. That meant he had probably headed south. Walking in that direction, the polar bear made his way to the likely route his teenage son would have taken after slipping away unnoticed. Stopping there, he pictured the layout of the circular city in his head. There were still too many people around.

The residential ring was fairly uniform, but once you reached the industrial ring things were a bit more unpredictable in their layout. The somewhat haphazard construction of the city's facilities, done at a time when survival was more important than aesthetics, meant that the outer section of Coldhaven did not follow any particular pattern in order to accommodate the large industrial facilities needed to run the city. This resulted in streets of inconsistent length interlaced between large structures that towered over the neighboring buildings.

While in general the children were instructed to stay away from these areas without their parents, most of the city's inhabitants knew the children liked to sneak away to play from time to time. For the most part it was harmless and as a result security tended to look the other way, the exception being when one of the kids was attempting to destroy property. As long as you weren't doing anything you weren't supposed to, they left you alone.

The architecture took on a significant shift as the shorter residential buildings gave way to large factories and other facilities designed to operate and maintain the city. While the central nexus housed everything needed to keep the city running, the industrial district was where raw materials were refined and surpluses stored for use in lean times like they one they appeared to be approaching now. An additional benefit was that the taller buildings in the industrial district helped to block some of the wind from making it into the residential area, and at the same time reflecting some of the heat from The Candle back to the center of the city.

It was not much, but in a world where everything outside was a huge sheet of ice he would take what he could get.

Catching a whiff of his son's scent, he recognized the small warehouse. The door was never locked as it had not been in use for months. Opening it gently he peeked his head inside. Always equipped with a flashlight he reached into his pocket and turned it on, making his way into the building. Shining the beam around, he found his son sitting on a wooden box that had been left behind from the last time this place had anything in it.

"There you are," he said. "I was looking for you."

Lucas looked up at him. "How did you find me?"

"I was a teenage boy once." Turning the flashlight off he waited a moment for his eyes to adjust to the lower light level. "I thought you might come here."

The younger polar bear let out a deep breath. "I needed to think."

"Are you still worried about the work detail?"

"It's not just that."

Joe sat beside his son. "Well, then what is it?" He nudged him gently. "Talk to me, son. I'm your dad. I love you."

"I know you do, and it's not you and Mom. You guys are great. It's just that I wonder what's left for Emily and me?" he asked.

"I don't understand." Joe wrapped his arm around the younger ursine's shoulders. "You mean the future?"

Lucas nodded. "No matter what, I'll have to get a work detail eventually. I accept that, just like I accept the fact that we'll have to deal with reduced rations sometimes. But what are we doing it all for?" he asked. "I mean, when you and Mom can't work anymore then they'll have folks like Emily and me take your place, but even if I love my job is that all I have to look forward to?" he asked. "Working every day until I can't anymore?" he sighed. "I know we all have to do our part. I just wish there was something more than just this."

Letting out a deep breath, Joe pulled his son closer. "I know the feeling. Your mom and I used to wonder the same things when we were your age."

"I don't want to sound ungrateful. I'm glad that we have a place to sleep and food to keep us going even if it's never quite enough," Lucas responded.

"I know." He looked at his son. "Trust me. You're not the first person to wonder if this is all there is.

Sometimes I used to wish they'd find something out there to indicate that we're not the only living creatures left on the planet. I don't know if it's loneliness or lack of surprises or something else entirely but I think we're hard wired to be curious. It's why some of the balloon teams keep going out there, because they want to go somewhere else, see something they haven't seen before." He sighed. "I wish I could tell you that there's more to your future than a work detail and a home, but if I did I'd just be lying to you. The reality is that this is the life we've been given, and any choices we might've had were taken away a long time ago. All we can do is keep going and hope that maybe one day we'll find out what it's all for."

Lucas nodded, rising to stand. "Does it get easier?"

"It does." He smiled. "For a long time I felt just like you did. Angry at the world, wondering why The Freeze had to take away any chance my generation had for the future. But you know what helped?"

"What?"

Joe stood and hugged his son. "You and your mom. I don't know what I'd do without you three. You and Emily make going out that door every morning worth it. Because I get to do it knowing I'm coming home to all of you." Gesturing towards the door with his paw, he shrugged. "So how about you and I head on home? Your mom is pretty worried about you."

Lucas swallowed. "She's going to kill me."

"I think this time you'll get a pass, though you may have to suffer some kisses from Mom when you walk in the door." Giving him a gentle slap on the back, he laughed. "Now let's get going before she sends the search parties after us."

"Okay, Dad."

Once they were outside, he closed the door and

followed his son as they made their way across the street. "I hope our talk helped."

Lucas nodded. "You know, I think it did."

"Good."

As they made their way back towards the residential ring and the part of the city they called home, Joe noticed his son's attitude already seemed to have improved. Walking faster and with little hesitation, he seemed to be calmer and more at ease. While he knew better than to assume the problem was resolved, at least for now it was no longer pressing quite so hard on his son's mind.

Turning on to the next street he was surprised to see the governor and her entourage taking an unscheduled tour of the residential ring. It was unusual to see her anywhere other than the central nexus given how much of her focus was spent on keeping the city running. She appeared to be speaking with one of her aides as she moved from one building to the next. The fur on the back of his neck rose sharply.

Sensing his discomfort, his son looked up at him. "What's wrong, Dad?" he asked.

"Nothing, just keep walking." He put his arm on his son's shoulder and they resumed making their way down this side of the street. He kept his attention forward as they approached the governor's entourage. He wanted to take an alternate route home, but he knew actively avoiding the government or its representatives could be viewed as a threat to the city.

While he had no way of knowing for what reason the governor was touring the residential area, he did not like the few possibilities that presented themselves. Although it was not unheard of for her to take morale boosting trips around the city this was usually done with much more fanfare. The dour expressions on most of her staff led him to believe that her reason was far more concerning. He gave her aide a nod of respect as they walked past.

Turning, the governor looked at the polar bears. "Pardon me," she said.

"Governor Cole," he said, with a nod of proper respect.

Scrutinizing him, she paused a moment. "Joseph Kennedy, with the maintenance team. Isn't that correct?"

"Yes, ma'am." Joe kept his gaze down but soft.

The arctic fox vixen stepped over to look at his son. "And this must be Lucas."

"I am," he replied. "My father speaks very highly of you. He says you've done a wonderful job keeping the city running."

She brightened at the compliment. "And I appreciate your service, Mister Kennedy. Your son is quite the bright young man."

"He takes after his mother." Joe smiled, giving his son a genuine look of affection.

Governor Cole nodded. "I can see that he does. How old are you, Lucas?" she asked.

"Thirteen, ma'am." He straightened up when giving his answer, something Joe noticed out of the corner of his eye.

Looking at her aide, the arctic vixen nodded. "I believe he was on the list, was he not?"

The aide reviewed the information at his fingertips and nodded. "Yes, ma'am, he was on the list for assignment to a work duty."

Joe froze. He had known it would be coming, but he did not think it would happen so soon. Parents were given no say in what work duty their children were assigned, nor could the children themselves refuse the order. In theory this was to keep it fair so that everyone was offered the same requirements, but with few exceptions the tasks assigned were nonnegotiable.

"Might I be permitted to take my son home before my shift?" he asked. "My wife has been very worried about him." He knew it would only delay the inevitable, but he hoped he could buy his son at least one more day before he would be forced to take his place in maintaining the city.

"We do have a rather busy schedule today, ma'am," the aide said, offering Joe a glimmer of hope.

Governor Cole looked at him and then at Lucas, before shaking her head. "Under the circumstances I'll permit you to be late for your shift. As you know we've been suffering a significant decrease in efficiency lately due to a number of recent vacancies and we need to make up the shortfall if we're going to keep The Candle burning." She sized Lucas up, looking at his body as if evaluating a piece of livestock. Polar bears were naturally strong and well built, easily able to handle some of the most brutal jobs in the city. While this would not have bothered Joe were it his own assignment, he had hoped to provide better for his son.

The aide offered a shrug as he handed her the clipboard. "The assignments, ma'am."

After reviewing the information for less than a minute, she nodded. "Very well, then. Starting tomorrow you, young Lucas, are assigned to The Candle's burn team. You'll report there tomorrow instead of your regular classes. Your father can instruct you how to dress and your supervisor will be expecting you. It's not a complicated job but it is essential to our city's operation."

Joe could not speak at first. Struggling to command his voice he at least managed to verbalize her title. "Governor," he said.

"Yes?"

He summoned all of his inner strength to speak to

her in a calm and rational voice. "Would it be possible to convince you to place my son on the maintenance team? Mike and I have been overworked lately and we could use an extra set of paws."

Hesitating a moment, she shook her head. "I'm afraid that won't be possible. We have no openings on the maintenance team. Unfortunately, we are suffering a shortage of new workers in almost every area and I cannot spare anyone from any section without a pressing immediate need."

"I understand," he said, defeated.

"Now I assure you he will be well trained and taken care of." Looking at Lucas, she continued. "I'm sorry to take you away from your classmates, but Coldhaven needs good workers and I need everyone pulling their weight. This city only works because everyone does their part to make sure we have a warm place to sleep and food in our bellies. I know it'll take some getting used to, but rest assured your contribution will be greatly appreciated." She turned to her aide once again. "See to it that his transfer is logged and his rations increased accordingly."

"Yes, ma'am." He nodded and wrote a note on the clipboard.

"Do you understand your new assignment?"

Lucas nodded weakly. "Yes," he replied.

"Excellent," she said. "They'll be happy to have you, I'm sure. If you're not certain where to go I'm confident your father can show you the way."

"Of course, Governor."

With a nod, she motioned for her entourage to resume their walk, her tail waving softly as they disappeared. No doubt they were seeking any children of the appropriate age to fill the gaps suffered from recent losses in the workforce. The harsh environment always tested the inhabitants of the last city on Earth, and many could not withstand it long enough to reach the day when they would no longer be needed. Those that did simply did not stop working out of concern the commensurate reduction in their rations would lead to an early death. So, for a few more ounces of food per day, they would keep working well beyond their limitations.

It was harsh, but when your very survival was at stake, there were few other options. Both of Joe's parents had died in the service of Coldhaven, doing their part to keep the city running. But while every job presented its share of dangers, nowhere was this truer than The Candle. The most visible structure in the entire city, it was this massive facility that ensured heat would reach every corner of Coldhaven and keep her people alive.

But the price it exacted for this life-giving warmth was measured in not only the amount of coal burned every day to hold back the cold, but in lives sacrificed to its operation. More workers died in the performance of their duties in The Candle than any other facility, with the overwhelming heat and aging machinery punishing those that kept it functional.

Requiring little skill to fill the machine with coal, it was also the most common tasks assigned to young people reaching the age of labor. During most years it was sufficiently staffed that most of the children were assigned to fill other vacancies, but every year at least a few of them were sent to pick up a shovel and fill the massive furnace with the fuel it demanded in order to run.

The average life expectancy of a candle worker was ten years. To most, being assigned to The Candle was almost a guarantee one would never see old age.

With a gentle squeeze on his son's shoulder, he looked down at the young polar bear and urged him forward.

Neither of them spoke until they reached the outside of the Kennedy family home, where Joe placed his paw on the handle but did not move to turn it.

Looking at his son, he smiled. "Son, for tonight I want you to just take care of your sister, okay?" he asked. "I'll tell your mom."

Lucas simply nodded.

Opening the door, Joe came inside, putting on his best poker face for his wife and daughter. "Hey, sweet pea. How's Daddy's little angel?" he asked, leaning down to kiss her on the cheek.

"I'm feeling stronger again, Daddy. It must be all the extra hugs Mommy gave me today," Emily said, proudly standing in front of the couch.

Laura smiled. "Yes, well, I had to give her extra since her brother wasn't here." She walked over and kissed him on the cheek. "Where have you been?"

Joe touched Laura on the shoulder, guiding her towards the bedroom. "Let the boy be, he's got to get ready for class." Putting on his best fake smile, he gave his son a supportive nod before making his way into the bedroom.

Turning around to close the door, he stared down at his paws for several long moments before facing Laura. "What's wrong?" she asked. When he did not answer, she pressed harder. "I know that look. Joseph Kennedy, you tell me what's wrong right now."

Joe opened his mouth as if to speak, but then closed it again. Sitting on the bed, he motioned for her to join him. "Please sit."

"Not until you tell me what's going on," she said.

With no choice but to tell her the truth, he sighed. "We ran into the governor today. She was recruiting young people to fill vacancies and she gave our son an assignment. Starting tomorrow he is to report to The Candle's burn team."

Covering her mouth with her paw, she fell to her knees as if she had been struck. Overwhelmed by her greatest fear, she started crying. "There has to be something we can do."

"I already tried to get him reassigned, she said there are too many vacancies to allow him to be moved," he said.

"Then try again," she insisted. "My son cannot work in that place." She shook her head. "I will not allow it."

"You know he can't refuse a work assignment." Failure to report to one's shift resulted in immediate cancellation of all of one's rations until the offender reported for duty. Repeated violations resulted in arrest and reduction of supplies for anyone in the person's family.

Furious with the futility of the situation, Laura swore into her paws. "Sometimes I wish we had never brought our children into this horrible world."

Wrapping his arms around his wife he looked her in the eyes. "Don't say that. Not ever. I love our daughter more than life itself, and you know I would give anything if it would get Lucas out of that place."

"We can't leave him there," she said.

"I know," he replied, holding her close. "I'll think of something."

"What?" she asked. "What could you possibly do to get our son away from that awful place?"

"I don't know," he said. "But I swear to you he will not die in that blasted furnace. I won't allow it."

Laura rose to a standing position. "I believe you."

Joe kissed her, pressing their muzzles together as he considered how he would keep his promise. Transfers from The Candle were not unheard of, but they happened so rarely it was almost a myth. The only way most people left The Candle was in a box, or charred beyond recognition. Few ever made it past their first decade in its service. "I promise, our son will be okay. He's strong, stronger than me. I'll see to it they take care of him."

Nodding, she moved past him to the door. "I don't want Emily to know."

"All right," he said.

Returning to the kitchen, Laura gave her son a kiss before starting breakfast. They would have just enough time to share a morning meal before he had to report for duty and Lucas would go to class for the last time. As his son offered to help his mother, Joe sat down beside Emily. Still holding her plush doll, she looked up at him. "Papa, is everything okay?"

"Yeah, sweetheart, why do you ask?" He did his best to keep his expression as neutral as possible, wanting to shield her from as much of the harshness of reality as he could.

"Everyone seems quiet this morning," she replied.

"It's okay, sweetheart. I think everyone's just upset about the governor's announcement, that's all," Joe lied.

Emily held her toy close, looking up at him. "You can have my rations if it'll help. Andre's too."

Joe smiled. "No, sweetie. You don't worry about a thing. I promise. We'll be okay." As Emily smiled back with that sweet smile only she could do, Joe wished more than anything that the words he spoke were the truth. Yet as he watched his family, he realized that for the first time in his life he had no idea how to keep his promises. Doing his best to project strength, he stroked his daughter's hair, wanting nothing more than to stave off tomorrow for a few more minutes.

CHAPTER THREE
HAZARD ALERT

Most days Joe was the last to wake up. On this particular morning, he had gotten out of bed before the sun had risen. He had even gotten up before even his wife had slipped out of the covers to start making breakfast. Joe, unable to get back to sleep, had walked into the combined kitchen and living room where his children slept, watching them as they dreamt.

Normally this comforted him, but he knew for his son it was the last pleasant dream he was likely to have. He sat down in one of the chairs by the table, watching them as they rested beside each other. He knew his mother often dreamt of the world before The Freeze, back when children could be children for as long as they wanted. Growing up in a safe world with a warm place to stay they could preserve their innocence for as long as possible. But here in

Coldhaven the survival of the city was primary above all other concerns, even the value of sentient life, because without the city there was no future.

For as long as Joe remembered that was all that there was to life in the city. Take care of us and we'll take care of you. But it was always a bit of a one-sided relationship. The city never took care of you if you fell. At best you would get a short period off from work duty provided you were not killed outright, and you were always expected to carry out your responsibilities regardless of other considerations when you returned to work.

It was a harsh way to live, but it was all they had. He had always been okay with it when it was his own life and his wife's, but all that had started to change when they had Emily and Lucas. Every morning he would watch them play he wanted nothing more than to shield them from the harshness of the icy world they were born into, to provide them a better life than he had been living. But he couldn't. There was nothing better here. This was all there was, and it killed him to admit that.

Just as he was about to try to get back to bed, Lucas opened his eyes. "Dad, what are you doing up?"

"I just couldn't sleep. Go back to bed, kiddo. You need your rest if you're going to be working in The Candle in a few hours," he said, coming closer.

"Dad?" he asked.

"Yeah?"

"I'm scared." The young polar bear made no effort to hide his fear.

Joe did his best to be brave for him. "I know. Just do what they tell you and follow their orders and you'll be okay." He earned a nod from his son but they both knew he was just trying to reassure him.

Lucas squeezed his dad's paw. It looked so small in

his palm. Rolling over, he turned away from his father. "I think I'm going to try to go to sleep again."

"Okay." He stood. "I'll be here when you wake up." And with that, Lucas returned to his dreams. For Joe though, there was no respite from the waking world. Left alone with his thoughts, he searched for a solution that would not come.

As Joe prepared for work, he turned to see his son dressed in his newly issued jumpsuit. Standing in the bedroom doorway Lucas picked at it uncertainly with a claw. With a small smile he looked at him and beamed proudly. "There's my son, the newest worker in The Candle. Enjoy having a clean uniform, son, it's the only time in your entire career there will be no stains anywhere."

"I'm not sure how to feel about that," he responded, entering the room.

Joe pretended to be shocked. "All of the real work in Coldhaven is done by people like you and me who like to get their paws dirty. Stains mean a job well done. Stains mean you've worked hard and the people respect it. Stains are a good thing."

"If you say so, Dad." Lucas shrugged and tugged at it. "At least it fits."

A fairly generic garment, it was made of thick material both to protect from the cold as well as to shield one from any minor injuries on the job. With long sleeves and a hood with holes for one's ears it was well suited for a variety of species. "It looks good on you."

"Thanks, I guess." He looked at his father. "Look, Dad, I know you did what you could."

Joe grabbed him by the shoulders and looked into his eyes. "Lucas, listen to me. You will be okay. Just do what you're told and come home safe."

Lucas nodded. "Okay, Dad."

"Now we'd better get going while we still have time. You don't want to show up late for your shift." Leading the way, he walked out of the bedroom to the kitchen where his wife embraced him.

"Now you two take care, understand?" She did her best to put on a brave face. "I don't want to have to visit either of you in the Infirmary."

"We'll do our best. Now Emily, come give your brother a hug before he goes off to work," Joe said. Emily complied, with her odd-looking plush toy under her arm as she did. "Good girl. Now Daddy will see you later. Do as your mother says, all right?"

"Yes, Papa," she replied.

With a smile, the two Kennedy men walked out the door. Making their way to the Workshop, Mike was already waiting outside when they arrived. "Morning, Joe. I've already got our list of assignments for the day. Lucas, the supervisor of the burn team wanted you to come see him when you arrived."

Joe took his son by the shoulders. "All right, Lucas, just go inside and do what he tells you. Follow all the instructions they give you and you'll be all right. I promise I'll come see you at lunch time, okay?"

"Okay, Dad." He smiled, walking into the Workshop and disappearing through the main doors.

Mike slapped him gently on the back with a reassuring smile. "He'll be fine. If there's one thing I know about Kennedy's is that they're tough. Now come on, we've got a lot of jobs today."

Looking one more time in the direction his son had gone, he turned and followed after Mike as they headed in to pick up their tools. Their first job was to repair a malfunctioning heating unit in one of the ration prep areas. Fortunately for them it was just a simple short and took less than five minutes to fix. Their next several jobs would not be so straightforward. They needed to track down a faulty valve that was allowing heat to escape somewhere in the residential area. This required them to stop at every valve and examine it for issues.

As Joe knelt to examine the hundredth such valve, he shook his head. "Everything's fine with this one."

Writing the information down on his clipboard Mike tucked it under his arm. "All right, then. One hundred down, four hundred to go."

"This is going to take forever," Joe muttered.

"Do you have somewhere else to be?" he asked.

"Well, no, but…" Joe looked towards The Candle.

"You're worried about Lucas," Mike finished. Joe nodded in response. "I get it. I've known him for as long as we've worked together. He's a smart kid with a good head on his shoulders. He'll be all right."

Joe turned away from the center of the city. "He might be, but I don't know if I will." He frowned. "I haven't been this nervous since I asked Laura to marry me."

Mike gestured for them to keep going to the next valve. "I know the supervisor of the burn team, he's a good man. He'll take care of him for you."

"Yeah, but what kind of a life is that for him? Shoveling coal into the furnace for forty years isn't exactly much of a future." The polar bear sighed. "I always hoped I'd be able to get him on the maintenance team."

In order to qualify Lucas would have needed at least two more years of schooling in addition to some on the job training, but he was unlikely to get that now. Once the need arose it was rare they would pull someone from work detail to send them back to school. Even if he had managed to convince someone with the power to pull him from the burn team, the longer he stayed there the more they would see him as essential to the operation of the massive facility, and there he would stay. Short of a miracle, there was little that anyone could do to change that.

"I could ask the supervisor to request him," the king penguin said.

"That's sweet of you, Mike, but unless you have some leverage I don't know about, there's no point. They'd never approve such a request and you know it." He frowned.

The bird shrugged. "You're probably right, but it's all I've got." He approached the fifth valve and knelt to inspect it. "This one's got a weakened seal." He entered the problem into the log. "It's leaking heat but not enough to cause the kind of readings they're seeing in the master control console."

"There must be more than one," Joe said, cursing. "We'd better replace it. If we don't, it's just going to get worse. Then we'll be back here in a week doing this all over again."

Mike nodded his agreement, turning the shutoff valve so that he could replace the damaged seal. Pulling out his tools, he handed Joe the clipboard while he did the work of removing the failing components and replacing them with fresh ones. Examining the faulty parts, he shook his head in disapproval. "These are definitely on the way out. Finish logging the repair while I switch them, would you?"

"Sure," Joe said. As he wrote the information on the maintenance log he looked up in time to see a balloon rising up into the sky from the perimeter of the city. With a large metal hull capable of carrying a fair amount of cargo, the occupants prepared to depart Coldhaven in search of additional supplies and other salvageable resources. A regular sight during all hours of the day, their mission was to scour the area around them for anything that survived The Freeze.

Consisting of teams of eight to ten people, they would regularly travel out over the ice for long periods carrying enough food and equipment to allow them to reach significant distances. Known as aeronauts, their primary function was to identify and collect anything useful that could not be manufactured or produced within the city. It was through one of these teams that the medication that kept Emily's condition in check had been found. Openings were rare, as in addition to being paid well for their services aeronauts were allowed to keep a percentage of whatever they retrieved.

Noticing his distraction, Mike tapped him with a webbed paw. "You still with me, partner?"

"Yeah, just thinking." He gestured in the direction of the departing balloon. "You ever wish you could do something else?"

Mike shrugged. "I suppose. I guess we all have at one time or another, but there's no point in fantasizing about things that will never happen."

"How do you know?" Joe asked.

"What?"

"How do you know you'll never get the chance to do something else? I mean, I know there aren't a lot of options in Coldhaven but have we all just gotten so used to the idea that there's nothing else that we don't even question it anymore?"

"What's the point when there's nowhere else to go?" Mike looked at him and leaned against a nearby streetlamp. "This is all there is. Dreaming of things that can't possibly be only leads to sadness."

Joe exhaled audibly. "You really think there isn't even the possibility someone else out there made it?"

"Oh, like my father who died spending his life looking for something out there instead of being here for us?" he asked.

"Look, I'm sorry if I touched a nerve. Just let me say this, please."

"Fine," he replied.

"Thank you." Joe placed a paw on his shoulder. When Mike visibly relaxed, he continued. "Lucas was asking me about the future and whether there was anything more to life than this." He gestured around him at the entire city.

Mike nodded sympathetically. "What did you tell him?"

"I told him that while I couldn't promise that there was anything else that he and his mom and Emily made it easier. That it wasn't all set in stone. And the entire time I was telling him that I kept wondering to myself if I was just trying to make him feel better or if there was any truth to the things I said."

The king penguin patted his friend on the back. "Of course there is. We may not be able to choose much in this life, but one thing we can do is decide for ourselves whether we're going to simply accept what we're given or make our own happiness."

Joe smirked. "Did you rehearse that?"

"Every morning in the mirror." Mike gently slapped Joe on the arm. "Now come on, we've got a lot more valves to check."

The rest of the morning was pretty routine, with one of them checking the equipment itself and the other recording the disposition of each one. Two hundred valves later, the relative calm of the late morning was shattered by a massive explosion, sending the city into a state of chaos. Alarms began to sound everywhere throughout Coldhaven, triggering warning lights and emergency response protocols. Desperately searching for the source of the blast, Joe's worst fears were realized as he saw the column of smoke.

The Candle.

"Lucas," he said under his breath as he broke into a run. Rushing towards the central nexus he was vaguely aware of Mike shouting his name but could only focus on reaching his son as quickly as possible.

Arriving in view of the facility he was momentarily shocked at the scope of the disaster. Wounded workers lay everywhere as the few medical personnel were sorting out the dying from those they could save. Engineers hurried about in all directions while the fire suppression teams tried to get the blaze under control. He rushed up to Doctor Reed, who knelt over an injured squirrel. The young rodent had been badly burned.

"What happened?" he demanded.

"I don't know," the red panda said, while continuing to treat the young worker. "Some kind of system failure."

"Have you seen Lucas? Do you know where he is?" He scanned the injured but so many of them were hard to recognize with the state of their injuries. Though he could identify a few ursines, none of them appeared to be his son.

Doctor Reed shook his head. "I don't have the slightest idea, he's probably still inside." Desperate, Joe rushed towards the entrance. "Hey, you can't go in there!"

The second he entered The Candle he felt the heat rush towards him. Without the systems to properly regulate the temperature it was being released unevenly all throughout the city. That included inside The Candle itself. Bracing for the warmth he pushed into the facility looking for the central core, where he knew the burn team would have been stationed. "Lucas!" he shouted. "Lucas! It's Dad!" He called out again and again but there was no response.

Moving deeper inside, he passed several workers and emergency personnel who tried to caution him, but he ignored their pleas. Entering the central core, he could see the primary flow regulator had blown, causing the system to overload and go critical in seconds. They had likely not even had time to identify the problem before the automatic systems kicked in and triggered the emergency status.

Feeling his fur get soaked with sweat the irony did not escape his notice that after a lifetime of being cold he might burn to death trying to rescue his son. Pushing it aside he moved onto the catwalk when he spotted him. Trapped under a broken piece of metal, Lucas was not moving. "Lucas!" he shouted again.

Descending the stairs to reach him it was even hotter. Swearing under his breath he took off his jacket and walked forward towards his son. He was unconscious but still breathing. Trapped under the debris, he would die from the smoke if he couldn't get him outside within the next few minutes. He reached to move the piece pinning his son and cursed as it felt hot to the touch. Wrapping his jacket around the metal he lifted with all his strength, but he was not close enough to pull his son free.

Losing hope, he looked up to see a webbed hand on his son's motionless form. "Mike! What the hell are you doing here?"

"Chasing after your crazy ass. Now come on, let's get Lucas and get the hell out of here. You lift and I'll pull!"

Nodding, Joe braced himself, shifting the metal out of the way as his partner pulled the younger polar bear free from the debris. Lifting him over his shoulder, Joe motioned towards the exit. "Come on! We're almost out!" Hurrying after Mike, the ursine rushed back towards the triage area.

Once outside, he shivered as the familiar cold rushed back into his fur again. Rubbing himself, he cursed at the realization he had left his jacket behind. When Doctor Reed spotted them, he pointed to a stretcher on the ground. "Put him right here!" Doing as instructed, Mike laid him down gently and stepped back. "Pulse is strong, I don't see any obvious injuries but it's too soon to tell."

"Is he going to be all right?" Joe asked.

"He's probably got some smoke in his lungs, but I think you got to him just in time." He looked up at him. "I know you're worried but you need to give me some room to work."

Mike took him by the shoulder. "Come on, we'd better get out of their way."

Casting another look at Lucas, he allowed himself to be pulled out of the path of traffic. With his son safe, he turned his attention to The Candle itself. The residual heat dumped into the system, even in the case of a catastrophic disaster, would linger for several hours before it dissipated below the levels required for survivability. In the meantime the backups would maintain essential systems to allow time for damage control. Even so, if they were not able to repair the main systems Coldhaven would be in for some very hard times indeed. Regardless, the loss of manpower was significant. There was practically no chance of Lucas being transferred now, a possibility already remote before the accident.

Resisting the urge to go and ask the doctor for progress, he sat down in the snow. Paralyzed by the thought of his son going back there he could only pray that his injuries would allow him the time to recover. Exhausted, he had never felt more helpless than he did at that moment.

TWELVE HOURS LATER

Work details had been cancelled for the rest of the day. Until The Candle could be assessed for damage and repairs affected it was not advisable to restart the massive furnace. For the time being supplemental systems provided the necessary heat in critical areas such as homes and the medical facilities. It was a stopgap solution at best, but it was all they had until they could refuel the main furnace and get it burning again.

A temporary treatment area had been set up in one of the large warehouses along the main steam pipes routed along the spokes of the city streets. Most of the wounded had been taken here to centralize and simplify their care. Rows of cots were set up along with some chairs for their loved ones while the medical personnel of the city saw to their recovery. It was crowded, but the most efficient way to treat everyone under the circumstances. At least while the reactor was offline no one would be required to report for duty there until it was cleared by the engineers.

In truth Joe hoped it was down for a while as the longer it was out of service the longer his son would have to recover from his injuries. The burn team was never more essential than after a disaster, and they would be expected to meet their responsibilities even with the reduced manpower as a direct result of the accident. That said, the disaster response teams were still clearing the debris from the interior. When that was done it would be up to the engineers and the maintenance crew to assess the damage. As soon as the cause was determined and repairs conducted, it would be fired up again without delay. Such was the nature of the city that relied on a single heat source for their very survival. God forbid if it ever failed completely.

Holding a vigil at his son's bedside, he and Laura sat together waiting for him to wake up. Being no warmer at home than in the medical facility temporarily set up to treat the wounded, Emily lay curled up in a blanket beside them. Sleeping, she occasionally stirred long enough to shift position before falling back asleep again.

Lucas was alive, though he had not escaped unscathed as evidenced by the bandages on his forehead. Evidently, he had been knocked back by the initial explosion and then trapped under the debris. It was only fortunate positioning that kept him from being crushed under its weight.

Many of his coworkers had not been so lucky. The injuries from the accident ranged from more than half a dozen deaths to some broken bones and other similar injuries. Almost half the burn team had been rendered useless by the magnitude of the disaster. The loss of the primary flow regulator had caused the system to go critical almost instantaneously, so rapidly that even the automatic systems could not properly compensate for the sudden violent shift in conditions.

Joe and Laura had not left their son since the incident, with one or the other being at his bedside every moment in case he woke up. Taking turns to use the restroom or retrieve the family's rations, they had waited most of the night for any kind of information from the doctors. Overwhelmed, it had taken this long for them to get all the wounded in one place and stabilized, to say nothing of treatment and recovery. Anyone with any medical or engineering experience at all had been called into service to do what they could.

Watching his son, he held Lucas's paw and squeezed, hoping the young bear could feel his father's presence. He rested his head on his other paw, wishing he had fought harder to keep him out of The Candle. Maybe if they hadn't run into the governor that day, he might have had one more day of innocence. Or maybe the accident would have simply happened a day later. Either way, it did no good to consider what might have been. As always, all he had was the choices in front of him.

He felt his wife's touch on his arm as the doctor approached. Eager for news, the parents stood together awaiting his prognosis. Taking up a position at the head of his bed he examined his chart before at last addressing the couple. "Mr. and Mrs. Kennedy."

"Doctor Reed, how is he?" Laura asked.

The red panda returned the chart to its position by their son's bedside and nodded. "He's doing well, all things considered. He got tossed pretty far by the initial explosion, it seems to have knocked him away from the worst of the disaster, but other than the konk on the noggin he appears to be in good shape. Now there is a possibility he may have a concussion or other related injuries but there's no way to tell until he wakes up."

"And how long is that going to take?" Laura clung to her husband's arm.

"That's up to him. It could be in five minutes, it could be tomorrow. He's got to come around on his own," he said.

"Is there nothing you can give him?" she asked.

Doctor Reed sighed. "I could give him a stimulant but considering how scarce medications are I'd rather not unless there's no alternative."

Joe hugged his wife tighter. "It's okay, honey. He'll wake up on his own time, he always does." He smiled, hoping the attempt at humor would relax her. She smiled weakly but it was clear nothing would displace her worry until he regained consciousness. "Thank you, doctor."

"If it helps, his vitals look good. I'm almost surprised he's not awake already." He touched his forehead. "He's young and strong, I wouldn't worry too much."

Joe smiled. "Part of the territory, doc."

The red panda nodded. "The governor is headed down here to assess the situation for herself. From what I understand she's already been through The Candle and they should have a plan for repairs by now." He offered a reassuring smile. "If you'll excuse me, I have other patients to attend to."

"Of course, thank you doctor." He nodded once more as the red panda resumed his rounds. A few days ago, news of The Candle's status would have reassured him, but with his son on the burn team it meant he would have that much less time to recover. The city did not offer exceptions for injuries or illness. The expectation was that it was a duty one performed regardless of personal circumstances or physical condition until one no longer could, and only those old enough would be allowed half ration exemptions.

Presented under the guise of resiliency, it was encouraged that work never stop out of a drive to keep their people focused. Before he had children Joe had never questioned that directive, but ever since Emily and Lucas had been born he knew one day he would have to face the difficult trial of watching his children go to work when he knew they were not in any shape to do so. He just had never thought it would be so soon.

Feeling pressure on his paw he looked down to see his son's eyes flutter open. "Dad?"

"Lucas?" he asked, leaning over him. "I'm here, son. We're all here. Your mom and Emily are worried about you." He tried to put on a brave smile, but he knew he was tearing up. He didn't care. He was so overwhelmed with joy that his son was awake. "How do you feel?"

"My head hurts, but other than that I think I'm okay," he said, trying to sit up.

Joe gently kept his paw on his shoulder. "Son, I think you'd better stay in bed for now. You just woke up from a pretty bad hit to the head."

Laura squeezed his other paw. "We were so

worried."

"I'm okay, Mom, I promise," he said.

"The doc told us you got knocked around a bit but you escaped the worst of the blast. What do you remember?" Joe squeezed gently.

Lucas shrugged. "Not much. I was working, shoveling coal into the furnace when an alarm went off. I didn't know what it meant, but everyone started shouting and running around all at once. I tried to find shelter, but before I knew it everything just seemed to go white and then you were all standing over me."

Joe exhaled deeply. "The primary flow regulator blew. The Candle went offline right after that. Mike and I ran inside to try to find you. We pulled you out as soon as we could." He wrapped his arms around him.

"Thanks for coming for me, Dad," he said.

Joe hugged his son again. "I'll always come for you." He smiled. "Think you're up to a hug from your sister?"

Emily came over to her father. He picked her up and sat her on the bed where her brother was recovering. "I'm glad you're okay," she said, embracing her sibling.

"Me too," Lucas replied.

Joe looked up as conversation increased on the other side of the room. Governor Cole had arrived. Flanked by her entourage on either side she entered the treatment area and held up her paws as everyone grew quiet to hear what she had to say.

"My friends, we have faced disasters in Coldhaven before. It is no exaggeration to say we are not strangers to adversity. Against all odds we have forged a life here in this icy wasteland and pushed back the cold with everything we've got." She paused for a moment. "There have been tragedies, and we have lost good people in our fight to keep our city going. We lost nine workers on the burn team and dozens are injured from this latest catastrophe." There was a lot of nodding from the crowd as she let that sink in. After a moment, she continued. "Repairs are still ongoing as we assess the damage and attempt to ascertain exactly what caused the system to suffer a temporary shutdown."

Joe looked up at her statement. He had been inside The Candle. He knew this was no temporary shutdown. It was an overload of the primary flow regulator, one of the most critical components to the city's survival. For reasons he could only guess, Governor Cole had chosen to keep the true scale of the accident from the people. Skeptical, he continued to listen.

"To that end, I ask you all to prepare to return to your shifts as soon as possible. We are working to bring the furnace back online and restore primary heat, but until then I must ask for your patience and cooperation." She put on her warmest smile. "I have been your governor for ten wonderful years. During those years I have learned what a strong and determined people you are. I know that we can weather any challenge the cold throws at us, and with your help we can do so again." A cheer from the people drowned out any other noise for several seconds.

Having lived through several governors, Joe understood that sometimes for the sake of morale it was necessary to bend the truth to keep the people moving forward, but at the same time the failure of such a critical component brought their very survival into question. Nevertheless, true or not he did not know what he could do about it. Exposing her deception would do no good even if he had the ability to prove it. Despite his misgivings, he remained silent. She had her reasons. Now was not the time to make a scene.

Governor Cole looked down for a moment, her ears folded in humility. "I want to thank all of you for your hard work and dedication." She gave a look of determination. "Rest well. Your people will need you soon. The reactor goes back online the moment repairs are complete." She smiled as another cheer rippled through the crowd.

Joe watched as she began to walk through the area, speaking to each injured worker and their family one at a time. She reached out and took their paws, saying something before moving on to the next.

Laura touched his arm. "Do you think she knows when The Candle will be back online?"

"I don't know," he said, wrapping his arm around her.

The governor was still several rows away from them. He did his best to hide his concern knowing the true scale of this latest disaster. Of course, the city had several replacement components for anything critical, but if that were all, then why lie about the true state of the massive furnace that was the key to their very survival? Before Joe could theorize about the answer to that question Governor Cole approached with her entourage in tow.

"It's good to see you all," she said, bowing slightly.

Joe nodded. "Governor Cole." He narrowed his gaze, his ears swiveling forward slightly.

"I'm glad to see young Lucas awake." She looked at him with a smile he was almost certain had to be false sincerity. "How are you feeling?"

"I'm feeling stronger," he said.

"Good, because Coldhaven is going to need strong young men like you in the coming days." She squeezed his shoulder. "Are you ready to get back to work?"

"Governor Cole," Joe said, stepping closer. "The men and women here need more time to recover."

"I agree," she said. "However, as much as I would prefer to give them more time, I'm afraid we don't have that luxury. A severe storm is headed in our direction and the temperature is dropping rapidly. Scouting teams have already reported dangerous conditions on the outer range of our expeditions. We need The Candle operational as soon as possible and I need every worker I can get to man their stations in two days."

"Two days! You can't possibly—," Joe began. He very nearly declared the impossibility of repairing the primary flow regulator in less than four, but stopped himself.

Governor Cole leveled her gaze at him. "Something to say, Mister Kennedy?" she asked.

Swallowing, Joe knew if he exposed her lie without evidence all he would do is get himself arrested. He shook his head. "I apologize, ma'am. I just know my son's injuries are too severe to return in two days. He requires more time."

"While I sympathize, Mister Kennedy, I, like my predecessors before me, cannot make exceptions based on our personal feelings. I have ordered the reactor brought online in two days, and I am requiring every member of the burn team to be there when it is. Failure to report will result in reduction of rations, until such time—," she started.

"I'll be there," Lucas interrupted.

"Lucas!" Joe replied, more forcefully than he'd intended. Even if his son were not injured, he would not want him anywhere near The Candle given what he knew. A faulty primary flow regulator, especially one that had blown without warning, indicated a serious problem unlikely to be diagnosed in such a short time. Certain that any repairs were temporary stopgaps to keep the furnace burning he was desperate to keep his children as far away from that place as possible.

"Dad, it's my decision," Lucas said. "You can count on me, Governor Cole."

Satisfied, she nodded. "Thank you for your loyalty,"

she said, before the arctic vixen walked off towards the next family. Several people lingered, staring at Joe from the corner of their eyes for moments after. Waiting until she was clearly out of earshot, he turned towards his son.

"Lucas, you can not go back there," he said. "Trust me."

The younger polar bear looked at his mother and father. "I do, Dad. But I also know that if I refuse Governor Cole can make life very difficult for our entire family, and we can't afford that."

"That's not something you should have to worry about," he said.

"And maybe in the world before that might have been true, but we don't have a choice," Lucas replied. "I have to be in that facility when it comes back online," he paused, "whether I'm ready or not."

As much as he wished he could disagree with his argument, Lucas was correct. They had few options other than to comply. Faced with the reality of the situation, Joe slammed his paw down on his son's bed as he prepared to walk away.

"Where are you going?" Laura asked.

"To play the only card I have left," he said, giving her no further answer as he walked after the arctic vixen. Waiting until she had finished speaking to another family, he stepped in front of her. "We need to talk. Now."

"As you can see, I'm quite busy." The vixen's ears flattened, and her tail swished defensively.

"We can have this discussion here, or we can have it somewhere more private. Your call." He glanced at her entourage. "I was inside The Candle."

With all eyes on the two of them, she acquiesced. "My office. Now."

Governor Cole's office was the tallest building in the

central nexus. Positioned close to The Candle both for optimum heat and to allow her to observe the operation of the facility from nearby it was the only structure in the entire city that could be classified as comfortable even on the coldest days. It was perhaps the single building in which people worked without jackets or other warm clothes.

The front entrance was a set of double doors, designed to insulate the building from the cold environment outside. Led by the arctic vixen, Joe traversed the lobby and began the climb up several floors towards the governor's office. The building was six stories tall, one of the highest in the city. Her office sat at the top, along with the central control from where all of Coldhaven's main systems could be monitored. It was here that she would have access to information about everything going on within the perimeter from resources to manpower.

Of all the places in the city that reminded Joe of the stories his mother told him, this was perhaps the most like the world that came before. One of the first buildings constructed when the city was established, it was one of the few assembled with old world technology. Along with The Candle, it represented one of the last remnants left behind from the world prior to The Freeze.

In every other building he had ever been inside there were no decorations, no frills, nothing of any kind that did not serve a purpose. Everything was present because it served an essential function. Here, there were reflective tiles on the floor and gold trim around the doorways, things that did little other than to enhance the look of the building. The stairs were marble instead of metal, providing a beautiful look rarely seen in a city built on functionality.

Of course, Joe knew these were all simple leftovers of pre Freeze architecture, but after the event that had changed the world no one would think to make a building such as this, with all of the ornate decorations that made the building more pleasant to look at but served no practical purpose. As he caught his reflection turning the corner to ascend the next set of stairs, he realized how different the lives of the people outside really were from those who ran the city.

His clothes were worn and showed signs of long days out in the cold, whereas Governor Cole's reflected someone who had never known the cold as something other than the thing you experienced between work and your quarters in the government residences nearby. As he watched her step in front of him he wondered how many of her relatives were assigned to the burn team.

"And here we are," she said. Reaching the top of the stairs she threw open the double doors and entered. Joe stepped into the center of the office, immediately feeling out of place in the well-kept workspace. Governor Cole sat behind her desk, which was arranged with built in monitors and equipment to allow her to survey the city at her leisure. A wide circular map of the layout of Coldhaven dominated the area behind her, and a large window filled the outside wall. A monitor to her right held information she had been reviewing likely in preparation for her next council meeting. A few taps of her control console and it defaulted to status updates on The Candle.

Two more security men stood behind her. She held up a paw and without turning her head, spoke to them both. "Thank you, gentlemen, please wait outside." Though hesitant, they complied. Once they were alone, Governor Cole gestured towards him with her paws. "Say what you have to say, Mister Kennedy," she said, keeping her gaze firmly on him.

"I want my son transferred off the burn team. Put him anywhere you want but get him out of The Candle."

"We've already talked about this." Her ears pinned back.

"I'm bringing it up again," he replied. "He is in no condition to walk back into that facility, not in two days and not in a week."

Governor Cole let out a deep breath. "I can see that your mind is made up on this, but my answer is still the same. I cannot spare anyone even if I wanted to, especially following this latest incident. I need everyone where they are." Her tail waved behind her in slow gentle motions. "Now you're a valuable member of the maintenance team and I would like to satisfy your request, but the moment I authorize his transfer then there will be a million more and I cannot encourage a labor crisis, at any time."

"Moving my son will not encourage a labor crisis," he replied.

The arctic vixen shook her head. "Perhaps not, but all eyes are on us and The Candle right now, and a transfer would draw unnecessary attention."

"I see," Joe said. "Then you leave me no choice."

Governor Cole leaned forward. "Be very careful, Mister Kennedy."

"If you don't authorize my son's transfer, I'll see to it that everyone in Coldhaven knows what really happened in The Candle," he said.

Neither spoke for a full thirty seconds after he laid his cards on the table. Joe had never felt such stillness, not even out there in the cold. He knew that by making that declaration he had put everything on the line for his son, including his whole family's future. Whatever happened as a result of this meeting there was no going back. He swallowed, keeping as still as possible as he waited for her response.

Governor Cole looked down at the surface of her

desk. "Or I could have you arrested for threatening the well being of this city. I could throw you in a hole so deep no one would ever find you."

Joe knew he had played a dangerous card, but there was no going back now. "Then why don't you?"

"For the same reason you didn't declare your proof in front of all those people in the Infirmary, assuming you even have any in the first place. You know as well as I do that the morale in this city is far thinner than most people think, and if you made such a statement even without proof it would plant a seed of fear in people's minds, one that once it grows no one here would be able to stop it." She turned around towards the map. "Keeping this city going has always been about careful management of the truth. Do you know how close this city has come to destruction?" She looked over her shoulder. "How many times we've come within a razor's width of catastrophic systems failure?" she asked. "Of course you don't. And why? Because you have the luxury of ignoring anything other than your little piece of the puzzle."

Joe relaxed slightly, though he remained silent as she continued.

"I can't arrest you without your family and coworkers asking me questions I would prefer not to answer. Nor can you go public with what you think you know without causing significant ripple effects. So it would seem to me that we are at an impasse," she replied.

"Then what do you suggest?" Joe took a step forward.

"Under the circumstances I will overlook this incident and allow you to return to your duties. Lucas will remain on the burn team and he will report for duty as soon as it is back online. Once you leave this office you will forget we had this conversation and you will speak of this no further. Provided you make no additional efforts to disrupt Coldhaven then I will consider the matter settled, but if you tell anyone anything that suggests we do not have full control of the situation then I will see to it that you are held responsible, am I clear?"

"Yes, ma'am." He let out a deep breath, aware that at the moment he had no other moves to make. In truth he was relieved his fatherly frustration had not separated him from the very family he was trying to protect. Blinded by his desire to keep his son safe, he had taken a foolish risk and shown his paw in the process. No longer certain he knew what to do next he was grateful when she dismissed him.

Walking out of her office he descended the stairs, suddenly feeling weak and helpless in the face of forces far beyond his ability to confront. Silently and without even acknowledging security, Joe walked out of the government building and into the cold. Looking up towards the center of the city he came face to face with a sight he had only witnessed a handful of times in his life.

The Candle was dark. Towering over the city it was silent and still. The gentle rumble that was the city's perpetual heartbeat, a constant symbol of its struggle against the snow and ice, was absent. It was a stark reminder that without the furnace all that stood between them and the fall of the last city on Earth was the backup systems working throughout the night to keep their city warm until it could be restarted. Faced with the deafening silence, he made his way towards home, driven on by the chill wind.

CHAPTER FOUR
NOT WORTH SAVING

Despite his best efforts, sleep proved elusive for Joe. Faced with multiple problems he couldn't solve, his responsibilities weighed heavily upon him. He'd been powerless to ease his son's burden and perhaps had even made it worse. Nor did he have a solution to Emily's ongoing medical care. The medicine he had bargained for would not last much more than a few days at most. Even if the doctor's efforts to help him were not discovered, he had known from the outset it would do little more than delay the inevitable.

Refusing to accept that there was nothing he could do, Joe searched his thoughts for a solution that would not come. Stuck with the same limited options, he stared at the ceiling wondering if there were any possibilities he had not considered. Try as he might, if there was a way out of this, he could not find it. He sat up, leaning forward over the side of the bed. Feeling his wife's paw on his back, he turned towards her. "I didn't mean to wake you."

"You didn't," she told him. "I couldn't sleep either." She sat closer resting her muzzle on his shoulder. "Emily is getting weaker. She tries not to show it, but I can tell. The medicine isn't working like it used to. She needs something else."

Joe frowned. "I don't know if there is anything else, and even if there was, we can barely afford it as it is." He placed his paw on top of hers, sharing his strength as they sat in the darkness. "I've failed her."

Laura wrapped her arms around him, sharing their body heat. "No, you haven't. You have been the best husband and father that I could have asked for. Never once have you ever failed to take care of this family." She smiled as she climbed off the bed and stared out the window. "I just wish this world was not so harsh and unforgiving," she said. "I remember when I was a little cub my mother would tell me stories of the world before, when everything was green and the world was a place of so many possibilities."

"Mine, too," Joe said. "My entire life I grew up hearing those stories. For the longest time I thought I was lucky to have never seen it myself. This way I could not miss what I had never known. It was comforting, for a while. I could tell my parents always felt a certain sadness in knowing they would never see a beautiful day ever again." He frowned. "I felt so fortunate, certain I could never feel that kind of pain. I thought nothing could ever hurt like that." He looked towards the door. "But then I had Emily and Lucas. And from the day they were born all I wanted was for them to be safe."

Laura held her husband close, looking into his eyes. "There must be something we can do."

Joe clasped her paws in his and leaned in close. "I give you my word. I will find some way to keep our children safe. I don't know how, but I am not giving up without a fight."

"I know you will," she said. "I love you, Joe."

"I love you too." He kissed her, wishing it would last forever. When they finally drew back, at last he felt the pull of exhaustion, and in her arms he fell asleep.

His dreams that night were fragmented. Visions of Emily, Lucas, Laura, and Coldhaven flew through his mind. Much like his conscious thoughts, his dreams refused to focus on any one subject, feeling like a constant barrage of disconnected images. He knew he was not in the waking world by the way he felt, falling helplessly as the world grew further away around him.

Attempting to cry out, no sound emerged from his muzzle. Pointlessly screaming at the top of his lungs the lack of a response from his body left him feeling powerless. Desperate for anything he could control, he flung his arms out in the hopes of grasping on to something.

Without warning, he found himself flat on his back. Getting up, he did not recognize the strange place he found himself. It was Coldhaven, of that much he was sure, but wherever he stood he could not identify where he was and he knew every inch of the city like the furs on his paw. Distorted and twisted, it was bent as if seen through a layer of glass.

Taking a step, the world spun. Dark and ominous, the shadows around Joe seemed to reach out as if trying to grab him from the void beyond, though whether they were trying to help him or harm him he could only guess.

Searching for someone, he attempted to call out, but once again his voice would not come when he commanded it. Dropping his shoulders, he walked forward, sensing movement just out of the corner of his eye. Suspecting there was a presence he opened his mouth even though he knew nothing would happen, but then stopped. Whatever it was, Joe could not identify its nature. All he knew was that it was dangerous.

Moving as fast as his legs would carry him, he ran in the opposite direction, searching for something familiar. No matter which turn he took it only seemed he was getting farther and farther away from anything he recognized. Cursing, he was about to panic when he saw Emily in the distance.

"Hurry, papa!" she called.

Sweetie, I can't find you!

"This way, quickly!" Emily's voice again. Following her calls he turned a corner and saw her walk inside a building. Uncertain where she was headed but knowing he could not stay here, he followed. Pushing his way through the door, he found himself standing in the Governor's office.

Gone was Emily, as was any sense of dizziness or danger. The Governor stood there with a serious look on her face. Before her was a version of him, standing there with a look of frustration. Suddenly, realization dawned.

This was earlier today.

But why would his mind return to that meeting? There was nothing special about it that he could recall. He had tried unsuccessfully to bargain for his son's safety though unless his subconscious had a cruel sense of humor, he did not know why the image of his daughter would take him here. Walking around himself, he could tell from the presence of the security guards it was from the moment when he had first entered the office, before she had dismissed them and left the two of them alone. His other self stood still as a statue, with the Governor looking up at him with her arm half raised in the air.

Walking to the window he saw The Candle, broken and in a state of disrepair. The massive furnace that provided heat to the entire city was not simply offline, but building towards an overload. He banged on the window to try to warn someone even though he knew no one could hear him. Desperate, he called to the two frozen figures in the office. Even his other self would not react to anything he did. Frustrated, he grabbed his other self and shouted in his thoughts at himself.

Wake up! What are you looking at? The furnace is going to blow, don't you understand!? Lucas and Emily are going to die!

The mention of Emily's name triggered a memory in the back of his mind. The image of his little girl had led him to this memory. Why? What was its importance? Looking at his face he could see his eyes were not on the governor, but on the monitor beside her.

She had changed it but for a split second it had showed something else, something other than The Candle's current status. Confused, he searched his memory.

What was she looking at?

Whatever it was, it was clear she did not want anyone to see it. He had only seen it for a second out of the corner of his eye, but something in him knew it mattered. Rushing once more to the window, he saw the explosion had begun. Starting at the base of the furnace the ball of fire had grown ever so slowly as if it was traveling at a fraction of normal speed. If this were the waking world the devastation would have taken only seconds. But for some reason he was dreaming of this moment with only a short while to parse out its meaning.

Returning to the monitor it was blurred and hard to read. He had seen it, but most of it had not made sense to him. As he struggled to recall what it had shown he knew that at least one thing on there had settled in the back of his mind. Fighting to bring it to the forefront he stared at the screen using all of his will to summon the information to his conscious thoughts.

I'm running out of time.

Certain he did not have long, he saw the Governor's paw start to move towards the button that would change the monitor. Returning to the window, the flames had already climbed halfway up The Candle. Desperate, he rushed once more to the blurred display. No matter how he tried, the information would not coalesce. Moving to where he stood he closed his eyes and pictured the screen in his memory. There had been a file with one word in particular standing out.

What did it say?

Joe cursed, the sound not manifesting his frustration as he ran once more to the window. Almost completely engulfed in fire, the building that was the very lifeblood of the city had now nearly completed its fiery destruction. Knowing this was his last chance, he returned to where his other self stood and looked at the monitor. In the split second he had seen the screen, he had recognized the name of the file. It was a single word.

Garden.

Garden, he mouthed to himself, moments before time resumed and the window shattered, sending him to the ground in a hail of broken glass.

Sucking in air like he was surfacing from a deep dive, he sat up quickly, finding himself in his bedroom, his sleeping wife by his side. Turning to see he had not disturbed her slumber, he got to his feet paws and went outside. Reassured that The Candle was still in one piece, he went back into their home and returned to the bedroom.

Making his way to Laura's side of the bed, he silently opened the drawer. Reaching inside he pulled out the two small glass bottles containing Emily's medicine. The first was empty, without even a drop of liquid inside. The second contained enough for a few more days, at best. Once that was gone, there was nothing to keep his only daughter from succumbing to her chronic illness.

Looking over his sleeping wife, he made her a promise. He would save Emily and Lucas, no matter what it took.

Unable to sleep, he threw on his clothes and walked out the door.

Making his way around the residential ring, he knew the way to Doctor Reed's unit by heart. Even though he suspected there was practically no chance his meeting with the doctor would go any better than his earlier one with the governor, he had to try, for Emily's sake. He was already pushing his luck with the doc the last time, but there had to be something he could do. For his children, no price was too high. Even if it meant risking his freedom, he would buy her another week.

The doctor lived in an apartment towards the east section of the residential ring. His position as a medical practitioner entitled him to comparatively luxurious accommodations in one of the few apartment buildings in Coldhaven, with the logic being individuals who served essential functions warranted slightly larger living spaces. Due to the large amount of materials required there were few buildings of this type present in the city, but the trade off for their construction also meant they required less energy to heat as opposed to the individual homes.

As such they tended to be filled with people whose skills were difficult to find and somewhat problematic to replace and were often the first places to have heat and other utilities restored in the event of an issue.

Joe entered the building, ducking into the stairwell

and making his way up towards the fourth floor. At this hour most people were still fast asleep, but given that he wasn't supposed to be here anyway it would make it easier to say what he had to say and slip out without anyone noticing. Pushing the door to the stairwell open a small crack, he peered out into the hall. No one was there, as expected.

Attempting to be as quiet as possible in his thick boots, he walked down the hall to the doc's apartment and gently rapped on the door. "Doc!" he whispered. "Doc!" He rapped a little more firmly, careful to keep it as quiet as he could. He was about to try for a third attempt when the door opened to a very bleary-eyed red panda. Wearing a wrinkled shirt, it looked like he had gone to sleep in his clothes. "I need to talk to you."

"Joe, it is four o'clock in the morning. Can't it wait?" he asked.

"Please, doc, it's important."

The red panda looked at him as if he were about to say something, but then exhaled and turned around, going back inside. Taking it as an invitation he entered and closed the door behind him.

"Well, since neither of us is going to get any sleep tonight, would you like a cup of coffee?" Doctor Reed asked.

Joe nodded. Coffee was rare in Coldhaven, with most residents lucky to experience it once a year on average, if at all. One of the rarest of the premium items, he was somewhat surprised when the doctor offered it to him so casually.

Taking a seat on the sofa he waited as the red panda moved to prepare the hot beverages. Pulling out a pair of mugs, Doctor Reed said nothing while he gathered the sugar and cream and set them out on the counter. Once he had gotten the process started, he looked up at Joe with a frown on his face. "I think I have a pretty good idea why you're here."

Feeling guilty, Joe looked down at his boots. "I know I've got no right to ask, but the medicine has stopped working. Emily's getting weaker, doc, and now we have even less time than we thought."

Leaning forward on the counter, he rested his paws on the tile surface. "How much do you have left?"

"Just the bit you gave me the last time I came to your office," Joe replied. It was a short supply to start with, Emily's situation made it even shorter. Laura had been doing everything she could to stretch the supply, but it was hard to stretch what you barely had in the first place. "My wife says she isn't responding as well as she used to. I need something else."

"There is nothing else," he said. "Joe, I've given you all the medication I can, and even more than I should have."

"I know you've gone out on a limb for me, doc, and I appreciate it, more than I can say," he paused, "but I'll do anything I have to, to save Emily's life." He looked at the doctor with wide, pleading eyes. "Whatever it takes."

Doctor Reed pulled the coffee carafe out of the machine and poured the dark liquid into the matching mugs. "How do you take your coffee?" he asked.

Taken by surprise, he had to think about it. "Cream and sugar," he replied after a moment. Prepared as requested, the doctor presented him with the precious drink before taking a seat on the opposite couch. As Joe stared into the steaming beverage, he wondered how much else the city had, but kept carefully isolated from people like him. No wonder they kept the lower class out of the apartment buildings. "Thank you."

"You're welcome," he replied. Considering his request, the doctor crossed his legs and leaned back. "Listen, Joe, I sympathize, but even if there were more powerful medications that could treat your daughter's condition, I can't give you anything else."

Joe knew what he was going to say before he even had a chance to say it. "The resource allocation algorithm."

Nodding, Doctor Reed took another sip of his coffee. "Every time I dispense medication it has be logged in the system. Resources are incredibly tight especially when it comes to medication. Now the bottle I was able to give you last time was old so I flagged it as expired, but if I try that on something else, they're going to notice. The truth of the matter is that your position does not entitle you to higher level medications without government approval."

Not wanting to waste the precious resource, he drank some of the coffee, but the luxury of the experience was soured by the reality of the situation he faced. Joe had always known that resources had to be carefully spread around so that there was enough for everyone. Everything, from the food they ate to the clothes on their backs, was carefully portioned out based on their age, gender, species, health, and so on, which was all calculated through an algorithm that was used to determine how much value any individual offered to the group as a whole.

While never referred to in public everyone knew that you were only given as much as you earned. It was why people kept working well past their prime, because the moment they were deemed nonessential the system would reduce all of their allocations accordingly in favor of those still contributing to the overall survival of the population. Before Emily was sick, Joe had never questioned the value of the method of resource allocation. Everyone understood that supplies were limited and rationing what they had was the only way to make sure there was enough for each person in Coldhaven.

It was also why theft and misappropriation of

anything was such a severe crime, with few things being seen with more disdain than taking someone else's fair share, regardless of the reason. People had been killed over a single strip of bacon. Punishments for taking something to which you were not entitled were harsh and often permanent. Meant as a deterrent, being a known offender was practically a death sentence. Merchants would refuse to do business with you and your rations were often contaminated or otherwise tampered with, never to the point that they were unusable, but a cut in your jacket or an excessive amount of salt was not out of the question.

Yet he would risk it all to see Emily grow up healthy and happy. Nothing was more important to him than the well-being of his wife and children.

"Would any of those higher-level medications help my daughter?" he asked.

"Joe," the doctor replied, pleading with him to drop it.

The polar bear set down the drink. "Please, doc. I need to know."

Hesitating, the red panda carefully considered his answer. "There is something I have that *might* help. Now I meant what I said earlier, this is not a treatment or a cure. But one of the higher tier medications I have has been known to extend the effectiveness of the medicine your daughter is currently on up to twice or even three times as long as the normal drug on its own."

"Then I need it," he said. "Whatever you want, I'll do it."

"It's not that simple," Doctor Reed replied. "I can't give it to you even if I wanted to. The higher-level medications are carefully monitored, especially those in limited supply. If they discover it's missing all hell will break loose. I can't fudge this one, Joe, not even a little. Now I sympathize with you, you know I do. But they are not going to authorize the dispensing of such a rare medicine for the daughter of a member of the maintenance team and I think you know that."

The doctor's statement hit him like a ton of bricks. Even though he knew he was just a cog in the machine he had never thought it would come down to such a simple matter as a number in a computer. He knew the doctor was right, even if he were to give it to him, he would never be allowed to keep it, and they would both be punished for misallocation of critical resources. Getting his paws on it would do Emily no good as she would never be permitted to take it as children were considered resources and her health would reduce her to a likely burden on the system as a whole.

Were he the governor his dilemma would not be an issue, Emily would already be on the medication and her old drugs would have lasted her years longer. But he had burned that bridge pretty badly already, and going to her was not an option. Joe had never cursed his life more than at that particular moment, when the world seemed to tell him as a whole that his daughter was not worth saving.

Feeling his chest tighten he pulled open his thick coat and fell to his knees. Breathing heavily, he struggled to calm himself but the thought of losing Emily was too painful to even consider. Robbed of all his strength, he could do little more than stare at the floor, bracing his body with his thick paws. He could not let his daughter down, no matter what it took. If there was even the slightest chance he could save her, he would cross heaven and earth to give his little girl more time. But if the doctor could not help, what else was there to do?

Struggling to accept the harsh possibilities before him, Joe was about to give in to his despair when he felt the doctor's paw on his shoulder. Momentarily distracted from his dark and foreboding thoughts he looked up at the red panda searching for the slightest glimmer of hope.

Doctor Reed knelt down beside him and exhaled. "I can't give you the medication, but there is a possible way you might be able to get it."

Energized, his eyes widened as he turned towards the physician with hope once more. "Anything," he said. "Just help me save my daughter."

After considering his answer for a moment, the doctor finally nodded. "Okay. I hesitate to mention this because it's a long shot in the first place. You understand that what I'm about to suggest is not a guarantee, just a possibility."

Joe knew his options were already limited. A slim chance was better than no chance. "I understand."

Doctor Reed looked towards the door as if he thought someone might be listening, before taking a seat on the sofa and encouraging Joe to follow suit. "You know that the balloon teams scout the ice looking for resources, raw materials, anything that might be useful that we either don't have enough of or simply lack the capability to manufacture, right?" he asked.

"Of course." Joe had regularly seen the balloons going up and out over the ice, and returning with valuable cargo on a regular basis.

His tail waving gently on the carpet he nodded. "Well, they've been particularly useful with medications. More than half my stock consists of things brought back by the balloon teams." Taking another sip of his coffee, he held the mug between his paws. "You've heard, I'm sure, that they're trying to assemble a few more, right?"

Joe nodded. Picking up his forgotten cup of coffee he drank a little more of the precious liquid. Still warm, it filled his chest with a gentle heat that restored some of his composure as he listened to the physician. Having only tasted it a few times in his life he had forgotten how reassuring a simple cup of this stuff could be. Holding it in his gloved paws, he looked up. "Yeah."

"What you don't know is that they found something on their last expedition. One of the balloon teams conducting a survey of an unexplored patch of ice found what looks like an old United States military vessel. A big one." He looked at Joe with a shrug. "It's been there a long time, but as far as they could tell they didn't see any sign it's been touched."

"You mean it's intact?" he asked. "Is that possible?"

"There's a lot of ice out there. We're still finding useable salvage four decades later. Now there's a possibility, and I stress the word possibility, that that ship might have what you need to keep your daughter alive," the red panda said.

"The team didn't board it?" he asked, confused. One of the unspoken benefits of volunteering to serve on a balloon team meant you got to keep some of the spoils. It was never discussed in polite company, but it was viewed by the government as fair compensation for spending weeks out there freezing your fur off for potentially nothing. Given the possibility that you might return empty pawed caused some to eschew joining a balloon team in favor of a more comfortable job, where at least you were guaranteed hot meals and a warm place to sleep. Still others chose to volunteer for the possibility they might discover some lost treasure from the old world or additional resources to bolster their family's limited supplies. No matter the reason, more often than not the balloon teams would return with precious spoils and tales of a world frozen in ice by a disaster still barely understood as more than just a simple phrase.

While a small number still harbored the scientific

curiosity as to what had turned our planet into a frozen ice ball, few still seriously searched for it four decades later. Knowing the possibility of finding it was so remote, and even if they discovered the cause it was unlikely they would be able to reverse the damage, such expeditions were frequently bumped in favor of resource collection teams.

There were a number of theories as to what had caused the initial disaster, but the more time passed the less interested anyone seemed to be in discovering which possibility was the correct one.

The doctor shrugged as he responded to Joe's latest question. "Their cargo hold was full. It was on their way back that one of the scouts spotted the ship in the distance. They went in for a quick look, but it was determined the next team to go out would explore the ship."

"When is it leaving?" he asked.

"In a few days. They're still trying to gather a few more members before they dispatch the team. They've been having a hard time finding enough people with this recent incident in The Candle. On top of the casualties and the injured it's made people less eager to explore so it's slowed things down a bit," the doctor said. "I only mention this because if that ship does have the medicine that can help your daughter, I'm sure you could request to keep it in exchange for your participation."

"I see," Joe replied.

"Now obviously you'd have to give up your job on the maintenance team, but I know some people. I could arrange it, but I'd need your answer now." The red panda looked at him with a firm but gentle stare.

Joe considered the choice he'd been given. If he remained, there was virtually no chance he could guarantee Emily's health would remain stable. Nothing he had would be worth the medication she required for even the possibility of survival. Nor was it likely he would find what he needed somewhere else in the city. Medicine was not for sale and it was even more expensive on the black market. Faced with limited options, he was not thrilled with the idea of being away from his wife and family for a full week but if he was lucky, when he came back he could buy Emily a little more time. What scant medicine she had left would have to stretch even further, and likely she would be very weak by the time he returned, but it was the best chance he had.

"Get me on the next expedition." He extended his paw and shook the doctor's in return. Joe knew Laura would not be thrilled with his choice, but he would accept her anger if it meant keeping his family together for as long as he could. First, he needed one more thing.

*   *   *

One of the few luxuries in Coldhaven was the bar that sat on the interior edge of the residential ring. It had little in terms of choices, but what it did have it presented plenty of it. As such, it was a frequent hangout for people looking to drown their sorrows and warm their bones. Provided you had the coin, you could drink to your heart's content, though you were still expected to report for your shift the next morning.

The interior was not much to speak of, but it was warm and it was comfortable. Entering the front door, Joe attracted little attention as he made his way to the bar and placed a few coins on the counter. "Two beers, a booth, and some privacy," he said without looking up.

Taking the coins, the bartender gestured towards the back. There was a booth isolated from the rest that unless you got really close you couldn't hear any conversation over the general background noise of the bar. Most of that came from the jukebox in the front, as it was one of the few places in the city you could hear real music from before The Freeze. The majority of the people that came in here seemed to like it, as it was always playing some tune or another.

Unzipping his coat, he sat and let out a deep breath. The bartender came over and delivered the two beers in large glass mugs, one of the few containers that never felt tiny in Joe's paws. Holding it he indulged himself in a sip, so rarely having the chance to enjoy anything other than his rations. The taste was pleasant and refreshing. It had been so long since he had enjoyed a beer, he allowed himself a brief smile as he hoped it would have the same effect on his guest. If he was going to pull this off, he would need the extra incentive.

The other party arrived a moment later, with the bartender gesturing towards the back booth. One of the other benefits of his present seat was in addition to comparative privacy one could also see the front door through a mirrored surface allowing him to know immediately when his partner arrived. Sliding the beer towards him as the king penguin took the seat directly opposite Mike stared down at it suspiciously.

"Okay, what do you want?" he asked.

"What?" He placed a paw on his chest in mock offense. "What makes you think I want something? Can't a guy just spring for a beer for his friend out of the kindness of his heart?" he asked.

Staring at him with a deadpan expression, the avian was unconvinced. "Nice try, but I know you too well."

"I don't know what you're talking about," Joe replied.

"Oh really? The bar tells me that you don't want our wives to know about whatever it is you're here to ask me. The beer says I won't like it or that it's probably worth several favors, possibly both. And the fact that you won't just come out and say it tells me that you're afraid I'll say no." He looked at him with a tip of his mug. "Or am I wrong?" he took a sip of the beer.

Joe shrugged. "You're just paranoid," the polar bear said.

"All right, then why don't I go and tell Laura about this little rendezvous." He moved to exit the booth.

Joe's paw stretched out to stop him. "Okay, you win."

"I knew it." The king penguin pointed to his chest. "Now will you just drop the act and tell me what the hell is going on?"

Looking down at his gloved paws the polar bear heaved a heavy sigh. "You're right. I owe you the truth."

"Oh boy." Mike leaned back and indicated the mug. "I suspect this is going to be a two beer favor at the very least."

Raising his paw towards the bartender, he nodded and a moment later delivered a second beer to each of them. Joe nursed the first one, taking a sip to gather his courage for what he knew was going to be a significant request. Staring into the refreshing liquid he steeled himself resolving to be as up front with the king penguin as possible. "Mike, we've known each other for a long time, right?"

"Long enough," the avian replied.

"And you know I wouldn't ask if it wasn't important," he continued.

Mike set his beer down on the table. "Joe, just tell me."

Letting out a deep breath, he nodded. "I've decided to join the next expedition," he said.

"The balloon team?" he asked, placing both webbed hands on the table.

"Yeah," Joe confirmed.

"Why?"

Joe looked down at his beer, taking another long pull from the mug. Clacking it down on the table he stared right into the penguin's eyes. "Because it's the only chance Emily's got."

"I thought she was on that medication," he said.

"She is, but it's running out and there isn't any more. The doctor says he's got a good lead on something that might help her but the only way I can get any of it is to be on the balloon team. If I don't join that next expedition the doc says I may as well kiss Emily goodbye." Joe lowered his gaze down to his paws, gripping the beer in both hands. "He says he can get me on the new team but they're not going to leave until they've got a full crew. And if we wait too much longer, they'll assign it to another group."

Mike considered his statement, putting the pieces together. "And you're one man short."

Joe nodded, drinking the rest of his first beer in one long pull. Placing it to the side he cradled the second, while his friend stared long and hard into his own mug. "I wouldn't ask if I had a better choice."

"Do you have any idea what you're proposing?" the avian asked. Swirling the liquid around, he took a deep sip before he continued. "You're suggesting we risk our jobs and our families' futures on the off chance that this lead, whatever it is, might have what you need to save your daughter. Do you even know what exactly we're looking for?" he asked.

"Yeah, I do." He slid a piece of paper across the table. "The doc says where we're going should have shelves of that stuff. Enough that I can keep Emily alive for a while, maybe even put her in remission."

Mike sipped some more of his beer. "You know it's

a long shot."

"I'm out of options, Mike. This is her last chance. I can't do anything for Lucas, but I can do something for Emily, and given the choice between slim chance and no chance I'll take slim chance *every* time," he said, tapping the table for emphasis.

The penguin rubbed his beak between his fingers. "And you're willing to risk everything to find out?"

"For my family, I would walk to the other side of the Earth and back if it meant keeping us together." He took the piece of paper, returning it to his pocket. "I know I've got no right to ask you to come with me, but I can't go out there every day pretending everything's okay when I know full well it's not."

Mike nodded, finishing his first mug. "You know I love Emily. Lisa and I think the world of her. She's the sweetest little girl I've ever met, the kind that she and I might like to have ourselves one day." He paused a moment, staring off into space. Taking another drink, he sighed. "Are you sure the doc's information is good?" he asked.

"As sure as I can be," he replied. "It's a risk, a big one, but it's the only shot I've got."

The king penguin looked down at his remaining beer. "And if we don't do this then Emily's done."

"Pretty much," he replied.

"Okay." He took another pull, downing the rest of his beer in one shot. "But if my wife kills me, I'm haunting you."

"Agreed," he replied. "Thanks, man."

"Don't thank me yet," he replied. "We haven't even gotten on the balloon team at this point."

Joe avoided his gaze. "About that," he replied.

"You're kidding," the king penguin rolled his eyes.

"The doc needed an answer right away," Joe said,

earning himself a smack from the avian.

"And what if I had said no?" he asked.

"Then they would have charged you with failure to report for duty and thrown you in prison," Joe said. "But I was pretty sure I could get you to say yes."

Rolling his eyes, Mike shot him a playful glare. "You play dirty, Joe Kennedy."

"I do not," he said in mock offense. "I simply wagered that you'd never be able to say no to Emily."

The king penguin jabbed a finger into Joe's chest fur. "Don't think you're not going to pay for this sooner or later."

Joe held up his paws in surrender. "Trust me, that'll happen when I tell Laura where I'll be for the next few days."

"Do you have any idea how you're going to break the news?" he asked.

The polar bear rose to stand and shrugged. "With my hat in my paws and my tail between my legs."

"You don't have a hat, and you're a bear," he pointed out.

"Exactly," Joe said.

"Ho boy. You sure you'll live long enough to get into the balloon?" he asked.

Joe shrugged. "Only one way to find out," he replied. "Wish me luck. See you at the launch point."

"Yeah," Mike replied.

With that, Joe walked out of the bar and began his trek towards home. When he arrived he could hear the kids playing, but it was clear that his wife was slamming pots and pans onto the stove. Joe cursed as he realized the people at ration distribution had likely changed his allocation the moment he had switched to the balloon team. No doubt his wife was currently dealing with the challenge of how to prepare a meal for four from the meager rations provided to balloon team members.

Swallowing hard, he pulled open the front door and went inside. "So, I guess you heard," he said.

Laura glared at him. "Oh, you mean how you left your job on the maintenance team to become a wandering nomad looking to find old world leftovers? No, I hadn't heard a thing. I had to find out from the ration center when they gave me this to cook for four people." She held up a tiny piece of meat and a small bag of vegetables. "How am I supposed to support our family on this?" she asked.

Joe lowered his muzzle. Unlike most of the city-based jobs, the rations for the balloon teams were distributed keeping in mind that most of the time they were scouting the ice for old world salvage. As a result, a large part of their ration allocation was diverted to this so they could be out longer before needing to resupply. The trade off was their city-based rations were much smaller, usually only enough for one or two people, assuming that the worker in question was out scouting and receiving bonuses from their work. This of course made the transition somewhat complicated as it would be a week before he would potentially return with supplies, if he returned at all.

Serving on the balloon team was by no means safe, as once they were outside of the protection of the city's warmth their only tether to home was the radio they took with them. In the event of damage or trouble, it was extremely unlikely aid would be able to reach the team in time to do any good, not to mention the balloons were not typically designed for rescues, needing to be loaded very specifically to have enough supplies to sustain the crew as well as space for any items recovered.

"You can give my share to Emily and Lucas tonight," he said without hesitation.

Laura stopped cooking and set the small rations aside. "I'm not even mad about the rations. I just don't understand how you could make a decision like this without even telling me."

"I know," he replied.

"The maintenance team was a good job. We always had enough to get by, and I never had to worry about your safety." She covered her muzzle with her paw. "Now every time you and Lucas walk out that door I wonder if you're ever coming back." She started to cry, burying her face in Joe's chest. He held her close, feeling her breathing as they drew strength from each other. He could not blame her for her feelings. He had time to consider his choice and prepare. She had found out on the ration line.

Joe held her tighter. "I'm sorry you had to find out like that," he said.

"At least tell me why," she replied.

He held her close, sharing in her loving warmth before putting just enough space between them that he could look her in the eyes. "It's not public knowledge but one of the balloon teams found something on the way back. The doc thinks that whatever it is can maybe give Emily a fighting chance to make it, but the only way I can get any of it is to be on the team."

"I see," Laura said.

"With luck, I can get some of it and get back here before her medication runs out." Joe touched her face with his paw. "It's the only chance she's got." Neither of them was willing to even voice the alternative. Both of them knew there was not much of her medicine left. Even stretching it would be difficult with so little of it left, but it was the only option they had.

"When do you leave?" she asked.

"Tomorrow morning."

Her eyes widened. "Tomorrow?" She pulled away from him a bit. "Does Mike know about this?"

"Funny you should say that," he replied.

Laura's muzzle fell open. "You got Mike to join the balloon team too?"

"I had to!" Joe said. "They'd only take me if we had a full crew, so I talked the doc into taking him too."

"Oh, this just gets better and better. You're going to make me go white with worry," Laura responded, while resuming her cooking.

"You're a polar bear, you're already white." Joe smirked.

"That's enough out of you," she said. "Have you thought about what you're going to tell the kids?"

Joe nodded. "The truth. I figure they're old enough they deserve to know what's going on."

"You think they can handle it?"

"Maybe not, but there aren't a lot of excuses I can use, Laura," he said.

"I know, but this is going to hit them hard." She motioned towards the bedroom door. "You'd better tell them before dinner."

The door opened as if on cue. "Don't bother. We heard everything," Lucas said, emerging with Emily right behind him.

The younger Kennedy sibling hugged her father around the waist. "Papa, I don't want you to go."

"I know, sweetie, but I have to. Doctor Reed thinks I can find some medicine to make you better," he said.

Emily squeezed him harder. "But what if you don't come back?"

"I promise, sweetie, no matter what I will come back to you. I swear it." He held her close. "I just need you to be good for mommy while I'm gone, okay?"

"Why don't you tell her the truth?" Lucas said. "That you think this is a long shot and whatever you find out there won't save her life."

"Lucas!" Laura shouted.

"Emily's going to die and you know it. It's just that I'm the only one in this family willing to face reality. She won't make it and neither will I." Pushing his way past his father, he rushed out the door.

Running after him, Joe called out. "Lucas! LUCAS!" Despite being seconds behind him, he was gone from sight when he emerged. Falling to his knees, he breathed the cold air while snow gathered on his nose. After sitting there for a full minute, he felt his wife's paw on his shoulder.

"Joe, come back inside."

"But Lucas," he said.

"When he's this angry you know you'll never find him. Now come back inside and spend some time with your daughter. You'll need all your strength if you're going to keep this family together." She looked at him with gentle eyes when he rose to stand once more.

"I love you, Laura Kennedy," he replied.

"I love you too." Taking her paw in his own, he turned and walked back into the house.

CHAPTER FIVE
THE EXPEDITION

BALLOON TEAM EIGHT
AREA DESIGNATION: SECTOR 47

Floating above the frozen seascape below, a large balloon proceeded further away from the city towards the perimeter of the previous team's search grid. Following the last group's return course, the six members of Balloon Team Eight kept alert for signs of their intended destination.

Consisting of two levels, the lower deck served as cargo and storage space, with a small area for the crew to bunk down two at a time. The upper area was the bridge, captain's cabin, and what passed for the mess hall, which really was just a table towards the back of the main section which doubled as a conference space. Cramped and barely comfortable, it served its purpose, but only just.

Studying the maps at the rear of the bridge, Joe sipped his coffee more for the warmth than anything else. It was nothing like the fine blend he had enjoyed at Doctor Reed's apartment. In fact, it barely qualified for the designation, but it was one of the few 'perks' of serving on a balloon team as it was deemed essential supplies, due to the warmth it could provide given the heating systems on the balloon were minimal at best.

Wrapped in a thick coat and heavy boots, he stared down at the line indicating their current course. The previous team had reported seeing something resembling a United States naval vessel somewhere off the coast apparently lodged in the ice. On the one hand, at least that meant it wasn't going anywhere, but at the same time it could present its own set of challenges. One thing that had been drilled into their heads repeatedly was to make no assumptions on the ice. Just because it looked solid did not mean that was even remotely the case.

Given the fact that there was no help if they got in trouble out here it was made abundantly clear to everyone that no allowances would be made for stupidity. Everyone was expected to do their jobs and obey the captain's orders without question if they wanted to share in the spoils. To that end, side conversation had been relatively minimal the entire two and a half days they had been traveling.

It was not that Joe minded the silence so much as it was he simply missed the conversation with Mike that made every day that much more enjoyable. Before Lucas had been assigned to the burn team, he had thought he would work maintenance until the day his paws could no longer pick up a wrench. Of course, nothing was going to be the way it used to be, not anymore.

The balloon shook slightly as the captain turned the wheel to the left, just enough that Joe could feel it. "Kennedy, altering course two degrees to port. Slowing to one half." The captain was terse, generally only speaking when necessary. Evidently, he did not see any purpose to idle conversation. A muscular tiger with dark brown hair, Joe had known nothing of his record other than the fact he had been well regarded by the rest of the crew. Dressed in a thick jacket with the insignia of his rank, he was really the only member of the team wearing anything 'official'. Mumbling about the cold, he rubbed his gloves together, shifting his feet paws to keep warm.

"Two degrees port, aye." Writing down the course correction and adjusting the map, he looked up to see the captain looking straight at him. "Something else, sir?"

"Go outside and check on Rush," the tiger ordered, blowing into his paws. "We should be approaching the object fairly soon."

Sliding off the bench he stood with a nod. "Yes, sir." Walking outside he pushed open the metal door to the small railing that ran along the perimeter of the upper level. Closing it behind him to minimize the heat loss, he made his way up the length of the bridge to the forward observation area where Mike stood with a telescope and a pair of binoculars hanging from his neck.

"Captain wanted me to get a status report," Joe said, standing on the open walkway that led to the small area where the king penguin made his observations. Shielded from the wind, it was little more than a glass alcove with an open side facing the bridge, where Joe currently stood.

"My feet are frozen to the deck and my beak has ice forming on it," he said with mild disdain. "I think our dear captain assigns me out here on purpose." He poked a webbed finger into Joe's chest. "The man is a tyrannical taskmaster."

"He's not that bad," the polar bear said.

"Easy for you to say, he likes you." The king penguin rubbed his arms. "He hates the crap out of me."

"He does not hate you," Joe said. "He probably just thinks you've got the best eyesight of the group."

"That is such a stereotype. You know not every bird can see for miles with perfect clarity. I had an uncle once, couldn't see the beak at the end of his face. He died when he walked off a ledge, cracked his head right open."

"I thought penguins were supposed to be good with the cold," he replied.

"Yeah, normal cold. Ground level cold. This is a whole different thing." He rubbed his webbed hands together for warmth.

Joe gave him a friendly slap on the back. "Tell you what, next time I'll take the shift out here."

"Deal." He looked back into the telescope.

"Have you found what we're looking for yet?"

Mike shook his head. "Not so far. Their report said it was right around this area so it shouldn't be much longer."

Joe nodded. "I just hope it has what we need."

"If what they say about the target is true, it probably has that and more. Any idea exactly what it is?" he asked.

"Just that it's a US naval vessel, but that's it. No indication as to size or class." Joe shrugged. "I guess the last team didn't think it was important."

Mike rolled his eyes. "Well, I doubt it'll matter. There can't be that many navy vessels stuck out here in the ice."

"So you would think," Joe agreed. "All right, I'm going to head back in and report."

"Do me a favor, next time bring me a coffee?" he

asked, pulling his coat tighter.

"Will do." Just as he turned to leave, Mike cried out in excitement.

"Holy shit!" He squinted into the telescope. "I found it! I think we found it!" He pressed himself against the side of the small space and encouraged Joe to look inside the eyepiece. Filling his vision was the main deck of a United States naval aircraft carrier.

"Holy shit," Joe echoed. "Look at that beast," he said, pressing his paws up against the glass. The large ship reminded him of a sleeping dragon, trapped in the ice at the waterline. The shape and size conveyed unmistakable power, only served to underscore the fact that even a ship as mighty as this was powerless against The Freeze. Whatever had caused it had even taken down such mighty behemoths as the one before them. Yet even in defeat the ship stood proudly, a reminder of its once great purpose. Joe looked down at the ship, almost unable to believe it was real.

Mike turned to face him. "You'd better report to the captain."

"Right," Joe said, turning and heading back into the bridge area. The tiger looked up at the sound of the door and shivered at the sudden chill wind let in by his return.

"What have we got?" he asked.

Joe stared straight at him. "The ship is directly ahead, sir. In another minute or two we'll be right on top of it."

"Understood," he replied. Pressing the intercom button he called down below. "This is the captain. We're approaching the target. All hands on deck, report to your duty stations."

"Captain Cutler, recommend we attempt to land on the center of the flight deck. It's likely to have the least obstructions and give us room to maneuver in case we need to leave in a hurry," Joe said.

"Good idea." He looked up as the first officer entered the bridge. Dressed lightly compared to the others to keep his wings free, the clothing he wore was specially designed to insulate his body. Having that thin and athletic build that most birds seemed to have by design, he did not know much about him other than the fact that this was his first tour as the second in command. "Whitmore, we're coming up on our target. Once we settle into position overhead I want you to anchor us in place. When that's done, get back up here and prepare the teams."

"Aye, sir." The gyrfalcon walked to the front of the bridge where you could see the area most likely to contain the ship's operations center. Coming in slowly, the balloon settled gently over the flight deck cutting all forward motion and gliding into position. Once the captain signaled all stop, the first officer offered a salute and walked outside, leaping over the railing and disappearing from view.

Joe stared after him a moment, reminded that avians did not fear the effects of gravity as much as those lacking flight capability. To them, it was simply another natural force. Taking a deep breath, he returned his attention to the matter at paw. Joe marked their position and arrival time on the map, picking up the radio and reporting it back to Coldhaven. Once that was finished, he gathered his gear and lined up with the others in the rear of the bridge area.

Captain Cutler stood before his assembled crew, looking at each of them in turn. "All right. You all know how this works. Two teams of two, one fore and one aft. Explore the ship, but be careful. Just because we don't expect to find anything alive down there doesn't mean it's not dangerous. Stay with your partner and provide regular reports. Check in if you find anything unusual." He turned to Joe. "You sure you wouldn't prefer Hawkins as your partner?"

Joe shook his head. "No, sir. I trust Mike with my life."

"As you wish. Whitmore, you and Hawkins are in command down there. Two hours. No more. Understood?"

"Yes, sir."

With the briefing concluded, the four crewmembers walked outside leaving the captain and the chief engineer down below as the only two remaining on board. While some considered the precaution unnecessary given the fact that Coldhaven was the only surviving city, the captain valued prudence over a slightly reduced mission time, given that provided his concerns were unfounded the most it would risk is a few hours extra. Watching from his perch on the bridge, the first officer simply glided down to the deck, making Joe momentarily jealous that bears would have to take the long way down, as would king penguins and squirrels.

Grabbing onto the rope, he used his gloved paws to control his descent, being the first to land on the deck with a gentle thump from his boots. Pulling out his rifle, he scanned the surface of the ship for any potential threats. Mike was next, landing behind him a few seconds later. Joining him, the three waited for Hawkins to touch down at which point Whitmore stepped before the group.

"All right, we have two hours to explore the ship starting now. Set your watches and be back here by the time the clock expires. Check in every fifteen minutes with the captain. Understood?" he asked.

"Yes, sir." Joe replied. The short time frame was also at the captain's request. While most of the other balloon teams put no such restrictions on their personnel, the tiger believed it was best to limit excursions to short bursts and do more of them, to keep the crew alert and refreshed between excursions. Whether there was another reason or not Joe did not know, but they would have days to recover all they could from the ship before they were due to head back.

Determined not to waste any of it, he offered a respectful salute to the first officer's team and gestured for Mike to follow him as they headed down into the depths of the ship.

The air inside was cold and still, having not been disturbed for some time. Activating his light, he shone it around as he descended the stairs, making his way forward at a slow and cautious pace. His breath visible, he could already feel the chill permeating his bones.

From behind, Mike's footfalls could be heard mimicking his own movements. "Remind me why I let you talk me into this?"

"Because you're a good bird who loves my daughter as much as I do," Joe said. "Now stay sharp, and be careful."

The king penguin scoffed and pushed past him. "I don't know what you and the captain are so worried about. There's nothing alive out her—" Mike stopped mid-sentence. Spread out on the deck before them, four bodies in naval uniforms rested in various positions lining the hall. Whether they had been killed by the initial disaster or died after Joe could not tell. Either way their faces were frozen in the last expression they had taken in life, never to move again.

Gently taking the lead once more, he put a paw on Mike's shoulder. "Just stay behind me, okay?"

"Yeah, sure," Mike said, humbled.

"We need to find the Infirmary." He looked at the walls, reading the various signages that marked their position within the ship.

"That's not going to be easy. This place is huge,"

Mike remarked. "It's hard to believe something this big could move under its own power."

"From what my mother told me they had a lot of big ships like this back then, though I never really thought I'd see one with my own eyes." Casting one last look down at the frozen sailors, Joe said a silent prayer before turning back to Mike. "Let's keep looking," he said, "and let these men rest in peace."

Nodding his acknowledgment, Mike took up a position behind him. The king penguin blew some warm air into his hands, rubbing them together to help battle the cold air inside the ship. Unlike Joe, webbed hands did not lend themselves well to gloves and mittens were not an option when manipulation of objects was necessary. Slowing his pace, he looked up at the polar bear. "What do you think it must have been like?"

Pausing, Joe turned and looked over his shoulder. "What do you mean?"

"I mean during The Freeze. What must these sailors have felt when the world suddenly turned to ice and the ocean itself froze over?" When Joe didn't answer, he shrugged. "Were they scared? Did they know what was happening?"

The polar bear flattened his ears slightly. "I don't know. There are a few people who were alive back from the days when the world used to be green, but none of them have ever known what caused it any more than we do." Joe exhaled. "And of course, in the years following the disaster, survival was a higher priority than history so most of the records from back then were abandoned in favor of more useful things like food and building materials." Wiping a small amount of frost from the walls he shook his head. "Whatever it was, it's probably buried under the ice like everything else."

"Maybe," Mike said, "although we've had forty-six years since then. Don't you think it's weird that none of the teams have ever found anything that might explain the disaster?"

"We don't even know if there's anything to find," Joe replied. "For all we know it was a natural phenomenon brought on by global cooling," he said. "They were doing a lot of crazy shit back then." Joe resumed walking.

Mike frowned. "That is true," he said. "People back then thought they could consume the planet's resources without consequence. Maybe it finally caught up with them."

Joe had barely heard his last statement, coming to a stop in front of a large metal door identified by the sign on the wall as the Captain's Cabin. Unable to contain his curiosity, he pushed open the door to peer inside. Frozen like a moment in time, everything was just as the captain had left it. So engrossed was he in the unusual sight he did not notice the sudden rush of footfalls from Mike's boots or the sudden impact of the king penguin's form colliding with his own until his friend cried out from his position on the floor.

"Damn!" he said.

"What the hell?" he asked, looking down at the avian.

"I looked up and you were gone," Mike said. "So I ran after you. Now will you help me off the floor, please?"

With one arm, the polar bear lifted his friend to stand. "Sorry."

"What's so interesting anyway?" he asked. "You were frozen in the middle of the hall. I thought maybe you'd iced over too for a second."

Joe shook his head. "Oh, I was just distracted by this." He motioned towards the sign. "I'm going to check it out."

"We still have to find the Infirmary," Mike reminded him.

"I know. I just need a minute. Besides, we still have over an hour." He stepped inside the spacious cabin, looking around at the various books and other assorted items filling the captain's quarters. Whoever he was, he was clearly a studious and efficient man, dedicated to his duty. The closet was lined with several spare uniforms, with each one looking like if not for the frost that it could be pulled out and worn at any moment. Joe entered deeper into the cabin, pausing when he found the captain's body, placed in his bed and covered in a blanket, frozen in peaceful slumber.

Mike paused. "Shouldn't he be on the bridge?"

"Most likely the crew placed him here after he died." Joe reflected for a moment longer before he turned to the captain's desk. Sitting at the computer, Joe pressed a key on the control panel.

"You know that's not going to work, right?" he asked.

To his surprise, the screen activated and the corresponding controls lit up to his touch. "Whoa."

"What did you do?" Mike asked.

Joe slid back a bit. "I just touched it, I swear."

The king penguin stepped back a few feet. "Maybe we should leave it alone, don't you think?"

The polar bear pressed a few keys, noting a flashing icon at the bottom. "It appears there's a log designed to play the next time someone activates the system." Starting to type, he prepared to access the recorded message.

"I don't know about this," Mike said.

Joe turned to face him. "You're the one that wanted to know what they felt. Do you want to see the message or don't you?"

Mike looked down the hall and then grumbled. "Okay, fine. But then we're out of here. Agreed?"

"Agreed," Joe replied. "Here goes nothing."

Pressing the enter key, the video began to play. A dignified looking elephant appeared on the screen dressed in his navy uniform.

"To anyone that finds this message, I am Captain Joshua Clark, commanding officer of the USS Abraham Lincoln. I am leaving this message in the hopes that it will one day be heard and perhaps in some small way help make sense of the calamity that has gripped our planet. Less than twelve hours ago my ship was incapacitated by a sudden extreme drop in temperature, severe enough to cause the ocean to freeze. Despite our best efforts we were unable to free ourselves or make contact with anyone back in the states, though if they were taken as much by surprise by this as we were I imagine they have their hands full. Nevertheless we have attempted to continue operations as much as possible in an effort to keep the ship operational but the prospects don't look good. My chief engineer has done all he can to keep the engines online but against the temperatures we're facing it's only a matter of time before the crew freezes to death. With limited supplies and no safe port reachable due to the lack of arctic gear, it's unlikely we'll survive more than a few days at most. To that end, I've ordered the crew to do all we can to leave as much information as possible for anyone who comes after us, including some emergency systems to power up the ship just in case someone with the will and the knowledge to do so finds this record. I'd also like to state that my crew carried out their duty to the very end, in the finest tradition of the United States Naval Service, and that each and every one of them served with distinction under incredible circumstances. If you find this, know that they have my heartfelt respect. Good luck and Godspeed." The screen returned to the menu.

Joe looked to Mike. "That's the last entry. There's a bunch of other information in here, mostly relating to the disaster the captain mentioned, though they don't seem to know exactly what caused it."

"As fascinating as that is, we need to find the Infirmary," he said. "We can come back here later if we think it's worth showing to the others."

Joe nodded his agreement. As much as he was curious to know what had caused the disaster, his daughter's survival was more important. Getting up from the computer, he turned the unit back off and offered a silent prayer to the captain before following Mike into the hall. Closing the door gently, he gestured for his companion to fall in behind him. "I think it should be this way."

The Infirmary was much like the rest of the ship, silent and empty. When they entered, there were several bodies on the beds, each of them wrapped in heavy blankets. All of the ship's medical personnel still wore their uniforms wherever they lay. It was clear they had kept trying to save their patients until the very end. Stepping into the room Joe could still see his breath as he exhaled, with the interior of the ship colder than the deck. As his footsteps pressed into the thin layer of frost, he left a slight trail through the room as he returned his mind to the task at hand.

"Somewhere in here is the medication Emily needs," he said.

Mike shrugged. "Any idea where they keep the good stuff?"

Joe opened a cabinet, then reached into his pocket for the list of things the doctor said he needed. Several of them were common medications, most of them in fairly decent supply as he grabbed pawfuls of the bottles and tossed them into a bag Mike had brought over. "Where did you get that?"

"Over there. Now keep grabbing anything that looks useful," the king penguin said. "The more we bring back, the more of that stuff you'll get to keep."

Joe nodded, knowing even the generic medications would do wonders for the people of Coldhaven. Using his whole arm, he dumped the shelves of medicine into the bags, spilling a few bottles onto the floor. Under the circumstances he was not in the mood to be delicate. Once he had gathered a fair amount of supplies for the city, he returned his attention to the list. There were several cabinets of medication. Odds were that the one he needed for Emily was in there somewhere. Pulling them all open, he continued to dump the medicines into the bag until it was practically full to bursting. Zipping it closed, he turned his eyes on the last cabinet. This one was locked.

No doubt it contained highly controlled substances. Mike came over with a bag full of medical supplies and looked up at him. "How are you going to get in there?"

As if in response, Joe grabbed the handles and pulled hard enough to bust the lock, sending pieces of metal clattering to the floor. Offering a shrug, he examined the contents within. Searching the names of the bottles, he at last came across the one he needed. Taking the bottles in his paws like they were gold, he stuffed them in his coat pockets. He wasn't taking chances the city would allocate them somewhere else. One way or another, Emily was getting her medication. Taking the rest of it, he filled another bag before the two were finally ready to make their way back to the balloon. "Let's go," he said.

"Lead the way," Mike replied.

With bags full of valuable medical supplies, they began their long trek back up towards the deck. It was slow going, but they had plenty of time before they were due to join up with the others. Retracing their steps, they followed their journey to the Infirmary in reverse, walking down the corridors using their earlier footprints as a guide. Turning another corner, Joe caught himself wondering how sailors managed to find their way around such massive seafaring vessels without getting lost.

As they approached the Captain's cabin once more,

he began to think about the final log the elephant had left behind. While it contained no practical information, such as what had caused the disaster or where it had begun, it nevertheless contained a unique and valuable historical perspective. Even if the rest of the computer records did not have evidence pointing to what might have caused The Freeze, Joe was certain the information in the computers on this ship would no doubt be of interest to those scientifically or historically minded among them. Perhaps there would be insights into the world that no one in Coldhaven had even considered.

Excited by the possibility, he could not help but slow down as they approached the cabin. "Do you think we should try to take their database with us?" he asked. "The captain did say there was a lot of information they had tried to store when the ship got caught in the ice. Maybe some of it points to what happened all those years ago."

The king penguin scratched his head for a moment before he caught on to what the polar bear was suggesting. "You want to try to recover the data?"

"Don't you think we should? I mean, we're here anyway." Joe offered a shrug.

"First of all, this is forty six year old technology. I don't know about you, but I don't know much about their computer systems. We might end up doing more harm than good. Maybe we should see if Coldhaven has a computer expert or something that could recover the data safely," Mike said.

Joe frowned. "I don't like the idea of leaving the information here. Besides, it would take weeks to get anyone else here and we may have already started the clock when we triggered the log earlier."

"And whose fault was that, mister peer pressure?" The king penguin angled his beak at Joe.

"You're never going to let me live this down are you?" Joe turned to look at his friend.

"Hey, you dragged me out here from my nice cushy job, I think I deserve a little friendly jabbing," Mike replied.

"Fair enough," Joe said. "Just don't let it get out of paw." He shrugged. "Now let's see if we can't get our paws on that data." Turning towards the doorway he stopped.

Mike bumped into him from behind. "Hey!"

"Sorry." Joe stepped to the side slightly. "Mike?"

"Yeah?" he asked.

"Was that door open when we left?"

Before Mike could answer a figure brandishing a knife leapt out from the doorway causing both men to scatter in opposite directions. "Holy shit!"

Joe pressed up against the wall as the figure looked at each of them. Dressed all in black military gear their face was covered with a thick scarf and goggles leaving long white ears as the only part of their face exposed. Before he could even open his mouth, the figure kicked Mike hard in the chest, sending him sliding along the icy deck before turning his attention to Joe. Holding his paws up, the black clad figure pushed past him and ran back towards the main deck. Running over to Mike, Joe extended a paw and hauled the king penguin to his feet.

"What the fuck was that?" Mike exclaimed. "I get kicked in the chest and he just pushes by you like it's nothing? That's balanced!"

His friend's wounded pride aside, he rushed into the captain's cabin to see what the figure had taken. On the screen were displayed the words 'download complete' and 'deletion in progress'. Joe bolted after him.

"Where the hell are you going?" he asked.

"He's got the records!" Joe did not wait for Mike as he ran down the hall. The rabbit had a fairly good lead over him but in order for him to have gotten on and off this ship there had to be some sort of support craft nearby. This meant most likely he was headed for the same place he was, the main deck. Taking what he assumed to be the most efficient route to the stairs, he climbed them in record speed and was rewarded with a glimpse of the small white tail sticking out of the figure's dark clothes.

Pursuing him out onto the deck, Joe looked in both directions but could not see where they had gone. The lack of footprints suggested they had not been through here since the snow had buried their initial entrance to the ship, but the only other place they could have gone seemed improbable even for a rabbit. Walking to the railing, he leaned over to check, seeing nothing. Without warning, a sudden weight landed on his back. Wrapping his legs around Joe's torso, the figure attempted to knock him off balance, but if there was one thing Joe knew is that it was hard to make a polar bear unstable.

With all of his weight, he pushed back against the hull of the ship eliciting a yelp of either pain or surprise from his would be attacker. Turning to face them, he moved to advance only to have the rabbit push both feet into his chest and kick with all his weight. Even as solid as he was, that much force was enough to knock Joe backwards a few steps. Arresting his momentum by grabbing the railing, he pushed off tackling the figure from behind as they turned to run. Wrapping his arms around their torso, he hauled the struggling bunny to his feet before pulling the scarf and goggles free.

As they clattered to the deck, he got his first good look at the mysterious figure. Her hair now exposed, a beautiful blonde snowshoe hare stared defiantly back at him. Taking advantage of his momentary distraction, she wrestled free only to come face to face with Mike.

"Going somewhere?" he asked.

From the other side of the ship, Whitmore and Hawkins arrived a moment later, cutting off any potential avenue of escape. Clearly caught, the female hare slumped her shoulders and allowed the gyrfalcon to take her into custody. Removing her knife and her handgun, he looked into her eyes. "I'll take those."

Saying nothing, she stared daggers at the group as they made their way back to the balloon.

With the prisoner secure for the moment, the crew gathered in the conference area. Standing in a circle, no one seemed willing to be the first one to venture a comment. After a long moment of awkward silence, the captain finally broke the tension. "What the hell happened down there?" Captain Cutler asked.

Joe shrugged. "We were exploring the ship looking for anything salvageable when we encountered her. She took us by surprise, but we were able to pursue her to the deck where we took her into custody."

Whitmore gestured to the items on the table. "This is all she had when we captured her." Other than the knife and handgun, a compass, matches, and assorted survival gear littered the table. Wherever she came from, it was clear she was used to life on the ice.

"And you saw no one else?" the captain asked.

Joe shook his head. "Not that I noticed. As far as I can tell she was alone. If there was anyone else on board we didn't see them," he said, gesturing towards Mike and the others.

Whitmore gave a nod of assent. "We searched the area directly around the ship. If there was anyone else with her, they're laying low."

Captain Cutler rubbed his chin. "Do you think she was already on board when we arrived?"

"If you're asking if I think it was a possibility she was living on the ship, the answer would be no. While it's possible she did arrive before us, the likelihood she could have been surviving on board long term is exceedingly remote without some kind of support," the gyrfalcon said.

"Which begs the question, what was she doing on board the navy ship in the first place?" he asked. "And where did she come from?"

"Right now I'm more curious about how she got on board. We saw no mode of transport and I can't possibly believe she got here on foot," Whitmore said.

"Do you suppose there's another settlement out there?" Mike asked.

"All the other settlements were wiped out by The Freeze," Captain Cutler said. "It's more likely she's just part of a renegade band of survivors that got lucky."

"For forty six years?" Mike made no effort to hide his disbelief. For as far back as they could remember, the government of Coldhaven had repeatedly insisted that there were no other survivors of The Freeze. With no radio transmissions or any other cities within reach to contradict that assertion it had long been accepted as fact. Mike's father had been well known for theorizing that it was possible others had survived the disaster, but with no proof and no one to validate his assumption it was never given much consideration. If this hare did come from somewhere else, it would change their perception of the world as a whole, and throw considerable doubt on the government's position.

"Regardless of where she came from, we have more pressing concerns, such as what to do now," he said.

"What do you mean?" Hawkins asked.

"Well, we obviously can't continue the salvage operation with our prisoner on board," Captain Cutler said. "Even if we had a place to hold her we can't spare the manpower or the resources to keep an eye on her for the duration of the expedition." He folded his arms. "Keeping her on board while we conduct an active salvage operation on this ship represents a significant security risk. Even if we were inclined to do so, I don't feel like watching my back for the next seven days running the risk that she'll escape and with her our only chance to get any answers, do you?" he asked of the group.

The captain had a point. Food rations were calculated for exactly six people for seven days. Any longer and they would have to break into the emergency supplies which came out of the team's salary should that be necessary. And while the majority of that reward was in the materials they retrieved, it was a significant risk to keep her on board the balloon for the entire week. Even if keeping her on the ship instead was an option, she would still represent a drain on manpower and resources as she could not be left unobserved for long. While heading back early would mean they would only return with the materials they had salvaged on their first run through the ship, it would also mean they would still come in ahead given they had not even consumed the expedition's allocated supplies. It was not much, but the longer they waited the more likely this was going to slide towards costing them more than it was worth. At least returning with the prisoner would net them some intelligence, as well as perhaps some additional resources from the government in gratitude.

However, it would also mean abandoning the salvage for the next balloon team, as they would not be sent out again for another two months. By the time they went back out, the ship would be picked clean by the other teams, and they would be back to searching the ice for anything of value. For Joe this was not a problem, as he had what he had come here to find. For the others, it represented a significant loss in pay.

"I don't know about anyone else, but I'm willing to take the risk," Whitmore said, obviously not wanting to give up his share.

"I'm not," Mike said. "I want to make sure I get home to my wife in one piece. Given that she's already kicked me once, I'm not looking forward to another surprise like that," he said, jabbing his finger towards the door to the captain's cabin. "Besides, the longer we stay here, the greater the probability that someone might come looking for her, and they may not be friendly."

Captain Cutler nodded. "She is wearing what looks like a uniform. That suggests she's got a base or something nearby. Odds are they're better armed than we are." Balloon teams regularly carried small arms in the event of possible threats, but if they ran into significant opposition they would be at a clear disadvantage.

Hawkins shrugged. "I don't know. I don't want to give up this salvage, but I don't want to sit watching the bunny for a week either."

Walker scratched his head. "Personally I want this job to end on a positive, whether that means we leave now and return with extra rations, a prisoner, and a little salvage, or stay the full seven days and cost ourselves a little of the bonus for our trouble. Either way makes no difference to me as long as I get paid."

All eyes fell to Joe. The polar bear looked up when he realized they were all staring at him, waiting for an answer. He knew that going back now would cost everyone on the ship to some degree, and even though he had the medication that would buy Emily a lot more time, he did not wish to bring it back to her at the expense of anyone else unless it was absolutely necessary. While it would get the precious resource to his little girl that much sooner, he was more concerned about what the hare's presence meant overall. Wherever she had come from, the fact that she existed at all cast serious doubt on what he had always believed was the truth. Faced with the possibility that there were indeed other survivors and settlements out there, it made every sacrifice their people had been asked to make seem hollow.

Knowing the others expected an answer, he looked up and cast a glance towards the door to the rear of the bridge. "While I'm certain there's a lot more useful salvage still left on the ship, what she brought with her may be more valuable than anything we'll find down there."

Intrigued, the tiger perked his ears up. "What do you mean?" he asked.

Picking up the only device he knew had nothing to do with cold weather survival he held up what he believed was a computer component of some kind. Small and plastic, the rectangle fit on his paw with room to spare. "Whatever she got from the ship is on here."

Taking it from him the captain shrugged. "What is it?"

"Logs and other information the captain and crew collected from immediately after The Freeze." He paused. "Now while it doesn't indicate that they knew what caused it, the information contained within might help us ascertain the source of the effect, or at the very least offer some clues as to how it started."

The tiger scrutinized it, wrinkling his nose at the small device. "As interesting as that would be I don't see how it helps us now."

Hawkins paused. "It might contain an inventory report for the ship's cargo." He tapped it with a finger. "Or even navigational charts that could lead us to additional salvage opportunities."

"Like locations of other precursor settlements," the

captain said.

"It also might answer once and for all what turned the planet into a giant ice ball. If we're lucky, maybe there's even a way to reverse it," Joe said.

"That's speculation at best, and even if it were true it has no bearing on the decision before us now," Captain Cutler said.

"Doesn't it?" Joe asked. "If we know there are tangible leads out there as to the origins of The Freeze don't you think we should investigate it?"

Captain Cutler shook his head. "It doesn't matter what I think. Whether we look into this or not is up to Governor Cole. Our priority is survival and the safety of our families. Now I've considered everything you all have to say, and I'm inclined to return to Coldhaven as soon as possible."

Whitmore slammed his hand down on the table, his talons scraping the metal. "Captain!"

"Save it, Whitmore. I know it's a pay cut for all of us, but I am not looking forward to babysitting her for six days while we scout the rest of the ship. We don't know who she is or how she got on board and I am not willing to run the risk of her escaping before we're done here. We have no idea how close any reinforcements might be, and I am not going to be the one to find out." The tiger looked at the rest of his crew. "Prepare the ship for immediate departure. We're going back."

The gyrfalcon frowned, shooting the captain one more irritated look before he regained his composure and nodded. "Yes, sir."

"I'm going to radio the city and inform them of our change of plan." He turned to Joe. "Mister Kennedy, log our course and then see to the prisoner."

"Sir?" he asked.

"You heard my order. Make sure she's secure and

see that she has food and water for the time being. Do not take her restraints off under any circumstances. That's an order," he said.

"Aye, sir." Joe took the key from the captain and opened the door to his quarters, shooting Mike one last look before he went inside.

Cuffed to a railing on the wall and sitting on the captain's bed, the snowshoe hare looked up but remained silent. In the light, she didn't seem half as threatening as she had inside the ship, but Joe knew better than to lower his guard. Despite her small size, she was stronger than she looked. Athletic and flexible, it was no wonder she had given them so much trouble. Her hair rested in a ponytail that had fallen over her shoulder onto her chest. Reaching forward to check her restraints, he stopped a few feet away. "I'm here to make sure you're secure and see to it you get fed."

"At least I know you don't plan on starving me to death," she said, not looking up.

He held up his paws in a conciliatory gesture. "I promise I won't hurt you." He leaned forward to check her handcuffs, confirming they were still locked tight.

The snowshoe hare smirked. "That's supposed to be my line."

"What were you doing on that ship?" Joe asked.

"You went through my stuff, you should already know." She stared out the window, refusing to acknowledge his glance.

Joe sighed. "I'm sorry about restraining you, but we don't know who you are and we can't trust you without them right now." When she did not respond, he let out a deep breath and shrugged. "We don't have much, but you have your choice of carrot soup or canned corn."

"Is that supposed to be a joke?" she said, looking at the can of carrot soup.

Joe looked down and then wrinkled his muzzle. "It's all we've got."

The hare nodded. "The corn, then."

"Corn it is." He opened the can and then set it on the small heating element just inside the captain's quarters and prepared a bowl and spoon for her. Pouring water into a cup, he handed it to their prisoner. "I assume I can trust you with this."

She tilted her head and looked at him. "It's just water. I'm not going to waste it if that's what you're thinking."

In truth, Joe was more thinking of her throwing it in his face and finding a way to get out of her cuffs before he knew what happened, but for the moment such a scenario seemed more like a theory than anything actually likely to happen. Relaxing slightly he waited as the corn heated up to an acceptable temperature. "I'm Joe, by the way. Joe Kennedy. I've been assigned to keep an eye on you until we get back to Coldhaven."

Her head jerked up at the mention of his home. She did her best to conceal her reaction, but Joe had already seen it in her eyes. She had heard of it before. "I'm Ellie." She looked into his eyes and lowered her shoulders. "Harper."

"Nice to meet you, Ellie Harper. I hope that at least for the next twenty-four hours, you and I can get along." He offered her a slight smile before turning his attention back to the corn, which had warmed up to a comfortably pleasant degree. Peering out into the main bridge area the others had returned to their usual duties. "It's not much, but it'll warm you up at the very least." Offering her the bowl, she accepted it with a graceful nod.

"Thank you," she said. "You're very kind, for whatever you people are doing here."

"We came to salvage supplies and equipment from

the ship for our city," Joe said by way of explanation. "It's how we found you."

"Salvagers," she said, neither approving nor disapproving. "We don't come across them too often."

"Who's we?" he asked.

Before he could get an answer the door opened and the captain peered inside. "Is the prisoner squared away?" he asked.

Joe nodded. "For now."

"Then get back out here. I need you to chart our course back to the city," he said, casting Ellie a sharp look. "You, behave and we won't have any problems. Become a pain in my ass and you can ride from a rope on the bottom of the balloon. We clear?" he asked.

"Crystal," she said, eating her corn.

Joe met her eyes one more time before returning to the table at the back of the bridge. Once the door was locked, the captain walked over to him with a slightly concerned look on his face. "Did she say anything?" he asked.

"Just her name. Ellie Harper," Joe said, which was true for the moment.

"Governor Cole has directed us to return with all possible speed. She's ordered the prisoner to be kept isolated until she can perform a proper interrogation herself," he said.

"That's a waste of time. She was talking, sir." Joe looked through the glass at the snowshoe hare.

Captain Cutler shrugged. "It was a direct order. Other than bringing her food and water, we are to have no contact with her until city security takes her into custody. Now, if you'll log our return path to Coldhaven, we can get underway."

Joe sighed and sat at the table. Glancing behind him at Ellie, he was bursting with questions. Though he had a feeling she had a great deal more to say, he doubted he would get the opportunity on the way back to Coldhaven. For now, he would have to shelve his curiosity and focus on the matter at paw. His questions would have to wait.

Charting the return course was much simpler, since they already knew where they were headed. Combined with an increased speed and a more direct route than the one they had taken to find the ship, they were back in the city in far less time than it had taken to get there in the first place. As they approached the familiar sight of The Candle, Joe looked up while the captain answered the radio. Standard procedure was for them to notify the city of their approach, not the other way around.

"*Good morning, team eight, welcome back,*" the official sounding voice said. "*We've got a priority notification for a member of your crew, Joe Kennedy.*" The captain abruptly turned to look at Joe as he listened to the person on the other end, and then nodded.

"Acknowledged, we're coming in now. I have a high priority report and a prisoner." A moment.

"*Did you say a prisoner?*" the voice said, surprised.

"I did. It's a long story, but we'll explain more when we set down," he replied.

"*I'm sure we'll be interested in hearing it, you're cleared for landing pad two. Proceed at minimal thrust. Control out.*" The radio went silent.

Tempted as he was to press for more details, Joe remained focused on his duties, knowing there was nothing he could do about whatever the notification was until he set his boots on the ground anyway. Concerned that it was something about Emily, he had to struggle to keep his attention on his job, making the last notifications on the map and entering their information in the log, until at last he felt the final bump of the ship being taken by the ground crew and being pulled into its landing position.

Once they were solidly locked into place he jumped to his feet. "I respectfully request permission to disembark, sir." He wanted to get to the bottom of this as quickly as possible. The ship would not be leaving for weeks. He could gather his belongings later.

"Granted," the tiger said. "See to that notification."

"Yes, sir." He rushed out to the deck, being joined by Mike who followed after him as he descended the gangway.

"Where are you off to in such a hurry?" he asked.

Joe didn't even turn to look at him as he responded. "They said I had a priority notification. I need to see what it's about."

Mike nodded. "Okay, don't worry about the balloon. I'll take care of everything." With a brief slap on the back, he rushed back the way they came.

At the base of the gangway, his wife stood with her paws held together in front of her chest. "Joe!" She barely waited until his boots had touched the ground when she ran into his arms, tears soaking her cheek fur. As she looked up into his eyes, he could not have anticipated what she said next. "Lucas has been arrested."

CHAPTER SIX
THE TIPPING POINT

Another day had passed before Joe and Laura were able to get an appointment to see the governor. He had learned from his wife that Lucas had been seen stealing medication, but that they had not found it on him when they had taken him into custody. That and his status as a member of the critically reduced burn team were the only two reasons he had not been exiled from the city already.

Waiting outside of her office Joe held Laura in his arms, doing all he could to comfort his wife during this crisis. Emily fortunately was at home, knowing little of what was going on other than her brother had been very busy, a lie her mother had fabricated to protect her a little longer from the potentially hard truth they might have to face should their son be forced to leave the city as punishment.

For now, his only hope was that Joe could speak to the governor on his behalf, though given how that had gone the last time he was somewhat less than optimistic.

Nevertheless, he had to make the attempt, if for no other reason than to try to spare his family the heartbreak. Squeezing Laura a little tighter, they both looked up as the Governor's assistant approached. The Maine coon cat purred softly brushing a stray auburn hair from her face. "Governor Cole is ready to see you now," she said.

"Thank you," Joe replied.

"We really appreciate this," Laura said, though he doubted she meant it as graciously as it sounded. Gritting his teeth, he kept his muzzle shut.

"Please, follow me." She opened the doors and entered the office with Joe and Laura in tow. "The Kennedys are here to see you, ma'am."

"Thank you, Miss Beckett. Please leave us," she said.

Her head tilted slightly at the order, but she did not object. "As you wish," she replied, bowing graciously as she withdrew from the room.

Joe strode forward and slammed his paws on the desk. "I want my son released."

"Your son's punishment has already been determined," she replied. "As much as I sympathize with your situation, I cannot make exceptions to the law."

"He's a thirteen-year-old boy!" Joe said, baring his teeth.

"His age is irrelevant," the governor replied. "Every person in this city knows full well what the consequences will be if they steal from our collective supplies. Now, I've already given him more consideration than I should have, out of respect for your long service to the city and your assignment to the balloon team. But he must be punished, and he will be."

Joe knew it was a long shot, but given the lack of alternatives he had to try anyway. "Grant leniency to my son. He only stole the medication to help his sister, who is chronically ill, and he knows we are low on her medication." He paused. "If I can convince him to give it back, would you consider releasing him?"

She only hesitated a moment. "No."

"Governor, please," Laura pleaded.

"If anyone discovers that your son stole medication and was not punished accordingly then we will have anarchy and I will not allow that. Not in my city." Her ears flattened and her tail drooped. "I know this is difficult, but returning the medication will not change the fact that he stole it in the first place, and that he was seen doing it by the city's guard." Rubbing the bridge of her nose she sighed. "Even if I were to grant him leniency, word would get out and I cannot run this city without support."

"That's ridiculous. You think that the actions of one boy will undermine your authority?" he asked.

"Watch your tone, Mister Kennedy. Now I will permit your outburst under the circumstances, but my patience grows thin. This is not a negotiation. This is merely a courtesy to you, his parents. Understood?"

He squeezed his paws enough to leave deep impressions from his claws, but forced himself to maintain his composure. "How is Lucas?" Joe asked.

Governor Cole nodded her head. "He's fine, for the time being. Your son is being held in the detention facility in the Industrial Ring where he will remain until either we recover the stolen medicine, or he decides to tell us where he has it hidden away."

"And then?" Laura asked.

"Upon return of the medication, he will be sentenced to exile and delivered outside of the city with the standard supplies," the arctic vixen said. The standard supplies, such as they were, consisted of little more than a sleeping bag, a tent, and a few days of food and water. Out there it wasn't nearly enough, but Joe suspected they were only given that much to assuage their guilt over sending one of their own off to die a slow painful death. To Laura's credit, she did not react other than to squeeze his paw that much harder as she took a seat while he remained standing. "Understand that I take no pleasure in this. It is not my desire to separate you from your son, but if I fail to carry out my duty then I will be punished by those who serve under me, and the person that comes after me would be far less sympathetic, I promise you that." Taking a deep breath, she continued. "Now I can assure you that he will be treated well for the next few days and when sentence is carried out that you will be notified so you can say goodbye," she said. "I'm afraid that's all I can do."

Laura fell silent, and while Joe knew she had a great deal more to say she seemed to realize that for the moment at least they were out of moves with the governor herself. Retaining her composure, she squeezed his paw one more time, wordlessly begging him for any kind of solution.

While Joe did not have much else to offer, he did have one option left to him. "I want to see him."

Governor Cole considered the request for a moment, looking at both Joe and Laura before finally nodding her approval. "Of course. I'll arrange it as soon as you're ready."

"We're ready now," he said.

The arctic vixen pressed a button in the control panel. A moment later, a male voice came back. "Yes?"

"This is Governor Cole. I am hereby authorizing Joe and Laura Kennedy to visit prisoner two two one. Please allow them access on my authorization." She stared down at the surface of her desk awaiting a response.

"Understood. We'll prepare for their arrival." The line went silent.

"Thank you," Joe said.

"Yes, thank you," Laura added.

Governor Cole nodded to them both. "I'm sorry I can't do more for you, but this is all I can offer."

"We appreciate it, ma'am." Joe nodded to her and then turned towards the screen he had only glimpsed the last time he was here. At the present time it only displayed temperature data for the entirety of the city, but he could not help but think that there had been something more going on at his last visit. Having no further excuse to remain, he ushered his wife gently towards the door as the pair exited out into the hallway.

Laura pressed herself against him. "Joe, what are we going to do?"

Wishing he had a better answer, he kissed the top of her head. "We'll figure it out. I don't know how, but we'll figure it out. I promise. First things first, though. We need to see Lucas and make sure he's all right. Once we do that, we can figure out our next step. We'll see him and then pick up our rations. Emily has to be hungry by then."

"What do we tell her?" Laura asked.

"The truth," Joe said. "That we're going to get her brother and bring him home." He held up a paw to forestall the inevitable question that would follow. "One thing at a time."

Nodding her agreement, she chose to say nothing for the time being. It would take them at least an hour to walk to the edge of the city, but at least it would be a pleasant walk. One of the benefits of living in a frozen wasteland, if there were such a thing, was that you were always dressed for the weather. Holding his wife close, Joe pressed against her to share their collective warmth. With her paw in his own, Joe walked alongside her away from the central nexus.

Following the radial streets towards the south section of Coldhaven, the facility was isolated from most other inhabited areas for two reasons. The first was security, keeping any violators of the law as far away from the rest of the population as possible. The second was that it was deemed that prisoners did not deserve the benefits of most of the rest of society and thus they were kept as far away from the central heat of the city as possible. It was for this reason the building had earned the nickname 'The Fridge'.

Shaped like a giant rectangle surrounded by a tall fence, it was easy to see why the name had stuck. With guard towers at each corner and a thick gate dusted with snow, there was little question as to what purpose the building served. Built in the first few years of the city, it had served as a deterrent to most people who would consider less than legal actions to ensure their survival.

Primarily intended to facilitate short term detentions, the prison was not large nor was it intended to house very many people. Consisting of five floors, the building was equipped with the bare minimum for the survival of those it held. Cold, dark, and windowless, it was far from a pleasant place to be. The majority of those serving a sentence here had committed some minor offense that when completed would see them returning to a productive role in the city.

However, in rare cases such as the one they now found Lucas in, the facility was used to hold people that for whatever reason could not be exiled at the time of sentencing. And while it was little better than the environment outside the city, it at least provided some breathing room for Joe to come up with something else.

Approaching the front gate, Joe and his wife stood a few feet away from the small booth out front. The two guards seated inside spoke through the small grate in the glass. "State your name and purpose."

"Our names are Joe and Laura Kennedy. We're here to see our son." The polar bear gave her shoulder a gentle squeeze. "Governor Cole called to say we were coming," he said.

Holding up a finger, the draft horse spoke into a receiver, and a moment later nodded to them both. "You can go inside." Pressing a button, the gate slowly slid open to allow them access to the rather small yard between the building and the fence. Entering with his wife's paw in his thick gloved fingers, he involuntarily shivered when it closed behind them with a loud clang of metal as the lock secured itself once more. Forcing his feet paws to keep moving forward, they entered the building and made their way into the lobby.

The other reason the nickname for this place was so apt became obvious the moment they had entered the building. The vast majority of structures in Coldhaven had heat radiating from the center of the city to provide a livable temperature. Supplemented by heaters in most every building on the colder days, The Fridge by comparison seemed to lack anything other than the most minimal insulation with little heat other than the warmth provided by the people inside and their own clothing.

The chill evident by the vapor of his breath, Joe pulled his coat tighter as they made their way towards the desk. Seated there was a black wolf inside a glass enclosure, one of the few areas within the building so far he had noticed any sort of heat at all. Already knowing why only the guard areas seemed to be temperature controlled, he made no comment about it as he approached. With a respectful nod, he waited until the muscular lupine looked up to acknowledge him before he spoke.

"You two are the Kennedys?" he asked.

"We are," Joe replied.

"Don't get many visitors here," the guard said. "Most of the time the people who end up here tend to not have too much family." When neither of them replied he shrugged and stood up. "Come with me." Ushering them into a small room, he locked eyes with Joe. "Wait here. Your son will be brought down in a moment."

The room was little more than a rectangle containing a table and some metal chairs. Certainly not comfortable, by any means, but at least they would get a chance to speak with Lucas. He had learned from his wife that Lucas had broken into the medical supply area and made off with two bottles of Emily's medicine, but she did not know any more than that. The only reason she knew that much in the first place was the result of the city guard's questioning when they demanded the stolen goods be returned.

Laura rubbed her paws together, looking around the room. "We can't leave our son in this terrible place."

"We won't, I promise." He knew he was in no position to make such an assurance, but he could not bear to see his wife suffer, especially not after all they had been through with Emily. Moving to embrace Laura, he held her close for several long moments until they were interrupted by the sudden opening of the door.

A guard ushered their son inside, looking at Joe as he spoke. "Fifteen minutes." With that, the door closed, and they were alone. Dressed in a drab prison jumpsuit and shackled at both the wrists and ankles, Lucas shuffled bare pawed towards the table. Joe's chest ached at the sight, wanting nothing more than to take him home to his family.

Laura pulled herself free, rushing to embrace her son as if she had not seen him in years. "Oh, Lucas!" Holding him tight, she squeezed the young polar bear until he began to squirm. "I love you so much."

"I love you too, Mom, but I kind of need to breathe," he said, his chains clinking against each other.

Recalling her own ursine strength she released him, meekly hugging him once more. "Sorry."

"Are you all right, son?" Joe asked. "They didn't tell us anything other than that you were here."

Lucas nodded. "Yeah, I'm sorry about that. I did what I had to do, just like you would have done."

Joe ushered his wife into one of the chairs. "We'll talk about that in a minute. First, how are they treating you?"

"Considering I've only been here a few days I'm all right. It's better than out there," he said, gesturing outside the city. Urging him to continue, Lucas looked up at his father. "The cells are pretty cold but at least I have a bed and a blanket, though it's pretty thin. They feed us twice a day but it's nothing like your cooking, Mom. I'm doing what I can to keep busy and stay warm, but I wish they'd tell me how long they intended to hold me."

Joe squeezed Laura's shoulder, knowing it was not easy for her to hear her son being treated this way. For her sake, Joe bore the brunt of their conversation. He knew as painful as it was to discuss, he would not get another chance to speak to his son before his sentence was carried out. "They're going to exile you, Lucas," he said. "The only reason they haven't done it already is because they want the medicine you stole."

Lucas straightened up. "For what, so it can sit on the shelf? They don't need it. Emily does."

Joe's chest tightened. It was an argument he had made in his head more times than he could count. If he hadn't found what he was looking for on the Navy ship, he might have stolen the drugs himself, consequences be damned. "I was coming back with something to help your sister. All you had to do was hold on a little longer."

"You didn't see her dad. She tries to hide it from us, but I know she's getting weaker." His eyes moistened and he clenched his paws. "Keeping her safe is all that matters. I'm her big brother. I won't let anything take her away from us."

Joe wanted nothing more than to wrap his arms around his son and tell him it was going to be all right. He gritted his teeth, foiled by his own helplessness. What Lucas needed was a plan to keep him safe, not false hope. "I need you to stay strong, for your sister. She's waiting for you to come home. After all, you're the only one who can calm her down when she's upset."

Lucas clenched his teeth and stared into his father's eyes. "I'm not giving it back, dad. No matter what."

"It wouldn't make any difference if you did," he replied. "The governor has made it clear she can make no exceptions to the law. One way or the other she intends to cast you out of the city."

Stunned, the younger polar bear's shoulders sank. He dropped into the chair beside him. "As long as it buys Emily some more time, then it's worth it."

"Not if it costs you your life," Laura said, speaking up at last. "You know your father and I have always found a way to take care of both you and your sister. Why couldn't you trust us to do it this time?"

Lucas stared down at his shackled paws. "It's not that I didn't trust you both. I know you'd do anything for us, but Emily was running out of time." He exhaled deeply. "I've been listening to you two." He looked at both of his parents. "When you talk to each other in the bedroom and think we can't hear. We can."

"Oh, Lucas," Laura said. "We didn't mean to concern you."

"I know you don't, but I love Emily too and I

couldn't stand by and let her die. Dad was going to be gone for who knows how long and even if you stretched out what medicine she has left, I know it's not going to last. It might not even have lasted long enough for Dad to get back," Lucas replied.

In truth, both Joe and Laura had known there was a possibility he would not return in time to give her the new medicine, whether it was due to weather delays or the simple fact that her current drug did not have nearly as much effect as it once did. Though neither one of them had been willing to voice the thought upon his departure, he could not deny it had crossed his mind. "Even so, it's not your responsibility to take care of your sister, it's ours," Joe said.

"In this family, we take care of each other," Lucas replied, staring at his father. "You taught me that."

Joe nodded, taking a seat beside his son. Grasping his ice-cold fingers, he attempted to warm them with his paws. "But I also taught you not to take chances, especially not here on the ice."

Lucas shook his head. "It wasn't supposed to go like this."

"What happened, exactly?" Joe asked.

The younger polar bear grew quiet for a moment. At last, he raised his muzzle and spoke. "I was going home after my last shift at The Candle when I walked by one of the storage facilities where they keep some of the medical supplies. No one was around so I broke in and took what I needed. On my way out, I ran into the city guard. I got away from them long enough to stash the stuff, but they caught me trying to make my way home."

"It's a good thing you didn't make it there," Joe said. Seeing his son's confused expression, he frowned. "If you'd given it to your mother and they found it in the house they'd have arrested her and Emily, too."

Shaking his head, Lucas slammed his paws on the table. "It doesn't make any sense! They could help so many people here if they just tried. But instead, they'd rather lock me up than help my sister."

"I know," Joe said, hugging his son. "I know." Taking a deep breath, he held the younger ursine gently and nodded. "Your heart was in the right place. Let's get that clear right now." He rubbed his back gently. "You're a good brother. There's no point in talking about what we could have done different. This is the situation we've got and we have to deal with it. For now, they're going to hold you here while they look for the medicine. I need to know where you stashed it."

Looking to his mother and then his father, he shook his head. "No."

"Son, if they find that before I have a chance to figure something out then they will exile you," Joe said.

"I know, but where I stashed it they won't find it for weeks," Lucas said.

"Are you sure about that?" he asked. "Because they are looking everywhere and I think it's only a matter of time before they track that medicine down. Now I know you don't want them to get their paws on it, but if they find it before we can come up with a plan then it won't do anybody any good, least of all Emily." Joe looked at his young son. "I know you think they can't find that medicine but I'm asking you to trust me. Tell me where it is, so I can put it somewhere safe." Lucas looked at the door and then leaned in close to whisper the information into his father's ear. When he pulled back Joe smiled slightly. "Smart boy." He gave him a gentle hug. "I promise you, we'll figure something out. I just need you to hang on for a few days while I come up with a plan."

With a nod, Lucas agreed. "Okay."

The door opened and the same black wolf appeared once more. "Time's up. I'm here to escort you back to your cell." Laura jumped up to hug her son one more time before allowing the guard to escort him out of the room.

Joe reached out for Lucas, their claws touching only briefly before his son was pulled out of sight. He felt a drip of moisture fall from his cheek to the table, freezing on contact. When they were gone, a moment later they were directed to leave the facility the same way they had entered. Outside once more, Joe and Laura started the walk towards the residential ring.

"Promise me you'll get him out of there." Laura pressed against her husband.

"I promise, I will not let them exile our son," he said. "I don't know how, but I'll come up with something."

Laura leaned against him. "I don't care what happens, as long as we're together." She held him close, kissing his muzzle.

Even though snow was falling all around them, Joe had never felt so warm in his life. Looking into Laura's eyes, he saw for the first time since he'd returned to Coldhaven renewed hope in her eyes. Smiling gently, he walked slowly towards the direction of their home. Arriving at their front door, Joe hesitated.

"Aren't you coming?" Laura asked.

"I have a few things to take care of before I go in." Joe offered her his most reassuring smile.

Laura, knowing he was not telling her out of an abundance of caution, nodded. "Just make sure you're home in time for supper. Emily has hardly seen her papa in days, and I'd hate for you to keep her waiting."

"Yes, dear," he said, giving her one last kiss before he made his way to the industrial ring. City guard members were crawling all over the place, but Joe was a familiar sight in the area. More than likely most of them had not yet learned he was no longer on the maintenance team, but even so he should not remain there any longer than necessary.

Keeping a steady pace as he walked, he knew it was not far to his destination. Even though he had walked this stretch of road countless times it seemed so much longer today given what was at stake. Joe knew the critical piece to his carrying this out was to remain calm and not give in to the anxiety bubbling just underneath the surface of his emotions. He rubbed his paws to disguise the nervousness, an act that in Coldhaven was as common as breathing. To buy his family as much time as possible, he had to get to that medicine before anyone else did.

As tempted as he was to break into a run, he knew it would only attract attention. Several members of the guard were combing through the area looking for the two tiny bottles of medicine that were the only thing keeping Lucas from being tossed out onto the ice. Joe could not let that happen. Nodding to a few of the men who might potentially exile his son he kept his face neutral. Ignoring him, they continued their search. At least that was one small favor.

Every member of the city guard seemed to be here looking for those two tiny bottles. Joe could not bring himself to be surprised given how precious such resources were considered to be within the city. Widely regarded as a worse crime than murder it was seen as a very affront to Coldhaven itself, with every person regularly being asked to sacrifice and accept the hardships as a shared burden made easier by the fact that the entire population was subject to the same limitations. Taken as a personal offense by most citizens Joe knew that some thieves never even made it to The Fridge due to 'accidents' during the attempt to take them into custody.

Knowing that if they caught him with the medicine

he would be arrested alongside his son, for the first time since he could remember he was grateful for the cold. At least it kept him from sweating. Passing another pair of guards on their patrol, he knew they were working from the outer edge of the city inward. Having seen their sweeps before, he knew the city guard liked their protocol, so he had a short while.

Approaching the building his son had taken refuge in after the citywide meeting, he slipped inside the small storage facility. Without a flashlight he had to wait a moment for his eyes to adjust. He had to move quickly as the city guard would be coming by in a few minutes. Walking forward, he spotted the box where his son had been sitting. Lucas would not have put it inside, that was too obvious. But he would have put it somewhere one was not likely to look at first glance. Looking up, he spotted the two bottles neatly placed on one of the rafters.

Climbing up on the box he retrieved them, confirming that they were indeed the medication that had kept Emily alive up to this point. Coupled with what they had, it would buy his little girl a good margin of time. Of course, this presumed he could keep it. Lucas was right in that the city had kept a stockpile of most supplies just in case, but given the fact that the governor had made it quite clear returning the medicine would make no difference with regard to Lucas's punishment, then it might as well do Emily some good.

Placing it in his pants pocket with the other vial from the Navy ship, he made his way back outside. Just as he turned to walk away, he heard his name called out and froze. "Joe? Is that you?"

Turning slowly he recognized the ursine as Valentine, a member of the city guard who he had met a few times in his travels around the city. A grizzly bear, he was muscular and well-built though his fur was more suited for warmer environments. Either way he was better off than his partner, a domestic cat who shivered as they stood there. "Do we really have time for a conversation?" the feline asked.

"We can spare a minute," Valentine insisted.

"Great, while I freeze my tail off," the cat complained.

Joe could not help but smile at the interaction as he greeted the pair. "Hello Valentine."

"I haven't seen you around much lately," he said. "Where have you been?"

Joe shrugged. "I've been working in other sections of the city the past few days," he lied. "They've been keeping us pretty busy after that incident in The Candle."

"Yeah," Valentine agreed. "Such a terrible accident. I'm glad we didn't lose more people." Looking at Joe, he frowned. "I'm sorry about what happened with your boy. That was a hell of a thing, surviving that and then being sentenced to exile." He extended a paw to squeeze his shoulder gently.

"It hasn't been easy to process," he said. "Laura's just beside herself. I wish I could be with her all the time these days, but you know how it is."

"Yeah, you have to report for work duty." He sighed. "Look, Joe, I'm not supposed to tell you, but we're looking for the meds your boy stole. Once we find it they're going to exile him so you might want to prepare yourself. I know its hard thing but it's only a matter of time before we find them." He wrinkled his muzzle and then looked at his partner. "Look, when we find it, I might hold off on reporting it for a day or two out of respect for you and Laura. Give your boy a little more time inside the city."

Nodding in gratitude, Joe did his best to appear appreciative knowing full well the medicine they were looking for was in his pocket. Working up his most genuine smile, he nodded. "Thank you."

"It's the least I can do for all you've done for the city." He raised a finger to forestall his partner's objections. "Now I can't do anything about it if someone else finds it first, but if you know where it is, I promise if you tell me I'll buy your son as much time as I can."

Joe fought the urge to tell him out of guilt or some sense of loyalty to the city, but if he was going to save his family everything depended on him not reacting. Steeling his face into a mask of impassivity, he shook his head. "I'm sorry, but wherever Lucas hid it, he didn't tell me."

Valentine examined him for a moment longer, before nodding and dropping his shoulders slightly. "I had to ask, you understand."

"Of course. Now if you'll excuse me, I have to get back to work," Joe lied.

Stewart twitched his whiskers and walked after him. "Hold on a second."

Joe froze. "Yes?"

"Where are your tools?" he asked.

In his haste to retrieve the medicine he had neglected to foresee this critical flaw in his cover story. So used to having his tools with him at all times it had not even occurred to him that he no longer carried them everywhere he went while on duty. Suddenly aware of their glaring absence, he had to come up with something, and fast. "I left them with Mike. He's waiting for me back in the residential ring."

Hesitating for a moment, the feline was interrupted by Valentine. "Okay. Then we won't keep you. Tell him I said hi."

"Will do," Joe said, offering a casual salute and walking off. Certain he could feel the cat's stare boring holes in his back, he did not relax until he was well out of sight.

Letting out a deep breath, he knelt in the snow for a moment as all the stress and anxiety of the last fifteen minutes came over him all at once. With his chest tight and his heart racing, he could not stand for another ten minutes as he fought to rein in his emotions. Fear of losing Lucas and Emily raged within him, a possibility he could not bear to consider. The memory of his son shackled and alone in that place gnawed at him. His children were in pain, and he could do little to ease their circumstances. He would do anything to keep his family together, but only the hope that he could figure out something kept him from collapsing completely.

He was not done, not yet. He still had some time, and he had to use it. Summoning all of his strength, he took a deep breath and resumed walking to his next destination. If his plan to get his family somewhere safe was going to work, he was going to have to prepare well.

At this time of the day the balloon hangar was mostly empty. Perfect for what he needed to do. Slipping inside, he looked up at the seven balloons currently docked in the massive structure. Held by their clamps and positioned next to a set of stairs that permitted access, they waited for their next missions.

Going into the maintenance room, he picked up a set of tools and scanned the area for signs of anyone present. Reasonably certain he was alone, he set to work sabotaging the other six balloons. It did not require much, a loosened connection here, an opened valve there, but it would take their crews time to diagnose and repair the problems. Even if Joe managed to take off without an issue, he could not risk the other balloons getting in his way. These subtle tweaks would prevent any sort of speedy pursuit without putting anyone at risk.

His work done, he returned the tools to the metal locker, taking care to be certain they were just as he had found them. Shutting it with his right paw, he found himself looking straight into the eyes of Captain Cutler. "Captain."

"Kennedy. I didn't expect to see you this evening."

"I just forgot something in my locker," he said. Holding up his gloves he shrugged. "Can't forget those."

Captain Cutler gestured behind him. "Central is still trying to decide what to do with us. So far they haven't decided whether or not they're going to keep us stocked or move all of our supplies to the other balloons, but I argued for them to keep us fueled and ready and to send us out on the next expedition. We're more or less ready to go, once we're topped off all we need is a few more days of rest and we can take the next trip out to the Navy ship. It's going to take at least three or four trips to clear it all out and that's optimistic, so I think we still deserve a crack at that pie, don't you?"

"Sounds good to me, sir. I know Walker will be pleased," he said, thinking of his crewmate's earlier complaint.

The tiger chuckled, baring his fangs slightly. "He still hasn't stopped complaining about having to come back early. Look, whether we do or not I just wanted to say you did good out there. You kept a level head even when faced with something unexpected, and you kept Mister Rush in one piece. You keep performing like that and I might consider you for the first officer slot one day."

"Thank you, sir." Joe nodded gratefully.

"You've earned it. As you can imagine it's hard to find good people these days especially for work like we do out there on the ice. And in case you hadn't noticed I can use all the good people I can get." He reached out and shook his paw. "Tell your friend he did all right too. If he wants to keep sailing with me I'd have no objections."

"Will do, sir." Joe smiled. "Sir, may I ask you

something?"

The striped feline paused. "As long as it's quick."

"What's going to happen to the hare?"

Looking around to be certain they were alone, the captain leaned closer. "I honestly don't know. The city guard took her into custody the moment we returned and I haven't seen her since. As far as I know they're taking her to The Fridge for the time being, but beyond that your guess is as good as mine." He shrugged. "I'm sure I don't have to tell you that the information I just gave you is not to be discussed in public."

"Of course, sir." Joe nodded affirmatively before turning to look once more at the balloon to which he was currently assigned. Lined up in a neat row, the aerial craft that made up the entirety of Coldhaven's salvage fleet sat silently like sentinels watching over the city, just waiting for the chance to be called to action. At the moment there were seven, with the first currently out making its way towards the ship to continue the salvage. To most they were little more than curiosities, but to Joe they represented the best chance he had to keep his family in one piece. But before he could put his plan into action he just needed a few more things. After one more look around he walked out of the hangar and back towards his home.

Laura and Emily waited for him at the table, having just heated their dinner. When he stepped inside the house, Laura kissed him before gesturing to his spot at the head of the table. "You're just in time."

Emily clutched her odd looking doll under her arm, and setting him in her brother's chair she smiled. "I thought since Lucas can't be here with us that Andre would keep his seat warm."

Joe smiled. "That's very thoughtful, sweetie. I know your brother appreciates it."

"When is he coming home, Papa?"

"Soon, baby. I promise." Joe smiled.

All of a sudden, there was a knock from outside. Alarmed, Laura moved over to Emily's side of the table. Meeting her concerned glance, Joe opened the door. Stepping aside, he allowed the two city guard members to enter. Recognizing them from earlier, he backed up a few steps. "Pardon the interruption," Valentine said.

"Can I help you?" Joe asked.

"I sincerely hope not, as if you can then I would need to arrest you by the governor's order. So far, we have been unsuccessful in locating the stolen medicine, and while we still have people scouring the area we are expanding our search to known associates, which includes you," Stewart said. "We were told you spoke to your son earlier, if he relayed to you where you could find the medication it occurred to us that perhaps you retrieved it and brought it here."

Joe balled his paws into fists. "I did nothing of the sort." He growled. "I don't know what you think you're doing, but I assure you I have no idea where he hid it." The polar bear gave them his iciest stare. "While you are free to search my home, I assure you that you will find nothing that does not belong." Staring at both men, he gestured towards the table. "Now as you can see, we were about to have dinner, so if you'll excuse us, I intend to have a meal with my family." Passing by the table, he slipped the three bottles of medicine into his wife's paw.

The two city guard members began to search the Kennedy home, looking through the various drawers and any obvious hiding spots while Laura and Emily sat close together, eating their meal and trying to ignore the men as they looked around. Stewart vanished into the bedroom, from which Joe could hear the sounds of drawers being opened and the bed being moved. When the feline returned he shook his head. "I found a single bottle of the medication, but it's nearly empty."

"That's the one my daughter was prescribed by Doctor Reed. You can ask him yourself." No doubt his wife had already tossed the empty one he had officially received from the doc. The one they found and mistook for the legitimate prescription was in fact the one he had begged for and so far had not been discovered as missing.

Valentine looked into his eyes. "You wouldn't hide it here, would you, Joe?" he asked. "I know you care too much about Laura and Emily to take them down with Lucas."

Joe avoided his glare. "Not in front of my daughter," he said.

Valentine looked up at Stewart. "Did you find anything?"

"Nothing of consequence," he replied.

With that, he looked once more at Joe and then at Laura's paw, which the entire time had been concealed under the table. Walking over, he pulled her wrist up to examine her clenched fist. "Open it."

Doing as instructed, she unfurled her fingers to reveal nothing more than her empty paw. "Satisfied?"

The two guards met each other's glance before Valentine let out a deep sigh and released her. "Apologies. Forgive us for disturbing you." Turning to his partner, he gestured for him to follow. "Let's go, Stewart. We have many more places to check," he said. Stewart looked once more at Joe before finally following Valentine out the door.

Once they were alone Joe let out a deep sigh. "That was close." Looking at Laura, he moved to the window to be certain the guards were gone before turning back to her. "When he grabbed your wrist I about had a heart attack."

"You thought I'd still be holding it?" she asked.

Joe shrugged.

"Oh, Joe, you may be an expert on this city, but there are a lot of things you've yet to learn." Laura flashed him a smile.

"Are you going to tell me what you did with them?"

"And spoil the surprise?" she asked. "Eat your dinner before it gets cold."

"Laura," he insisted.

She sighed and looked to Emily. "Well, what do you think? Should we tell him?"

Emily held up her toy. "It was Andre." Rolling him onto his tummy she lifted up his shirt to reveal a tiny zipper. Pulling it down she exposed the three tiny glass bottles inside her doll, where they remained safely hidden from prying eyes. Zipping it back up, she smiled.

"I take back everything I ever said about Andre, sweetie. From now on he's a member of the family," he said.

Smiling brightly, Emily began to eat her dinner.

Joe looked at his wife and daughter, the sight of their smiling faces only serving to underscore the absence of their son. Thinking of Lucas reminded him of how much stood between him and his family's safety, but that was a concern for another day. For now, they had kept things together for a little while longer, and all they had to do was keep doing it until the next set of problems presented themselves.

Though the fight was far from over, the next few days were likely to present a particular challenge, so until then he intended to gather as much strength as possible. Odds are he would need it.

CHAPTER SEVEN
NOWHERE TO GO

Mornings in Coldhaven were always abuzz with activity. The day started early, with most folks needing to pick up the day's rations before reporting for duty. Normally Laura would be the one to do this but today Joe had volunteered since he had errands to run anyway and thought he would spare his wife the trip. It was strange to Joe to not be on his way to the workshop as he had done every day before joining the balloon team. Yet one of the trade offs to working the balloons meant that when you were in the city you were one of the few people not required to hold down a regular work shift.

This did not mean you did not have responsibilities, of course, but contrary to most other full-time positions in Coldhaven, only half of the crew was needed to maintain the ship and its systems while docked in the hangar. Barring any particular complications the crew took turns monitoring the ship while the rest of the team was free to go about their business.

Wrapping his coat around himself, Joe stood in line waiting for the rations for his family. Shivering slightly, he shifted his boots in the snow in an effort to generate a little warmth. Noticing his discomfort, a German shepherd standing behind him leaned forward. "You've got to keep moving, it helps."

"I'm not used to standing in line," Joe said.

"I can tell. I do this all the time, so I'm used to it." He extended a paw. "Name's Alexander Scott. I work in one of the shops in the residential ring." Dressed in a dark blue insulated jacket and a white shirt, the German shepherd was slightly shorter than Joe with a neat haircut and well-groomed fur. Looking at the proffered paw he could tell from his manicured claws that he was definitely someone that spent most of their working hours inside. As he reached out to take it the canine smiled in response. "I don't think I've seen you here before."

"My wife usually does this," Joe explained.

"Ah, that explains it," the canine replied. "Confirmed bachelor here. No one to pick up my rations but me."

"Oh," Joe said, not sure what to say to that.

Recognizing his discomfort, the German shepherd held up his paws. "Oh, it's no big deal. I rather like it actually, having a place to myself. It's small, but it's mine." He gestured towards the line, which had been moving steadily since he arrived. "So, what do you do?"

Joe opened his mouth to answer, but then remembered he was no longer carrying a wrench everywhere he went. "I'm on Balloon Team Eight."

"Ah, an aeronaut," he said, his eyes brightening. "I bet you've got some stories to tell."

"You have no idea," Joe said. Interrupting their

conversation, he turned as it was his turn at the front of the line. "Picking up for the Kennedy family, unit 42." The skunk at the counter nodded, consulting her notes before calling out Joe's order. Another person behind her passed her a parcel which she handed over to him. "Thanks," he said, taking it in paw.

Wrapped neatly in a package tied by string, it contained all of the food and resources for a family of four, minus the usual allowance for him being on the balloon. As he tucked it under his arm Alex stepped up to the window and received his own. Hurrying to catch up to Joe, he looked up at him with a smile. "So what did you see out there?" he asked.

"A lot of ice," Joe replied.

"The rumors say you saw a lot more. They say that you found something alive." When Joe did not respond, he continued. "Is it true?"

Joe shook his head. "All we found was an old, abandoned Navy ship." He shook his head, recalling the Captain's order about the hare.

"Then why did your balloon come back four days early?" he asked. When Joe did not respond he shrugged. "Look, you go out on a normal salvage operation and you come back ahead of schedule with no explanation, people are going to talk."

"I don't know what to tell you. We just had some maintenance issues and had to turn back early," Joe shrugged and kept walking. Whether the German shepherd believed him or not he could not tell, but even he had to admit it sounded suspect. Seeing that he was not likely to learn anything from Joe, the canine turned and walked away.

Joe stared in the direction he had gone for a few moments longer. He hated lying to anyone, but he knew admitting the truth would probably cause more trouble than it would solve.

His thoughts turned once again to the word he had recalled in his dream, and the image he had caught a glimpse of in Governor Cole's office. Garden. What did it mean? What was she looking at before he had come in to see her? Knowing he would not likely find answers to his questions walking around the city he dropped off the rations with Laura and made his way to his next stop at Mike's house.

The king penguin lived not far from Joe in a similar sized unit in the residential ring. Like him, he was off for the day so Joe knew he would be there when he arrived at the front door. Knocking with the back of his paw, he waited patiently for his friend to answer.

Mike appeared dressed in a long-sleeved shirt and thick jacket, looking up at the polar bear with a slightly tilted beak. "Joe? What are you doing here?"

"I need to talk to you about something," he said.

"Is this something I'm going to like?"

Joe frowned. "Probably not."

Letting out a deep sigh, Mike gestured for him to enter. "Okay, come on inside."

Joe gave his friend a grateful nod, casting a glance around before making his way inside the house. Mike's home was set up similar to his own, with the same basic design being used many times during the early days of Coldhaven's existence. Taking a seat at the table, the polar bear waited while Mike poured them each a cup of water. Handing one to Joe, he accepted it gratefully. "Thanks."

"So what brings you to my place?"

"I came to ask you about your dad," Joe replied.

"What about him?" Mike took a sip of his water.

Joe held the cup between his paws. "He was on one of the first balloon teams, wasn't he?"

"Yeah, back before they ironed out the kinks. It's a

wonder he came back at all sometimes. But he served on the balloon team for a couple of years until they discontinued the program for a while." Mike shrugged. "Why?"

The polar bear raised his head. "Do you still have his research?"

Mike straightened up suddenly. "Dad's old logs?" He nodded. "Yeah, of course I do. Lisa wanted me to get rid of them a few times but I couldn't bring myself to do it. No matter what people thought of my father I always believed he was on to something." He sighed. "He could just never prove it."

Joe nodded. "I need to see everything he had."

"Why the sudden interest in dad's research?" he asked. "I mean, I don't mind, but if you're going to dig into my family's history, I want to know what's going on. After all, we've been friends for as long as I can remember." Mike leaned closer, bringing his beak to within inches of Joe. "Please."

"They're going to exile Lucas."

"Shit," Mike said.

"The governor told me herself. He was caught stealing and the only reason he's still within the city is because they can't find the medicine he stole. Now I can't let that happen, but before I can go in and get him, I need to have someplace to go. Staying in the city isn't an option. Not only do they monitor all the supplies, but there are only so many places to hide and I can't do that to Laura and Emily, not forever. Your dad talked about places he thought were likely to survive any sort of event like The Freeze, and I need to know if any of them are within range."

Mike blinked a few times while he considered what the polar bear had just said. "That's a pretty big ask."

"If I had any other options I'd consider them, but I'm running out of time and I need to find a safe haven for my family," Joe responded.

He looked down his beak at Joe. "Well, whatever you plan to do, I'm with you all the way."

"What?" Joe replied, surprised. "No, Mike. I can't involve you in this more than I already have. You could get in trouble just for giving me this information." He rose to stand. "If they find out that you told me where to go, they'll arrest you too."

"Then we'd best make sure they don't find out," he said. "I don't know what you've got up your sleeve, but even if you're the luckiest son of a bitch in the world you're going to need help to pull it off," Mike said. "And I just got myself into some pretty deep shit, didn't I?"

"Probably," Joe admitted.

"You know, some days it's not easy being your friend, Joe Kennedy." He squeezed his shoulder with a webbed hand.

"Sorry."

"I'll say one thing for you, at least you keep life interesting," he said.

"I'm not doing it on purpose," Joe insisted.

Mike chuckled. "So, what's your plan?"

"Get Lucas and get out of the city," Joe replied.

"How?"

"I don't know yet," the ursine admitted.

"What are you going to do when you get him out of there?"

Joe shrugged. "I'm working on that."

"Since there's really only one way out of the city, I expect you're going to steal a balloon. How were you planning to operate it by yourself?" he asked.

"Laura knows how to navigate, and I can fly it as long as I don't have to do any crazy maneuvers. I think I picked up enough from the captain during our trip out to the Navy vessel," Joe said.

"And you have no idea where you're going once you get it into the air," Mike said. "Not as of yet, no," Joe replied.

"This is going to go great," he said.

Joe frowned. "Look, a week ago my biggest problem was what size wrench I needed. I'd say I'm doing pretty good all things considered. Now are you going to help me or keep making snarky comments?"

"I don't recall those being mutually exclusive," Mike pointed out.

"I hate you," Joe said.

Holding up his webbed hands the penguin laughed. "Okay, okay, I'm sorry. Let's handle one problem at a time." He ducked into the bedroom, returning a moment later with a detailed map of the city. "Okay, this is Coldhaven." He looked at Joe. "You're going to need a clean way to get in and get to Lucas."

"Right. Having been there to see him, I can tell you the front door is not an option," he said.

"Definitely not, not if you want to get to him unnoticed." Mike paused. "There has to be a way in there, something they wouldn't anticipate."

"And preferably something that won't set off any alarms."

Mike jabbed at the map with his talon. "The access vent on the bottom level. There's a tunnel that runs underneath the building where they're keeping Lucas, it was installed long before they ever knew there was going to be a prison there when they were originally laying out the city. Now it's not very big, you're going to have to squeeze in, but you should still fit." He held his arms apart to indicate the approximate width. "It's there for maintenance access so you should be able to get it open from inside."

Joe looked up. "Wait a minute. Those tunnels are normally filled with steam from the transfer pipes."

"Yeah, and?" Mike prompted.

"So, I'd like to still have my fur after we get out of there," Joe said.

Mike held up a finger. "I'm getting to that. Now the prison doesn't use a lot of heat but that actually works in your favor. Whenever you're ready to go in and get Lucas, I can divert the steam to another part of the city and blow some of the steam hubs. It won't kill anybody but it'll cause a hell of a noise."

"Not to mention a huge headache for the maintenance team," Joe said.

"They won't be happy with us for sure, but I still have some guys in the Workshop that owe me some favors. That'll get you in, and it'll also do double duty in that it'll divert most of the city guard and general population away from your section of the city," Mike said.

"Definitely a good thing," Joe agreed.

"Now I hope you got a good look at the layout of that building because I can't help you once you're inside. You have to find Lucas and get out before the diversion is discovered and they figure out what happened." He gently rolled up the map.

"How long will I have?" he asked.

"Ten minutes at the most." He shrugged. "It's the best I can do."

"I'll figure it out," he said. "Next?"

"Where you go is up to you, but you're not going to be able to run straight to the hangar and take off. They'll be in high alert after you bust him out, so lay low for a while until they loosen the security restrictions a bit. They don't have the manpower to maintain security over the whole city at the same time, so all you need to do is stall until they move on from that section of the Industrial Ring," Mike said.

Joe nodded. "Seems easy enough."

"Do you have any idea where you're going to hole up?" he asked.

"Substation fourteen," the polar bear said. "It's been offline since the Candle blew. The entire section has been evacuated."

"Okay. Well, once you're ready I'll volunteer to be assigned to the hangar to perform maintenance on our balloon. It's still loaded from our expedition, so at least we won't have to worry about supplies," Mike said.

Under normal circumstances balloons were empty upon their return. Given their early arrival back in Coldhaven, inventory had yet to be completed to determine what supplies they would need or what they had already consumed. Until this was finished the ship would not be restocked but nor would they remove any of it either. No doubt by now they had removed the limited cargo they had retrieved on their first run through the ship. It would not be much longer before they conducted a review of the supplies. The remaining craft would be empty of food and other essentials until their crews were ready to ship out so they would have no choice but to take balloon eight. That suited Joe, as he already knew the ship well enough from his time aboard. "We'll make it work."

"Now assuming that we're able to get to the hangar in one piece I can hit the remote activation sequence to open the hangar doors and launch the balloon. Once we're clear, then we just need to get far enough away from the city that they can't track us," the king penguin replied.

"What about pursuit?" Joe asked.

"It'll take them some time before they can get the other ships fueled and ready. Now the other balloons aren't any faster than ours, so as long as we can get out of range before they can launch, it should be near impossible for them to follow." Mike folded his arms. "We just have to make sure we get as much of a head start as possible."

Joe nodded in agreement. "Now all we need is a destination." He looked at Mike across the table.

The king penguin touched his beak in contemplation. "Hopefully some place we can get to before we starve to death."

"That would be preferable, yes." Joe sat down and leaned back in his chair.

Mike walked into his bedroom and returned a moment later with expedition maps, folders, and assorted documents that Joe recognized as having been compiled by Mike's father. Covered in the elder penguin's handwriting, it represented a treasure trove of information about the vast snowy wasteland and beyond.

Spreading them out with his webbed hands, the avian looked at Joe. "These are all my dad's notes and reports from when he was on the balloon team. Now I wasn't able to get all of them after he died, but hopefully there's enough here to give us a potential lead on a destination."

Joe began looking through the information, flipping the pages on some of the logs looking for any indication the elder Rush had seen something other than endless fields of snow in his travels. Unlike modern balloon expeditions, in the first few years it was deemed the priority to map the ice rather than search for salvage.

Most of these missions had produced little more than topographic maps of the area. Future expeditions had explored the region surrounding the city up to the maximum range of the airships, but other than a lot of ice and snow few signs of habitable areas had been found outside of Coldhaven. No matter how many teams went out to explore, all they found was ice as far as the eye could see. Despite finding nothing that would back up his theory, Jonathan Rush had refused to accept the possibility that nothing else was out there.

Going out for trip after trip, he served on the balloon team until his death one particularly frigid evening out on the ice. Returning with his father's body, the captain had given Mike and his mother all of Jonathan's personal effects along with the research they now held in their paws.

Looking down at one of his father's old maps, Mike laughed quietly to himself. "If only dad could see us now."

"I bet he'd encourage us," Joe said.

"Hell, he'd want to come along," Mike replied. "He always believed there was something out there. It kept him going, gave him a reason to get out of bed every morning. I suppose he'd have to be sure, to go out on those balloons each time. But he never found what he was looking for." He lowered his beak.

Joe leaned forward. "But we will. I promise." He looked at some of the maps. Recalling his dream, he spotted a note scrawled in the margins. "Did your dad ever talk to you about something called The Garden?"

Mike looked straight at Joe. "Where did you hear that?"

He pointed at the note on the map. "He wrote it here on the map from his fourth expedition."

Coming over to look he placed a webbed hand on the corner. He took a deep breath and then nodded. "He used to talk about a place he'd heard about called The Garden. Supposedly it was an area theoretically shielded from the disaster, but even he wasn't sure if it was real or just a rumor. He looked for it a couple of times but if it does exist it was well out of range. Why do you ask?"

"I have reason to believe he may have been right," Joe said. "Unfortunately I don't know anything more than the name."

"Well, even if it is real most of dad's research is based on decades old information and educated guesses. We might not have the luxury of finding a safe harbor before we have to pick a direction," he said.

The polar bear frowned. "Yeah, I know, but I'd like to have at least a vague idea of where to go even if it's a long shot. I'd rather not go through all the trouble of getting my family out of here only to freeze to death in a balloon hundreds of miles away."

"Neither do I but unfortunately this is the best we've got," Mike said. "It's not exactly like we have a guide that can tell us what's out there."

Joe raised his head suddenly. "Maybe we do."

Mike looked up, confused. Realization dawning, he snapped his fingers. "The bunny girl."

"Exactly," he said, standing up. "Not only is she the only person who's been outside of the maximum range of our balloons but wherever she came from has to be survivable."

"If you're already there busting out Lucas, it shouldn't be too much extra trouble swinging by and picking her up too. Just one problem. How do you know you can trust her?" he asked.

Joe frowned. It was true he did not know if the bunny girl would cooperate or not, but in his view they did not have a better alternative. They needed a guide, and they could use the help piloting the balloon. She could handle herself, of that he was sure. He would just have to hope that her desire to get home was enough to convince her to cooperate with him.

Though he had not spoken with her much during their return to the city, he had sensed that she was as surprised to find him as they were to encounter her.

Whether that was by accident or design, either way she had answers to questions only someone from outside the city could provide. In any event, she represented their best chance at survival. Once they left the city, there was no turning back, for any of them.

"We don't, but without her we're just stabbing in the dark," Joe said. "We need her, one way or the other."

Mike nodded, unable to argue the point. "I don't disagree. I just hope she's all we hope she is."

Joe shrugged. "I don't know. Either way, it's all we've got. Pack as much of this as you can't bear to part with and store it in your locker at the balloon hangar. When we go we won't have time to come back here and get it." Mike nodded. "Now if you'll excuse me, I have to take care of a few more things. We get started tonight at seven."

"You just make sure you're at that steam vent when it's time. We won't get a second chance at this."

Nodding, he hugged his friend tight. "Trust me. That's the one thing I'm absolutely sure about."

*   *   *

Gathering his tool belt, he reviewed everything he would need in his mind. Knowing he was not likely going to be able to come back here he would have to be certain everything was in place before he left the house. Perhaps that was why all three of them had been so quiet at dinner that night. Each of them had silently realized that this was the last night they would be sharing a meal at this house. It barely even deserved to be called a house, being built of little more than metal scraps and other things. Yet for the last thirty years of his life this was the place Joe and his family had called home.

Two rooms and barely enough space for a family of

four, he had raised Lucas and Emily from cubs here. The walls were poorly insulated and there were only two windows, but it kept the chill out and was tall enough that Joe could stand normally without having to bend down in the doorways. Laura had cooked their meals in the kitchen, less than six feet from where he was standing. In that same space his children had shared the small couch that served as their bed, and they ate their meals together at the table that took up most of the little furniture they had.

It was not much, but it was a good life, and one Joe had thought he would have until he died. Yet such was not to be the case, with everything he knew slipping away faster than ice melting inside The Candle. Sweat beaded up on the back of his neck at the thought of leaving the city. As he lifted his wrench, feeling the weight of it in his paw, he felt his wife enter the room behind him. Turning to face her, he slipped the wrench into his belt and took her in his paws.

"You're sure about this," she said.

"Not really," Joe replied, "but we don't have a choice. We have one window to do this, and we can't afford to fail."

"The prison will be heavily guarded. We should expect a lot of resistance." Laura flexed her paws causing her claw tips to glint in the light.

"I wish I had something more deadly than a wrench," Joe remarked.

"Are you kidding? I've seen what you can do with one of those. It may be more handy than you think."

Joe held his paws up, surrendering and conceding the point as he continued his preparations. Wrapping his scarf around his neck, he watched his muscular lady bear as she prepared to change her clothes as well.

As much as Joe would have preferred otherwise, a large amount of this plan depended on luck. No one was allowed into the prison unless they had business there, and in all of the years Joe had served on the maintenance team he had never been allowed inside the prison, with the city guard having a special division of the Workshop specifically for their needs. Other than his trip there with his wife to see Lucas, he had no idea of the interior layout of the building.

Fortunately, he had a good mental picture of the first floor and knew the size of the building from having passed it so often over the years, so he was not entirely blind in that regard, but one way or the other he would have to find his way through the building without the benefit of advance knowledge.

Laura had chosen a pair of thick pants, a warm shirt, sturdy boots, and a thick jacket to cover her upper body. Nodding in approval, she opened the dresser drawer to remove a small pocketknife. Belonging to her father, Laura had kept it with her ever since his death, keeping it near her as one of the few pieces of him she had left. "Okay, I think I'm as ready as I'll ever be."

Joe nodded. "Either way it's almost time to get going." He motioned towards the kitchen. "We should wake up Emily."

Laura led the way into the kitchen where their little girl was sleeping. She gently shook her awake, smiling as she knelt beside her. "Wake up, sweetie. Mama and Papa are going out for a little while. We need to drop you off someplace safe while we take care of something."

"Are you going to go get Lucas?" she asked.

Laura glanced at Joe. "Yes, we are." She pointed to the chair beside her. "I've laid out your clothes, now get dressed real quick and let's get going."

A few moments later, they were standing outside of Mike's house holding Emily in Joe's arms as he knocked on the door. Opening the door, Lisa stood there with Mike visible behind her. "Oh, it's you."

"Nice to see you too. Sorry to drag you into this, but we need someplace for Emily to stay while we go get her brother," Joe said.

Lisa accepted Emily into her arms with a growl. "I still think all of you are insane for doing this. And don't think that I'm okay with you dragging my husband into your little agenda either. The only reason I don't turn all of you into city security is that I don't want to be responsible for orphaning your little girl. I won't stand in your way, but I will not let you put my husband in any more danger than you already have. After tonight, he's done, understood?"

Joe nodded. "Loud and clear." He shifted from one foot paw to the other as Mike came out to join them. "Sorry."

"She's just scared. To tell you the truth, I am too. But I couldn't live with myself if I didn't try," Mike leaned close to Joe's ear. "I've made all the arrangements. At exactly seven our window begins. I'll be doing everything I can to keep the attention off of you for as long as possible."

"Thanks, Mike," Joe said. "We really appreciate it."

"Pay me back by getting your boy out of there," he said. "This is really going to suck if it all turns out to be for nothing."

Joe gestured towards the prison. "Well, we'd better get in position. We're going to need every second we can get."

Mike slipped on his jacket and came outside with them. "Good luck."

"You too," he said, shaking his hand before the two parted ways. The closest access point would be not far from the prison itself, close to the street outside. Once the steam went off, they would have to get in and get out in ten minutes and not a moment more. If they failed, they would be trapped inside with the only other way out being through the front door, protected by several armed guards and who knows what other security measures.

As Joe walked in the direction of the prison, he checked one more time to make sure the wrench hung from his belt, the symbol of everything he had ever put into this city. Now it was time to put it to a different purpose, saving his son.

INDUSTRIAL RING
COLDHAVEN PRISON FACILITY A.K.A. THE FRIDGE

Observing the grate from across the street, Joe could see the steam rising from it into the air, a side effect of the city's temperature regulation system. The moisture coming from beneath the city was a constant sight throughout Coldhaven, serving as one of the many reminders that the critical systems were functioning as they should. With Laura at his side, Joe waited for that to change.

It seemed ironic that after so many years of keeping the city running that his family's survival would depend on causing those same systems to malfunction. He had spent most of his life trying to prevent exactly what he and Mike were about to cause.

They did not have to wait long. Seconds later, the steam ceased to flow, and Joe moved quickly across the street. Using his wrench to pry the grate up, he placed it aside and dropped into the tunnels. Crawling beside the pipes, he and Laura made their way underneath the prison. It was only a short distance until they arrived at what he assumed to be the maintenance closet, responsible for directing heat to the few parts of the building they kept warm for the guards.

Due to the extremely high temperatures of the access tunnels, there were no locks on the grates anywhere in the city. When they were in operation, the heat level was so high it was deemed impossible for anyone to use them without having the steam rerouted. Of course, they did not have friends on the maintenance team.

Under normal circumstances, rerouting the steam had to be done from one of the main control consoles in the Workshop or The Candle. Carefully coordinated, the steam in the city had to be constantly regulated in order to keep everything within acceptable tolerance levels. Done correctly, this would prevent any interruptions in the system other than the intended location. Usually only done in small sections of the city to allow maintenance, it was designed to keep the city running under all circumstances.

In an ideal world the city could function indefinitely for hundreds of years, but as Joe knew, things were not ideal. The government's stubbornness with proper maintenance procedures had forced them to come up with creative solutions over the years to keep the city running, and their resistance to prolonged shutdowns had opened cracks in the system. It was those cracks Mike had intended to exploit.

Lifting the grate quietly off its mount he climbed out into the steam room, lifting his wife up after him. They took up positions behind the door, waiting for their opening. Joe knew that steam was like an animal, always looking for freedom. If it was not allowed to release properly it would find a way, whether you wanted it to or not. Right at that very moment Mike was diverting the steam to hub number fourteen. Both Joe and he knew it was desperately in need of a total teardown and rebuild. As soon as the steam was diverted there, all they had to do was wait.

Gripping his wrench in his paw, Joe signaled Laura

to get ready. An explosion in the distance went off like a starting pistol, signaling the start of their window. Powerful enough to be felt even this far inside the building, the vibration was soon followed by emergency alarms. Loud klaxons wailed throughout the city, alerting every citizen throughout that a serious situation was developing.

Given the critical nature of The Candle and its related systems, any incident of this type tended to generate a certain amount of panic. It was exactly that Joe was counting on. With a second and then a third explosion, the alarm became more insistent, and he listened for the sounds of shouting as the prisoners became more agitated. It would take some time for the guards to get them under control.

With one last look at his wife, Joe pulled open the door and hurried up the stairs to the prison levels. The facility was in utter chaos, as the few inmates they had begged to be let free, but Joe was only interested in two.

His back to the stairs, a single guard attempted to regain control of the panicked prisoners. Attacking him from behind, Joe drew the wrench across his neck and cut off his supply of oxygen. Struggling against the much stronger polar bear, the skunk reached for his radio, pressing the transmit button to call for help. It clattered to the floor as his body went limp and he lost consciousness. Joe dropped him to the ground and removed his security key.

The radio crackled to life. *"Position three, respond."* A moment. *"Position three, respond! This is the Warden, we may have a security breach on level two. Prepare for intruders."*

"Shit." Joe scanned each cell, searching for the one that contained either his son or the hare. Laura did the same, checking the doors on the other side as they made their way up throughout the building.

Arriving at the fourth floor, they found their way blocked by two guards armed with batons. Joe lowered his wrench, growling and baring his teeth. Swinging it towards the closest one, he struck him hard enough against the arm to hear an audible crack. The guard yelped, dropping his baton to the ground. Joe prepared to swing again, but the injured fox tackled him with his shoulder, pushing him off balance.

Stumbling backwards, he fought to regain his footing. He shifted his balance as the guard attempted to anticipate his next move. Joe advanced, moving to swing but before it could connect the guard grabbed his wrist, attempting to overpower him. Using his superior ursine strength, he roared and used his other paw to slam him into the wall. Dropping to the floor, he moaned.

Laura had managed to cut her opponent, with a line of blood dripping down his face. He held his baton menacingly, growling. With a quick strike of his weapon, he delivered a hit to her gut. Doubling over, she stumbled and fell to her knees.

Moving to his wife's defense, he held his wrench to block the next downward strike. The second guard kicked him hard enough to elicit a grunt. Joe blocked the next couple of hits, but this lion was fast. He was testing his defenses. Trying to disable his speed advantage, Joe reached to grab his uniform but was instead rewarded with a blow to the ribs. His large frame reduced the overall impact, but the pain was enough to make him wince.

A wide swing from his wrench caught the lion off balance, sending him to the ground. Joe moved to step on his chest, but he rolled out of the way before his weight pressed down. Rising to a crouch, the lion swung his baton again, only to have Joe smack it away with the back of his paw. Joe looked at him and then at Laura. He couldn't be stopped here.

Taking a chance, he threw the wrench at his head,

forcing him to duck out of the way. As he did, Joe tackled him from below, pressing him against the wall. With a hard punch to the chest, he pressed his weight on his chest, placing a paw at his throat. "Where is my SON?!" he demanded.

The guard stared at Joe defiantly. "I'm not telling you anything!"

"Wrong answer," Joe said, squeezing his claws tighter, drawing blood.

"Joe! We don't have time for this." Laura called out, having recovered. She retrieved their weapons and moved to join him.

Seeing that the guard was not going to comply, Joe restrained him with his own cuffs and moved to check the cells. Just as he was about to advance to the next row, he stopped. Though the window, his son sat on the bed staring at the wall. Joe unlocked the door with the access card and pulled it open. "Lucas!"

"Dad!" He jumped up and ran to his father, hugging him tightly. "What's going on?"

"We're breaking you out," he said. Leading him out of the cell, Lucas hugged his mother before following him down the hall and up the stairs.

"Isn't the way out down?" he asked.

Joe nodded. "We have one more person we need to get, the bunny girl they brought in earlier."

Lucas pushed into the lead. "Then follow me, I know where they're keeping her." Running up the stairs, they reached the fifth floor which was deemed the high security wing. Using his key, Joe granted them access.

Very few people were ever kept on the fifth floor, usually reserved for the worst of the worst. It was rare that a capital crime ever occurred in Coldhaven, but if it did, they were held here until they could be exiled. Joe ignored the other inmates and followed his son to the last cell on the end. "This is the one?" Joe asked.

Lucas nodded. "I heard the guards talking about her."

Joe reached for the keys when another pair of guards emerged from the shadows. Before he could even bring his wrench up the first tackled him to the ground. Both the keys and the wrench clattered to the floor as he wrestled with the large wolverine. Attempting to push his opponent off of him, he caught sight of Laura as she pulled her knife on the panda before her. Unable to help her, he growled at his attacker, trying to gain the upper paw.

From behind, Lucas struck the wolverine with the wrench. Whirling around to face the young polar bear, he abandoned Joe and went after the teenage ursine. Overpowering him, the prison guard squeezed his wrist until Lucas dropped the weapon onto the ground.

If he knew what was going to happen to him, he might have reconsidered his actions, as the sight of his son being attacked drove Joe to his feet paws in an instant. Letting out a roar that shook the walls, the wolverine did not even have time to turn around as Joe struck him from behind, baring his teeth in fury. "Get off my son!" he shouted, throwing the wolverine hard onto the floor. With a swift kick, Joe delivered a stunning blow.

Catching his breath, Lucas placed his paws on his knees. "Thanks, Dad."

Turning towards Laura, she kicked the panda hard in the chest. In retaliation, he swung back with the baton. Grunting as she blocked it with her forearm, she punched the guard with her other paw. Before he could recover, she thrust her knee into his chest hard enough to send him wheezing.

Breathing heavily, she gestured towards the cell. "As

fun as this has been, how about we get what we came for and get out of here?" Laura asked.

Nodding his agreement, Joe picked up the keys and his wrench and opened the cell door. Still dressed in her military blacks, the bunny looked up at him, meeting his glance with a neutral expression. "I have to admit I didn't think I'd be seeing you again," she said.

"I'll make you a deal. We get you out of here, and you take my family back wherever it is you came from," Joe said.

Rising to stand, Ellie nodded. "Agreed."

CHAPTER EIGHT
RUN LIKE YOUR TAIL IS ON FIRE

Emerging from the cell, the female hare looked towards the end of the hall. Kneeling to search the guards, she frowned upon discovering they were only armed with batons. Taking one, she stood. "Lead the way."

Once he had deposited the two guards inside Ellie's former accommodation, Joe closed the door and took the lead, turning back the way they came. "The only exit is down on the ground level. Now that they know we're here, odds are it's going to be a lot harder getting out than it was getting in."

"Then let's not waste time." Descending the stairs, they made their way down towards the first floor, as Ellie spoke to Joe. "They took that hard drive I was carrying. I need to get it back."

"They're probably keeping it downstairs. We'll look for it on our way out," Joe said, assuming they likely kept it somewhere near the spot where they had emerged from the basement.

Without warning, Ellie stopped and held her baton to block Joe's movement. "Hold on." Ellie's ears twitched as she listened, her finely tuned hearing gathering information about the situation below. "A large group of well-armed men just arrived, and one woman in heels."

"Governor Cole," Joe said. "They're blocking our exit, and they've probably got guns."

"How many?" Laura asked the hare.

"At least six. More than I can take with just this." She held up her borrowed baton.

"All right, change of plans. Split up and head upstairs," Joe said.

"Up? Don't we need to go down?" Laura touched her husband's arm.

"Right now, we're the only thing running loose in here. We need to give them something else to chase. Laura, go with Ellie. Lucas, stay with me." Using the confiscated keycard, Joe began to open each of the cells with an occupant. Heading up the nearest staircase, he heard shouting as the city guard engaged the panicked prisoners.

Alarms and klaxons continued to render the scene inside the Fridge utter chaos. Guards and prisoners ran every which way while the two polar bears weaved through the corridors. As he had hoped, several of the prisoners took out their fears and frustrations on their captors. It would not last, but hopefully it would split their forces enough so that they could slip through the confusion.

Lucas let out a distressed yelp as one of the prisoners

grabbed him. "Dad!"

Joe struck the fox on the forearm hard enough to elicit a crack and a cry of pain as his wrench made contact. He ushered his son forward, holding the tool up in a warning gesture. "We need to regroup with the others. Keep moving."

"But…"

"I won't let anything happen to you, but we have to keep going," he said, earning him a nod from Lucas. Joe ascended to the fourth floor opening each cell on his way, catching a glimpse of Valentine as he ducked around a corner. "Shit."

He felt his chest tighten. They had been seen. He was sure of it. Joe ushered his son down the corridor in the opposite direction they had been headed. He froze as his path was suddenly blocked by the grizzly bear with a wicked grin. "End of the road."

"I don't think so." Joe rushed him, using his weight to force Valentine to shift to the right. With a strike of his wrench, he delivered a swift blow to the other bear's midsection.

A roar of pain was followed by a hard strike from the back of his paw. Too close to use his handgun, Valentine held up his claws and assumed a combat stance.

Joe raised his fists defensively. He shook off the momentary dizziness and watched his opponent. All the grizzly bear had to do was slow them down. Their options were limited, and the more time they wasted the greater the chance they wouldn't be getting out of here. He had to make a move. Joe swung his wrench, missing by several inches.

Valentine countered, thrusting his knee into Joe's chest. The wrench clattered to the floor and his body exploded with pain. He struggled to breathe, trying to shout for Lucas to run. He felt the other bear grab him by his coat and slam him against the wall. "Looks like I was right."

Striking him from behind, Lucas brought the wrench down on his upper back. "Don't touch my dad."

Joe coughed, taking the wrench back. "Thanks." He kicked Valentine in the chest, taking his handgun while the other bear moaned on the floor. "Come on." Searching the hallways for a clear path, he pushed through the disorganized prisoners to the stairwell. Looking up, he caught sight of Ellie and his wife. "Are you two all right?"

"We ran into a couple of city guard members but nothing she can't handle," Laura said, gesturing to the hare.

Ellie held up the baton for emphasis. Seeing the handgun in Joe's belt, she took it from him. "No offense, but I think this is better off in my paws than yours."

"Be my guest," he replied. "Let's get out of here while we can use the chaos for cover." The group descended the stairs, making their way down to the first level. As they emerged from the prisoner area, they found themselves surrounded. Governor Cole stepped forward, her eyes squarely on Joe.

Putting himself between her and his family, he raised his wrench. "I'm taking my family out of here," he said.

Governor Cole remained stoic holding a paw up to pause the guards. "I'm afraid I can't allow that." Stepping forward slightly she kept her eyes on Joe, as did the guards with her. "Surrender, now, and I promise you won't be harmed."

"No, we'll just be exiled to die slowly out on the ice," he replied.

Holding out her hands in a gesture of concession, she nodded. "That is the punishment for your crimes." Indicating his family, she shook her head. "Far preferable, I would think, then watching your family die here and now on the floor of the Fridge."

"You'd kill us for attempting to rescue my son?" he asked.

"The question is whether you would by refusing to surrender." She indicated the guards around them. "There's nowhere to go. You can't escape. Stand down or I will do what I must to end this."

Lowering his wrench, Joe carefully considered the situation. They were all armed with batons, but like Valentine, they kept their guns holstered. In a fair fight, they were outmatched. So why didn't they simply kill him and be done with it? He looked over his shoulder at Ellie. Enlightenment filled his eyes with confidence. They didn't want to kill her by accident. Whatever they were planning, she was essential to it, or so they thought.

What Joe needed to do was distract the governor and her people long enough for Ellie to make her move. The odds were good enough that they could get to their escape route before they were able to catch up with them, but they were running out of time. Joe had no idea exactly how much of their window remained, but if they failed to make it to the maintenance tunnel before it expired the only other way out would be through a lot of guards. He had to keep their attention. "Governor Cole, why are you here?" he asked.

"What?" the arctic vixen looked up at him in surprise.

"The leader of Coldhaven doesn't usually respond to a prison break, unless you were already on your way," he said. Keeping his glare focused on her, he pointed towards the white vixen with the wrench. "You were coming for Ellie, weren't you?" he asked. "In fact, I bet you were already on your way when the guards triggered the alarm."

"An interesting theory but hardly relevant," Governor Cole said.

"Considering the things you've been keeping from

the rest of the population I'd say it's highly relevant." He looked around at the armed escorts surrounding her. "Do your guards know what you've been hiding from us?" he asked. "Or have they not been kept informed of your private agenda?" Joe watched her for any reaction. If she was alarmed, she did not show it. The woman had an incredible poker face.

"My guards know where their loyalty lies, with the people of the city and their survival. It is people like you who threaten that, refusing to accept the laws that have been put in place since this city was founded," Governor Cole said, baring her teeth as she spoke.

"I never wanted to defy the law," Joe said. "You made that necessary when you arrested my son."

"And now you and your wife will join him," she said.

Tightening his grip, he stared into her eyes. "They will, but not where you think." He swung his wrench as hard as possible in a wide arc. "NOW!"

Ellie drew her gun, firing shots at the city guard on either side of the group. Several of them went down, clutching their wounds. The rest scattered, taking cover behind nearby walls and furniture.

Her eyes wide, the governor fell as she scrambled for cover. Her jacket fell open as she backpedaled, blindly searching for sanctuary. A small black object bulged from her pocket. "Batons only!" she ordered, clearly not wanting to risk killing the hare in the crossfire.

"GO!" Ellie commanded, firing a few more shots to keep the guards at bay.

Joe ushered his wife and son down to the basement, holding the door as he called after the white hare. "Come on!"

Ignoring him, Ellie walked up to the governor and removed something from her jacket. "This belongs to me," she said, keeping her weapon trained on the vixen. Backing up, she kept her aim directed straight at her forehead, following Joe and closing the door behind them.

Speaking over his shoulder as they descended the stairs, Joe expressed his irritation. "What the hell was that about?"

"She had the hard drive, the one I took from the Abraham Lincoln. I couldn't leave without it," she said.

"That was risky, I hope it was worth it," he said.

"If it has on it what I think it does it just might be," she replied, running after him to catch up with his family, who were already by the steam room door.

Joe could hear the sound of the guards thundering down the stairs. They would be on them in a few moments. Looking down at the tunnel he could tell the steam had not yet kicked back on, but they would not have much more time. Ushering his wife and son in first he gestured for Ellie to enter the tunnel. "Go!"

The snowshoe hare dropped in after Lucas and hurried to crawl down the length of the tunnel, with Joe going after her, closing the grate behind him. His heart racing, he kept his eyes on the steam pipes knowing that if they failed to reach the end in time this tunnel was going to become fatally hot in a matter of seconds. Silently he hoped that the guards were not foolish enough to come in after them. While there was a possibility he and his family would make it out in one piece, anyone that came after them would be caught in the system reset.

Shouting became louder behind him when two of the guards dropped into the tunnel. Joe cursed as they continued their pursuit, their growls echoing inside the crawlspace. He gritted his teeth, resisting the urge to look behind him, instead hurrying on all fours to the exit.

Lucas climbed out first, followed by Laura. He

watched Ellie's white head disappear from view, crawling faster to clear the tunnel knowing he had little time left. Practically vaulting himself from the opening he rolled onto his back, panting for breath. A few seconds later, a loud rumbling sound was followed by the sudden burst of steam and horrific cries of pain which soon gave way to silence.

Putting his paw on his chest, he found himself embraced by Laura and Lucas as he fought to catch his breath. Unable to form words, he just held his family close to him as they rocked gently in the snow.

Standing above them, Ellie cast a glance towards the prison. "As much as I hate to break up the family reunion, we really need to get going."

Joe nodded, rising to his feet as he led the group away from the building and opened a hatch around the corner. Motioning for them to go down, he followed last, closing the grate behind him.

Dropping off the last few rungs of the ladder, he looked around at the lighted path that seemed to go on forever in all directions. His companions waited for him as he approached, all of them looking to him. Taking the lead, he pointed forward. "We take this path down straight through until we reach the next intersection, then take a right and follow it all the way around the city to section four of the residential ring."

"What is this place?" Ellie asked.

"These are the maintenance tunnels. They run parallel to the steam distribution system to allow us access to the rest of the city in the event of extreme temperature drops. The idea behind it was the maintenance team would call in the area they needed access to and they would shut down the appropriate section from the Workshop. Under normal circumstances they're not used very much, but that makes them perfect for our needs," Joe said.

"And they run throughout the entire city?" The white hare walked beside Joe.

"That they do. You can get anywhere from anywhere using these tunnels. Now eventually they'll catch on when they realize they can't find us above ground but for now we should be reasonably safe. All the same, let's not loiter around any longer than necessary." Joe looked at Ellie as she removed her magazine from her pistol and examined the remaining ammunition.

"Six shots left," she said.

"Let's hope we don't have to use them," Joe replied.

"I tend to doubt we'll be that lucky." Ellie slid the magazine back into the gun and replaced the captured weapon in her holster.

Joe slowed his pace, preoccupied with how much had changed in such a short time. For most of his life he had never raised a paw to another. Yet the likelihood that they would be able to get to safety without a fight was looking more and more improbable. People would die. A few of them already had. He had been prepared for that possibility the moment he had committed to rescuing Lucas. So far, he had managed to avoid ending anyone's life directly, but he knew he no longer had the luxury of pulling his punches if the situation called for it.

Feeling a presence at his side Joe looked to his right to see Laura gently hanging on his arm. "Are you all right?" she asked.

"That was going to be my question," he replied. "I'm still in one piece, at least." He touched his chest as if confirming there were no injuries. "So far."

Letting out a deep breath, Laura rested her head on his arm. "When that steam came back on, I swear I thought my heart was going to jump out of my chest," she said.

"You and me both," Joe admitted. "That was way

too close."

Laura nodded in agreement. "I'm just grateful we got our son out in one piece." She looked ahead towards Lucas. "If anything had happened to him, I don't think I could've handled that."

Joe turned towards her, his expression becoming serious. "It's not over yet. We've still got a long way to go before we're out of the snowstorm. Lucas is strong. So is Emily. We'll make it."

"Do you really think we can get out of the city?" she asked.

"We've made it this far, haven't we?" Joe pointed out. "Breaking Lucas out of The Fridge was the hard part. Now all we have to do is avoid being caught, steal a balloon, and find a safe haven somewhere out in the frozen wasteland."

"Oh, is that all?" Laura asked. Shaking her head, she looked at him with an impish smile. "You certainly know how to reassure me," she said.

"It made you smile, didn't it?" he asked, booping her on the nose.

"Hey!" she protested.

Ellie stopped at the next intersection. "You two coming?" she asked, prompting Joe to take the lead once more.

"Sorry." Joe turned right and followed the gently sloping tunnel on the path around the city. "If we keep walking, we should hit our destination in a couple hours."

The blonde lapine looked at Joe. "How soon can we get out of the city?" she asked.

"It depends," he replied.

"On?" she prompted.

"You in some kind of a hurry?" Joe stopped and looked at her.

Ellie pulled out the hard drive she had taken from the Navy ship. "I need to get this back to my people as quickly as possible."

"And I want to get my family to safety, but we can't leave while they're out there combing the city looking for four highly recognizable fugitives." Joe regarded her with a stern look. "Now I understand your urgency but if we try and escape the city now, we'll just end up right back where we started."

"No, you don't," Ellie insisted. "My people are on their way. They are getting closer every second and they haven't heard from me in over twenty-four hours. If I'm not at the rendezvous when they arrive, they won't wait."

Joe stepped closer to her. "And when were you going to tell me this?" he asked, quiet enough so the others didn't hear.

"I'm telling you now," she said.

Letting out a frustrated sigh Joe pointed a finger at her chest. "How much time do we have?"

"I don't have an exact schedule but not long. A few days at most," she said. "If we can't get out by then, then it won't matter."

Joe touched his paw to his forehead and then back to her. "And there's no way you can get word to them?"

"Not from here. The city guard took my radio when you captured me," Ellie said.

Joe frowned. "They probably stripped it for parts, tech like that is pretty valuable these days."

"Bastards," she said.

"All right," Joe said, "I think we can still get out in the time we have but before we take one more step, I need to be damn sure there's nothing else you're keeping from me. We clear?" he asked, pointing a claw at her.

With a sigh, she nodded her agreement. "We're

clear." As they continued to walk, Ellie turned to Joe once again. "I'm just not used to trusting people out here on the ice," she said.

"Well, if you're going to escape with us, you're going to have to learn to start." Joe walked ahead to catch up with his wife.

"Everything okay?" she asked.

"I think so, just working out the details," he said. "It's fine, I promise."

Laura stared at him for a few moments longer before finally exhaling and returning her attention to the path ahead. "Okay, I'm going to trust you here for the time being, but if there is a problem I expect you to tell me."

"I swear to you, you will be the first to know." For the moment, there was little he could do either way. Until their escape was complete, he had more immediate concerns. The city guard would be keeping an eye out for the Kennedy family, making it almost impossible to remain undetected the longer they stayed in the city. Their only viable option was to get to a balloon and get as much distance between them and Coldhaven as possible.

For now they still had no idea where they were but the longer they waited the less likely they would be able to make a clean getaway. Their best chance rested with getting to the balloon hangar before the city guard figured out what they were up to. Caught between his desire to take his family to safety and his overabundance of caution Joe directed his energy into walking towards their destination, deciding that if he was going to be anxious, he would at least put that energy towards something useful.

No one spoke for the rest of the journey, and perhaps it was just as well. While it was unlikely that anyone would be using these maintenance tunnels unless the surface temperature fell low enough to make it inadvisable to remain outside, it was still probably a wise precaution to minimize the possibility that anyone would overhear them. Picking up the pace, Joe drove the group towards the opposite side of the city.

Arriving at their destination, Joe stopped to double check the signage painted on the wall. Confirming they were at the junction closest to their destination, he held up a paw to signal the group to stop and gather around. Once he was certain they were exactly where they were supposed to be, he gestured for them to climb the ladder and made the gesture for quiet.

Taking the lead, he put his boot on the first rung and began to ascend. Reaching the street level, he listened for sounds of anyone nearby, but given the late hour it was unlikely anyone would be in the area. Though there was still the possibility of patrols walking around the city, Joe knew he would have to take the risk sometime, and pushed the grate up.

Looking around, he scanned the immediate vicinity, letting out a deep breath as soon as he was certain the coast was clear. Moving the grate free, he climbed out onto the street, extending a paw to his wife as she followed. Waiting patiently, once Lucas and Ellie had joined them, he replaced the grate and started walking.

The substation was unremarkable, being little more than a square box of a building with few features to distinguish it, appropriate given its utilitarian purpose. Joe approached the door reaching into his pocket for the access key. Leftover from his years as a maintenance tech, the door opened obediently for him with a gentle click. "Come on." Making his way inside, he guided the group into the main room before closing the door behind them. "We should be safe here, at least for a little while."

"What is this place?" Ellie asked.

"It's a substation designed to route heat and power throughout the city. At the moment it's shut down to conserve resources, so we shouldn't have any unexpected company. It's not perfect, but it'll do." Joe looked at his wife and son. "You two all right?"

"All things considered, I'd say so," Laura replied.

"I'm fine, Dad. Thanks for coming to get me." He smiled weakly.

"Wasn't even a question," he said. Squeezing his son on the shoulder, he looked around. The room was mostly filled with pipes and monitoring equipment, the only furniture being a metal table and chairs in the corner of the room. With no resources being actively routed through the building, the entire place was silent and still. Emerging from the back room a figure appeared, causing Ellie to draw her weapon.

Holding his webbed hands up in the air, Mike stopped. "Whoa!"

Moving to intervene, Joe put his thick paw on Ellie's barrel. "Relax, he's with us." Meeting his glance, Ellie lowered her weapon. "This is Mike, he's a friend."

"Ellie," she mumbled awkwardly. "Hey, sorry about the, uh…"

"Don't mention it," he replied. "Everything go all right?"

Joe nodded, stepping aside so he could see Lucas. "We got what we came for."

"Good," he said. "I wanted to make sure you were all right before I brought Emily. The city guard is losing their shit over this. So far, they haven't alerted the public, but my guess is they're going to keep it secret as long as possible."

"That makes sense," Joe said. "Revealing a prison break doesn't exactly boost confidence in one's administration."

"Not to mention the fact that they don't want anyone knowing about me." Ellie folded her arms.

"Given how interested they are in what you know and what's on that hard drive of yours they aren't going to make it easy for us to get out of here," Laura said.

"Maybe not, but we have one advantage. I know this city better than anyone in the city guard. They can search this place from here until doomsday and they'd never find me. We can steal a balloon if we play it right. We just need to find an opening large enough for us to slip through."

"Or make one," Mike said.

"Exactly."

"Right now they've got the area around the Fridge sealed up tight, but it's only a matter of time before they figure out you're already outside of their perimeter. Whatever you do, you'd better do it soon." Mike took a seat in one of the metal chairs.

Joe nodded, noticing that Ellie had walked off towards a window on the second floor. Staring out of it from the side, she kept out of sight while looking over the massive city of Coldhaven. Silently, she held herself as her hair rested over her shoulder, breathing deeply while she collected her thoughts. Joe touched his wife on the shoulder as he moved to approach her, taking up a position just on her left.

"Is the place where you come from like this?" he asked.

Ellie looked in his direction, having not noticed him until he spoke. Lowering her head she kept her ears close together in contemplation. "No," she said. "Where I come from it's nothing like this." She turned away from the window. "I guess I've spent so much time out on the ice I'm still not used to being out from the cold."

Joe leaned closer. "What's it like out there?" he asked. "I've only been out the one time, so I don't know."

He shrugged. "And even that got cut short."

The blonde lapine shrugged, looking off into the middle distance. "It's harsh, and sometimes unforgiving, but to find the things we're looking for we have to keep searching. I've spent most of my life out there, digging through the remnants of the old world for things they left behind."

"You're an explorer," he said.

"Among other things," Ellie replied. "I like to think of myself as a scout, searching ahead for signs of danger, making sure the others are safe." The hare shook her head. "It's why I have to get back there with or without your help, to warn the others and tell them what I've found." Letting out a deep sigh, she frowned. "It's not that I don't appreciate the rescue, far from it. I'm just not used to needing to count on someone else to get the job done."

Looking into her eyes, Joe offered a warm smile. "Look, I know you don't trust us yet and I can't say I blame you. I'm taking a lot on faith with you too," he said. "But you can count on me doing whatever I have to in order to protect my family, and right now that means helping you. I can't give you any guarantees but one thing I do know is that you and I need each other, and we're both going to have to rely on the other sooner or later."

Relaxing her ears, she allowed them to fall slightly and lowered her paws to her sides. "Fair enough," she said. Rejoining the group, Joe looked to her once more.

"Now, I do believe you've got some storytelling to do." Joe said, leaning against a set of pipes. "If we're going to help you get home, I think it might help if you told us about where you come from."

Ellie took a deep breath. She stared at the others for a long moment while she gathered her thoughts. Looking at Joe and then Mike, she began her story. "Where I come from isn't a place, exactly. I'm an advance scout for a train that has been traveling the surface of the Earth since The Freeze began. Originally designed to transport people around the world, it was coopted to save the population from the catastrophic disaster. Built by several nations in cooperation, it was modified to make it impervious to any atmospheric changes and converted to facilitate the evacuation of the world's population to a theoretical safe zone we now call The Garden."

"Do you know what caused The Freeze?" Joe asked.

"Unfortunately we don't know any more than you do. All of our information regarding the event itself comes from what little we've been able to piece together during our expeditions. While we have determined that it was not a natural phenomenon, unfortunately that's all we've been able to confirm for certain," Ellie replied.

The origin of The Freeze had been a subject of debate for many years among the people of Coldhaven. While interest in the subject had waned over time, there were some like Mike's father who had never given up their curiosity on the subject. Countless theories had been circulated but with no proof and no ability to confirm any of them they were viewed as little more than amusing ways to pass the time for those that cared to consider it at all.

To most the subject was not relevant as no matter what its origin, it would not change the fact that it had happened, nor would it make their hardships any easier to endure. As a result, most chose to drown their sorrows in what little alcohol was salvaged from the ice and pay the matter no further attention.

Among those that did, the most prevalent theory was that it was a result of climate change, with most of the nations at the time consuming significant resources with little effort to counteract the effects. It was theorized that some invisible point of no return had been reached causing massive global temperature changes which resulted in most of the planet becoming covered in ice and snow.

Other theories included the possibility of a nuclear winter blocking out enough of the sunlight that the temperature drop triggered a new Ice Age, or that an asteroid had struck the planet causing similar effects, but neither of these ideas had gained significant traction due to the lack of any evidence in either direction.

Joe personally had never given the subject much thought, but unlike the previous generation he had never known the world before The Freeze. Life inside the city was all he had ever experienced, having no memories of grassy fields or warm sunny days filled with carefree people going about their business. Every day in Coldhaven was about survival. The weather never changed, with the cold being a constant threat to the people of the last city on Earth, always reminding them of the danger that sat ever present just outside their door. When you were always one step away from your potential demise, one had little time for theories.

It was not that Joe had never been curious, but between his work on the maintenance team and caring for Emily and Lucas it had never been more than an idle consideration.

That is, until Ellie.

Joe looked up. "You're saying it was artificial?"

Ellie nodded. "That's what our research suggests. We've found numerous reports indicating it started in specific places but we have no idea where those places could be or even where to start looking." She shrugged. "For all we know, those places may not even be the point of origin."

"And even if they are, who knows if you'll be able to gather any useful information after all this time," he said.

Mike gestured to Ellie. "You mentioned a train. Is that how you got here?"

Ellie shook her head. "Yes and no." Sliding the metal table to the center of the space she drew a line with her finger. "The train is almost constantly moving, traveling along a network of tracks built all over the planet. It only stops when we've found something worth investigating or when we return to The Garden. Originally designed to be much larger than its current form, we use it to explore the ice much like you do with your balloons."

"We found her on board the Navy ship my balloon team was assigned to salvage," he explained. "Of course we didn't expect to find anyone else there."

The blonde hare folded her arms. "I could say the same." She took a breath and continued. "We'd identified the ship as a potential resource. I was sent to investigate and report back. I was just about to do that when your team found me."

"Where is the train now?" Joe asked.

"It's in the area but it isn't going to stay that way. We need to get to it while it still is." Ellie looked at Joe while he considered the matter.

"Surely the train isn't going to leave you behind?"

"They may not feel they have a choice," she said. "My last known position was the USS Abraham Lincoln. After my arrival I went radio silent and they haven't heard from me since. They'll send someone to look for me, but with no sign of my whereabouts and no idea where I am they won't wait forever. Standard protocol is to wait for a signal and assign a rendezvous point. We have to get out of the city and get ahead of them before they move out of range."

Joe leaned forward, interlacing his fingers. "And if you fail to make that rendezvous?"

"Then the train continues on course," she said.

Throwing his paws up into the air, Joe sighed. "This just gets better and better," he said, not bothering to hide his exasperation. "How long do we have?"

Ellie considered the question for a moment. "Not long, a few days at most. They're taking a pretty circuitous route through the region in order to avoid being spotted by any of your balloon teams but we've only got a short window to catch up with them before they start heading back in the opposite direction."

"And our balloons speed is nowhere near fast enough to overtake them," he said, finishing her unspoken thought.

"Exactly. The only chance we have to intercept them is to find them first," she replied.

From beside him he felt his wife's paw on his wrist. Looking in her direction, he could see the concern in her eyes. Though she did not wish to say so in front of the group, he knew she had her doubts. She smiled weakly, but it was clear the prison escape had left her rattled. Laura steeled herself, closing her eyes momentarily, but he still felt a tremor as she squeezed harder.

"You all right?" he whispered.

"I am so far from all right I don't even know what all right is anymore." She pulled her paw away as Ellie glanced in their direction pretending that she hadn't heard. "I just want to go home."

"I know," Joe said. "But we can't let them find us. We've come too far to turn back now."

"I don't even know what we're running to." She lowered her muzzle. "We have no idea what's out there. Here we had safety, security."

"I know, but they're not going to let us stay anymore. Not with Lucas, and if we remain here Emily will die. I know out there is a big unknown, but it's the only chance we've got." He gave his most supportive smile.

Laura sighed and flattened her ears. Staring at the floor, it was clear there was nothing else to be said at this point.

Both Ellie and Mike noticed the unusual mood shift between the spouses and looked at him curiously. "Everything okay?" Mike asked.

"Not really," Joe replied. "But we have more important things to worry about right now. Like how to avoid those patrols between us and the hangar."

"Well, I hope you can come up with a solution because if not, this is going to be a real short trip." Ellie folded her arms.

"You let me figure out how to get us out of here. Your job is making sure we catch that train," he replied without hesitation.

Ellie nodded her agreement. "If you can get us out of this city, I can take it from there."

Joe nodded once more and turned to his friend. "Mike, do you think you can get the balloon ready in time?" he asked.

The penguin lowered the corners of his mouth in the avian equivalent of a frown. "It's going to be tight, but I think I can do most of the prep work before you make your run. I think our best bet is to take balloon eight. It's already mostly fueled and loaded with enough supplies that we should be okay until we reach the train. Provided we get out of the hangar with enough of a lead we should be able to outrun any pursuit."

Ellie's ears perked up. "What kind of reaction should we expect?"

"Governor Cole won't be happy about losing a balloon or you. More than likely, she'll send everything she has after us," Joe admitted. He looked over at Lucas, who since his rescue had been uncharacteristically silent. He stood in the corner, not really paying attention to the conversation but unwilling to be separated from his parents. Still dressed in his prison clothes, his shoulders drooped as he rubbed his arms.

Mike held up a webbed hand. "The plus side is that the other balloons aren't any faster than ours, and as long as we can reach their halfway point the other balloons will be forced to turn back."

"Just in case, we should probably load up our balloon with as much fuel as possible, don't you think?" Laura added, looking between Mike and her husband.

"No, if we try to refuel it'll raise too many suspicions. We should have enough to reach the point of safe return." Joe touched her shoulder. "Fuel is very carefully watched. Even if we wanted to, any attempt to refuel an inactive balloon is going to be met with questions."

"Besides, it's almost impossible to do by myself and the rest of you are too conspicuous even if you weren't wanted fugitives." Mike tapped a talon on the table. "I got a look at the fuel gauge before we disembarked. There's enough to get beyond the point of safe return but the less time you need to find the train, the better."

Letting out a deep breath, Ellie nodded. "I know the route the train is taking. We can intercept them before they get too far ahead of us, but it'll be close."

"All right." Mike looked at Joe and shook his friend's paw. "Well, I'd better get back before I'm spotted. I'll bring Emily after the morning bell, and we'll figure out our next move."

"Be careful," he said. With a wave towards the rest of the group, the penguin turned and left. Once he was gone, Joe locked the door behind him.

"I recommend we stay out of sight until we're ready

to head to the balloon. We can't risk the possibility of alerting the city guard to our location. Nobody goes outside until your friend gets back. Agreed?" Ellie asked.

"Agreed." Joe didn't like the thought of being in one place for too long, but at least for the moment there was nowhere else to go. For now, it would do. It had to.

Ellie tapped her gun with a paw. "I recommend we have someone on watch at all times as well. If they do find us I don't want to be caught unaware."

"I'm not much of a soldier." Joe could tell his wife was uncomfortable with Ellie even without looking. He only hoped the lapine couldn't pick up on it. Like it or not, they didn't have a choice.

"With any luck we won't need to fight, but I'd rather have a few seconds warning then none."

Seeing Ellie's point, he nodded. "All right. You and I will take the first watch. Lucas, you and your mom get some rest."

"Dad…" Lucas opened his muzzle but then closed it.

"There's nothing else we can do until Mike comes back. You need to save your strength. Emily's going to need her big brother." Joe took off his jacket and gave it to his son.

He pulled it tight around him. "Okay." He followed his mother into the next room and sank onto the couch. Pulling his knees against his chest, he rested his muzzle on them and curled himself into a ball.

Joe's chest tightened, wishing there was something he could do or say but knowing there was nothing. Joining his wife in the doorway, he followed her glance out to where Ellie stood.

"Are we sure we should put our trust in her?" Laura asked, looking towards the main room.

"Maybe not, but the only other alternative is to go without her, and I don't think we'd last long out there without a guide," Joe said.

Laura frowned. "What about the maps the balloon teams use?"

Joe shook his head. "Even if they covered the full area around the city, they only extend so far outside Coldhaven. Without Ellie we're flying blind and that's no better than staying here."

"I know," Laura started.

"I get why you're hesitant to trust her, but she did help us break Lucas out and she's been trustworthy so far," he said. Taking a deep breath, he looked into her eyes. "What is this really about?"

"I'm worried about Emily."

"Lisa and Mike will take care of her. They won't let anything happen to our baby." He said it as much for her as himself, knowing it was important they not let their fears get the better of them.

Laura sighed. "I hope you're right."

Joe opened his muzzle to say something reassuring, but nothing came. He watched as she walked over to their son and sat beside him. Stroking his head, she held him close and began to sing a lullaby. Most nights he would declare himself too old for such things, but given all they had been through, he offered no protest. Resting against his mother, Joe should have drawn comfort from the sight, but all it did was fill him with anxiety.

He was taking his family away from everything they had ever known on the slim chance that there was something out there. Certainly, Ellie's presence suggested that life outside was possible, but what right did he have to put them all through that risk? Despite its faults, Coldhaven had been safe, and it had been protected. But to keep his family whole he would need to risk all their lives to do it.

One way or another, they were set on their course now. All that remained was to see it through.

It would be at least ten hours before Mike returned with Emily. Until then, there was nothing to do but wait. Wait for what, he was not sure. Regardless, he doubted he would be getting much sleep in the night ahead. Putting on a brave face for his wife and son, he gave a nod before returning to the main room.

Looking around, he initially saw no sign of the hare until he looked at the stairs up to the second level. Seated on the metal steps, she was reading what appeared to be some kind of book. Stepping closer, he leaned in to see what it was. The cover indicated to him it was some sort of history book from before The Freeze. "Where'd you find that?" he asked.

Ellie closed the book and gestured at the inactive console. "I found it in a drawer. We don't have too many of these on the train," she said. "I'm surprised that it's in such good condition."

"Some of them survived The Freeze, others have been brought back by the balloon teams," Joe said. "Most of us don't really have a lot of time for reading, but I have been known to crack a book or two."

The snowshoe hare looked sadly at the book in her paws. "It's almost unbelievable how much we've lost."

Joe nodded, understanding her point of view. For those with the luxury to consider the matter, so much had been abandoned when the world became a frozen ice ball. Countless books and music and everything in between had been left behind in the mad scramble to save as many lives as possible. Whatever had caused The Freeze, there was no question what it had taken. Billions of lives had become buried in the snow, their experiences lost to history. Only a few hundred thousand had survived the disaster, and those that had kept only memories of the world that came before.

And with the older generation dying off, soon there would not even be that much left to remind future generations that there was a world before all this. Joe thought once more of his mother, telling him of things he could only imagine, that were as real to her as the wrench in his paw.

One of the lucky ones, she had been one of the first people to have a place in the last city on Earth. Abandoning everything she had ever known, she had gone with her husband to hopefully find shelter from the deadly cold that was approaching from all directions. One of the first ones to make it to the city, she had only brought with her two things. A necklace her mother gave her and a photo album, filled with images from the world before The Freeze.

Every night after he went to bed, he knew she poured through those images, drawing strength from a world he had never known but she could never forget. And now Joe found himself in the same position, forced to abandon everything in order to preserve his future.

Looking at Ellie, he waited until she returned his glance. "I want to ask you for a favor."

"Me?" Her ears perked up in mild surprise. When she regained her composure, she nodded. "Go ahead."

"I want your word that no matter what happens, my family goes with you to the train," he said.

Not understanding, Ellie tilted her head. "Yeah, we have a deal, remember?"

"I mean in case I don't make it out of the city." He stepped closer to be certain no one else overheard their conversation. "I want your word. Now I intend to do everything I can to get us all out of the city in one piece but if it comes down to it, I need to know my family is safe." Joe and Ellie continued to stare at each other as she considered his request.

"All right, you have my word. I'll keep your family safe, as long as you keep your end of the bargain and get us out of this place, because it won't matter if we miss that train," Ellie said.

Joe frowned in agreement. "We miss that train, we're all done," he said. Heading up the stairs, he took up a sentry position on the second level, followed by Ellie a moment later.

Leaning against the wall, he attempted to get as comfortable as possible while remaining alert. Even if he did not get any sleep, he knew he had best conserve as much of his energy as possible if he was going to get his family to the train intact.

Thinking of Emily, he stared out the window silently hoping that she was safe. Now that they were all fugitives she would be in as much danger as the rest of them, but Mike would do everything within his power to keep her hidden until they could be reunited. Even so, he found himself wishing he had been able to retrieve her despite the fact that for the moment she was safer anywhere else.

Knowing there was nothing he could do until Mike returned, he pushed the thought out of his mind and stared into the street below. Tomorrow they would have to find a way to get to the balloons and escape the city before Governor Cole and her people could respond. Compared to that, the prison break was the easy part.

CHAPTER NINE
ONE WAY OUT

The worst part about being separated from Emily was the waiting. During Lucas and Ellie's rescue he had not had time to worry about his daughter or the danger they were all in. Now that Mike had left to make preparations and the city guard were scouring the city looking for the fugitives, they had no other choice at the moment but to stay put and keep out of sight.

Pacing back and forth, he walked the length of the walkway before turning around and heading back in the other direction. Squeezing his paws, he at least attempted to generate some heat in the inactive building. Given the fact it was shut down it meant that they could not run any power or heat through it lest they give away their position.

Turning towards him, Ellie placed a paw on his chest. "You do that any more you're going to wear a hole in the metal."

"Sorry." He looked at the lapine scout, knowing it served little purpose. At least it gave him something to occupy himself. "I just need something to do."

"You want to do something? Keep a lookout for your friend."

Letting out a deep sigh, Joe nodded, returning to his regular post since his wife had woken him a couple of hours ago.

Staring down at the street below Joe searched for any sign of Mike. The king penguin was fifteen minutes overdue from his scheduled return. While there had been no outward signs of anything unusual Joe could not help but worry that something had happened to him after his departure last night. Wiping the tiredness from his eyes he fought to remain alert and ready. He had gotten a few hours sleep last night at Ellie's insistence. Despite his stubborn desire to remain on guard she had reminded him that he would be no good to his family if he were exhausted. Relenting, he woke his wife up and had managed to get some rest despite the concerns plaguing his thoughts.

Looking down at the lower level, Laura and Lucas had woken up in anticipation of Mike's return. Both of them were seated at the metal table in the center of the room. He offered a reassuring smile as his wife glanced up, doing his best to project confidence before returning his attention to the window.

Ellie held up a paw, narrowing her gaze before nodding to Joe. "He's back." Descending the stairs, they both met him at the door, pulling it open as he slipped inside.

"You're late," Joe said.

"Couldn't be helped." Mike rubbed his webbed hands together. "Patrols have been increased since you all went underground. I had to take a lot of back ways to get here undetected. They're stopping everyone now." He offered a weak smile. "Besides, I didn't want to take any risks with cargo this precious." He opened his coat, revealing Emily wrapped up against his chest.

"Emily!" Joe exclaimed.

"Daddy!" Practically jumping from Mike's arms, she rushed into her father's embrace. Joe felt all of the fear and panic over Emily's safety melt away as he pressed his muzzle into her face.

"It's so good to see you, sweetheart!" he said.

"Daddy, you're crushing me!" she replied, giggling as he loosened his grip.

"Sorry, baby girl. I just missed you so much." Joe set her down as he knelt in front of her. "I'm so glad you're safe."

"Uncle Mike watched over Andre and me." Emily held up her doll before hugging it tightly against her chest. "We missed you too."

Ellie placed a paw on Joe's arm. "As much as I love reunions, we need to discuss our next move."

With a sigh, Joe nodded. "Emily, I need you to go with your brother into the next room while the grown up's talk about some things, okay?"

"All right," she said, following Lucas into the back office.

Standing in front of the metal table, Mike unfolded a map of the city. Hand drawn, it was one of the tasks required of anyone who worked on the maintenance team. In order to keep the city running one had to know the ins and outs of every street and system in Coldhaven. After enough time most of them had it committed to memory, but it never hurt to know your way around.

"Okay, let's have it," Joe said.

Mike exhaled deeply. "Security has been increased

throughout the city. They're doing their best to keep it low key but it's only a matter of time before they figure out where we are."

"With our knowledge of Coldhaven we can keep ahead of them for a good long while though sooner or later we're going to run out of places to hide." Joe frowned. "We have to get to the balloon hangar as soon as possible."

"That's going to be a challenge. Patrols are currently sweeping the outer rings, moving inward along the spokes of the city one section at a time. For now, their search pattern is fairly widespread, but the closer they get to the center of the city the tighter their net is going to be," Mike said.

Ellie furrowed her brow. "Then we need to slip through one of the gaps while we can."

Mike pointed towards her. "Yeah, but finding one we can use is going to be a challenge."

"Okay, so what's our best option?" she asked.

Joe looked down at the map and considered the matter carefully. The balloon hangar was normally unguarded, save for the regular personnel. With most of the citizens believing that Coldhaven represented the only life on Earth there was little reason to assign security to it under typical circumstances. The harsh environment outside meant there was little reason for anyone to use a balloon other than the salvage teams. It was also the reason exile was such an effective punishment. With few resources and even fewer safe havens it was a death sentence to go out there without a plan. Yet it was out there that represented their best chance to stay together, with Ellie and her people.

The prison break meant that any critical facilities likely had some sort of security around them now, though with a city this large it was impossible to guard them all with equal measure. The city guard numbered a couple hundred people at most, and while they were searching the outer rings their personnel were stretched even further. Of course, the balloon hangar was placed within the industrial ring, meaning that it was currently in the path of their investigation. Getting to it would not be easy.

The biggest problem was that getting a balloon launched took a minimum of ten minutes under normal circumstances, and that was with coordination from the ground team. While it was theoretically possible to do it much quicker provided one was willing to ignore certain safety requirements, it would still take longer than they were likely to have once they got into the building. Should the city guard react faster than they were able to get the balloon released from the ground clamps and into the air, the journey would be over before it started.

Mike and Joe looked at each other. "We could try…"

"Yeah, but that's risky." Joe frowned.

"But we know they can't secure them all."

"Maybe not, but even if we're lucky enough to get one headed in the right direction…"

Ellie slammed her paws on the table. "Guys! Care to let the rest of us in on your little brainstorm?"

"Sorry." Joe waved his paw apologetically. "What we need to do is try to get on board one of the underground supply transports. If we're lucky, it'll take us right past their patrols to the vicinity of the hangar. Once we're past the bulk of their forces, we just need to get inside and initiate the launch sequence. With the balloon already fueled and loaded, we should be able to get it free fairly quickly," Joe said.

"You don't sound especially confident about that," Ellie replied.

"Well, the problem is that releasing a balloon isn't the sort of thing that goes unnoticed. Once they know where we are it won't take them long to descend on us like a pack of angry timber wolves." Mike frowned.

"What we need is a distraction," Laura said.

Both men turned to her at the same time. "What are you thinking?"

Laura rubbed her muzzle with a paw. "All we need is a few minutes, right?"

"Yeah, the more the better." Mike threw up a webbed paw in exasperation. "Getting one of the balloons free is hard enough with a team on the ground. We've got to release the docking clamps, start the balloon's engines, and open the hangar doors before we can even start to get out of here. If any part of that process gets interrupted, then the whole plan fails."

"Okay, so we need to keep the city guard busy long enough for us to get airborne." Laura paused. "What's the minimum amount of time you need to launch the balloon?"

"Best case scenario?" Mike prompted. "Eight minutes."

"Eight minutes?!" Ellie exclaimed.

"Look, this isn't exactly a standard procedure. These balloons were designed for exploration and reconnaissance only, not getaway vehicles. Given the fact that there are only four of us, I'd say eight minutes is optimistic." Puffing up his neck feathers, Mike let out a chirp of frustration.

Joe held up his paw in an effort to diffuse the situation. "All right, eight minutes it is. Now we just need something to keep the city guard off balance for at least that long."

Laura looked at Joe. "What if we blow up the fuel depot for the balloons?"

"It'd provide a hell of a blast," Joe said. "But whoever does it is going to have to run to the hangar before the balloon lifts off. Once we release the clamps there's no stopping it."

"I'll volunteer for that job," Mike replied. Joe looked up in surprise. "Look, I'm the only one we can spare, and besides, no one else has the expertise to do it other than you and me."

Joe grabbed his arm. "You're not expendable."

"Trust me, I don't plan to get left behind, but one of us has to do this if we have any chance at all of getting out of here." As much as Joe hated to admit it, he had a point.

"Well, it's not an ideal plan, but it's the best we've got," the snowshoe hare said.

"It'll have to do." Guiding a talon over the map, he illustrated the sequence of events. "First, we need to take the tunnels to the nearest access point. We hop on a transport and get as close to our destination as possible. I'll head off and provide the distraction while the rest of you head to the hangar. Once there we need to release the docking clamps and start the takeoff sequence. Now it'll be tight, but as long as we don't waste any time, we should have just enough of a window to pull this off."

Joe nodded. "Ellie, I'm going to need you to handle the launch doors. Laura, you'll be on the bridge running the startup sequence. I'll take care of the docking clamps."

"I don't know how to operate the equipment," Ellie said.

"The launch doors are easy. All you have to do is pull the lever. Laura, I can run you through the startup routine. I'd do it myself but one of us needs to release the clamps and I'd rather have you up in the balloon with the kids." He placed a paw on her shoulder.

"All right," she said.

With a nod of his beak, Mike began to fold up the documents once again. Tucking them into his coat pocket he exhaled audibly. Sensing his hesitation, the two men waited until the others had become engrossed in other things. Mike led the way to the upper walkway.

"You okay?" Tilting his muzzle towards the bird, he leaned in slightly.

"Just crossing my talons hoping that this plan will work," Mike said. "There are a lot of variables that we just can't account for." He sighed. "And even if everything goes exactly according to our best case scenario there are still a lot of things that could go wrong."

"Tell me about it," Joe agreed. "If my children weren't at risk, I wouldn't even consider it. I wish I could say I knew it was the right thing to do. All I'm sure of is that my family won't survive if we stay here. Our only chance is to get us away from Coldhaven and beyond their reach."

Mike nodded. "Once everything's in place we'll have exactly one shot at this."

"Then we can't afford any mistakes." He looked down at the others. "My family means everything to me. I can't lose them, Mike, I won't."

"We won't let that happen." Placing a webbed hand on his arm, he gave it a squeeze. "We just need to stick to the plan."

"Speaking of which, there's one thing we haven't talked about," Joe said. "What happens to Lisa after we're away?"

Mike lowered his beak. "With any luck, she'll live a long and happy life here, without me." After a long pause, he sighed. "She left me, Joe. When I wouldn't abandon you all, she threw me out and made it pretty clear not to come back."

"I'm sorry," Joe replied.

He answered without looking up. "It's okay," he said. "We haven't seen eye to eye on anything since this whole thing started. At least she'll be safe here, which is more than I can say for the rest of us."

"Mike..." Joe looked into his friend's eyes.

"Lisa made her choice, and so have I." He sighed. "I'm okay, really."

Joe tended to doubt the truth of his friend's words but decided not to press further. "Okay. Just promise me if you need to talk, you'll let me know."

"Tell you what, we'll talk about it when we're all safe and sound on that train of hers." He slapped Joe gently on the back.

Turning towards the door, he noticed Ellie giving him a pointed stare, lingering on him as he approached. "We need to talk."

"Can't this wait?" he asked.

Ellie shook her head from side to side. "No, it can't."

Letting out a deep breath, he looked to his family. "Ellie and I have to speak in private. Stay here until I get back, okay?" Lucas gave no reply. A nod from Laura was his only consolation.

Following her outside, Ellie walked into the building across the street. Joe followed a few steps behind, his eyes on her back as they descended down into the basement, where they were not likely to be overheard. "This will do."

"What's this all about?" he asked.

She held up the pistol she had taken from the guard. "Do you know how to use this?"

Joe hesitated. "I know how it works."

"You've held one on a salvage operation. It's not the same thing." Lifting her arm, she selected a spot on the wall and aimed her gun as if to fire it. "People always think they're ready until they're face first with the reality of it. When I met you on the ship I saw the hesitation. You held the rifle in your paws, but you weren't ready to use it. I saw it again when you came to get me out." She held up the handgun and then placed the weapon on a nearby table.

Inhaling deeply, Joe looked down at it with uncertainty. "I've never shot anyone before."

"And I hope you never do, but given what we're going up against I need to know you can if you have to." She paused as she folded her arms. "We're going to be going up against people who will not hesitate to shoot you if given the opportunity. Now I don't expect you to be an expert marksman, but I need to know if I can count on you in a fight."

"Is this really necessary?" he asked.

"You tell me. Back then in the prison, if you'd had the gun instead of me, would you have fired it to protect your son?" she replied in return.

Joe looked at the weapon and considered the question. He had always been a gentle person, never once in his entire life had he needed to turn a weapon on another living being. Yet ever since Lucas had been arrested, he had done things he never would have considered before and likely would have to continue to do so to keep his family safe. With the revelation that his entire life would never be the same he had been forced to adapt and this would be just one more thing he would have to master if he was going to protect those things most dear to him. "I don't know," he said.

"An honest answer," she replied. "I can work with that." Ellie held up her own weapon again. "Do you know what this is?"

"A gun," he replied simply.

"Yes, but it's also a decision. Most people know if they're going to fire it before they ever put their paws on one. When you pick one up you have to accept the fact that there are lethal consequences to using one of these." She popped out the magazine and emptied the chamber before handing it to him. "The first thing about guns is always treat them like they're loaded. Even if you know they're not it's important you respect the power they represent." Watching him hold it in his paw, she took up a position beside the polar bear. "Never put your finger on it until you're ready to fire." She then took it from him and slid the magazine back into the handle. "And when you do, be sure you commit, because you can't change your mind halfway." Pulling the slide back, she handed the weapon to Joe. "You ready to practice loading and unloading?"

Joe swallowed and gave her a nod. "Show me what I need to do." Over the next two hours Ellie gave Joe a crash course in how to use a handgun effectively. The more he listened the more certain he was that she was the only way his family was going to stay safe. Following her every instruction, by the time they were finished he was moderately proficient at its operation. And while he still held out hope that they could escape the city with a minimum of casualties, Joe knew that nothing would stand between him and his family's safety.

In a few hours, Joe would be saying goodbye to everything he had ever known. Putting his faith in Ellie, he could only hope that his decision was the right one.

The timing of their escape was intentional, with Joe waiting until nightfall when the Industrial Ring would be shut down for the evening to conserve the city's heat. Residual steam would keep the tunnels warm for some time, enough for them to make it to their destination.

When at last the time arrived, Joe gathered up his family for the next stage of their journey. Lucas had changed into some clothes Mike had brought with him, though his mood still seemed subdued, not that he could blame him.

Laura stared wistfully at their surroundings, as if she would miss the city after they were gone. Indeed, both of them had been born, fallen in love, and had their children here. But this place was no longer a sanctuary, not for them.

A tightness rose in his chest at the realization that if all went according to plan, he would never see this place again. Emotions warred within him at the thought. Though he knew he had little choice, he could not purge the weight of the finality of what he was about to do, nor could he ignore the fact that he was making a decision that would forever change his family's future.

Steeling his resolve, he knelt before his young daughter. "Okay, sweet pea. We're going to go on a long trip. I need you to be good for your mom and me, all right?"

"Where are we going?" She clutched her doll tighter.

"Someplace we can be safe, where they'll have medicine to make you all better," he said. "Daddy's friend is going to take us somewhere warm, somewhere we don't have to beg for what we need to survive." He cradled her head. "I know you're probably too young to understand all this, but Daddy is doing this for you. Now we're going to go down below for a little while. I need you to stay quiet and stick close to your brother, all right?"

"I'll cover the rear once we get down below," Ellie said, pulling the grate open.

Emily peered into the darkness and shook her head. "I don't want to."

Joe gestured to Laura to go first. "Emily, I know you're scared, but we have to."

She again shook her head. Clutching her doll tighter, she sat down and refused to budge. Up on the second level, Mike frowned. "We got a patrol coming down the street. We need to move."

Tensing up, sweat began to build on his forehead. He took her paws, trying to project fearlessness despite the tremors in his grip. "Daddy won't let anything happen to you."

"No!" she said, pulling away from him. Mike dropped into the hole, while Ellie ran up to the second level.

"They're getting closer. We need to go, now." She hurried down the stairs, swinging her legs onto the ladder.

Joe reached out to pick her up when Lucas sat beside them. "Son, go ahead without me."

"I can help," he said, ignoring his father's pleading glance and taking Emily's paws in his own. "Remember when we were playing hide and seek with the other kids, and you had to stay real quiet?" he asked. When she nodded, he continued. "We have to go down below, because we're hiding and we can't let them find us, okay?"

She timidly lifted her head. "Okay…"

"Now follow your big brother, all right? I'll make sure nothing can hurt you." He moved to the ladder. "I'll go first. Just do what I do." Slowly he disappeared from sight.

Emily moved to the ladder, clutching her doll with one arm, and after a moment she followed Lucas down to the others.

Casting one more glance at the door, Joe climbed in and pulled the hatch closed moments before he heard voices and footsteps from the room above. Staying silent, he descended the ladder into the massive labyrinth of tunnels beneath the city. Though the thick walls and ceiling would cushion any sound, it would not be long before they realized someone had been here and where they went.

Turning his attention forward, he touched Lucas on the shoulder as he made his way up to Ellie. To get to their destination they would have to maneuver their way through the endless tunnels that provided the city with heat. Once a place Joe visited for work, they were now a lifeline to guide his family to safety. Taking a moment to orient himself he pointed down the tunnels. "This way," he said.

"You sure about that?" Ellie asked.

"I've spent years maintaining this city. I know it better than the back of my paw," he said. "Trust me. No one knows this place better than I do." Joe took the lead, guiding the group away from their temporary haven and on to the staging area for the next phase of their escape.

"Stay close," she ordered, drawing her weapon as she guarded the rear.

The lighting down here was subpar at best, but it functioned well enough for him to find their way. Following the alphanumeric codes along the walls, Joe could read them like signposts. The transfer station they were seeking was some distance from their current position but once they reached it, they merely needed to board one headed in the right direction. He glanced at his daughter, her fear of the dark momentarily forgotten while her big brother held her paw.

Though she had always been daddy's little girl, she and her brother shared a unique bond between them. No matter how scary things got, Lucas could always make his sister forget about her troubles for a little while and just be a little girl. He smiled at the moment of calm among such trying circumstances and wished for nothing more than for his children to simply have a life free of burdens, at least until they were old enough to handle such things.

Turning down another of the tunnels, he signaled for the rest of the group to follow as he headed towards one of the areas of the city not currently in heavy use. Designed for storage of supplies, this part of the city had few active steam hubs. Consisting entirely of warehouses, there was little point to providing heat to them when there were so many other sections of the city in far greater need of the precious resource. As such few people were ever seen in this area, which made it perfect for a transfer station.

Joe could tell they were getting close just by the fact that he could feel the cold in his lungs. His breath visible in the chilly air, it was evident that not even the steam tunnels in this section provided any significant heat.

"Are you sure we're headed in the right direction?" Ellie asked.

"We're almost there," Joe assured her.

"Good, because I'm about to freeze my tail off," she said, rubbing herself to generate a little additional warmth.

"It's not going to be much better where we're going," Joe replied. "This is all warehouses."

"Great," Ellie said. Looking around at the rest of them, Ellie turned to Joe. "Aren't the rest of you cold?"

Laura shrugged. "We're bears. Thick fur and muscles tend to hold the heat in better."

"The cold doesn't really bother us," Joe agreed.

"Lucky you," Ellie said, pulling her jacket in a little tighter. "If it's all the same to you I'll be glad once we get someplace warmer."

Joe offered a sympathetic smile, gesturing ahead of them. "Maybe if you tried moving a little more it'd warm you up," he suggested.

Ellie shook her head. "At this point I doubt hell could warm me up," she said, trying to bury herself in her coat as much as possible. She lifted her head, stopping abruptly. "Wait."

"What is it?" Laura asked.

"Someone's coming this way," Ellie said, her sharp hearing alerting her to the approach of an unknown party. She gestured for them to hide in a maintenance alcove as a single guard scanned the tunnels with his flashlight.

Joe held up his finger for quiet as Lucas wrapped his arms around Emily and gently rocked her back and forth. He gripped his wrench in his paw, ready for anything. After a moment, Ellie relaxed her shoulders slightly.

"He's moving towards the center of the city," she said. "We're clear to move, at least for the moment. We should probably expect more patrols like that the longer we're down here."

"They probably know how we're moving around by now," Joe replied.

She stepped out into the tunnel and reholstered her stolen weapon. "If they know that, they might know where we're headed."

"It's not hard to guess, there's really only one way out of Coldhaven," Mike pointed out.

"That may actually work in our favor," Joe said.

"How do you figure?" He placed his webbed hands in his pockets.

"They're probably waiting for us. My guess is they'll have enough of security to make it look protected, but not so much we won't approach." Joe folded his arms.

"A lobster trap," Ellie said.

"Exactly. They'll wait for us to get inside and then once we can't get back into the tunnels, they'll spring the trap." He clapped his gloved paws together. "We just need to be faster than they are." He resumed walking towards the transfer station.

From his thigh there was a gentle tugging on his pants. "Daddy, I'm tired."

He knelt before her. "I know, sweetie, but we can't stop. Tell you what, I'll carry you for a little while, okay?" Joe picked her up and held her against his chest. "Just hang on to me and don't let go, all right?"

Emily did as he instructed and immediately curled up against him. He kissed the top of her head as they approached the next junction.

Ellie paused again. "There's a checkpoint setup just

around the curve."

"Damn it," Mike said. "Can we get around them?"

Joe shook his head. "Possibly, but we'll have to take a longer route and there's no guarantee they haven't blocked off that way too."

"Is there a way to sneak past them?" She listened carefully. "There are two guards standing stationery and a third patrolling the tunnel."

Joe looked up. "Maybe, but it won't be comfortable, and it'll be tight." He reached up to a set of thick pipes above him. Testing them, he handed Emily to her mother and climbed on top of them. "All right. Everyone do what I do and go slow." He knew their movement would be slightly cushioned by the sound of the industrial equipment above the surface, but all it would take was a single unexpected noise to reveal their position. He reached down to pull up Lucas, and in turn he pulled up Mike. Laura handed Emily to Joe and pulled herself up with Ellie providing a temporary stirrup with her paws. At last, the hare jumped up and pulled her body on top with the others. "We need to crawl the length of this tunnel on the pipe. Stay quiet."

He clutched Emily to his chest like a precious treasure, moving as quickly as possible with one paw. He shuffled his knees on the pipe, silently gritting his teeth as he moved along the hard surfaces. Making slow but steady movements he inched ever closer to the guard's position, watching them below as they stared down the tunnel for their prey.

So far, they had not noticed their presence. He gently held his daughter to his chest, feeling his heartbeat with the exertion. Forcing himself to move, he crawled forward until almost the entire group had passed the checkpoint. Joe exhaled, but his relief was not to last.

The groan of straining metal brought him to a

sudden state of alertness. The guards looked around but so far, they had not seen them.

"What was that?" one asked.

"It's probably just the pipes," the other replied. "Things are always making noises down here."

Joe listened and soon identified the source of the sound. The supports holding the pipes up were starting to crack. Wordlessly he moved faster, trying to clear the guard post before the pipes gave way.

Buckling under his weight, the entire thing collapsed, dropping Joe and Emily right into the middle of the guards. "AH!!!"

"Oh shit, it's them!" the one guard said.

"Emergency alert, section— Unh!" the second guard's signal was cut off by a shot from Ellie's handgun.

Joe rolled out of the way of the first guard as Mike dropped down to the tunnel floor and wrestled with the arctic fox. Emily began to cry as Joe picked her up, pressing her to his chest. "It's okay, baby, I'm here."

Mike grunted, taking a hit to his torso. He gripped the baton, struggling against him as Ellie kicked the guard in the back of the head. Delivering a spin kick before he could recover, Ellie sent the guard into the wall. "Thanks."

"You're welcome."

Joe's breath caught in his throat as the last guard approached. Gripping his wrench in his paw, he aimed for his head and hurled it as hard as he could. It struck its target with a satisfying clunk. He breathed heavily as Emily continued to cry.

Lucas ran over to his sister while Ellie knelt before Joe. "Nice shot," she said, returning the wrench back to him.

Joe looked down at the tool. "It comes in handy sometimes." He rose to stand, replacing it on his belt.

Ellie kicked the arctic fox in the chest one more time.

"We'd better go before they realize we've breached their perimeter." She knelt down and removed the extra handguns and magazines from the downed guards, handing a set to Joe.

Joe nodded, gesturing forward. "Come on, the transfer station is right up ahead." Approaching the massive underground hub, trains moved supplies all over the city. Underneath the surface, they were protected from the elements allowing materials to be allocated wherever necessary. Most of them were filled with the essentials, but anything the city needed other than steam could be routed through here.

"We need one heading to section G14," Mike said, as he studied the signage above each track indicating its destination.

Threading their way through the numerous waiting trains, Laura stopped and paused at one marked 'Priority Cargo'. Indulging her curiosity, she undid the latch and slid the door open. "Joe, look at this."

"Found something?" He stepped in front of the open door and paused.

Laura turned to Joe. "The cars are full of metal. What would they be doing with all that material?"

Turning his muzzle towards her, he shrugged. "The only possibility I can think of is that they're building something."

"What could they be building?" she asked. "We haven't had a major expansion project in years. Why would they be devoting such a large amount of resources to whatever this is?"

"That, I don't know. But the amount of steel and other materials they're rerouting is way more than you need for any kind of repair." Pointing to the labels on the cargo pallets he tapped the floor of the car for emphasis. "Material of that grade is usually only reserved for top priority projects."

"As fascinating as this is, we really need to keep moving," Ellie declared.

"Yes, of course." Joe walked back to his daughter and picked her up in his arms. "Emily, I need you to keep an eye on Andre for me, okay?" He leaned in close to her muzzle.

Emily looked around and held her doll tightly. "Andre says he wants to go home."

"We can't, sweetheart. Daddy knows you're scared, but he won't let anything happen to you. I swear it." He pressed his muzzle against hers. "You believe daddy, don't you?" A pause. "I've never lied to you." He touched his paw to her much smaller version. "We'll be okay."

"Okay." She tucked her doll against her coat. "I'll make sure Andre stays quiet."

"Good girl." He looked up as Mike returned to the group.

He gestured behind him with a webbed hand. "Good news, I found one headed in the right direction on platform ten."

"The preface of good news suggests that there's also bad news," Joe replied.

"You'd be right. The supply transport is right near an active patrol. We have less than three minutes to get everyone on board before it pulls out of the station."

"Shit. We need to move fast and carefully. Stay quiet and watch the supply trains." Turning to the snowshoe hare, he nodded. "Ellie, find us a way through."

Ellie took a deep breath and observed the patrol. They moved back and forth scanning the area for the fugitives. When she spotted an opening, she made her move. It was a careful ballet, needing to time both the patrols of the soldiers as well as the numerous small trains transporting cargo across the city. One needed to avoid being seen while at the same time evading the oncoming projectiles that could turn a polar bear into jam. Once the guards at the nearby checkpoint turned back to walk in the opposite direction, she sprinted, leaping over the tracks in a signature lapine move, dashing across before they'd even completed half of their circuit.

Turning to his wife, Joe nodded. "Just like that."

With a look of sheer disbelief, Laura slapped him on the arm. "If you think I can do that, you've got another thing coming, mister."

Joe smirked, and then waited until the guards turned. "Go!"

Laura did not waste any time, hurrying towards the tracks as quickly as possible. Running across, she made sure to step carefully on the slats between the tracks and on to the other side. A few more seconds and she reached Ellie's position moments before the guards turned around again.

"I'll go next," Mike declared. Moving with surprising swiftness, the penguin hopped from one hiding spot to the next, joining the ladies as they worked to climb up onto the platform.

"Your turn," Joe said, looking at Lucas.

The young polar bear gave his dad a doubtful expression before taking a deep breath and running towards the tracks. Joe kept an eye on the soldiers as they had their backs turned to them. It was only when he heard a sudden gasp that he saw Lucas had his foot stuck in the tracks. Trying to pull it free, he was hidden from the view of the soldiers, but he would be hit by the oncoming train if he did not escape before it passed.

Cursing, Joe dashed out the instant the soldier turned his back, rushing out to Lucas with Emily in his arms. Ellie rushed to meet him, taking his little girl while Joe used his superior strength to wrench his son's foot free. Grabbing him with both arms he rolled out of the way seconds before the train sped past their former position. Breathing heavily, he sat up and pushed Lucas forward. "That was too close," Joe said.

"You're telling me," Lucas agreed. Meeting his father's eyes, he smiled. "Thanks."

"You're welcome." Joe kept his face positive, glad no one could sense how terrified he had been. Lifting his son up onto the platform, Joe cursed as the alarm for imminent departure sounded. "We gotta go!"

Ellie passed Emily up to her mother before vaulting onto the platform with uncanny agility. Her ears perked up as she drew her weapon. "They've seen us!" She opened fire at the patrol, taking one soldier out with her first shot.

Laura hauled Joe up to the platform, embracing him for a moment before the two polar bears rushed towards the car. "The door is jammed!"

Joe grabbed the handle and pushed with all his strength, forcing the mechanism to release with a violent snapping of metal. "Get in!" he called out. Pulling Laura inside, he ushered his son and daughter into the car. Mike leapt across the gap seconds before the massive vehicle began to move. "Ellie, come on!"

Ellie cast one more glance at the soldiers as she ran after the car. Stunned, they fired at her, missing by inches as she jumped into the open doorway. The supply transport pulled away, leaving them behind.

Joe gave the snowshoe hare a hearty pat on the back as she slowly caught her breath. "Thanks for helping me with Emily back there."

"I had a feeling what you had in mind. I thought I'd better make sure you had time to do it." The lapine nodded as she sat on a nearby crate.

Laura stepped up beside him, looking into her husband's eyes. Casting a glance towards the hare, Ellie continued to gather her strength as the supply car brought them closer to their destination. "I'll say this much for her, she knows her stuff."

"That she does," Joe agreed, thinking back to their first meeting on board the Navy ship. His surprise aside, Ellie was a capable fighter, and had the others not shown up when they did it was quite possible, she would have made her escape, and they would be on their own right now. Despite the short time he had known the lapine he suspected her to be someone he could trust and she in turn appeared to trust him, at least for the time being.

"I just hope we can get out of the city in one piece," she said without meeting his glance.

"So do I," he admitted. "But they're not going to let us go without a fight. Especially not as long as we have Ellie."

"Why do you think they care so much about her?" she asked.

Joe shrugged. "She represents a threat to their authority. Anyone that's aware she exists knows that the city leadership has been lying to us for decades."

Laura shook her head in confusion. "Why would they do that?"

"Control," Joe stated. Seeing his wife's confusion, he continued. "Consider all of the things we've just accepted for the good of the city. Longer shifts, reduced rations, harsh punishments. All of those things were instituted by the government for the greater good of Coldhaven, and in every case they were accepted without question because we knew the only alternative was freezing to death out here."

Even such things as the perks had been limited

among the general population in the name of their collective survival. Things like coffee and fresh meat were rare treats ostensibly as a reward for loyal service and taken away when one stepped out of line. Joe recalled how surprised he had been when he had visited the doctor and seen not only his living space but the comparative luxury of his personal quarters. He had never seen where Governor Cole lived but he suspected it was even more luxurious than that.

The arctic vixen had always sold her policies as hardships shared by all of the people of Coldhaven, but Joe could hardly recall any time when she herself had rolled up her sleeves and left her heated tower other than to recruit people for more laborious work. Indeed, that was what she was doing when she had seen him and Lucas that morning inside the residential ring and changed Joe's life forever.

Whether she had intended to or not she had set Joe on a path that now he had no choice but to follow to its end. Wherever it led he could no longer accept the things he had once taken for granted.

"But what would that get them?" Laura asked.

"Our loyalty," Joe said. "No matter what they do they convince everyone that it's a noble sacrifice for the benefit of everyone. No one complains, no one resists, and no one looks too deeply into what they're doing."

Laura frowned. "We can't be the first ones to think like that though."

"We're not," Joe replied.

"But without proof you've been unwilling to cross the line and openly defy them," Ellie pointed out, joining the conversation. "By telling you that they're the only option they make resisting too risky to consider. Rather than openly defying their authority the best you can do is gather information and move things around a bit," she said, offering a shrug.

Joe exhaled deeply as he considered Ellie's point. Coldhaven was relatively peaceful but how would that change if people knew there were other options? No doubt a significant number of people would demand action. Suddenly it became clear to Joe why they had spirited Ellie away so quickly upon their return to the city. If word got out of her presence, then the people would realize what Joe had the moment he had seen her. They were not alone. While the revelation had not truly settled in until later, for the first time Joe could no longer be certain what he knew.

Ellie's mere existence had thrown everything he had believed into question. No longer was he certain that the sacrifices asked of him were for the greater good or even necessary at all. His experiences in the last few weeks had thrown his entire world into doubt, with the only thing he was sure of being the fact that he could not remain in Coldhaven.

The snowshoe hare not only represented a fundamental game changer for Joe but also the chance that for the first time in his life he might be able to choose his own destiny. Going with Ellie represented the only possibility he had of keeping his family together and his children alive, but more than that it offered the possibility of a fresh start. For the first time in his life Joe would be able to determine his own path forward.

"Yeah, but there's got to be more to it than that," Laura said.

"There is," Joe responded. "The city is dying." At that statement they all turned to look at him.

"What do you mean?" Laura asked.

"Think about it. The Candle has been experiencing more and more system failures. The maintenance team has been constantly dispatched throughout the city to keep the heat distribution system running. The reduction in food rations along with the conscription of additional labor to keep the city operating for a little bit longer. They know that we're running out of food, fuel, and resources and they need more of all three. And I know of only one place to get them."

Ellie's ears drooped. "The Garden."

"Exactly," Joe said, pointing a claw at their hare companion. "That's why Governor Cole had those files in her office."

"But if they know about the Garden then why do they need Ellie?" Laura asked.

"Because they don't know where it is," Joe answered for her. "More than likely, they were aware of it from the plans put in place before The Freeze."

"And the information they have doesn't go about mentioning the coordinates," Ellie said, reasoning it out.

Joe nodded. "Likely for security reasons at the time," he said. "So the only way they can find it is through you."

"Couldn't they just follow the tracks?" Mike asked.

Ellie shook her head. "The tracks crisscross the entire planet. They'd have no way to know where the train was headed without the information in its databanks."

Pulling his wife closer with his paw, he offered a reassuring smile. "Once we get out of Coldhaven, we just need to get far enough away and then we'll be home free. The balloons have a maximum range of a few thousand miles. Once we pass the point of safe return they'll have to turn back."

"And if they don't?" Laura pressed a paw into her husband's chest.

"One problem at a time," Joe replied. "Try to put it out of your mind for now. We'll be safe soon enough."

"Easier said than done," Laura replied.

On that, she and Joe were in complete agreement.

"All right, we ride this train until it gets to G14. Then we just need to find someplace to hide while Mike takes care of the fuel depot. Once we get to the balloon, we launch as quick as we can and get out of the city before they can pursue. After that, it's up to you." He looked towards Ellie. "I just hope your people are where you say they are."

"They will be," Ellie said without hesitation.

"Well, I guess one way or another we'll find out," Joe responded. Walking over towards his family, he looked at the trio huddled in the corner. "You all okay?"

Laura nodded, doing her best to appear confident. Although she did not let it show, Joe knew she was as frightened as he was. Squeezing her two children, she looked up at him. "We'll be all right."

Emily looked up at her father, the young cub smiling brightly. It always amazed Joe as to the adaptability of his daughter, and her eternal optimism. A part of him wondered if perhaps it was simply the fact that she didn't know any better, but he chose to believe it was because she was a bright light and nothing would dampen her spirit. "Andre says he's scared, but I told him my daddy will get us someplace safe." She squeezed her doll close. "I know you'll keep your promise."

He reached out a paw to give his daughter's cheek fur a gentle caress. "You bet I will. Tell Andre he doesn't have to worry about a thing." Smiling, he waited until he was no longer in view of her and allowed his expression to fade. Although he wanted to project courage for his children, he could not allow them to see the doubts he harbored. There were still a lot of things between him and the way out of here, and until they were safely away, he would not be able to relax. Perhaps not even then.

Sensing a paw on his arm, he turned to see his son Lucas. "Everything okay, son?"

The younger polar bear looked at him. "Dad, I want you to know that you can count on me."

Looking at his son, he turned his muzzle down towards him. "I know I can. I'm relying on you to keep your sister safe."

Lucas frowned, apparently not satisfied. "I can do more than look after Emily. Let me help you and Ellie."

"You already are by looking after your family. Look, I need you to keep your mom and sister safe. I've given you the most important job of all. I wouldn't trust it to anyone else." Joe looked towards his wife and daughter.

Lucas shook his head. "What you need is someone to watch your back." He gave him a pleading look.

"Lucas," he started.

"Forget it," Lucas said, turning away and returning to his mother.

Opening his muzzle, he took a breath as if to speak but then thought better of it. It was not as if he did not understand his son's desire to make a more active role, but as a father, he had always wanted to keep his children safe as long as possible. Almost losing him in the Candle explosion had shaken him to his core. He could not run the risk of Lucas getting killed, not if he could help it.

CHAPTER TEN
BALLOONS

The last time Joe had boarded a balloon it had been as the navigator. This time he, Ellie, Mike, and Laura would have to perform the jobs of the entire crew while at the same time racing against the clock to get out before anyone could do anything to prevent their escape. It was going to be complicated, he already knew that, but just how complicated remained to be seen.

He stood on the rooftop of a nearby building aiming his binoculars towards the balloon hangar. Patrols walked around the building in a regular pattern. Covering the perimeter, it was apparent they were expecting this move. Once Mike triggered the explosion at the fuel depot, it would be time for them to make theirs. Feeling a paw on his shoulder, he turned, expecting Laura but paused when he recognized Ellie.

"You here?" she asked.

"Huh?" Joe replied.

"Are you with me?" she asked. "I know you're not used to things like this, but I can tell you from experience it doesn't get any easier."

Joe nodded, looking over at the others. In a brief moment of calm before the storm, his wife held his daughter in her arms while they waited for the signal to go. Laura offered him a reassuring nod, staring into his eyes while they steeled themselves for what was to come. Standing beside his mother, Lucas remained standoffish. Lowering his muzzle, he straightened up. "You can count on me."

"Good," Ellie said. "When things start happening, we're going to need to move fast. You and I are going in first. Your family can follow behind. We only have a short window so make sure they keep up."

The polar bear exhaled audibly. "Once we get inside, you and I will work on clearing the way out of here." Turning to his wife, he continued. "Laura, the maps are in Mike's locker. Grab them on your way up. The startup routine will take a full six minutes. You're going to have to begin the moment you get inside the cockpit." He offered her his best supportive smile. "It's just like we talked about."

"That's a long way from actually doing it," she responded. He nodded sympathetically.

"While you're running the startup routine, we're going to have to release the docking clamps and open the doors. All that is going to create a hell of a lot of noise, so it won't take them long to realize the fuel depot is a diversion," Joe added. "With luck we'll be pulling away before any of them can get back to the hangar."

Ellie shook her head, her long ears swaying with her hair. "I'm not relying on luck. Everyone knows their jobs. Stay focused, get it done, and get out of here. That work for everybody?" she asked. Both polar bears nodded their agreement. "Good. Then let's get this show on the road."

"Mike should be at the fuel depot by now. Once he's inside, all he should need to do is remove the safeties and…" A large explosion nearby indicated Mike had completed his task. "That." Sirens filled the air as shouting and alarms could be heard in the direction of the depot. Below, the city guard looked around in a moment of confusion as they debated their next course of action. Reacting to something being said over their radios, the people patrolling outside the balloon hanger stared at each other as if waiting for one of them to make a decision. He looked at Ellie for the signal to go, but so far she had not moved.

Still as a statue, her ears perked up while she listened for the sounds of the nearby patrols. Momentarily envious of her superior hearing, he looked to her, waiting for any sort of reaction. She held up her paw indicating they needed to wait.

Looking again through his binoculars he could tell the members of the city guard were alarmed. Shouting and people running back and forth seemed to be predominant as more reports came in over their radios. The emergency alert had unsettled them, but they needed it to pull them out of position. Lowering the binoculars, he handed them to Ellie while he crossed the distance to the rest of the group. "Once we start moving, I want the three of you to stay together. Lucas, keep an eye on your sister. You understand?"

"Yes," he replied.

"Good." Joe squeezed his wife's shoulder. "We'll be all right. Just stay close to each other and follow my lead."

Returning to Ellie, the snowshoe hare kept her finely tuned senses on the activity near the balloon hangar. "They're spreading out," she said.

"Isn't that what we want?" Joe prompted.

"Yeah, but if we go too soon, they'll spot us, and we'll have a running firefight all the way to the balloons and you and I don't have a lot of ammo. Get everyone ready, we're going to have to move as soon as we have an opening." She checked her pistol while the others gathered up behind her.

Joe exchanged a concerned glance with Laura before drawing his weapon and taking up a position behind Ellie. "We're good to go."

Ellie acknowledged his statement with a slight tilt of her head. After a few more seconds, she waved her paw forward. "Go! Go! Go!" She leapt down the stairs skipping more than half of them at a sprint, turning and descending to the ground level at a rapid pace.

Hurrying after her, he attempted to keep up with the faster hare, barely rounding a few of the curves. Once his boots had hit the ground, the polar bear fought to keep up, closing the gap between them in a short amount of time. The pair dashed across the open space between the building that had been their starting point and the hangar.

Arriving at the door, Ellie entered first. She scanned the interior listening carefully for sounds of anyone present. After a moment, she nodded to Joe.

He ushered his family to join them with an urgent wave of his paw. As soon as they were inside, he locked the door behind them. "That won't keep them out for long, but it'll buy us a little time at least."

"Then let's get started. Keep your eyes open, we may not be alone here." She continued to scan the area, listening for signs of anyone who might stand in their way.

Looking up, he saw the seven massive balloons that filled the long rectangular building. Each of them numbered and prepared for launch they were always kept ready for salvage, rescue, and reconnaissance. Barring the one currently absent, the remaining balloons stood ready for action.

Joe silently thanked standard procedure for keeping the balloons always inflated. Had they needed to prepare it they never would have stood a chance at getting out of the city before they were stopped. He watched Laura as she grabbed the maps and hurried up the steps with their children to the cradle that housed Balloon Eight. Silently towering over them like a sentinel the balloon stood ready for the final steps of their escape.

Pointing Ellie towards the control room he headed up to the launch platform. "All right, we need to release all four of these clamps before we can maneuver. Ellie, get on the doors."

The snowshoe hare nodded, running her paws over the panel inside the control room. Interrupted by a flashing red light and an unfriendly sounding buzzer, the lapine looked up. "Uh oh," she said. "We have a problem."

"What's wrong?" Joe asked.

"The remote door activation sequence isn't working," she replied.

"Keep trying," the polar bear said.

"I am, it's not responding."

Joe looked up towards a raised platform on the other side of the hangar. "You're going to have to release the doors manually."

"We're already cutting it close," Ellie cautioned.

"And if you don't get those doors open nobody is going anywhere," he responded, gesturing towards the panel. Joe handed the hare a radio. "You'll need this."

"Thanks," Ellie said, taking it and turning it on. "I'm on channel four."

Joe adjusted his radio to match. "Ellie, can you hear me?" he asked to confirm. The snowshoe hare held it in front of her muzzle as she ascended the stairs.

"*Loud and clear,*" she replied, her voice conveying her exertion.

On a panel visible from anywhere in the hangar there were two indicator lights on the status display which currently glowed red. Indicating both the status of the docking clamps and the doors above them, they were going nowhere until both had changed to green. Looking towards the raised platform to monitor Ellie's progress, he pressed the button on his radio. "How's it looking?" he asked.

"*I can't make heads or tails of this,*" she said.

His ears perked as a metal grate lifted off the floor beside the platform where Joe stood. "Anyone call for a mechanic?" Mike asked, emerging from an underground tunnel. Normally designed to allow the fuel pipes to transport their contents directly to the balloons, Mike had used it as an impromptu escape tunnel. Reaching down to pull his friend up, he gestured at the two red indicator lights.

"Would you give Ellie a hand with the doors?" he asked.

"I'm on it," he said, running up to join her. Taking the radio from the hare, he looked up and placed it in front of his beak. "*I'm going to initialize the door release sequence, stand by,*" he said. Below the avian pressed several commands into the control panel followed by a rather loud mechanical clack as the doors above began to open up and slowly contracted as the panels slid out of the way, revealing open sky. One of the lights changed to a pleasant green allowing Joe to breathe a silent sigh of relief.

One down, one to go.

"Great job, Mike. Now both of you get down here," he said.

"*On our way.*" The two hurried down onto the maintenance platform. Taking up the opposite position,

Mike looked across to Joe.

Grabbing onto the release lever, Joe flipped up the safety latch and motioned for Mike to do the same. Once the levers were released, they pulled in unison, causing a significant heavy clunk as the massive metal clamps released their cargo. The balloon remained in position, held in place by several ropes meant to keep the ship level until the crew was prepared for takeoff.

Moving to the next set of clamps, Joe's radio suddenly buzzed to life with Laura's voice. "*We have a problem.*"

Joe did not have to ask what his wife meant as several city guard members made their way into the hangar. "Damn it," Joe said, looking to Ellie. "You're up."

The snowshoe hare nodded, taking her weapon and walking over to the edge of the maintenance platform. Aiming her pistol, she zeroed in on the lead guard and opened fire. The bullet struck him in the chest, sending him to the ground as it impacted his armor. Taking cover behind a large tool chest, she fired several additional shots forcing the city guard to scatter.

Looking around for Mike, Joe had lost sight of him in the chaos. Forcing himself to focus, he did his best to put what was happening outside out of his mind as he concentrated on his task. All of this wouldn't matter if he couldn't get the docking clamps released.

Returning his attention to the lever in front of him, he gripped the handle and kicked the latch free. Pulling it, he was rewarded with a loud metal clank as the third clamp released. There was no time to celebrate, however, as the firefight continued to rage not far from where he was standing. Somehow Ellie had managed to keep the city guard distracted with only her handgun. Moving towards the last clamp, he roared as a bullet grazed his arm. Gripping the wound, he could smell the blood as it stained his coat a dark red. Swearing, he moved to the last clamp and cursed as the safety latch stubbornly refused to move.

It was then that Joe recalled the reason why the safety clamps had to be released in pairs. Normally this was done all at once by the ground crew, who would time their efforts in a well-rehearsed routine, but with Ellie otherwise engaged, it had slipped his mind. The balloon was pulling unevenly on the last clamp, trying to break free from its bonds. Even without the engines active, the wind from the open roof was pulling and pushing the balloon in different directions. The safety ropes would keep it in place, but it would be near impossible to release the final clamp under these conditions.

Trying once again to pull the safety latch free, he felt pain from the bullet wound. No doubt the injury had damaged at least some of the muscles in his arm. It would be difficult, though he had no choice but to keep trying. Joe grabbed the latch again, only to look up in surprise as Mike appeared at his side. "Mike!" he shouted.

"You can't do this alone!" he shot back, pulling the latch free with their combined strength. "Now let's get this done and get out of here."

"No, I can do this," he said.

Mike gave him a soft tap on his arm. The pain made Joe wince, baring his sharp teeth. "I trust I've made my point. Now help me with this clamp."

Joe swore and complied, as the two pulled together on the large lever. With a loud metal clack, the last clamp released, and the balloon pulled upward, held in place only by the safety lines tied to the railings around the cab. "That's our cue to get out of here."

"You won't get any argument from me," Mike agreed. A gunshot pierced the air from an unknown direction.

Joe's head whirled around to see where it had struck. His muzzle fell open as a red stain grew from the center of Mike's chest. "Mike…"

"I don't feel so…" He collapsed onto the platform, his webbed hand touching his wound.

"Stay with me!" he shouted, looking up at the shooter. Stewart raised his weapon and hissed. Joe roared, his eyes watering with rage as he swung his wrench hard enough to knock the handgun from the feline's shaking paw. Terrified, the cat backed away, but he could not escape as Joe grabbed him by the chest and bodily threw him from the platform into a table. He knelt back down beside his friend. "Mike, hang in there, we'll get you help on the balloon…" He shook him gently. "I need you to stay with me!" He looked up. "Ellie!"

The hare did not need a radio to hear him, even over the din of the gunfire around her. Turning and sprinting towards the balloon, she shot up to the platform and felt the king penguin's neck. "He's gone. We got to go!"

"We can't leave him!" Joe grabbed at Mike's body.

"If we don't get out of here, he's going to have a lot of company!" She fired another shot at the city guards. "It's now or never, Joe!"

Casting one last glance at Mike, he hurried up to the cabin. Ellie had already cut the safety lines holding the balloon in place, allowing it to rise up through the sky doors and into the open air. Returning his wrench to his belt, he gave his family a reassuring nod. "Strap in, everyone, this is about to get bumpy." He trudged forward towards the pilot's station and momentarily hesitated at the complex controls to the massive craft.

"You sure you know what you're doing?" Ellie asked.

"We're about to find out," Joe replied. Closing his eyes and doing his best to summon his recollection of the takeoff sequence he took a deep breath and opened them as he flipped the first switch. The rumble of the engines could be heard as the propellers started to spin. With the balloon now idling, Joe turned his attention to the navigation system. Checking a few of the settings he began the process that would guide them out of the city, setting the controls to the proper positions.

Ellie joined him at the control console. "How long until we get moving?" the snowshoe hare asked.

"I'm working on it," Joe responded. "This is a complex machine. It takes more than a few buttons to get her going." Joe felt his paws become sweaty as he struggled to remember the rest of the sequence. His anxiety filling his chest, he felt his wife's paw on his shoulder as Laura wordlessly provided him her strength.

Calmed and emboldened, he nodded to her as he returned his attention to the matter at paw. Checking the panel one more time, everything indicated it was ready. Either the balloon would maneuver, or it wouldn't. Closing his eyes as he flipped the last switch, the panel flipped to green. "YES!" he shouted.

Ears perked, Ellie turned towards the side of the balloon. "They've stopped firing."

"Isn't that a good thing?" Laura asked.

Stepping to the railing, Ellie's ears drooped as she spun around. "They're trying to launch some of the other balloons."

"Damn it." Joe squeezed the yoke harder.

"I thought you sabotaged the rest of them," Ellie said, coming to stand behind Joe's chair.

"It's not an exact science!" Joe pushed the throttle forward. "We need to get some distance between us and them as quickly as possible." Ascending away from the balloon hangar, Joe knew it would take them several minutes to ready any of the remaining six balloons for pursuit. That gave them some time, but they could still be prevented from leaving until they were out and clear of the city. Continuing to climb, he began a gradual upward turn as he pulled the balloon around to head over the city.

"Shouldn't we be heading away from here?" Laura asked.

Joe nodded. "The Navy carrier where we picked up Ellie is in the opposite direction. We take the long way we might not make it out before they can shoot us down."

"Can they do that?" Laura asked.

While Coldhaven was generally unarmed given its supposed status as the last city on Earth, it was an unofficial secret that several weapons emplacements were positioned around the border of the city to shoot down any potential incoming threats. While no one outside of the government was supposed to be aware of their existence, the necessity for regular maintenance had meant the crew in the Workshop had been responsible for keeping them in good working order. Joe simply nodded.

"How long before we're clear of the city?" Ellie asked.

"At least seven minutes." At her incredulous look he shrugged. "These things weren't designed for speed or maneuverability."

"Clearly," she replied, deadpan.

Leaning over his shoulder, Laura spoke softly. "Are we going to be all right?"

"Ask me in seven minutes," he replied.

Ellie walked to the observation windows and scanned the skies around them. "We've got company, two balloons coming up behind us."

"All right. As long as we can stay ahead of them, even if they're operating at full capacity their top speed shouldn't be any better than ours," Joe said. "However…"

"However, what?" Ellie frowned.

"If they work together, they can try to force us down or even attempt to board the balloon depending on how badly they want us." Joe gripped the yoke and altered course. Soaring over the massive city, he tried to keep the gap between the three of them but every time he would attempt to maneuver, one or the other would move to cut him off.

Joe called over his shoulder. "I need the rest of you to tell me what they're doing!"

Laura pressed her paws against the window. "The port balloon is accelerating!"

"The starboard balloon is trying to outflank us!" Ellie shouted.

Joe increased speed another ten percent and drove the balloon towards the center of the city. Both enemy craft moved to follow. "All right, they want to chase us, we're going to make them work for it."

His wife touched his shoulder. "Joe, what are you doing?"

"Getting us some room to maneuver." He pushed the balloon closer towards the towering sight of the Candle. Given their limited altitude they would have to thread the needle through the taller structures of the Central Nexus to escape. Hopefully, the gamble would provide them with some breathing room and maybe give his sabotages some time to work.

"The port balloon is closing!" Laura said.

Ellie gripped the back of Joe's chair. "The other one is trying to cut us off!"

Joe angled the front of their craft towards the cluster of residential buildings that surrounded the Candle. "Let's see how they handle this." Sacrificing some speed to improve maneuverability, he gritted his teeth as they raced towards the city center. The starboard balloon did the same, altering course to try to close the distance between them while the port craft increased speed to prevent evasive maneuvers. As the space between them narrowed, they closed on the Central Nexus.

Ellie swore. "They've got us boxed in!"

"Not yet they don't!" He swerved the balloon hard around a tower, forcing the other balloon to slow to avoid a collision. As the second pursuer increased speed, a sudden explosion and a puff of black smoke emanated from the rear of the now disabled craft. "Ha!"

Her ears raised, she smirked. "Better late than never, I suppose." Ellie turned her attention towards the remaining enemy craft. "They're coming around from the side!"

Joe gripped the yoke and pushed the balloon towards the other ship, aiming the nose at the forward section of their remaining pursuer. At first refusing to give ground, at the last second the pilot swerved, clipping one of the towers as the balloon suffered a puncture, losing air as it descended towards Coldhaven. "That was too close. Hopefully they won't launch any more before we're safely out of the city."

"I don't think we'll have to worry about the other balloons," Ellie remarked, ears flattening.

Before he could ask her what she was talking about Joe turned his head in time to see something slowly rise into view. "What the hell is that?"

Ellie frowned over her shoulder. "I think we figured out what they were building."

Joe locked the controls and walked to the side of the bridge. Visible from outside the window was a dangerous looking jet black dirigible. Sleek and designed for combat, it was both fast and deadly, more than a match for their exploratory balloon. The hostile craft fired two shots past their port side. They were not close enough to hit but near enough that the message was clear. Joe cursed as he ran back to the pilot's console and maxed out the engines. "Hang on!"

Ellie gripped the railing with both paws as the balloon surged forward before settling into a more consistent acceleration. After a moment it once again appeared to taper off and settle into a steady speed. "That's it?"

"That's it." He looked at the controls. "The engines are at the red line. This is as fast as she's going to go."

Laura looked at her husband. "There's no way we can outrun them."

Ellie cast a glance at Laura and then at Joe. "So what are they waiting for?"

Joe shrugged and looked at the snowshoe hare. "The fact that they haven't shot us down means that they want us in one piece. With luck that also means they're not willing to fire on us directly, which gives us an advantage."

"Not much of one," Ellie argued.

"True, but in a straight up fight we'd be burning on the ice right now. That first shot was a warning." The polar bear offered his wife his most reassuring smile. As if to support his theory, less than a minute later a radio transmission forced its way into the cabin. At the same moment, two more dirigibles assumed a position in their path, leaving a small space between them.

"This is Captain Raniel Parr of the Dirigible Nova. *You are hereby ordered to stop and return to the balloon hangar. There will not be a second warning. Stand down or you will be fired upon."* The male voice spoke with authority, clearly indicating someone with experience.

Reaching for the handset, Joe placed the microphone in front of his mouth. "Negative, Captain. I intend to leave Coldhaven with my family one way or the other. If you intend to stop us then I welcome you to try because I'm not slowing down." Replacing the handset back on the console, he kept the balloon steady and planted his boots on the deck keeping an eye on both in case his hunch proved to be wrong.

Neither dirigible moved as the distance between them steadily decreased. Joe's paws held firm to the controls, never taking his eyes off the enemy craft directly ahead. The bridge had become completely silent as everyone waited to see what the dirigibles would do. Joe held his breath as the final stretch disappeared and the balloon sailed harmlessly between them.

Emerging on the other side Joe loosened his grip on the controls slightly. It was only then he realized how tightly he'd been holding on. Breathing heavily, he knew it was not over yet. "Positions!" he called out.

Ellie narrowed her eyes. "Dirigible one is to our left at seven o'clock, dirigible two, five o'clock. The third is directly astern. They're holding position."

"Why aren't they still coming after us?" Laura asked.

"Because they don't have to," Ellie stated. "They know where we're going." Approaching the main control panel, she pulled open an access door and yanked something out of the console. "I've disabled the transponder, but it won't be hard for them to figure out where we've gone. We need to get as much distance between us and them as we can while they gather their forces because I guarantee you, they will be coming."

"I'm reducing speed slightly so we don't burn out the engines." Joe gently slid the throttle back a notch.

"What's our position?" Ellie leaned forward over the control console.

Joe turned to check the navigational readings. "We're passing over the city perimeter now." Locking the controls, he turned to face the group. "Everyone all right?"

he asked.

"We're in one piece," Laura replied.

"We're fine, dad," Lucas agreed.

Picking up Emily, Joe hugged her against his chest. Rubbing his muzzle against hers he gave his beloved daughter a lick before once again becoming serious. "All right, everyone. We may be clear of the city but we're not out of the blizzard yet. I've set our course to follow the general direction towards Ellie's train. Once we've taken care of the immediate issues we'll settle on an exact heading. Laura, I need you to inventory our supplies. See what we have, what we can take with us, and what's useful. There should still be plenty of food on board so maybe you could prepare something for us in the galley. Ellie, you and I need to check the ship's systems and make sure we didn't do any damage to the balloon on our way out. While we're at it I'd like to confirm the coordinates of your rendezvous with the others and figure out exactly how this going to work."

"Assuming we can maintain this speed it shouldn't take us long to rendezvous with the train," Ellie said.

"Lucas, take care of Emily." He folded his arms. "Any questions?" he asked. When none came, he nodded. "Let's get to work."

Joe took a moment to watch over the others, knowing they were doing their best to hide their collective uncertainty, which he admitted to himself that he shared. Somewhere out there was a moving train traveling over the frozen wasteland. Its purpose at present was to scour the world for salvage and potential clues to what had caused the disaster. It was here Joe was hoping he would find the next safe haven in his fight to keep his family whole. But as much as he trusted Ellie, he hoped he had not made a catastrophic mistake by following her out here.

His entire life up to this point had been one of

routine and familiarity, with each day much like the last. For the first time he found himself without any of the comforts of what he once knew, with the path before him uncertain at best.

From this moment on he was leading his family into uncharted territory. They were headed places no one from Coldhaven had ever seen, and he had no idea what to expect. Up until now Joe had the luxury of being too busy to consider his family's future beyond the immediate moment. With several hours until they arrived at their destination, for the first time he found himself with no clear idea what was coming next.

CHAPTER ELEVEN
RENDEZVOUS

Gliding towards their destination Joe monitored the instruments on his display panel with careful precision. His limited experience notwithstanding he was fairly certain he had a reasonable comprehension of balloon navigation. For the last several hours he had remained on the bridge, careful to monitor their speed and direction.

The kids had gone below to get some rest. He had insisted Laura go with them, leaving him and Ellie as the only two on the command deck. Seated at the table in the back, the snowshoe hare's attention was concentrated on the maps before her. Brow furrowed in concentration, her ears remained sharply together as she looked down at their projected course.

Locking the controls into place he turned around and joined her, sitting on the other side. "Everything okay?"

Ellie looked up suddenly, her ears relaxing and

separating a few inches when she noticed Joe's presence. "What?" she asked, before processing what he had said. "Okay might be a little bit of a stretch, but we're under control. According to my projections we should intercept the train in about an hour." She set her pencil down.

"And then what happens?" he asked.

"Then I introduce you to Daniel, and we do our best to outrun those dirigibles." Ellie fixed him with a hard stare. "Under no circumstances can we allow those things to follow us back to the Garden."

"That's one thing we're in absolute agreement on," Joe replied. "I just have no idea how we're going to do that."

Ellie folded her arms. "Our first priority is to get to the train and put as much distance between us and them as possible."

"I've been pushing the engines at full since we left the city. Although based on the look of those black dirigibles I think it's only a matter of time until they catch up to us."

The snowshoe hare looked up at Joe. "They're probably already on their way. I wouldn't be surprised if they're following us just out of visual range."

"So what are they waiting for?" he asked.

"They know where you found me. Most likely they're hanging back, waiting for us to meet up with the train before they make their move. We have no idea of their capabilities, but I'd be willing to bet they've got scanning equipment measures beyond what you've got in here." Ellie leaned back against the wall. "They've been preparing for this for a long time. Coldhaven didn't just come up with those dirigibles. They've been designing and constructing them for who knows how long."

Joe grew silent as he considered what Ellie had said. He had not had time to think about it during the escape, but it was hard to deny her logic. The black dirigibles were faster, stronger, and more advanced than anything he had ever seen before. The only reason they had made it out of the city in the first place was the fact that at least until they reunited with the train, they still had value to them. Once they linked up with Ellie's people, their value to Governor Cole disappeared.

And then there were the dirigibles themselves. Longer than the exploratory balloons and jet black in color, it was clear they were designed for combat and nothing else. Armed to the teeth with more weapons than Joe could count, in open air they were faster and more maneuverable than the craft they currently flew. Unknown in number and capabilities they would be a significant challenge to overcome.

Now understanding the reason for the massive supply chains traveling in secret under the city's surface, Joe wondered to himself how it was possible they could construct such things without anyone knowing. No doubt somewhere they had a specialized facility for the design and construction of these assault dirigibles as well as a hangar from which to deploy them. Faced with the city's eventual death it was clear that Governor Cole had chosen to defy their fate, no matter what sins she had to commit along the way.

Joe turned away from Ellie as he considered the fact that had he not met her, he might still be back in the city believing every lie Governor Cole had told him.

Sensing his melancholy, Ellie put a paw on his own. "It's not your fault." She smiled softly. "You had no way of knowing what they were planning."

"No, but I should have. The increased demands on the Candle, the system failures, the ration reductions all pointed to something going on and I just sat there thinking it was business as usual. How could I not have realized they were building a war fleet under our feet, planning to take what they didn't even try to ask for?" He shook his head. "All this time I thought the balloon teams were going out there to find more food and medical supplies for the people, but half of that material we saw was probably from other expeditions. If I hadn't been on that Navy ship…" Joe trailed off.

"But you were, and we don't have time to fret about what might have been. We're being chased by a fleet of assault dirigibles who would think nothing of taking the Garden and its resources by force. Now I know you've had a lot thrown at you since we met but I don't have time to deal with regrets. Your wife and kids are counting on you and so am I. You're smart, you can take care of yourself, and you don't give up. Now we are a long way from being out of the snowstorm so I need to know if I can depend on you."

Joe took a deep breath and nodded. "I'm with you."

"Good." She squeezed his arm. "Because we've got a long way to go before we're safe."

Offering a slight smile, they returned to the matter at paw. "The one saving grace I can anticipate is that they have the same aeronautical limitations that we do."

"In English?" Joe prompted, not understanding the finer points of dirigible flight mechanics.

Ellie leaned back slightly. "Their limited on their maneuverability. Now don't get me wrong, they're damn fast compared to us and they can fly circles around us in open sky, but in tight quarters they're just as clumsy as we are. If we can get them boxed in then depending on how many of them there are, we might be able to turn the situation against them."

"That's easier said than done," Joe said. "Assuming we make it to the train, what kind of weapons capabilities does it have?"

Her ears perked, she lowered them slightly. "It's unarmed."

Turning towards her, Joe raised his muzzle in alarm. "I thought you were a military craft."

"We're a reconnaissance expedition, not a combat unit. Sometimes during salvage operations we run into trouble but we can usually outrun it. Joe, the train was originally a civilian craft. We've repurposed it for our use, but we never anticipated surface to air combat scenarios. Now, overall we're faster than they are, but they can still give us a hard time, not to mention the fact that they outnumber us from the start. We do have one advantage they don't," Ellie said.

Joe leaned in, intrigued. "And that is?"

"The train is armored. Now that armor was designed to protect it from environmental hazards but it will stand up to a significant amount of small arms fire. If they have anything bigger in those things we can take a pounding for a little while, but if nothing else it'll buy us time when we need it most." Ellie walked over to the window and looked out over the ice.

Joe returned to the control stations and rested his paw on the safety railings at the bottom of the console. "Those things looked pretty tough to me," he said. "How do you know they don't have armor?"

"I don't, but I know military tactics. Craft like the ones we saw on our way out of the city need to be fast and light. Armor seems great in theory but it adds a lot of weight, something predators like them can't afford. Add to it the additional materials needed to armor your dirigibles and the likelihood of encountering other hostile aircraft, and…" Ellie threw up her hands in a demonstrative gesture.

Joe nodded. Whether their purpose was tactical or exploratory, the basic nature of all of Coldhaven's aerial transportation rendered it vulnerable to same kinds of hazards. The challenge rested in finding a way to exploit them without endangering themselves in the process. Ellie's train, for all its capabilities, was limited in its defensive options. Their main advantages being speed low to the ground, powerful armor, and the harsh environment providing some measure of protection against anyone attempting to board it meant that they could delay any effort to seize control of the train. However, lacking the ability to freely maneuver they could only alter course at a switching station which meant that strategy and planning would be key to their success.

No matter what they did, there were still a small fleet of assault dirigibles on their way to intercept the train. Assuming they were fortunate enough to disable or destroy all of their pursuers, there was a chance they would be able to keep them from getting close enough to determine the Garden's location, but that entirely depended on them being able to deal with their pursuers before they crossed the final switching station. Once that happened they would no longer need the train's computers to locate their future home.

"What do you think about our chances?" Joe asked.

Ellie paused, considering the question. "I don't know. We have the experience and we know the territory ahead a lot better than they do, but on the other paw they've got the numbers and tactical superiority. Right now I'd say it's even money."

Joe sighed. "We'll have to see what we can do about that." A chilly breeze made him aware of the door opening and Emily walking onto the command deck, rubbing her right eye with her paw, Andre tucked under her arm. "Emily, what are you doing up?"

"I couldn't sleep. That engine is noisy." The young polar bear cub looked up at him. "Can I stay up here?"

Joe shrugged. "Your mom is probably wondering where you went."

"But I want to stay with you," she whined.

Scratching gently behind her ear, he picked her up in his arms. "Okay, sweet pea. You can stay with me for a few minutes, but then I'm taking you back to your mom, okay?"

Seeing that there was no way she was winning this argument, Emily surrendered. "Okay, daddy."

Smiling warmly, he bounced his daughter against his chest. "Aunt Ellie and I were just talking about our plan for keeping you safe."

"Aunt Ellie?" the snowshoe hare prompted with a smirk.

Joe shrugged helplessly out of his daughter's field of vision and held her against his chest. "I'm going to find us someplace we can all live together away from all of this." He offered his young daughter his most reassuring smile. "I promise, we'll be okay."

"Even Andre?" she asked, holding up her furless doll. Running a claw through his hair, she held onto him tightly.

"Yes, even Andre." Taking on a smirk of confidence, he stood taller. "No one is going to mess with your daddy. Not when he's got his mama bear and her cubs to protect."

Emily giggled. "My daddy will scare all the mean people away."

"Rarr," he said, making a playful growl. "Feel better now?"

She nodded.

"Okay then. I'm going to take you back below decks where you can stay with your mom and brother until we're ready to disembark." He turned to Ellie. "You okay to take over?"

Ellie rose from her seat at the table. "Go. Be a father."

With a grateful nod, Joe headed outside and descended the external stairs to the lower level towards the balloon's crew cabin and cargo area. Pulling the door open he entered and made his way towards the door to the sleeping arrangements, which was mostly a series of bunk beds arranged in a tight formation. Both his wife and son had taken the other two bottom bunks, given that bears tended to take up a fair amount of space.

Despite his best effort to enter silently his wife and son stirred at his arrival. "Are we there already?" Laura asked.

"No," Joe replied. "I just had a visitor upstairs."

Taking her daughter into her arms, Laura gently admonished her daughter. "You know better than to interrupt daddy while he's working."

"But Andre wanted to see the bridge," she offered by way of explanation.

"I don't care what Andre wants. You shouldn't go anywhere without letting your mother know." She quickly let her muzzle curl into a smile and licked her daughter's cheek. "We'll let it go this time, but next time ask mommy first."

Joe shrugged. "It wasn't a problem. She just wanted to see me, so I let her stay for a few minutes and then brought her back to you."

"You indulge her too much sometimes," she said, though it was clear she did not consider herself an exception to that. Letting out a deep sigh, she smiled. "Though it's hard not to with a face that cute."

Joe looked down at Emily as her mother put her on her lap. It was moments like this it was almost possible to forget she was stricken with a chronic condition that if left untreated would eventually result in her death. Yet now, happy in her mother's arms and surrounded by her family, she seemed like any other normal girl. Joe felt his muzzle quiver as he reached out to touch her. Setting a reassuring paw on her shoulder, she turned and looked up at him.

"I hope wherever we're going is someplace nice," she said.

"I don't know, kiddo, but wherever it is will be fine as long as we're together." It occurred to Joe he had not asked Ellie much about her home, being occupied with more pressing matters since her rescue. What little he knew was that it was fertile and survivable there, which was far better than where they had come from. All that he cared about was keeping his family together. As he looked around and noticed Lucas had disappeared, he sighed.

So much for that.

His son had been distant and moody since he had not allowed him to help with the escape. To Joe, it had been too risky. It was dangerous no matter what role he had played but to him he could not accept it if Lucas had died because of an order he had given. It was not as if he did not trust his son, but if a bit of moodiness was the cost of keeping him alive he would pay it gladly.

Watching Emily and her mother he realized for the first time that his children might actually get a chance to grow up at a normal speed. In Coldhaven, as soon as you were old enough to hold a tool you were pressed into the workforce in the name of survival. From the age Lucas was now to the time you couldn't perform your duties you were asked to bear those burdens for the good of the city. Idle citizens were not permitted within Coldhaven under any circumstances. Even medical exceptions were rare and often limited in their scope.

Had they remained in the city, even Emily would

have been pressed into service when she had reached the right age, regardless of her frailty. Illness or no she would have been required to do as her brother had and taken any job that Governor Cole had assigned irrespective of the level of danger. Framed in the guise of necessity and fairness it was how Coldhaven ensured only the strongest received the benefits of its protection.

Laura looked up at her husband. "Any idea how much longer it'll be until we rendezvous with the train?"

Joe shrugged. "Not a clue. Ellie guided me towards where she thinks the train should be but we're still too far away to reach them by radio." He placed a paw on her shoulder. "She assures me we should be in contact soon. Given that the train is constantly moving we may have to adjust our course once we narrow down their current position."

Laura nodded, letting out a deep sigh. "They're never going to let us go, are they?" she asked, meaning Governor Cole and her people.

As much as he wished he could offer her some comforting news, the truth was that even if they were able to shake their pursuit it was unlikely they would give up the search. Governor Cole and those in control of Coldhaven knew that capturing the train and harvesting the information from its databanks was the best chance for their own survival. Knowing firsthand what a person would do to protect their own, he doubted Governor Cole would do any less to ensure her city and its people survived.

Silently Joe contemplated how they would be able to outwit the fleet of assault dirigibles following behind them like ghosts in the night. Stalking them in the endless field of white it was only a matter of time before they caught up with them.

"No," Joe admitted, seeing no point in lying to his

wife. "They'll follow us as long as they think we can lead them to the Garden."

Laura sighed. "I just hope Ellie and her people can help us."

"Once we've met up with the train, she and her commanding officer will do everything they can to keep us all safe." He did his best to project confidence despite his own doubts about whether or not they would be able to shake their pursuit. If Laura saw through his façade she did not let it show. Changing the subject, she looked down at her daughter.

"Do you think they can help Emily?" she asked.

"Ellie tells me they have significantly advanced medical facilities on board the train, better than anything we had access to in Coldhaven. But until their doctor gets a chance to have a look at her she couldn't give me any guarantees." He offered a shrug.

Laura pulled her bag closer to her. "Well at least we have plenty of this." She removed Emily's medication from it and prepared a dose. Holding the syringe in her right paw, she looked into Emily's eyes. "Hold still while mama gives you your medicine."

"Andre says he doesn't like the needles." She blocked her mother's efforts with her doll.

Kneeling in front of her, Joe smiled. "Now sweetie, you know that you need this to keep you healthy." Taking her paw in his own, he looked at her. "Now I'm going to show you a magic trick. As long as I'm holding your paw, you won't feel any pain." Smiling warmly, he brought his nose close to hers. "I promise."

"Okay," she said, squeezing his much larger palm while Laura gently pressed the needle into her flesh. Once she was done, she removed it and returned it to the bag.

"There, all done." Laura licked her daughter's cheek.

"You were very brave."

"I had my daddy," she said, leaning into him for a hug. Squeezing her back, he wanted the moment to last forever. Eventually, she pulled back and he let her go, rising to his feet. "If only our other child was as easy to manage," he said.

Laura offered a supportive smile. "He'll forgive you eventually." Gesturing with her muzzle out towards the rear of the craft, she shrugged. "Right now he just wants to help his sister and his family so badly, can you blame him for being a little frustrated?" Laura looked at him with a gentle expression.

Joe smiled to himself. "No, I suppose not." He walked over to his wife, gave her a lick on the cheek, and rubbed Emily's forehead. "You be good for your mother."

"I will, daddy," she replied.

Rising to stand, he looked towards the rear of the craft where Lucas had disappeared. Making his way through the lower deck of the balloon he passed the cargo area and entered the cramped engine room. Peering through the tiny windows it was there he spotted his young son, standing outside leaning on the railing.

Turning around he walked to the nearest access door and moved to join him. Saying nothing at first, he rested his forearms on the rail and stared out over the ice. "Quite a view, isn't it?" he asked. Out in the vast expanse between landmarks there was nothing but a sheet of white below them, covered by blowing torrents of wind and snow. Particles of frozen water danced in the air above the ground like pixies as they cruised across the chilly landscape. Uninterrupted by anything artificial it was a subtle reminder of the beauty of undisturbed nature. Reclaimed by the cold, the world had become an arctic gallery of icy masterpieces.

Lucas turned away from him without responding.

The young polar bear was half his size but trying to act as if the cold winds buffeting them on the outer deck did not affect him in the slightest. Joe was used to it, having worked outside much of his life, but he knew it was harder for his son who lacked the mass to withstand it for long. Moving to block the wind, he waited.

Joe tried again. "You did good back there," he said.

"I didn't do anything," Lucas protested. "I just took care of Emily."

"I know you don't think like that's an important job, but there are only two people in this world I trust with your sister's safety, and you're one of them." He reached out a paw to touch him but refrained.

"But I can do more than that, dad. I can help you keep her safe out there if you'd just let me do it." Lucas turned around and stared at him, tears in his eyes.

Joe's face melted into a wistful frown. "There are a lot of things out there that you aren't prepared for. Governor Cole and her people will do anything it takes to ensure their side survives. To keep you kids safe I'll do whatever I have to, but I don't want you and Emily involved."

"Look around, Dad, we're already involved. Like it or not we're in this scruff deep just like you are. I get that you want to protect us but you can't be everywhere at once. Sooner or later I might have to get my paws dirty and I can't do that if you don't trust me." Lucas paused. "At my age, Coldhaven assigns me a job. They pretty much consider me an adult with all the privileges and responsibilities that come with it. If they trust me to be an adult, why can't you?"

His son made some rather salient points. As much as he wished to shield them both from the danger they were in, it would not be possible to do so completely, no matter how much he might want to. Looking at Lucas, he let out a deep sigh. "You're right," he said, surprising the younger ursine. "I know I can't protect you from every danger, and that sooner or later you're going to have to stand on your own two ~~feet~~ paws. I just hoped it was going to be a little longer before that happened." He wrapped his arm around his son. Lowering his muzzle, he narrowed his gaze. "When did you get to be so smart?"

"I learned from the best," he said.

Giving his son a tight squeeze he tousled his hair with a paw before letting him go, a wide grin on his muzzle.

"Ah, dad!" He brushed his claws through his wheat colored hair, returning it to normal.

"Sorry," he laughed. "I couldn't resist."

Lucas's face softened into a chuckle. "I guess it's okay. Just this once."

"Got it, I'll never do that again," he said, paws in the air. Leaning against the railing, he turned to Lucas. "So are we good?"

Lucas nodded. "We're good. I just hope that next time you need me, you let me help."

"You'll get your chance, I suspect sooner than either of us would like." No sooner had he straightened out than an alert came from over the speakers.

"*Joe, report to the bridge. We've got trouble.*" It was Ellie.

"I gotta go," he told his son, who nodded. "Get inside before you freeze your fur off." Properly admonished, Lucas did as he was told. Joe rushed up the external stairs to the bridge, pushing his way onto the command deck. "What's happening?"

"I was right. I contacted the train less than two minutes ago. The moment I did, we had three contacts pop up behind us." The blonde hare returned her attention to the controls.

Joe slid in beside her, looking at the sensor display.

"Range, ten kilometers and closing. Time to intercept, five minutes."

Ellie frowned. "It'll take us three to get to the train."

"They can outrun them, can't they?" Joe asked.

She answered with a nod. "They can, but not until we're on board."

"So where do we land?" he asked.

Ellie lowered her ears. "We don't." Taking a deep breath, she explained. "If we stop long enough to board the train those assault dirigibles will be on top of us in seconds. We may as well hand them the train ourselves." She directed the nose of the balloon down ever so slightly.

"What are you doing?" Joe asked.

"I'm decreasing our altitude so we can get into position. Once we're above the train they're going to match our velocity so we won't bounce off when we drop down to the roof." Seeing his apprehension, she turned to look at him. "I don't like it either but it's our only option if we're going to get out of here in one piece. Get your family ready to go, we're going to have to do this quick."

Joe swore under his breath as he rushed back out and down the stairs. Bursting into the crew quarters he looked at his family. "Everyone, jackets on. Bundle up, we're going to have to hurry."

"What's going on?" Laura asked.

"The black dirigibles are back. We have to move fast if we're going to outrun them." Working to get Emily's jacket on, he offered his most reassuring smile. "We're going to have to do something pretty scary, hon. I want you to promise me you'll keep Andre safe, okay?"

Emily looked at her father with clear anxiety, but after a moment, she nodded. "Okay, daddy. I'll look after him."

"Good girl." He zipped up her coat and turned to

Laura and Lucas. "Ready to go?"

"As ready as we'll ever be," Laura said. "So what's the plan?"

"Trust me, you don't want to know," he replied, carrying Emily in his arms up to the top of the steps. Returning once more to the command deck he motioned for the others to sit at the back table. "Time until we're in position?"

"Almost there," Ellie said, pressing the nose down a little further. The deck tipped forward as the balloon dropped another step towards the speeding train below. Through the front window Joe could see a bright silver-gray object cutting through the center of the field of white beneath them. Like a sword cutting through the mists of snow, the train shone brightly like a beacon to the small group in the balloon. "I'm going to need you up here, Joe!" Giving his daughter a kiss, Joe rushed forward to the command console. Ellie braced, struggling to maintain their approach. "I'm doing my best but this thing is hard as hell to maneuver. Keep our course steady and ease her over the train."

"Got it," Joe replied, taking the controls into his paws. With gritted teeth and flattened ears he held the levers tightly. Winds buffeted the balloon trying to force it off course, but Joe refused to allow the balloon to fall out of position. Growling as he resisted the forces of nature, he looked forward at the train as it centered itself in his field of view. "That's it!"

Ellie picked up the handset and spoke into it. "This is Ellie Harper, we're in position. Richard, get ready for us!"

"*We're ready when you are,*" he said. "*I'm opening the hatch right now.*" The gentle masculine voice then disappeared as Ellie replaced the unit in its cradle.

"I don't suppose this thing has autopilot?" she asked.

"Not for something like this," he said.

Ellie shook her head and then gestured for the door. "Go!"

"I'm not leaving you!" Joe shouted.

"No, you're not, but one of us has to hold this thing in place until the last second and I'm the most qualified," Ellie argued.

Joe shook his head. "I'm stronger than you are. My family needs you to survive, one way or the other. They can afford to lose me if it comes down to it, but they can't lose you. Take care of them," he said.

Ellie looked as if she was going to argue, but with time being short, settled for something profane and grabbed Laura's arm. "Let's go!"

Emily jumped from her mother's arms and clung to his leg. "Daddy, no! You have to come with us!"

"Ellie, get going!" he shouted. Turning to his daughter he spared a second to reassure her. "I'm going to be right behind you, I promise! But I have to hold the balloon in place until you're safe! Now go with your mother!"

Grabbing Emily in her arms, the snowshoe hare bolted out the door, leaving it open, flapping in the wind. The cold wind stung his face, even through his thick white fur. Joe cursed and held on tight to the controls, bracing his body and spreading his feet paws wide. The balloon groaned in protest, and he could hear the cables and metal screaming at the forces being pressed against it.

Outside, he could see the others on the front of the balloon at the observation post. Ellie threw a rope over the edge and with Emily on her back, dropped down onto the top of the train. Lucas was next, giving his mother one last look before he too disappeared from sight. Laura was last, closing her eyes as she hurled herself over the side. Joe waited a few seconds until he at last heard the sound of the radio crackling to life.

Ellie's voice rang through the speaker. *"Joe, we're all down, get your furry ass off that balloon!"*

Locking the steering controls into place he wasted no time rushing out towards the front of the fragile craft. Taking one quick look below, he saw the train rushing through the frozen wasteland twenty feet below him. Cursing, he spotted Lucas sticking out of a hatch on the top of the train. He was shouting something but through all the wind and the screeching metal he could not make it out.

Taking a deep breath, Joe thought of his family and leapt. For a moment after he left the deck of the balloon's crew compartment he felt weightless as time slowed to a crawl. He was hyper aware of the train beneath him, his son shouting from the hatch, the balloon flying behind him, and the assault dirigibles in pursuit. No sooner had he turned his head then gravity reasserted itself and he fell. Grabbing the rope with both paws he gripped it just enough to slow his descent, landing on the roof of the train a bit harder than he intended.

Suddenly the train swerved along a curve in the track, throwing Joe off his feet paws and sending him stumbling towards the side. As he felt himself hurled forward by his momentum he saw out of the corner of his eye the balloon pull away as it continued straight on its original course. No sooner had he begun to fall than he felt a paw grip his sleeve and pull hard. Balancing on the edge of the train, he became aware of another pair of paws pulling against his coat and yanking him from the edge with a sudden reversal of direction. With a yelp and a tumble of bodies Joe fell into the train, landing on the deck in a tangle of limbs resembling the pipes in Coldhaven's larger hubs.

Sitting up, he looked face first into Ellie's perfectly

white tail. "Oh."

"Can you get off me, please?" she asked. Rolling over as he moved, she sat up against the wall. "You're heavier than you look."

Joe shrugged. "Sorry, I wasn't exactly planning to fall off the train."

"You okay, dad?" Lucas asked, looking to his father in concern.

"Yeah, I'm fine," he said, straightening up. "Just a little shaken up, that's all." He smiled. "Thanks for grabbing me."

Ellie's next comment forestalled any possible response the young ursine might have made. "Come on, we've got to get to the engine car."

Joe nodded. "Laura, Lucas, you two stay here with Emily. We're not out of the snowstorm yet."

Laura gave her husband a quick lick on the muzzle. "Good luck."

"Thanks," he replied, before dashing after Ellie through the various cars of the train. Joe could not help but be awed by all the advanced technology that filled the spectacular vehicle. Despite his curiosity he forced himself to keep moving forward. There would be time for that later. Keeping his eyes focused on Ellie, he stayed close behind until finally they arrived at the first car that the snowshoe hare needed to input an access code to enter.

After keying in the digits, she passed through with Joe close on her heels, moving around the side of a display table showing the train's current location as well as the three pursuing Coldhaven dirigibles approaching from behind. Joe even caught the symbol representing their former balloon off to the side and increasing in distance from their course with every passing moment. Entering the engine car Ellie walked up to the zebra at the side console on the left.

Looking over his shoulder, the dark haired equine did not spare any of the pleasantries as he gave his next order. "Ellie, take the other console. You, whoever you are, stay out of the way."

Joe did as instructed, remaining on the side of the engine car towards the rear as the crew went about their jobs. Observing silently, he marveled at the complexity of such a fantastic machine. As the train cruised along its track he could tell it was designed for both speed and durability. Bracing himself against the wall as it rocked gently, he listened to everything that was being said.

"Noah, accelerate to maximum speed as soon as we pass the next curve." The zebra whipped his head behind him to call out to Ellie. "Harper, where are those dirigibles?"

"They're at two kilometers and closing! The lead dirigible is moving ahead of the others, trying to match our speed," she said.

"They're going to try to board us," Joe said.

Shooting him an irritated glare, the zebra snorted in response. "How long until we hit the curve?"

Noah looked down at the panel, indicating their current course and speed. "One minute."

"Maybe we should slow down?" Ellie suggested.

Noah shook his head. "Any slower and they'll be on us before we can accelerate."

Ellie gritted her teeth, her ears flattening against the back of her head as she shot Joe a look that said 'hold on'. Joe did as suggested. The snowshoe hare checked the readouts and called out to the zebra. "One kilometer to intercept. They're within weapons range," she announced.

"They won't fire on us, not unless they think they can do it safely. They'll wait until after we pass the curve." Joe leaned forward towards the zebra. "Trust me."

The zebra considered what he had to say for a

moment before finally turning and pointing at Noah. "Briggs, get us around the turn. The moment we're clear you push the engine as hard as it'll go! Understood?"

"Yes, sir," the sandy haired ram nodded. Flipping a few more switches Joe could hear the train surge with power as it started to hit the curve. With a sudden jolt Joe was thrown against the opposite wall, unprepared for the sudden shift in direction. The train rattled along the tracks at a brisk pace, taking the bend with considerable speed. Holding on to the safety railings, Joe looked ahead as they approached the end of the current stretch of railway line. Holding on tightly, Joe prepared for their imminent acceleration. "Increasing to maximum speed!" Noah pushed the lever all the way forward, and the train surged ahead like a racehorse finally free of its restrictions.

Pressed against the back wall of the engine car he waited for the forces to equalize as they pulled away from their pursuit. Letting out a deep breath, Joe waited silently for someone to speak.

"Engines holding at maximum acceleration, sir, but I wouldn't recommend holding it for too long," he said.

The zebra turned towards Ellie. "Report?"

"The assault dirigibles are falling behind, sir. They can't keep up with us, not at this speed." She smiled.

"Good." Sitting forward he rose to a standing position. "Noah, keep us at max speed until we're out of sensor range. Then drop us to half."

"Yes, sir," the ram replied.

Turning his attention back to Joe, the zebra looked him up and down with skepticism. "And who is this?"

"Joe Kennedy, sir." He gave a humble nod and extended his paw, though the zebra did not take it.

"Ellie?" he prompted.

"He's okay. Joe helped me break out of Coldhaven

after they picked me up on the Navy ship. I promised him we'd take him and his family to safety." Ellie remained at her post, looking between the two men for any sort of response.

Joe hesitated to say anything, not feeling it was his place to weigh in when he clearly did not hold any authority here. While he did not believe the zebra would toss his family out on the ice he nevertheless did not wish to antagonize anyone by assuming he was welcome. Out of an abundance of caution he remained quiet while the striped equine considered his status.

After a long pause he held a hoof tipped finger to his muzzle and spoke. "All right. Considering the situation, we could probably use your expertise. You know these people chasing us better than anyone we've got. For now we'll consider the matter settled pending review." He turned to Ellie. "Assign them a cabin and start showing Mister Kennedy how to operate the train's systems."

"I don't understand?" Joe said, opening his muzzle before he realized he spoke.

The zebra turned towards him. "I don't carry passengers on my train, Mister Kennedy. Either you're a member of the crew or you don't stay. I don't have the resources to support anyone who isn't pulling their own weight. Understand me?" he asked.

Joe nodded. "Yes, sir."

"Good. Ellie will get you settled and once you are, you and I can have a conversation. I suspect you and I will have a lot to talk about." He gave Joe a firm nod, walking past the two of them towards the door. "Oh, and one more thing. Welcome to the train."

CHAPTER TWELVE
WELCOME TO THE TRAIN

Even though Joe had seen it from the outside, it was still awe inspiring to walk through the massive moving machine that was Ellie's train. Silently he marveled at the use of space as well as the advanced technology that filled each section of the fantastic vehicle. Each one was filled with more wonders than the last, making Joe anxious about his ability to learn its systems.

He and his family followed behind the snowshoe hare through the next several cars which seemed to be the crew quarters. Distinguished from the functional sections of the train by wood panel accents as well as a side hall instead of a central pathway, they were clearly designed for comfort as well as functionality. With four units per car, each one could house several crew members and passengers. Passing by a number of doors with nameplates, Ellie led them through to the fifth such car, stopping at a door with no label before turning around towards the Kennedys.

With a flourish of her arm, she indicated the empty cabin. "Here it is, home sweet home. Or as I like to call it, Cabin 5C." She touched a panel at chest level and with a gentle whoosh the door slid open allowing them access. Taking a step inside, she allowed the ursines to enter and look around. "It's not much, but for the time being it should suffice."

"It's wonderful," Joe replied. "Thank you."

"Unfortunately, these units don't allow for a lot of privacy but there's a small washroom in the sleeping area. It's designed for crew rather than families so there are four bunk beds but at least you each get your own. The living area has a sofa and a little bit of furniture but it's pretty sparse. Meals are at nine, twelve, and six in the dining cars, though if you need something they can fix you a meal but I'd try to be on time if I were you."

Joe nodded. "We'll keep that in mind."

"You're free to eat in the dining car but if you prefer you can take your meal back to your cabin. For now, you're free to settle in and get comfortable. I have duties to perform but I'll check on you in a few hours to make sure you're getting along all right." Ellie indicated a panel on the wall. "If you need to you can contact anywhere on the train through that panel though for the time being it'll remain offline until we can get you an access code. All the same it would be appreciated if you use it for essential business only."

Setting Emily down, he squeezed Lucas on the shoulder. "Why don't you and Emily check out the bunk beds?"

"Okay, dad," Lucas replied, taking his sister's paw. "Come on, Emily, let's go pick out our beds."

Joe turned back to Ellie. "You said your train had a doctor?" he asked, once he was certain the kids were otherwise occupied.

"We do, she's in the car between the crew quarters and the lounge," she said, jerking her thumb over her shoulder. She'll want to see all of you for a basic workup just to make sure there's nothing being brought in by any of you or vice versa as well as a general health assessment. When you see her, you can ask her any questions you have." Twitching her whiskers, she gestured towards the door. "Do either of you need anything else before I go check on our status?".

"I think we'll be all right," Laura said. "Thank you."

Ellie nodded. "You're welcome."

The door slid closed, leaving them alone. Joe let out a deep breath, pacing the length of their small living area. Looking at his wife, he stopped to take her paws in his. "So what do you think?"

Laura shrugged, turning her head towards the sleeping area where their children were giggling and apparently having great fun trying out each of the beds one at a time. "We're here and we're together," she said. "That's all that matters to me."

"I just wish it hadn't cost so much," Joe said, thinking of Mike. "I never should have gotten him involved."

Understanding, Laura rubbed her muzzle against his. "I know how you feel." Laura wrapped her arms around him. "But we never would have made it without him."

Nodding in agreement, Joe embraced her tightly. "I just wish he could have seen all this."

Lucas emerged from the other room. "Hey dad, you've got to check out these beds!"

At his son's beckoning, he followed into the sleeping

area. Two rows of bunk beds fit in the room with just enough space for two aisles wide enough for an adult. Joe tested the mattress with a paw, before looking to his wife. "Which one do you want?"

"I'll take whatever's left over," she said.

"Emily wants the one by the window. She's on the bottom, I'm on the top." Lucas stood beside his sister, the pair having already laid claim to them.

"Then I'll take the top by the door," Joe said.

"Don't be ridiculous. You take the one on the bottom," Laura replied.

"I just thought you wouldn't want to have to climb up and down every morning," he said.

"Yeah, and can you see yourself up on the top? You'd bang your head all the time, and I can't have you scrambling your brains every morning. You're the only thing holding this family together," she said.

Joe shrugged. "Well, I don't know if I'd go that far," he replied.

"Take the bottom bunk," she said, poking his chest with a claw.

"Yes, dear," he replied.

"Now that that's settled, how about we wash up before we get this nice train all dirty?" she asked. Her suggestion was met with halfhearted groans from her kids, who walked over to the small washroom as they began to clean the dirt and other things from their fur.

Joe smiled. "They're good kids."

"That they are," she replied. "We raised them well." She smiled. "Maybe it's not very motherly of me but I'm half tempted to be the first one to try out that shower I saw in there."

"Go right ahead," Joe said. "You've earned it. The kids can wait their turn."

Laura smirked. "You're a good animal, Joe Kennedy." Once the kids emerged from the washroom she excused herself to go take a shower, closing the door behind her. Alone with his children, Joe sat down on one of the bunks. Looking at Lucas and Emily, he offered a reassuring smile.

Sitting beside him, Emily clutched her doll in her arms. Pulling her against him, he wrapped his large paw around her side, grateful for her very presence. Taking the seat opposite, Lucas placed his claws together and looked up at his dad. "What's going to happen to us?"

Uncertain how to answer the question, Joe hesitated. "I don't know just yet, son. I've made an agreement with the captain to stay on board for the time being, but what will happen after that is up to him for now."

Lucas sat forward. "He wouldn't throw us off the train, would he?" his son asked, obviously concerned.

"No, I don't think so, but all the same we're guests here for the time being so I want you to do as I say as long as we're on board, okay?" Joe looked at both his children imploringly.

Lucas looked at his father and nodded. "Okay."

"We saved Ellie, and that earned us some points, but until I know what's going on I'd prefer not to push our luck. The fact that we're here at all is a bit of minor miracle and I don't want to tempt fate by being ungrateful." He sighed. "I need to speak to the captain and then as I understand it Ellie is going to teach me how this thing works." Joe gestured around at the train. "In the meantime, I need you two to stay here until I come back."

"Dad," Lucas said, looking around. "I was hoping we could explore a little."

"I understand, but for now I need you two to stay here where I know you're safe. You'll get time to take a tour later, if we have the opportunity. I promise." He looked out the window as the train whipped across the frozen landscape, seeing nothing but endless white outside. Joe wondered to himself if the entire world looked like this other than the Garden, a perpetual field of ice and snow. He remained with his children until his wife emerged from the shower.

While she held a towel around her midsection she gestured for Lucas to take his turn, smiling at her husband. "That shower is amazing. Not only is the water hot but there's this button inside that dries your fur in minutes. I can't remember the last time I felt that good."

Joe embraced his lady bear and kissed her on her muzzle. "I can't wait to try it."

The door chime sounded, and a crewman entered. "Apologies for the interruption, sir, but Captain Hall will see you now."

Turning to acknowledge his statement, Joe nodded. "I'll be right there." When he had gone, he turned back to his wife. "I'll only be a short while."

"Okay," she said.

Tugging on the sides of his jacket, he turned and walked out the door. The painted dog took him down the length of the train to the room he had passed earlier on his way to the engine, the one with the computerized display in the center and screens on most of the walls. No doubt this here was the command center, for lack of a better term, with all sorts of sensor data from the train's myriad systems being routed to these monitors.

Standing at the opposite end of the room were Ellie, Noah, and the zebra he assumed must be Captain Hall. His black hair was tied into a neat ponytail, flowing gently down his back. Both Captain Hall and the ram were in uniform, with the zebra's being dark blue while Noah's was more of a shade of beige. Ellie was still wearing her field uniform from earlier, though it appeared it was not the same one as it bore none of the scars of their escape.

Joe entered and took his place on the other side of the table, waiting for them to address him while the painted dog left to perform his duties. Keeping his paws at his sides, he kept his eyes forward as Captain Hall entered some commands into the control panel.

Looking up, the zebra gave him a nod. "Mister Kennedy, thank you for coming."

Joe offered an awkward smile, initially not sure how to respond. Finally, he looked to each one in turn and spoke. "Reporting as ordered." He had heard it from one of the city guard a long time ago while he was performing some repairs. It seemed appropriate.

"As you know we have a bit of a problem." He gestured towards the table, where images of the assault dirigibles appeared along with footage of the train's escape. "What can you tell us about these enemy vessels?"

"Unfortunately, not much. I didn't even know they existed before we made our escape. But what I can tell you is that they're fast and agile," he said.

"Any weaknesses?" he prompted.

Joe nodded. "One, that I can think of. They may be tough but they're not very maneuverable in tight quarters. If we can find a way to limit their movement, we may be able to use that against them."

"Do you agree?" he asked, turning to the hare.

Ellie nodded. "Yes, although I'm not sure how."

"One thing at a time," he said, tapping a hoof tipped finger on the table. "We should be prepared to encounter them again. What sort of response can we expect?"

"They'll probably favor an aggressive strategy," Joe said. "As far as they're concerned the Garden is their only option. They'll do whatever's necessary to get their paws on it."

"We know that we can outrun them if we have to," Ellie said, getting the conversation moving again.

Noah chimed in at this point. "Yeah, but that's only on comparatively smooth ground and assuming we can run the engine at full for long enough to get some distance on them. You know given their intention to seize the train they're not going to be far behind us."

"There's also the fact that we have no idea how many of them they have," Captain Hall stated.

"I may be able to help you there." Joe met the captain's glance. "Back in Coldhaven I was part of the maintenance team. While I never worked on the assault dirigibles I know every inch of that place like the back of my paw, and given the fact that no one outside of the city guard was aware of their construction it means they had to build it underneath the surface, and there is only one area large enough to be converted for use as a construction facility and hangar bay." He paused. "Given the size of the space I'd say they can't have more than six."

Captain Hall nodded, touching his chin. Pacing behind the table, his hooves made gentle clacks on the deck. "That's still some pretty steep odds."

Noah nodded. "And that's not our only problem. We blew the secondary command processor running the engine at full for that long. If we plan to do better than half speed, we're going to need another one."

"Fortunately for us, I have an idea on where to get it," Ellie said. She entered a few commands into the console, bringing up additional tracks in the area. "According to the train's database there's a depot up ahead that should have what we need. The manifest indicates it should be full of parts for the train as well as general supplies and possibly a significant medical stockpile. The only catch is we'd have to divert our course to get to it."

Noah tapped one of the consoles on the wall. "Assuming those dirigibles max speed was what we observed during our last encounter, I can calculate the approximate time we'd have before any possible intercept. Though, of course, it would be just a guess."

Captain Hall spoke over his shoulder. "How long, Noah?"

"Assuming we arrive on time, we should have two hours to recover any useful supplies before we run into trouble." He shrugged.

"That's fairly tight," he said. "Not to mention we'd be sitting ducks as long as we were stopped there."

Ellie looked at her commander. "I can handle it, sir." She looked up at him, ears perked straight up. "Let me take a team. We'll clear the facility and pull our most urgent needs before the window closes."

The zebra appeared to hesitate for a moment as he looked from Ellie to Joe. At last, he nodded. "All right. We need those supplies, but I don't want to sit there a moment longer than necessary. No frills. Essentials only, clear?"

"Clear," Ellie replied.

"Am I correct in assuming you intend to have Mister Kennedy accompany you on this salvage op?" he asked.

Ellie tilted her head slightly. "I could use him. He's capable for a civilian and he's been on the ice before."

"All right." He looked at Ellie. "We arrive in ten hours. Get him as up to speed as you can before then," he said.

"Yes, sir."

"Dismissed." He turned back to Noah as the two continued to discuss the train's operational status. Ellie walked towards the rear door, taking Joe's arm in her paw as they left. Following her out, he waited until the door closed to speak.

"You want me to go with you on a mission?" he asked.

"We're shortpawed and I need someone to back me up," she said.

"Yes, but I'm not a trained soldier." Joe looked at her in curiosity. "Wouldn't one of these people be a better choice?"

Ellie shrugged. "Maybe, but it's important the captain sees that you can be a contributing member of this crew. He won't throw you out on the ice but if he thinks you're a burden he won't hesitate to dump you somewhere else." She looked down for a moment. "You did good back there. Your intel on the number of dirigibles will be very useful."

"I just hope we can find a way to deal with them before we get where we're going," he replied.

"One thing at a time," she said. "Even if they noted our heading it'll take them a while to reacquire us. We can use that time to our advantage. Now we've got a lot to do and not a lot of time to do it. The first thing I need to do is get you familiar with the train's basic systems."

Joe stepped in her path and held his paw in front of her chest. "Before we get to that, I have a few questions I'd like to ask you."

"Go ahead," she said.

"Not here," he replied, leading her back to his cabin and opening the door. Laura and his children were waiting, sitting on the sofa with all of them looking much cleaner than when they had boarded. Joe gave his wife a half smile as he took a seat on the arm. "All right, Ellie. Let's start with the Garden. What exactly is it?"

"It was one of several proposed settlements crafted in the early stages of the disaster. We knew that our planet was freezing and that we didn't have a lot of time to do anything about it. So the world governments got together and formulated a plan to save as many people as possible."

"The train," Joe said.

"That was part of it," Ellie admitted. "It was already almost completed by the time the disaster occurred. Out of the available options it was deemed the safest way to move as many people as could be brought on board through the rapidly deteriorating conditions. The oceans were impassable, and the skies weren't much better."

Laura rubbed her paws together to generate some heat. "So what happened next?"

"Scientists had identified several areas they thought might be survivable after it was clear the cold was here to stay. One of them was the train's home base, a place we designated the Garden."

"I learned about it shortly before I met you," Joe said. "It was mentioned on some information in the governor's office."

"I'm not surprised," Ellie continued. "Not long after the disaster occurred, several options were considered to try and save the remaining population. A number of them were developed in tandem by different entities before alliances broke apart and everyone started fending for themselves. One of them was your city. A good portion of the survivors of the initial disaster went there. A few went to other locations either because they thought they stood a better chance or because they didn't want to share. In any case, most of them preferred to keep to themselves and in the decades following survival was a higher priority than anything else." She folded her arms. "It was deemed our best option as it was originally designated as a seed storage facility prior to the disaster."

"How does that relate to Coldhaven?" Laura asked.

Ellie looked straight at Joe. "Your husband knows."

Laura turned to him. "Joe?"

Joe nodded. "Coldhaven was constructed where it was due to its proximity to significant deposits of coal and other natural fuel sources. It gave the city and its people access to practically limitless quantities of energy."

"Only it's not so limitless anymore," Ellie reasoned.

"Coldhaven has almost doubled in size from its initial design parameters. Now while the city can heat that much area due to the massive output of The Candle the problem is that it's consuming fuel at an exponentially higher rate." Joe waited a moment for the truth of that revelation to sink in among the group. "That's why they've been establishing more balloon teams and why they've been so determined to keep the Candle running at full power."

Lucas stood, placing a paw on Emily's shoulder. "Dad, what are you saying?"

"Coldhaven is running out of time. By my estimation, they'll be unsustainable within three years," Joe said.

The group fell silent at the pronouncement of their former home's eventual fate. The massive city, home to over fifty thousand people, would run out of fuel and then become as cold and dark as the rest of the frozen wasteland. The government would do all it could to stave off revealing the truth for as long as possible, but nothing they could do would prevent it. When at last they could conceal the reality of their situation no longer, the population would begin to panic. Once that happened, it would only be a matter of time before they would lose control and chaos would consume what was left. A few might survive in the remnants of the large city but most would likely die in the death throes of the once invulnerable Coldhaven. Those left after the initial destruction would prey on the others for the smallest scraps, and in that which was once the last beacon of civilization, all that would remain would be animals fighting for whatever remained.

Ellie shook her head. "Which means they have nothing to lose, and that makes them dangerous."

Joe touched his paw to his chin and turned to Ellie. "Would it be all right if I studied the train's upcoming course?" he asked.

The snowshoe hare considered the request and offered a shrug. "I'd have to clear it with Captain Hall, but I don't see why not."

"What are you thinking?" Laura asked, curious.

"I don't know yet," Joe said. "But if we're going to outrun those dirigibles we're going to need every advantage we can get."

Ellie nodded her agreement. "The sooner the better. It'll take us a few weeks to get back to the Garden, but if we haven't lost our pursuit by then I know Captain Hall won't allow us to get close enough for it to be identified. We're supplied and equipped to last a good long while out here if we have to, but the longer we've got them on our tails the greater the chance they'll gain access to the train, and I know what'll happen if they get too close to the command cars."

Leaving the rest unsaid Joe did not push as he suspected he knew what Captain Hall would do to keep the secret of the Garden's location from those who would threaten it. No doubt the loss of the train would be a crippling blow to the people up there but better to buy them time than to lead a hostile army to their doorstep. While he had no way of knowing what sort of defenses they had, if any, he knew that the Coldhaven dirigibles would not hesitate to inflict maximum damage when their survival was at stake. That was something he could not allow.

Wanting to change the mood of the conversation,

Joe looked at Ellie. "What's it like up there?"

"At the Garden?" she asked. Facing the entire group she sat on the opposite bunk. "It's the most beautiful place you've ever seen."

Emily's eyes grew as big as saucers. "Really?"

"Really," Ellie replied. "It's a warm and sunny and green all over, full of lots of things I bet you've never seen before."

"Like what?" Emily asked.

"Do you know what a tree is?" she asked.

Emily shook her head.

"Well, a tree is like a really big plant, except it's tall and sturdy and you can climb all the way to the top." Ellie held her hands out trying to pantomime the shape of a tree. "Some of them are so tall you almost can't see where they touch the sky."

"No way," Lucas said.

Ellie shrugged. "Fine, don't believe me, but then you can't climb on them."

"Do they really get that tall?" Lucas asked.

"Taller." Ellie smiled. "There are a lot of things you kids are just going to go nuts over up there. I bet you've never had fresh fruit. Up in The Garden, you can just walk up to a tree and pick them."

Laura smiled warmly at the idea. "Fresh fruit. It's been so long since I've had any."

Joe thought fondly to the rare occasions they would get special rations in Coldhaven. From time to time, especially when morale needed boosting or there was some sort of holiday, the general population would get their only opportunity for fresh food, or what passed for it around the city. Every year in the spring Joe and his family would each receive a single apple which represented the harvest from the limited orchard that the city had managed to cultivate in the greenhouses.

Most of the time rations were very carefully controlled depending on both your usefulness to the city as a whole but also whether or not you had any marks against your record. Even if you were spotless the quality of the food was never what Joe would have considered exceptional. It was clearly most often frozen and later thawed out or otherwise preserved and even on the rare occasions they would get something like bacon and eggs they were obviously of lower quality than the city's elite tended to get.

It hadn't started out that way, at least not initially. But over time the better ingredients tended to be allocated towards those viewed most essential to the city's continued survival, and this generally meant anyone with irreplaceable skills. Doctors, computer experts, things like that tended to get the best food and supplies, with the leftovers relegated to everyone else.

Particularly as time went on, however, it was clear that many of the essential personnel were animals in high level positions and not the people that actually kept the city running. Of course, they were always told that they were valued members of society but in truth individuals like Joe and his family were generally given just enough to keep them in line.

For years he had never had reason to question this arrangement, but perhaps it was just the fact that he had feared to do anything that would endanger his daughter's access to her critical medication. It was why he had never questioned Governor Cole's policies, not directly, in any case, and why he had always been content with things as long as his family was taken care of.

It was where he would still be now, had Governor Cole not threatened Lucas with exile.

"I promise, when we get back to the Garden, I'll

show you guys fields of the stuff," Ellie smiled.

Sitting beside Emily, he wrapped his arm around her. "How are you doing, kiddo?" he asked.

"I'm okay. A little cold, but I'm all right." Emily clutched Andre close to her chest. "I've got Andre to keep me warm."

Stroking a paw through her auburn hair he offered his best reassuring smile. "Then I know my daughter is in good paws."

"Hands, papa. Andre has hands," Emily insisted.

Wrinkling his muzzle, he shrugged. "As long as he makes you happy, sweetie. That's all daddy cares about." He gave her a gentle rub on the back and stood, letting Lucas take over for him.

Ellie let out a deep breath. "Well, I don't know about you, but now that I'm back on the train I'm going to get some rest in my own bed. I suggest you all do the same."

"But it's still light out," Emily said.

"Your dad and I have a long night ahead of us, and considering what you've been through so far I think you all could use a little sleep." She got up to leave. "Joe, I'll be back to get you in six hours. We'll see the doctor then. After that, training begins."

Joe watched her leave and took a deep breath. "All right, you heard the lady. Let's get some sleep." As soon as his head hit the pillow, he was out.

Six hours passed far quicker than Joe would have preferred. He awoke to a sound he did not recognize, sitting up and making his way to the entrance. Touching the control with his paw, the door slid open to reveal Ellie with a mild smirk on her face. "There you are."

"What? Is it six hours already?" he asked.

Ellie smiled. "Afraid so, big bear. You learn quick on this train to sleep light. If you and your family are ready,

I can take you to Doc Thurgood before we get to training."

Joe yawned, his muzzle opening wide. "Sorry. Give me five minutes." He stepped back inside, closing the door. Gathering his clothes, he woke his son and gave his wife a kiss on the cheek before carrying Emily out into the hall. "Lead the way," he said, the others following behind him.

Ellie gestured towards the rear of the car. Following her, they passed through a few more residential sections before entering the second half of the train. It was clear the rest of the massive machine was more utilitarian than the cars designed for the crew's comfort. Arriving at the doorway to the waiting area, she pressed the entry control and indicated for Joe to wait while the others went inside. "Just take a seat in here. I'll be back for you when you're done."

Joe nodded and followed after his family.

The medical car was similar to the residential cars with the exception that the treatment area consisted of two of the cabins combined into a single unit, with the third making up the area where they now sat. Decorating the walls were a few images of flowers as well as an artist's rendition of the train. Filling the corners between the seating were a few planters built into the car itself. Laura sat with Emily on the sofa while Lucas occupied himself with staring out the window at the frozen landscape.

Joe was still getting used to the idea that he was on a constantly moving vehicle. With the exception of the balloon, he had never been anywhere that moved on its own. Unlike that other mode of transportation the train had a constant gentle vibration as it rolled along the tracks that he had not quite grown accustomed to just yet.

For their part the children had seemed to adapt quickly, remarkably unaffected by their experiences since leaving the city. While both he and Laura still had their reservations, for the moment at least they had little choice but to continue on and hope for the best. Despite the apparent good fortune of their current new home, Joe knew he and his family were still at risk. The danger had not passed though it was tempting to relax given the comfort of their surroundings. Nevertheless, he could not allow himself to drop his guard completely. Not until he was sure Laura, Lucas, and Emily were safe.

Attempting to distract himself from his thoughts he glanced around the waiting area. The room was the epitome of efficiency. Every inch of space was perfectly utilized with everything precisely where it belonged. Even the reading material out in the waiting area was deliberately arranged in two neat piles. Joe had only been in a few such places, but it was a stark difference to the haphazard nature of Doctor Reed's office.

He considered looking at one of the books on the table when the door slid open to reveal a beautiful black furred wolfess with a stethoscope around her neck. Paws in the pockets of her pristine white lab coat, she stepped out into the waiting room and addressed the group. "My name is Doctor Rachel Thurgood. I'm told you four are my patients?"

Joe stepped forward. "Yes, ma'am." He swallowed. "My family and I were told to report here for a medical examination."

"Then you're in the right place," she replied. "How about we start with you?" She stepped aside and gestured into the treatment area.

After sparing a glance to his wife and what he hoped was a comforting smile to the kids, he dutifully stepped forward into the examination room. Much like the waiting room everything was neat and organized, but he supposed when space was limited one had little choice but to be as efficient as possible. Waiting for instructions, he stepped inside and noticed the doctor wrinkling her muzzle. "Something wrong?"

The lupine physician hesitated a moment, then sighed. "Your clothes smell."

"Sorry, doc, but I haven't exactly had a lot of time to do laundry during our escape. This is the only set I have." He felt mildly embarrassed by the admission even though it was not as if he had many changes of clothes to begin with. Perhaps it was just the apparent difference between his old world and his new one, but it was clear he had a lot of adjustments to make. He only hoped he was up to the challenge.

"I'll see if the quartermaster can't find you something else to wear, if only while we're cleaning your clothes." She held up the stethoscope. "Lift up your shirt." When he complied, she pressed it against his chest. Listening carefully, she held it there for a short while before at last allowing it to drop against her white coat. "Your heart sounds good." She looked into his eyes. "Any medical problems you're aware of?" she asked.

Joe shrugged. "Not really. Not with myself, anyway. My daughter has a chronic condition, we've been managing it but the only thing that works is a medication that we have been lucky enough to find here and there up to this point." He handed her the bottle. "This is what we've been giving her. It's not a cure but Doctor Reed said it would keep it in check."

Holding it between her fingers she examined it for a moment before returning it to his paw. "I'm familiar with it. We have some on board but as you say, it's not a cure." She shrugged.

"Is there one?" Joe asked.

The wolfess leaned back against the counter, her ebony locks falling over her shoulder as she considered her response. At last she nodded. "I think so."

Joe stood up from the exam table. "You don't know?"

Doctor Thurgood held up a paw and sighed. "As I'm sure you're already aware the condition your daughter has is fairly rare. Now while they were developing a cure when The Freeze occurred, records from that time are pretty sketchy. Most of the materials I've read from back then suggest that they did develop one, but whether or not they distributed and in what form is another matter. Now our supply network is pretty well equipped but even if we find it, it may be a while before it's viable. That medicine you've been giving her should keep her stable for the time being."

"Is there anything else we can do?" Joe asked.

Doctor Thurgood shook her head. "Stay in one piece and hope we get lucky."

"That's it?"

"I'm afraid so," she replied. "Look, I know I don't have to tell you that even if we're fortunate enough to find a supply of this stuff it may not be as simple as giving her a shot. Now I'll do everything I can to try and help your daughter, but I just want you to understand what we're up against here."

Joe nodded. He had known from the moment Doctor Reed had diagnosed her with the illness that it was going to be an uphill battle. It was a chronic condition and chances of her survival were slim, but long odds or not, Joe had known from the start he was not going to let her go without a fight. "Just do what you can."

"I will." She walked over to the counter and made some notes in his chart. "Well, from my preliminary exam you seem to be in relatively good health. I've still got to look at the rest of your family but as it stands I feel comfortable certifying you for duty."

"Thanks, doc."

"Don't thank me yet, they work us pretty hard on this train," she said cheerfully.

"I'm pretty used to a hard day's work," Joe replied.

Doctor Thurgood waggled a claw at him. "That's right. You four are from that city, aren't you?"

"We are. I was from the maintenance team for a long time," he said. "It was only recently I transferred to the balloon team. That was how I met Ellie."

"That must've been a story," she replied.

The polar bear smirked. "You could say that."

"So what do you think about our train?" she asked.

"It's impressive," Joe admitted. "I've never seen anything quite like it."

"We're very proud of our girl. She's not perfect, but she's carried us through more than our share of scrapes." The physician ran her paw along the smooth metal walls.

"How long have you been on board?" Joe asked.

"A few years," she said. "I've never really been one to enjoy staying in one place all the time, so when the opportunity came up to serve as the train's doctor, I took it. At least this way I get to see the world, such as it is."

Joe nodded, looking out the window at the frozen landscape beyond. "What's it like out there?"

Doctor Thurgood paused, wrapping her arms around herself as she considered her answer. "Well, I don't get out there as much as the others, but it's cold and harsh and it will kill you if you're not careful." She let out a deep breath. "But, what we're out here to find can only be found out there somewhere."

"And that is?" he asked.

"Answers. To the only question we've ever asked." She lowered her ears and allowed her tail to still.

Joe remained silent, unsure if he should press further.

Deciding to pursue another avenue of inquiry, he moved on. "Do you think the captain can get us to the Garden?"

"You can bet on it." Doctor Thurgood did not look up.

"I hope I get to see it," he said.

"You will," the wolfess replied.

"You seem awfully sure about that." Joe had to admit as much as he hoped she was right he could hardly believe they had made it this far. They still had a long way to go between here and safety, and there was a lot they had yet to overcome. Although Joe would fight for as long as he was able, he could not help but be humbled at the magnitude of the tasks ahead.

Doctor Thurgood took off her stethoscope and set it on the counter. "Look, I know you haven't been here very long, but Captain Hall knows what he's doing. He's taken this train out onto the ice more times than I can count and every time he's brought her back safe and sound. Now when it's time to worry I'll let you know, but for now, you just take care of that family of yours and do your part to keep this train running, understand?"

Joe nodded.

"Good." The lupine physician gestured towards the door. "Send in the next patient, if you please."

"Will do," he replied. Taking a step outside, he looked to his wife and gestured behind him. "Your turn."

Touching his arm as she passed, Laura gave him a warm smile. "See you in a minute."

Joe placed his paw on hers, returning the gesture before rejoining his children in the waiting area. No sooner had he given Emily a kiss on her cheek than Ellie reappeared in the doorway.

"All done?" she asked.

"Yeah, I suppose." He shrugged and looked at his

kids.

"If you'll come with me?" She gestured for him to follow her into the hallway. Upon sensing his hesitation, she let out a gentle sigh. "Doctor Thurgood will take good care of your family. You won't be gone long."

Joe looked at his children before getting up, offering them an apologetic smile. "Daddy's got to go to work. I'll see you guys later."

"Okay, dad," Lucas said, wrapping his arm around Emily.

He followed Ellie down the hall towards the rear of the train. She led him to the dining car which was largely unoccupied other than a few crewmembers. Most of the space was consumed by several booths running the length of the wall, and a kitchen area behind a counter which was currently unoccupied. Indicating one of the stools with her paw she began to rummage around the cabinets. Opening each door, she worked her way through them until at last she found what she was searching for. Pulling out a bottle of single malt scotch, she held it up for Joe to see. "I learned during our last journey that the captain liked to keep a little something special in his allocation." She pulled out a pair of glasses and set them out on the counter. "Join me?"

Joe gestured for her to proceed and watched as she poured the two drinks before resealing the bottle. Turning back to Ellie he held up the glass but did not drink from it. Instead for a moment he simply held it in his paw, swirling it about and watching the liquid move around inside the container. "You know I don't think I've ever had scotch before." He shrugged.

Ellie's ears flattened slightly. "Never?"

"It's not exactly like this stuff can be found anywhere, you know. Most of our stock is stuff that got stockpiled before The Freeze. Sometimes on special occasions or after something big they'd break open some of it to raise morale, but I was always working."

"Oh, then you're in for a treat," she said. "I haven't had any of this for years. Sometimes we find some of it out there during salvage missions. If we're lucky they even let us keep a bottle sometimes." Ellie held it under her nose and sniffed it gently. Letting out a pleasant sigh, she held it up. "Cheers."

Joe followed suit, the liquid working its way down his throat as he swallowed the scotch. Closing his eyes and twitching his muzzle he made a slight face before looking at the small container. "Interesting," he said.

"It's good, isn't it?" she asked.

"Considering it's the first time I've had it I don't know. It wasn't entirely unpleasant," he said.

Ellie opened the bottle again and poured them each another drink. "On the train we have a tradition."

"Oh?" Joe asked.

"When someone falls, we have a drink and a toast to remember them." She slid his glass over to him. "I can think of no better reason to pop open one of these bottles than that."

Joe smiled slightly, looking down at the liquid. "I wish Mike was here to share it with me."

"I know. But when we can't do anything else for them, the only thing we have left is to honor their memory." Ellie gave him an encouraging nod.

Joe pulled a photo out of his coat. "Mike and I have been friends since we were young," he said. "You don't meet a lot of new people in Coldhaven. All the kids tend to get stuck together by default since there are only so many of us. You grow up with the same twenty or thirty kids until it's time for you to start contributing to the city. If you're lucky, you'll get along with most of them. If you're not, you end up getting beat up a lot. One day I ended up finding myself on the receiving end of a fist when one of the other kids decided he wanted my rations. He almost got them too, until Mike came to my defense. From that moment on we always knew we'd be partners. When the time came to choose a task for apprenticeship we chose the maintenance team together."

"He sounds like a good friend," she said.

"He was." He stared into the glass. "I remember the first time we showed up to the Workshop. It was our first shift. We were so excited. Finally, we would get to see how the city breathed. We were going to learn every bit of how it worked and fix it all."

Joe looked down at the photo, taken at their completion of the apprentice program. It was the only formal acknowledgement they received other than the set of tools they were allowed to keep pending their official graduation from the program. The pair stood together, the toolboxes at their feet, with each one holding a tool up into the air. Both Joe and Mike smiled widely for the camera, which someone had managed to get working for one of the more well to do citizens and had needed a reason to test it. With the press of a button, the light on the top flashed and a moment later a small square of paper emerged from the bottom.

Holding it like great treasure, Joe had sworn he would keep it with him always, with Mike joking that maybe the photo would be worth something someday. "He was a great mechanic, always knowing what was broken and how to fix it. He was a hell of a partner, too. For all the years we worked together he always had my back. No matter what I was into, I never had to work very hard to talk him into going after it with me." Joe laughed. "I still have a hard time believing he was willing to follow me out here."

Ellie's ears perked up slightly. "I don't."

Joe raised his muzzle in confusion.

"You two have been through a lot together. Whether he knew what he'd be signing up for or not he was willing to follow you out here either way. Where I come from we call that loyalty. It's not easy to find, especially now, and well worth its value. Now I haven't known you as long as he has but in the short time I've been in your company I've seen what you're willing to do to protect those you care about, and that is why I agreed to take you with me. We need good people, and you certainly qualify." Ellie offered a slight smile.

"Thank you," Joe replied, not certain what else to say.

"You're welcome," Ellie said.

Taking a deep breath, he sighed. "To Mike. The best and most loyal friend I could have asked for. He was always there for me, no matter what I needed, and I'll miss him greatly. He never met a problem he couldn't solve or a piece of machinery he couldn't repair."

"To Mike."

Clinking their glasses together, Joe swallowed the liquid, his thoughts diverting to what lay ahead. Once they arrived, they would have a limited time to find what they needed and hope they could outrun the dirigibles. Regardless of the outcome, all he could do was follow the path he had set them upon no matter where it led.

CHAPTER THIRTEEN
SALVAGE

Making their way to the abandoned facility, the four snowmobiles sped across the frigid landscape. Their riders proceeded towards the entrance which was dominated by a rather thick looking set of metal doors. As they approached, the quartet came to a stop and stepped off. Ellie pulled her goggles off her face for a better look. Bringing her radio to her muzzle, she pressed the transmit key. "Team Leader to Captain Hall. We've arrived at the facility. It appears undisturbed."

"*Acknowledged, team leader. Even though it's unlikely anyone's breached the doors be prepared for anything,*" the zebra said.

"Yes, sir." Ellie gestured for the others to approach.

The radio crackled to life again. "*This is Noah. Ellie, we've got two hours on the clock. If you haven't found what we need by then we're going to have to pull out.*"

"Understood," she replied. "I'll signal when I'm ready for you to bring the train in." Closing the channel, she replaced the radio back on her belt. Turning to her team, she looked at the large eared fennec equipped with a tool bag under his arm. "All right, Richard, it's your show."

The fennec stepped forward with a snarky grin. "Prepare to be amazed." Opening the door access panel, he entered several commands into the keypad. After a moment, the massive metal doors in front of the facility pulled apart and allowed them access. Looking up to the others, he stood proudly. "Am I good, or what?"

Doctor Thurgood walked past him with a pat on the shoulder. "Thanks, now can we get to work, please?"

Sighing, Richard rolled his eyes. "So underappreciated."

Ellie shot them both a look of reproach. "Stay focused. I don't want any fooling around until we're back on the train, got it?"

"Yeah, I got it." Richard lowered his ears, suitably chastised.

Joe approached Ellie as she took point, scanning the shadows with her weapon. Once they were far enough ahead of the others he whispered into her ears, knowing she could hear him quite well. "Was that necessary?"

"Out here we depend on our wits and our team to keep us alive. A moment's distraction could be the difference between life and death. It may seem harsh but out here I am responsible for all your lives until we step foot back on the train." Taking a few steps forward, Joe took that to mean that the discussion was over. He certainly appreciated the gravity of her position. Things looked different when others depended on you to keep them alive.

Following behind her he kept his eyes on both the area in front as well as the position of the rest of the team.

Both Richard and Doctor Thurgood pulled up the rear, the black wolfess watching their tails.

The space beyond the entrance was a large open area with a bridge crossing a wide chasm leading to the levels below. Joe leaned over the railing, unable to see the bottom in the massive darkness. The only light making its way into the structure was coming through the skylight above them.

Ellie stepped forward and activated her flashlight on the end of her rifle. "Lights on, everyone. Looks like we're going to have to do this the hard way." Joe and the others followed suit, advancing over the large bridge.

Joe spoke over his shoulder to Richard. "How big is this place?"

"Pretty big," he said. "It was designed to support the train's operation for the long term but they weren't counting on a planetary weather event to freeze the entire world. The bulk of the facility is made up of hardened equipment and personnel support, but it was abandoned before it ever really came online so most of the good stuff should still be here." He shrugged. "Ideally we'd have time to strip this place clean, but given the circumstances…"

Joe didn't need him to finish. He stumbled forward as the bridge shook, sounds of straining metal reaching his ears as he gripped the railing. "That didn't sound good."

"Let's not push our luck," Ellie said. "Keep moving."

Once they reached the other side, Richard consulted his tablet. "That was a minor earthquake."

"You call that minor?" Doctor Thurgood said.

"The area must be unstable," he replied as if she hadn't spoken.

The radio crackled to life. *"This is Hall. We just detected a significant geological disturbance. Are you all right?"*

"Yes, sir, we're fine. We're a little shaken up but okay

to proceed." Ellie looked over her team with a nod.

"*Understood. Proceed with caution. Hall out.*" The radio went silent.

"All right, let's get what we came for and get out of here," she said.

Joe glanced back at the bridge before returning his attention to the path ahead. Rejoining Ellie at the front of the group he exhaled, watching his breath as it turned to vapor.

Ellie paused as they approached an intersection. "Which way?" she asked Richard.

The fennec looked down at his tablet. "Most of these facilities have a fairly common layout. What we need should be in parts and manufacturing, down to the left." Richard gestured with a claw.

"What about the medical supplies?" Joe asked.

"That should be down that way," he said, pointing at the other direction.

Ellie looked at her watch. Frowning, she addressed her team. "Okay, it's going to be tight, but I need us to split up. Joe, go with Doctor Thurgood. Get as much of the medical supplies as you can. Richard and I will handle the command processor. Be back in no more than an hour. I'm not risking missing our ride."

"Understood," Joe replied.

"Stay in touch over the radio," she ordered.

Gesturing towards their chosen direction, he nodded to the wolfess. "Shall we?" he asked.

Doctor Thurgood kept her eyes moving, searching the shadows for anything unexpected. The lupine physician held her flashlight up against her pistol as they advanced further down the hall. With her ears perked up and rotating she listened for signs of activity.

Joe once again took the lead, raising his rifle up to

search the darkness. "Expecting trouble?"

"Always," she replied, not taking her eyes off the dark shadows they passed. Shining her light into every crevice and corner she could find, Joe followed suit on the opposite side of the hall. The facility was deathly still with no sounds of any kind other than their soft footfalls as they walked. Joe could see a slight mist of frost covering everything he passed. The cold had penetrated the entire structure, all the way to its core.

Joe examined each room cautiously, pausing as he reached one of the doorways. Stepping inside, he shined the beam on a figure lying across the floor. It was feline, frozen to the point of being covered in a thin layer of ice.

Noticing he had stopped, Doctor Thurgood turned around to see what had captured his attention. "Joe?"

"I've seen dead bodies before," he said, "but nothing like this."

Doctor Thurgood nodded sadly. "Poor bastard probably got trapped here when the disaster occurred."

"Do you know how it happened?" he asked, more curious than ever about what had caused the world to freeze.

The black furred wolfess shook her muzzle. "No. What we do know is that it took years. It came up on the whole world at different rates and to different degrees. The few accounts we've found from back then all agree on one thing. It seemed to come from everywhere at once."

"In Coldhaven we rarely talked about what happened or how it started. A few of us were curious, but most of us old enough to remember didn't like to talk about it, and those that did didn't know much more than the rumors. My mother always told us stories about the world before the Freeze, but if she knew what happened she never told us."

Doctor Thurgood knelt over the body and looked at his face. "I sometimes wonder if they knew." She sighed.

"Did they see it coming or was it just like that?" she asked, snapping her fingers. She reached out a paw as if to touch his cheek but stopped inches away and pulled her paw back. "Hopefully there's something on that hard drive Ellie retrieved from the *Abraham Lincoln*."

Joe had completely forgotten about the piece of technology Ellie had recovered from the derelict Navy vessel. Connected to its computer systems, it contained a window into the world lost to the cold. A treasure trove of information, it had held its secrets for a very long time. Whether it contained any clues as to the cause of the disaster remained to be seen, but Joe could not deny his curiosity.

He wondered to himself which would be better. To be one of those who knew the end was coming and could do nothing to stop it, or to meet it so suddenly you scarcely had time to even properly curse your fate. Neither was particularly enviable, Joe decided. Either way you ended up dead.

"Do you think that if you knew what caused it that you could reverse the Freeze?" Joe asked.

Doctor Thurgood did not answer immediately. The black wolfess breathed in and out a few times before rising to stand. Turning to Joe, she placed her paws in her coat pockets. "Depends on who you ask. There are some that think we're wasting our time out here searching for answers. Others think it's the only way forward. Whether it's even possible or not, I don't know. All I do know is that we've been searching for almost forty years and we've barely scratched the surface of what caused the global weather event. Whatever it was, it's remained in effect ever since."

Joe wanted to inquire further but considered that perhaps now was not the time for a full on discussion. Feeling the cold in his paw pads he rubbed them together to restore feeling in his digits as he once again hefted his rifle and motioned for them to continue. Exiting the room, he considered the enormity of the event that would have to happen to change the weather for the entire planet. Whatever it was, it had altered the course of history and sent it down a desperate path with no obvious escape.

Something had frozen the world, and it had done so with such thoroughness that if the answer was out there it was probably buried under countless feet of snow and ice.

Before Joe could ponder it further, Ellie's voice came over the radio. *"Kennedy, Thurgood, status report."*

"We're approaching the medical ward now, Commander," she replied.

"Keep an eye on your time. We need to get back to the crossover bridge with a margin of error," the rabbit insisted.

Doctor Thurgood held the radio up to her muzzle again. "Acknowledged," she said, closing the channel.

The medical ward was identified by a pair of glass doors frosted with ice crystals. In the center of the doors was the image of two snakes curled around a winged staff. Joe recognized the symbol, having seen it before on the door to Doctor Thurgood's office. Stepping forward, he tested the doors but they did not budge. "I don't see a way to open it," he said.

Doctor Thurgood fired three shots into the glass and kicked it to shatter the fragile pieces into a shower of broken shards. Turning to a shocked Joe, she said, "We don't have time to be subtle." Stepping through in her booted paws she entered the space and examined the signage. "Any medical supplies should be this way."

Uncertain what to make of the mysterious doctor, he followed behind to what appeared to be countless quantities of various supplies and medical equipment. In awe, he stared at the bounty of things filling the shelves. Medication had always been scarce in the city, only dispensed for essential needs. He had been lucky Emily had qualified even though he always needed more of the rare and valuable substance. Fortunately for him few others suffered from the same condition as his daughter and so she was the only one drawing from the well, as it were.

Even so, he wanted nothing more than to free his little girl of this burden she had carried for almost her entire life, since she had caught it at a young age. Shaken from his reverie by the sound of Doctor Thurgood filling her duffel bags with as much as she could, he began to do the same.

"Anything on this shelf is good," she said. "We also need bandages, and any first aid supplies you can find."

"Got it," Joe replied, pulling an armful of antibiotics into the bag. Gathering enough to fill the first of two he had brought, he looked at the shelves for the medication that Emily would need to survive. "Doctor, would they have Emily's cure here?" he asked her.

Her tail stopped waving as she paused. "Unlikely." Hesitating a moment, she continued. "This is a maintenance and supply facility. The things stored here were for maximum utility and unfortunately your daughter's condition is fairly rare. While the odds are good that at least some of it made its way into the train's supply network or at least some facility we could access, it's doubtful it's here."

"Can you check anyway?" he asked. "Please."

Doctor Thurgood stood and nodded. "I'll see if I can't find anyplace they might store it. It would need to be refrigerated but based on the state of this place I can't imagine that'd be a problem."

Joe remained, gathering necessary supplies as he filled his second duffel bag. Once he was finished collecting everything on their list, he lifted his head up to listen for her presence. Hearing the sound of rustling paper, he approached her from behind. "Find anything?"

Her ebony furred tail waved slowly behind her as she scanned the listings. "Yes and no. These are the components we need but I don't know how to synthesize it. There should be instructions somewhere around here. However, I can't access it from this terminal."

"Is there someplace you can?" he asked.

Cutting off her answer, Joe heard his radio crackle to life. "*Thurgood, you headed back to the rendezvous point?*"

Doctor Thurgood pulled her own off her belt. "Hold on a moment."

"*Standing by,*" Ellie replied.

Hefting the bags over her shoulder, Doctor Thurgood gestured towards the doors. "We might be able to access the network from the command center, but it's possible the system may have degraded too far to bring it online." She sighed. "And then there's the matter of getting emergency power running."

"I have to try." Joe said.

Doctor Thurgood lifted the radio to her muzzle. "Ellie, Joe wants to try to access the medical database but the computers down here are shot. To get what we need we'd have to go to the command center. Do we have enough time to hit it before we need to leave?"

A few moments of silence. "*It'll be tight, but I think we can. Meet us at the rendezvous point.*"

"On our way," she said.

"Thank you."

"Don't thank me yet. There's no guarantee the system will cooperate." She picked up her duffel bags and headed out of the medical area.

Joe nodded. "I'll take any chance I can get."

"Fair enough," she said.

Walking beside her, he added, "I've spent my entire life trying to keep my kids safe. I'm not about to give up on them now."

Returning to the point where they first split up, Ellie and Richard were already waiting for them. The snowshoe hare turned to Richard. "How far is the command center from here?" she asked.

Richard consulted his tablet. "Not far. Getting in shouldn't be a problem, I'm more concerned about the status of the network." Letting out a deep breath, he continued. "These systems were designed to take a lot of abuse but there's a strong possibility we may not be able to bring the computers online at all."

"You have to try," he said. "For my daughter."

Richard nodded. "I'll do my best. I just want you to be prepared for the possibility it might not work."

Joe shook his head. "I'm not losing Emily. Not if I can help it."

"Lead the way, Richard," Ellie said, blessedly ending the conversation.

The matter being settled for the moment, Joe looked up at the solid metal doors that sealed off the command center. Unlike the medical area there were no glass panels. It was designed for security, to protect the facility from unwanted visitors. As Ellie stood guard, Richard knelt before the door controls. Entering a few commands, he looked up as the door slid open a few inches, and then stopped.

"Is that it?" the snowshoe hare asked.

Richard shrugged. "The servos must be jammed. Try the manual release on the wall."

Ellie walked over to a panel and tore it off, revealing a lever. Pulling on it and pushing it back up, the door slid open a few more inches. "Joe, help me." Taking one side of it, Joe pushed on the other, creating enough of a gap to open a space wide enough for him to enter.

Stepping out of the way, he followed the rest of the group inside the command center, which remained as cold and silent as the rest of the facility. As he shined his light around the room Joe scanned the various consoles, most of which had a member of the staff lying nearby. "They never had a chance."

"Most of the world didn't," Doctor Thurgood said. "I wish I knew what they were thinking."

"You think somebody did this on purpose?" Joe asked.

"I don't know," the doctor said. "But whatever caused this certainly made a hell of a mess."

Joe certainly could not disagree. Coldhaven had fought the frozen wastes for over forty six years and never made more than a dent with its reactor. No matter how much heat it generated the cold continued to push against the city's only defense.

Most of the time, Joe did not think of the cold much. He supposed after feeling it your entire life you simply got used to it, or at least stopped thinking about it all the time. It became an ever present threat you simply learned to live with, whether you liked it or not.

Relentless and uncompromising, the ice and snow rained down on the world in a perpetual barrage of winter fury. This was the world Joe had grown up in. It was the only way he had ever known.

"You know I've never seen a warm sunny day?" he said to no one in particular.

"You'll see one when we get to the Garden," Ellie promised. "Every day up there is warm and bright, and you can feel the sun on your face."

Joe tried to imagine it but was unable to do so. He had seen the sun his entire life but never once had he known the warmth the others spoke about.

Richard sat down at one of the consoles, attempting to bring the computer system online. Tapping several commands into the system, he frowned. "Main power is offline."

"Not entirely unexpected," Ellie replied. "How about the backups?"

"Maybe," he said. "Give me another minute."

Joe leaned over to Richard. "Can't you get it working?"

The fennec shot Joe an irritated look. "This is a little more complicated than turning a wrench. You're going to have to give me some space," he said. "These systems haven't been turned on in a long time. They may not come on at all."

Doctor Thurgood put a paw on Joe's arm. "Come over here with me. Let Richard do his work."

Joe reluctantly did as she asked, though his gaze did not leave the fennec's efforts. "I'm sorry."

"I understand where you're coming from, but you have to remember you're not the only one whose tail is on the line anymore. You're part of a team, and you need to trust us to come through for you." Doctor Thurgood offered a supportive smile. "I promise you we'll do everything we can."

Joe nodded, lowering his muzzle. "I know. Trust is just a little hard for me right now," he said.

"You trust Ellie, don't you?" she asked. "And you trust me."

Joe nodded again.

"Then trust us to do what we do," she said. "I promise you we won't give up. If anyone knows how to be stubborn, it's us."

"I heard that," Ellie said.

Joe could not help but allow a small chuckle. The

rapport between the train's crew reminded him of his own family. He supposed being out here long enough they became like one, sharing countless dangers in their quest for answers. Whether there were any to be had remained to be seen, but if there were, Ellie and her crew would be certain to find them.

Rubbing his arms to generate some warmth, Joe thought about Mike, and how much his friend would have loved seeing all this. Memories of the king penguin flooded his thoughts as he fought the urge to break down at his absence. Squeezing his palms, he felt a gentle touch on his shoulder.

"Everything okay?" the lupine physician asked.

"I don't know," he replied.

"Good answer," she responded.

Joe gave her a skeptical look. "How's that?"

"It's an honest one, isn't it?"

Joe nodded.

"Then it's a good answer. We deal with a lot out here and there isn't always time to process it. Things tend to get bottled up. The first rule about doing what we do is to make sure we're honest with each other. Because we can't make this work any other way," she said.

Joe relaxed slightly and nodded. "Thanks."

Richard looked up from the console. "I think I have something," he said.

All three of the others clustered around him. "Richard, don't keep us waiting," Ellie said.

The fennec tapped a few commands into the console. "I've got emergency power working, but it isn't going to hold for long. From what I can tell the computer does have a copy of the medical database, but it's encrypted."

"Can you crack it?" she asked.

Richard shrugged. "Maybe, if I had the train's

resources."

Joe leaned forward. "Ellie, we can't leave without that data."

"All right. Richard, copy as much of it as you can, we'll deal with it on the train," she ordered. With a nod, the fennec set to work copying the database. After a few moments, he offered a nod.

"I've got it," he said.

Ellie spun her paw around in the air to signal their withdrawal. Picking up her radio, she held it to her face. "Harper to the train. We're on our way back. Any sign of hostiles?"

"Negative, Ellie, but the longer we stay here the sooner they'll catch up with us. Get your butts back here ASAP."

"Understood," she replied, leading the group out of the command center and back the way they came.

The train wasted no time getting underway, surging forward at its best possible speed while he and Richard prepared to install the new part. Impressed at the train's advanced technology, Joe watched the fennec fox work. Placing the component into the train's systems he nodded in approval at the sudden surge of power. With a firm smile, he gestured to Noah, who pushed the train's speed up to half.

Turning over his shoulder, he examined the readouts. "All systems appear to be responding normally."

Captain Hall looked over his shoulder. "How long until we're back up to full speed?"

"My best guess is an hour or so. The engine needs time to build up its power levels and calibrate itself to accommodate the new part. Running all those systems checks is going to take time," Richard replied.

"Any chance we can shave that a little?" he asked.

Richard wrinkled his nose and shook his head negatively. "I wouldn't recommend it. We push the engine too hard before we've had a chance to give it a proper workup and we run the risk of causing the same problem all over again."

"Do what you can," the zebra ordered, receiving a nod from the fennec.

"Yes, sir."

Turning to Ellie, Captain Hall leaned towards her. "Nice work out there."

"Thank you, sir."

"Given the likelihood of our being intercepted before we reach the Garden, I'd like you to work up a plan for what we'll do when that happens," he said.

"Yes, captain."

Joe looked to the zebra. "Captain Hall?"

"Mister Kennedy?"

"Governor Cole is determined to get her hands on the train's data," he said. "Whatever she's got planned, I guarantee you she will come after us."

Captain Hall paused a moment. "What kind of strategy can we expect?"

"She's not afraid to take chances. To get what she needs she's willing to do just about anything if it means it'll give her a shot at getting what she's after. Whatever happens, don't expect her to back down." As much as he wanted to avoid a confrontation, Joe knew that the six dirigibles would chase them all the way to the other side of the world if they had to. Escaping their single minded pursuit would be difficult, if it were even possible at all. Nevertheless, they had no other choice but to try.

The striped equine considered him for a moment before he nodded. "Noted." He tossed his hair out of his face. "What can you tell me about the woman herself?"

Before Joe could answer, the voice of Doctor Thurgood came over the intercom. "*Joe Kennedy, please report to the medical car. Joe Kennedy, please report to the medical car."*

"We'll continue this later," Captain Hall said.

With a grateful nod, Joe gave Ellie a gentle touch on the arm as he left the command cars and made his way towards Doctor Thurgood's office. Empty except for the ebony furred wolfess herself, she gestured for him to enter. "Come on in." Sealing the door behind him, she waited for him to stand in front of her desk.

"What is it, doc?" he asked.

"I had my staff run your daughter's test results while we were gone, and I found something." She spun her monitor around for him to see.

Joe looked at the information, but not being a medical professional, he indicated his lack of comprehension with a shrug. "What am I looking at?"

"You're seeing the results of your daughter's current blood work," she said.

"And?"

Doctor Thurgood paused a moment. "I'm afraid it's not good news." She kept her face as neutral as possible, clearly trying to find a way to tell Joe something he almost certainly did not want to hear. Though he had not known her for long, Doctor Thurgood struck him as a good and compassionate physician. The fact that this news was so difficult for her to deliver only spoke to the seriousness of what she was about to say.

Joe braced himself as best as possible. "Tell me, doc."

The wolfess sighed, her tail slowing to an almost imperceptible stillness. "Your daughter's condition is degrading."

"What does that mean?" he asked.

"What it means, put simply, is that the medication that's been keeping her condition stable is losing its efficacy.

In short, it isn't working anymore." She frowned. "It's still doing its job, but she's been on it so long it's losing its effectiveness."

"So what do we do about it?" Joe asked.

Doctor Thurgood folded her arms. "There's only one thing that can help her now and that's synthesizing the cure. If I can't figure out how to formulate it…"

Joe placed his paw on her wrist. "You don't have to finish that sentence." Joe had always known how close he was to losing Emily. Contracting her condition at a young age, she had always been in danger of succumbing to the elements, even more at risk than most of the rest of the population. Only a bit of luck, her father's determination, and her young age saved her from an almost certain death.

In Coldhaven, there were no exceptions to the work policy. At age thirteen she would have been required to accept whatever job she was assigned. It was a practical certainty she would catch her death out there, no matter what task she was given. Her condition drained her of her strength, leaving her spending most of her time on the couch under the blankets. The medication kept her well enough to keep her comparatively healthy and active, but only so long as she remained as strong as possible.

Joe had done all he could to buy her time, but now it seemed his ability to do so had run out. Unless they could synthesize the incredibly rare medicine that could cure her condition once and for all, Emily would die and there would be nothing that Joe could do to stop it. Frustrated, Joe slammed his paw on the desk.

Sympathetic, Doctor Thurgood touched the sleeve of his jacket with her paw. "I promise you we'll do everything we can to help your daughter."

Desperate for any ray of hope, Joe looked into her eyes. "I can't lose her, Rachel," he said, using her first name.

"It's obvious you love her very much. I give you my word if there's anything I can do for her I'll do it. I've got Richard working on decrypting the information we brought back from the supply depot, with luck it'll have what we need." Managing her best reassuring smile, she dropped her arms back to her sides.

Joe nodded. "It has to. Because I don't know what I'll do if it doesn't." Unwilling to even consider the possibility, he stared deeply into her eyes. "Save my little girl, doc. I'll do the rest. No matter what it takes."

"I believe you will." The ebony furred wolfess gave Joe a reassuring look though he drew no significant comfort from it. Returning to their cabin, he hesitated at the door before finally pressing the button for access.

Laura was seated on the couch with the door to the sleeping area closed. She looked up as he entered, rising to greet him. "Joe," she said.

"I'm back." He turned his muzzle towards the closed door. "Are the kids…?" he started.

"They're asleep. Emily wanted to stay up but I told her she needed her rest." She smiled, stopping when she met his glance. "Joe, what is it?" she asked.

"She's getting worse," he said.

"But the medicine," she replied.

"It's not working anymore." Joe lowered his head. "Doctor Thurgood said it's buying us time, but it won't keep working for much longer."

Laura stiffened, pressing her head into his chest. "What are we going to do?" she asked.

"We may already have a solution to that. The doc has the cure but she needs time to figure out how to synthesize it. She's got Richard working on decrypting the information." He held her against him, his muzzle resting on top of her head. "I won't let anything happen to her, I swear." Joe held his wife as he stared out across the frozen expanse through which the train traveled. With a kiss on her forehead he said nothing further, knowing that their daughter's only chance rested with the train and her crew.

Doctor Thurgood had to develop the cure. There was no other option. He would not lose his little girl, not after all they'd been through. He would bring his family to safety, one way or the other. With a determination he had not felt since the first moment he'd held his young daughter in his arms, he swore he would save her. They had come too far to give up now.

CHAPTER FOURTEEN
CLOSING IN

The dining cars were perhaps the closest thing to a communal meeting place on the train. With most of the internal structure taken up by mission critical areas there were very few places for people to simply meet and talk. Other than their cabin, the dining cars were one of the few areas his family was permitted to go without the captain's permission. Doing his best to convey confidence, he smiled at Emily as he carried her in his arms towards an unoccupied booth.

She smiled back, blissfully unaware of what Doctor Thurgood had told him. Still clutching Andre in her paws she held the doll to her chest with a gentle squeeze. Emily's time was running out and this train was the only hope she had. Joe would do anything within his power to save her. The only problem was at the moment it was out of his paws.

Doctor Thurgood was still waiting to find out if the cure rested in the information they retrieved from the supply depot, but even if that proved to be the case it would be some time before it would be ready. And even if they got lucky, they likely would not have a chance to test it. Though he did not doubt they would make every effort to cure her condition there were no guarantees. Either way he knew that his daughter's fate was in the hands of their new companions. Looking around he could not think of any better people to entrust with her well being, yet he could still not stand the thought of being unable to help her when she needed him.

Setting Emily down in the booth, he slid in beside her while his wife and son took the other side. Looking around, Joe noticed the dining area was relatively unoccupied, with only a small portion of the crew present. Scattered among the various tables they appeared to be preoccupied. He could not blame them. In addition to the fact that they were far from home it was also a fact that they were being pursued by the people he had entrusted for his very survival less than a week ago. With Coldhaven searching for them it was only a matter of time before they would have to deal with Governor Cole once and for all.

He knew they were equipped with six heavy assault dirigibles, but despite their limitations they were still very powerful and agile craft. Well-armed and loaded with troops, they represented a significant threat, one that they could not allow to follow them anywhere near the Garden. With two rather substantial problems and no idea how to solve either one, Joe was not feeling very hungry.

Emily fidgeted in her seat, looking at the list of available items above the bar. Setting Andre beside her she looked up at her father. "Do we get in line?"

Joe wrinkled his forehead for a moment before comprehension dawned. "Oh, no, honey. Mommy doesn't have to get on a ration line here. You just tell them what you want and they'll prepare it for you."

Her eyes brightened as she pointed at the list. "I want some blueberry pancakes." She grinned. "With walnuts and syrup."

"Okay," he said. "Laura?"

His wife looked at the list and then back at him. "It's definitely not like it was back in Coldhaven." She paused for a moment and then smiled. "It says they have fresh fruit."

"Order what you'd like, all of you. Ellie said the train has more than enough stores for whatever you want." Joe still could not believe the significant amount of supplies the train carried in the two cars dedicated to food storage. With one car devoted to refrigeration and the other to dry storage they had significant resources for the crew's pleasure while they carried out their missions on the frozen wasteland. While he knew they were not limitless, at least according to Ellie it was rare that they would run out of anything before returning to base.

He could still hardly believe the advanced technology of the train. Equipped with systems he had never heard of the train was prepared for all sorts of scenarios. The cars they currently carried were only a fraction of the train's original length, as when it completed its original job of evacuation most of the cars were repurposed to serve as early habitats for the Garden's first group of settlers. Joe could hardly believe that the technology in the train existed before the Freeze, and yet they could not prevent the disaster that had forever changed the world into a ball of snow and ice.

Having accompanied Ellie on his first salvage mission she had told him afterwards that he had done well. Considering he had never ventured out beyond the limits of Coldhaven before he had to agree. He had taken his first steps out into the cold and had come back in one piece, but there was much more to do before his family was safe.

Laura had begun working in one of the train's maintenance crews. It was not much, but the two of them had agreed that one of them needed to stay on the train with the children at all times. With Joe being on Ellie's team for the time being that meant Laura had to hold down the fort and keep an eye on Emily especially. With her condition deteriorating it was only a matter of time before he would no longer be able to keep it from the children, and it was this he dreaded most of all.

Lucas for the time being had spent most of his time with Emily when his mother was on duty. He had asked once or twice to be assigned a job on the train, but Joe had insisted that his sister needed him more than the train needed an extra hand. He was not entirely sure that Lucas believed him, but in part he had to admit he was slightly afraid to let his son take the kind of risks he knew they'd be facing before this was all over. Perhaps it was due to the fact that he and Laura had needed to grow up so quickly that now that he had the chance to provide them with a real childhood he wanted to do so. Both he and his wife had gotten their jobs in Coldhaven at Lucas's age, and it was a few years later that they had met and married and started a family. But life expectancy within the city was a lot lower than he hoped it was in other places.

All things considered Joe had enjoyed the relative peace of the last few days. Of course, it wouldn't last, the dirigibles would catch up to them eventually, and when they did they would once again be running for their lives. He could only hope that the train and its crew were up to the task. While Lucas and Emily were up placing their orders, Laura returned with hers to sit with Joe.

"Anything?" she asked, glancing at her daughter.

Joe interlaced his fingers. "Not yet. Doctor

Thurgood is still checking. She's supposed to brief me before my next shift."

"I can't lose her, Joe. I can't." She looked up at him, her eyes moist with tears she refused to cry. "Not after we've come this far. The world wouldn't be that cruel."

Joe wanted to comfort her, assure her that there was no way he would let that happen, but unless Doctor Thurgood was right and they could formulate Emily's cure then there was nothing anyone could do to prevent it and they both knew it. Doing his best to convey the confidence he could barely feel, he took her paw in his and squeezed it. "Don't worry. Ellie and the others will come through for us. I know they will."

Before she could respond their children returned with their meals. "That looks good," he said, sniffing Emily's pancakes.

"They've got lots more, daddy, all you have to do is ask," she said.

"I'm not really that hungry," he replied, as Ellie entered the dining car.

Emily stared at her father. "Andre says you need to eat."

Opening his muzzle to respond, Ellie appeared over his shoulder, her paw on the back of the booth. "You should listen to her. If you're on my team you need to keep your strength up," she said.

"All right," he replied. "Since I'm clearly outnumbered, I'll have some breakfast." He rose from the booth, walking towards the counter with Ellie. "Has there been any news?"

She nodded. "Yes, but probably not the kind you're hoping for." She kept her voice low so no one else would hear. "We cracked the hard drive I got from the Abraham Lincoln."

"And?" he prompted, placing his order with the cook.

"We found a large amount of files in there on the train and its original mission, among other things. Apparently there's a significant archive of information in the ship's database. Some of it is corrupted, but we did find something that gives us a few more options than we already had."

"Such as?" Joe asked.

"Well, for one thing, the hard drive contains a map of a number of tracks completed after the train was launched," she said. "When the project was initially commissioned the tracks were completed by a number of different contractors and connected to the network as each section was completed. Now fortunately for us most of the work was finished before the Freeze but as a result there are large sections of the tracks that we've never seen before."

"Interesting, but I don't see how that helps us," he said.

"It doesn't, at least, not right now. But it may provide us a solution down the road," she said. Handing him a tablet, she touched a button with her finger. "This is a map of the train's current course. Take a look. You might see something we don't."

Joe nodded as he received his order and returned to dine with his family. Setting his plate before him he smiled once at his young daughter, though his thoughts continued to drift towards their next move. While they had no contact with the pursuing dirigibles since they had initially escaped their approach, the train was limited in its options for evasive maneuvers. They could delay the confrontation, but sooner or later they would have no choice but to engage the Coldhaven forces. No matter how Joe attempted to consider the matter, they were at a significant disadvantage.

Even without knowing their exact capabilities he knew they represented a significant threat to the train. Working together, their goal would be to board it in an attempt to gain control of its systems and unlock its secrets. No matter what course of action they chose, Governor Cole would not stop her pursuit of their new companions. If nothing else, she was relentless in her crusade for the survival of her people, even at the cost of someone else's.

"What's going to happen to us, dad?" Lucas asked.

Taken by surprise by his son's question, Joe answered honestly. "I don't know yet. We're following a track that will lead us where we need to go, but we can't do anything as long as the dirigibles are on our tail."

"Do we have a plan?" Laura looked at her husband, raising a fork to her muzzle.

"For now, the train is running at best possible speed away from our last point of contact, but the captain is working on a number of plans for what happens the next time we're forced to engage them." Speeding over the snowy landscape, Joe turned his head towards the window. Outside there was nowhere for the train to hide. Its best defense was staying just out of reach, but such a strategy would not last forever.

Joe considered their enemy, recalling the six dirigibles in pursuit of his newfound companions. Armed, fast, and extremely capable, they were no doubt well equipped to carry out their job of interception and attack. Yet everything had a weakness, everything. There was a way to disable them, he just had to find it.

Since the train had no offensive weapons, their best option would be to use the dirigibles against themselves. But the first time he had been piloting a balloon, and they had refused to fire upon them because they needed Ellie. Such would not be the case with the train. They wanted it, and they wanted it badly enough to do damage if they had to. They would pursue them with unmatched zeal as without the resources of the Garden, Coldhaven would die a slow death, eating itself alive.

Joe considered their options, examining the tablet he had been given with the train's upcoming routes. The same display that the captain had in the command cars, Joe observed their position along with several branches that appeared to go off in different directions.

There were several possibilities, as they were approaching an area with a relatively large number of switching points. Until they reached the hub they could alter their course depending on which track provided the best options. Ellie had said that the train could survive a fair amount of damage, but Joe knew it was best to avoid taking any if at all possible. The train was irreplaceable, and a critical asset to the Garden as well as the only chance of solving the mystery of the Freeze.

Whatever had caused it, Joe knew that the train and her crew were the only people still looking for answers. Should the train fall to her enemies, the possibility would be lost.

Joe knew that Governor Cole was desperate, and such desperation would drive people to act against the greater good for their own self interest. Even if he tried to convince her to stand down he knew that in order to maintain her house of cards she could not admit to the city she allegedly protected that there was a better way. As long as she could keep the people believing she was their only path to salvation she would not stand down.

A confrontation between the Coldhaven forces and the train's crew was inevitable, the only question was what the circumstances of it would be. Joe let out a deep sigh and examined some of the possibilities. The train was alone, with no help coming and with no option to change their plan if something went wrong. Whatever they chose would need to be carefully planned out and it would need to be something the dirigibles would never see coming. They were not foolish and would be watching for both the train and her crew to see what they would do in their effort to escape.

Thinking of his last encounter with the dirigibles he knew that their greatest point of vulnerability was in their crews. The ships themselves were very impressive. Tactically the six of them were more than a match for the train. But they would only do as their captains commanded. Joe did not need to know who they were to know they were members of the city guard, loyal to Governor Cole and just as determined as she to ensure their victory. They had been shown up by Joe, a member of the maintenance team, and a single soldier from the train. They would be angry, and they would want to purge that anger by capturing them.

That was how he would get to them. But how to use it?

The dirigibles had the advantage of firepower, maneuverability, and numbers. There had to be a way to neutralize all of those at once. As he considered their dilemma he absentmindedly poked at his breakfast. Occasionally the random forkful actually made it into his muzzle. After spending a long time staring at the map of the train's upcoming routes, he set the tablet down.

"Where are you going?" Laura asked.

Touching her paw, he smiled. "I've got a meeting with Doctor Thurgood to go over her findings. I'll be back later. Stay here and enjoy your breakfast."

"Okay," Laura replied. "Hurry back."

Joe nodded, heading towards the aft door. No sooner had he made it into the next car then he realized he was not alone. Turning behind him, he was not surprised to see Lucas following him. "Lucas, now is not the time."

"Then when is the time, dad?" he asked. "You said you'd let me help. I need you to keep your word."

"And I will, when I need you. Right now the best thing you can do is to watch over your sister," he said.

"She's got mom watching her. I can't do anything for her here and you know it. Whatever you two aren't telling us I know it's serious. You're probably going to Doctor Thurgood right now to talk about whatever it is behind our backs." Lucas glared at him. Joe wanted to deny it but all he could do in response was open his paws helplessly. "I know you want to keep us out of harm's way but it's not the right call. Let us help," he said. "Those dirigibles are coming after us and we are all at risk as long as the train is their target. Now I can't help Emily here but what I can do is help you."

Joe looked at his son, placing a paw on his right shoulder and beaming with internal pride. He nodded, and gestured for him to join him. "All right."

"Dad, I… What?"

"You're right. We're all in this together, and to keep you safe I might just need to count on you to do that. If you want in, then come with me. We'll talk to Doctor Thurgood together." Joe gestured for Lucas to precede him down the hall.

The ebony wolfess was staring closely at her monitor, not even looking up as they entered. If she was surprised at his son's presence, she covered it well. Not even missing a beat, she looked at them both. "Have a seat."

Joe remained standing. "What have you found, doc?" he asked.

"Well, I've combed through most of the information we retrieved from the supply depot. There is a file indicating how to prepare the cure," she said.

"That's good news, isn't it?" Lucas asked. "We can

save her."

"Yes, provided that I can synthesize it," she said. "It's a complex formulation and we don't have a much of a margin of error."

"So what's the problem?" Joe asked.

Doctor Thurgood frowned. "If I try to do this and I make a mistake, we could use up our only chance to make this work."

"So don't make a mistake," Lucas insisted.

"If only it were that easy. I wish I had more resources to test the process before giving it a try but a few of these compounds are hard to source and won't stay stable once I start," she said.

Joe clenched his fists, looking at her with desperation. "We can't just give up on this, not when we're this close."

"I don't intend to, but if this doesn't work then I don't know if we'll have enough to make another attempt. Now I'm going to do everything I can to keep your little girl alive, but we aren't in a good position here, Joe. Now I've got a few more files to research, but whether or not we proceed is up to you."

"It's my little girl," he said, helplessly.

"I know," she replied. "And I know the captain will do everything possible to ensure we all make it to the Garden." Touching him on the arm, she nodded. "And I'll do everything I can to keep your daughter in one piece."

"Thank you," he said. "You'll notify me if anything changes?"

"Of course," the black wolfess replied.

Before he could thank her for her efforts, the intercom crackled to life with the voice of the train's captain. "*All senior staff report to the command cars. Repeat, all senior staff report to the command cars.*"

"Gotta go." Joe turned to leave, stopping in the doorway. "Do what you have to."

Her ears perked forward, she nodded. "I'll be here when you get back."

With a nod, he left the medical car. From the vibrations in the floor he could tell the train had increased speed. Outside the window all he could see was the endless field of white whipping past as the train hurried along its tracks. Though the captain was skilled at controlling the tone of his voice, Joe knew enough to anticipate that whatever it was it was not likely to be good news.

Joe and Lucas were the last to arrive, with Ellie, Richard, Captain Hall, and his wife already present around the situation table. Both Ellie and the zebra appeared focused on the display.

Laura raised her muzzle as he entered, giving him a kiss on the cheek and taking his paw in her own. Saying nothing, she squeezed his just enough to let him know she was as uneasy as he was. The two polar bears stood off to one side as the captain addressed the group.

"Now that everyone's here, we can get started. Ellie?" he prompted.

"Less than ten minutes ago the long range sensors detected the presence of six Coldhaven dirigibles approaching from the west," she said, indicating the cluster of red dots approaching from the rear of the train. "From their current speed we can assume they're pushing their engines as hard as they can to catch up with us."

"But we can outrun them, can't we?" Joe asked.

"Under normal circumstances, yes, but with the damage to the secondary command processor it delayed us by a significant margin. On top of that, the engine still isn't at full capacity and likely won't be before they catch up to us." The fennec rested his paws on either side of the display table. "Now I can probably get the engines up to seventy five percent of its max capability before that happens but even if we had full thrust it wouldn't matter."

"Why not?" Joe asked.

To illustrate, Richard zoomed out to show the view of the train's current position as well as its course. As soon as he did, Joe immediately understood the problem. The dirigibles were headed straight for them, but the track the train was traveling on was curved over a large area. Even at full speed it would take them a considerable amount of time before they reached the next switching station. "The track we're currently traveling on is a long stretch with only a few points of divergence. Now while the train is normally fast enough to outrun anything out here, we can't beat aerial superiority. One way or another they will catch up to us, but we can make it as hard as possible for them."

Joe stared at the zoomed out view of the train and studied the landscape ahead. The point of intercept was marked on their current course, with three switching stations offering alternative routes through the region. While there was no way they could avoid the inevitable confrontation with the Coldhaven assault dirigibles, they were not without options. Concentrating on one in particular, Joe considered the possibilities as he listened to the others discussing their situation.

Noticing his interest, Ellie looked over in his direction. "Joe?"

"All of these lines represent tracks the train can travel across, correct?" he asked her.

Ellie nodded. "Yes. These are the tracks, and these are switching stations." She pointed to each of the three junctions that would allow the train to alter course.

Captain Hall tossed his mane, his gaze meeting Joe's. "Mister Kennedy?"

"You said there's nothing we can do to outrun them, right?" he asked.

Richard frowned. "Unfortunately not."

"And this indicator is the eventual point of intercept?"

A nod from the fennec. "Provided we don't alter course."

Joe brought his paw to his muzzle. "And if we do?"

"Either way we'd just be delaying the inevitable. We can't lose them, not like this," Captain Hall said.

"I don't want to lose them. As a matter of fact, we need to make sure they know exactly where we are," Joe replied.

Ellie stared at the train's course, clearly not yet understanding what he was thinking. "To what end?"

"We can assume they're going to follow us no matter what, right?" Joe looked around the table.

"They want the train, and through it, the Garden." Ellie folded her arms, her ears perked up and directed at Joe. "They'll follow us anywhere."

"With your permission, Captain?" he asked, receiving a nod from the zebra. Joe reached down to touch the display, sliding his finger along the train's projected course until he reached the second switching station. "We need to let them get close and take this track."

"There's nothing down there other than the Shadow Valley." Captain Hall offered a shrug.

"Perfect," Joe replied. "Once we get to this point, slow us down to half."

"We do that, they'll close the gap between us pretty quick," Richard pointed out.

Joe smirked. "I know. I'm counting on it."

CHAPTER FIFTEEN
INTO THE VALLEY

All eyes were on Joe as he stood confidently before the group. With the tip of his claw he drew their eyes to the valley that was the key to his idea. "We need to get them to close on us."

"That shouldn't be too difficult considering how badly they want to get their paws on the train," Captain Hall mused. "I assume you have a plan?"

"I do," Joe declared. "Before I joined the balloon team I worked on Coldhaven's maintenance team for years. We didn't always have the right tools or the proper equipment but one thing you learn pretty fast is how to improvise. If you don't have a hammer, use a wrench. If you can't repair, reroute." Joe looked at Ellie. "Now at the moment we are unable to outrun the dirigibles. No matter what we do they will catch up to us. We can't control that. But what we can control is where." He zoomed in the screen on the Shadow Valley. "Now we need to take them all out before we reach the Garden, right?"

Captain Hall nodded. "We can't risk leading them to it."

Richard frowned, his large ears flattening. "Unfortunately the train doesn't possess any offensive weapons."

Laura looked at them. "No weapons? Then how do you defend yourselves?" she asked.

Ellie rested a paw on the edge of the display table. "The train may not be armed, but at full speed there's nothing on the ice that can keep up with her."

"Hence our current dilemma," the fennec lamented.

Joe turned towards Ellie. "How many of those snowmobiles do you have?" he asked.

"Eight, altogether. Four for the team and a backup for each." Ellie folded her arms. "They come in handy for reconnaissance or going areas the train can't safely reach without attracting a lot of attention."

"What have you got in mind, Mister Kennedy?" Captain Hall asked.

"I'm proposing we set a trap. We take the train into the valley at half speed. The dirigibles will have to descend in order to follow us. Once they get close enough we wait until they get within three hundred feet," the polar bear said.

Richard straightened up. "That's almost close enough to board us."

"If this is going to work we need to make sure they don't have time to react." Joe pantomimed the train approaching the valley with his left paw. "Ellie, I know the train isn't armed but I assume you carry some sort of explosives on board in case of emergency, right?"

Ellie shrugged. "We do stock a limited supply of C4. What have you got in mind?"

Continuing to move his paw over the train's projected course, he illustrated his plan as he spoke. "As we approach the valley the snowmobiles break off and reach it ahead of the train. Each one of them lines the edge with as many explosives as possible. Once we reach the bottom, we slow down and the dirigibles will drop in after us. With luck they won't realize what we're doing until it's too late."

"Are you suggesting what I think you're suggesting?" the zebra asked.

"We trigger an avalanche," Joe said without hesitation.

Everyone spoke at once. Holding up his hand for silence, Captain Hall waited until the noise subsided to speak. "You realize that in order for this plan to work, everything has to go perfectly."

Joe nodded. "I do." He let out a breath and squeezed his wife's paw. "Once we get into position, the train accelerates to full speed. Once it does, we blow the C4. The resulting avalanche will bury the dirigibles in the valley. By the time they realize what's happening it'll be too late."

"It's a bold plan," Ellie said. "And one dependent on a lot of variables."

"Yeah, I know it's a risk, but we don't stand a chance against all six of those things and you know it," he replied. "We need to thin their numbers."

The striped equine tilted his head towards his engineer. "Richard, what do you think? Is it possible?"

"Yeah, it's possible, but I don't know if the train can handle full speed right now, and in the condition she's in it might just blow the engine entirely." He frowned.

Joe looked at the fennec. "We don't need to hold it for long, just enough to get clear of the avalanche."

Richard stared back at Joe with considerable hesitation. "I'll do my best."

"Now it's imperative that we do not trigger the explosives before at least four of the dirigibles are below the top of the valley. Once they descend into it they're going to lose a lot of maneuverability, so they can't suspect anything before we make our move." He glanced at each member of the group in turn. "We do this right, we can take them all out in one shot."

Laura held up a paw. "I don't mean to put a damper on things, but what if they don't take the bait?"

"We make sure they do," Joe said. "Governor Cole has followed us this far. She won't give up when she's this close. All we need to do is give her a little push."

"How do you plan to get them angry enough to follow us into the valley?" Captain Hall asked.

"Trust me, that's going to be the easy part." Joe held his breath as the train's commander considered his plan.

"Assuming we do this, how long is it going to take to get everything in place?" he asked.

Richard sighed. "I can have the train ready by the time we reach the valley."

"It'll take at least thirty minutes to load up the snowmobiles and another fifteen to get into position. To do this right we're going to need to use at least six." Ellie threw up her right paw in a noncommittal gesture.

"Be sure. We don't have a lot of room for error here," the zebra said.

"We'll get it done," she replied.

"All right." Captain Hall looked at Joe. "Proceed, Mister Kennedy." He pressed the button for the intercom. "Noah, prepare to change course."

"Understood," the ram replied. "We reach the switching station in fifteen minutes.

Get going, Ellie." Captain Hall returned his attention to the train's systems. "Mister Kennedy, assume your station."

"Sir?"

Captain Hall faced Joe with a look that brooked no argument. "You're the mastermind on this, which means I need you here, in the engine. You run the operation from my console on the left."

Joe hesitated, looking at Laura and Ellie. "I assumed I'd be setting the explosives."

"Setting the explosives is the easy part. You have to keep Governor Cole busy until we're ready to spring the trap. If she knows you're not on the train it'll divide her attention, and we need her focused on us." The captain was right, of course. Joe knew that to time the operation he would need the train's information at his claw tips. Though he wanted to go with Ellie to ensure the operation went according to plan, he knew what he had to do.

"Yes, sir."

"Dad," Lucas started, "Let me go in your place."

Laura looked at her son. "Are you sure that's a good idea?"

Lucas nodded. "I can help. Ellie can show me what to do, and you're needed here." He looked at each of his parents in turn.

Joe took a deep breath and at last nodded his permission. "You bring my son back in one piece, you understand?"

Ellie squeezed his shoulder. "Don't worry, Joe, we'll take care of it. You just do your part here."

As they turned to leave, Joe let out a deep sigh. "Good luck."

Ellie nodded. "To us all," she said. A moment later she was gone.

"This is where you prove Ellie right about you,

Mister Kennedy," Captain Hall said. "Report to your station."

He swallowed, turning to face the train's commander. "Aye, sir." Joe stepped through the door towards the engine, sliding into the seat the captain had been occupying when he first came on board. The console was impressive, displaying an overview of the train's status from engineering to communications and everything in between. From here Joe could see all of the information from every sensor on the massive vehicle, including a tactical display. On the far edge of the monitor he could see the dirigibles' current location, slowly getting closer.

He hovered his paws over the controls. Tightness squeezed the breath from his chest as he considered the details of his plan. He knew that it was risky, to say nothing of how many things could go wrong. Life in Coldhaven taught you harsh lessons about how cheap life could be out on the ice. Make a wrong move and you could find yourself dead along with countless others in a world where every day was a fight to survive.

Yet despite the risk Joe knew he could not afford to stand by and do nothing. Those dirigibles could not be allowed to discover the location of the Garden, and Governor Cole would never stop her pursuit of the train.

In a few minutes Ellie and her team would commence lining the valley with explosives. Taking a direct route, they would arrive at the Shadow Valley with enough time to set the trap. From there, all Joe would have to do would be to keep their attention focused on them.

Operating the forward console, Noah tapped his controls keeping the train at a steady acceleration as they approached the switching station. The ram looked back at Joe with a nod. "The train is at three quarters speed, arriving at the switch in ten minutes."

"Maintain current speed until we're fifteen minutes out," he said, marking the coordinates where he would put the final stages of his plan into motion. "Now we'll see how bad they want us," Joe remarked to no one in particular.

The train traveled along the tracks with the ever present red indicators displaying the fleet of six dirigibles slowly closing the distance between them. In the corner of his display, two numbers gradually decreased getting ever closer to zero. The top number represented the time until Ellie's team had to be finished with their job. The bottom number was the time to intercept. At the moment the numbers had a significant difference between them, but it was up to Joe to ensure that when the train reached the valley, those numbers matched as closely as possible.

To say he was nervous was an understatement. The rest of the train's crew at least had some training. They had been facing the challenges of the world outside for far longer than Joe. As he watched the information at his clawtips he could not help but wonder if he had made a mistake by following Ellie out here. Every action he had taken from the moment they had assigned Lucas to the burn team had been improvised. And yet despite all odds he had made it out of the city and reached the train, and now he was risking it all on a dangerous plan in a vehicle he barely understood.

Of course he knew on some level that he had no choice. He could no more have allowed Lucas to be exiled than he would have let Emily waste away from her disease. He would not let them. Not as long as he still had breath in his lungs. So he did the only thing he could do, and hoped he was doing the right thing.

Turning around to face him, Noah set the controls on automatic. The ram must have sensed his uncertainty, offering a sympathetic smile. "Nervous?"

"Is it that obvious?" Joe asked.

The ram smirked. "I'd be scared if you weren't. This is going to be a complicated operation. Even if things go perfectly there are no guarantees. Now I don't mean to scare you, but trust me when I say that out here you don't survive if you don't take chances now and then. The only way we make it, is if we trust each other and have each other's backs, because we're the only help out here."

Joe nodded, slightly comforted by his words. He turned from his station towards the pilot's seat. "What do you think about our chances?"

Noah inhaled. "Honestly?" He lowered his muzzle. "It's a shot in the dark, but it's the best we have right now. We're outgunned, and they know it. But out here it's not what you know, it's how well you can turn it to your advantage."

Resting a paw on the console's edge he leaned back slightly. "I'm used to working with whatever's at paw."

"Yeah, I can tell," Noah said. "It's a damn good plan, and one I think we stand a decent chance of pulling off, but I'm not going to lie to you, it's a hell of a roll of the dice. If the train's engine fails to hold or those dirigibles get in a lucky shot, this could end real quick."

"Thanks for the pep talk," Joe said, half kidding.

The ram chuckled. "We'll make it. Don't you worry about that. This train has been through a lot more than this and it'll be many revolutions more before she arrives at her final destination." He offered a reassuring salute and turned back to his station as the rear doors opened, revealing Captain Hall.

The zebra's hooves clacked softly against the metal deck of the engine. Taking up a position in the center of the room, he took in the three stations that made up the command center of the mighty vehicle. Starting with Noah, he turned his attention towards the ram. "Status, Mister

Briggs?"

"We're proceeding on course at three quarter speed. Arrival at the switching station in ten minutes," he reported. "Engineer Callahan reports the train will be ready when we need her, sir, but he cautions not to run the engines any longer than we have to at full for the time being."

Captain Hall seemed to consider the report for a moment. "Tell him that if the engine can pull us through this, we'll put in for a full maintenance cycle top to bottom when we get back."

"He'll like that, sir," he said.

"Just make sure he does his part. He has my authorization to do whatever he needs to in order to get us the speed when we need it." He gave him a solemn nod. "Ensign Hague, report. Any chatter from our friends behind us?"

The painted dog shook her head. "Negative, captain. They're maintaining course and speed but if they're talking to each other I can't break through their encryption."

"Keep trying." He looked at Joe. "You know Governor Cole better than anyone we've got. What can you tell me about her?"

Looking up at the captain, Joe leaned forward in his chair. "She's capable, determined, and utterly relentless when she needs to be. She likes to tell herself that she's acting in the best interests of her people but she knows that if Coldhaven finds out how close to the edge they are it'll devolve into chaos. The only way she can prevent it is if she gives them something else to focus on."

"The Garden," the zebra filled in for him.

"Exactly. Without it she has nothing to offer her people to offset the resources she's invested in these dirigibles, to say nothing of the manpower and equipment she's diverted to their construction," Joe said. "If she doesn't bring back the train and its secrets, she's done."

Captain Hall folded his arms and frowned. "Then there's no chance she'll turn back."

"I don't think so, no." Joe met the captain's glance. "Governor Cole has put all of her chips into this plan, which means she'll go as far as she has to in order to capture the train."

"And her people?" he asked.

The polar bear paused. "Given the level of secrecy with which these assault dirigibles were constructed and built, she most likely chose only her most trusted people to work on it. They'll follow her to the end of the earth if only because they're as deep into this as she is."

"If you're right, then we can use that against them," the zebra replied. "You understand what your job is once we get to that valley," he said, more of a statement than a question. "If they don't go for the bait, then we've wasted a perfectly good train route for nothing."

"I can get them to follow us if your engineer can keep us ahead of the avalanche," Joe said.

"Noah and Richard will keep us in one piece. You just set them up and Ellie will knock them down," Captain Hall stated.

Joe stared at the monitor feed which displayed what was going on in the snowmobile car. From there he could watch Ellie and Richard prepare the explosives that the salvage team would use to line the top of the valley in preparation for their trap. It would be a complex operation requiring both timing and precision, with the explosives needing to be placed at the right intervals to hopefully cause sympathetic vibrations. Too close and they would simply cause a sudden mess and little else. Too far apart and they would not cause a chain reaction. Done properly, they would trigger the explosions with just enough force to bury at least half of the dirigibles under the snow.

With nowhere to go and no time to climb they would be pulverized under the weight of the snow and ice. A part of Joe lamented the necessity of taking so many lives even in the name of self defense. Yet he could not allow Governor Cole to find the Garden or plunder its resources. She could have chosen to extend her paw in friendship, but instead she had determined that the only way to secure her people's future was through force.

For years she had controlled the people through the careful manipulation of information. Had Joe not encountered Ellie he might never have known what lay beyond the frozen borders of Coldhaven's reachable territory. And yet a small part of him almost missed the simplicity of life back within the city, but now that he knew the truth he could not turn away from it for a life that was long gone.

In less than an hour he would be risking everything on a play he knew was a big risk, but they were out of options. He would have to trust Ellie and Lucas to do their jobs, and the rest of the train's crew to keep them safe. All he had to do was distract Governor Cole for a few minutes.

Taking a deep breath, Joe resumed watching the timers. The next thirty minutes were both agonizingly slow and far too fast at the same time. Watching the monitors intently Joe held his breath as Ellie delivered a thumbs up gesture, indicating the hare was ready to begin. His son beside her, the young polar bear had switched his clothing for some deep winter gear. Dressed in the expeditionary uniform of the rest of Ellie's team, he subconsciously swelled with pride at his son's courage.

Placing a striped hand on his shoulder, Captain Hall activated the intercom. "Ellie, this is Captain Hall."

"*We're ready, captain,*" the snowshoe hare replied. "*All*

the snowmobiles are loaded and we're prepared to head to the drop points."

Lowering his darkened muzzle towards the microphone he spoke gently to her. "Be careful out there. Their primary attention will be on us but that doesn't mean they won't come after you as well."

"Just get the train into that tunnel before the avalanche hits, we'll do the rest." Ellie offered a salute to the camera as she gestured for her team to climb aboard the snowmobiles. *"See you on the other side."* Grasping the handles of her own machine she looked ahead at the side door of the train.

Lowering into position just a few feet above the ground, the wall became a ramp through which the small vehicles could depart the train as Joe had done during the salvage operation, and in a few seconds the snowmobiles had vanished into the snowy wasteland.

From his console he kept a careful watch on the green indicators that represented Ellie's team. Staying in close formation they sped ahead of the train towards the upcoming valley. Taking a more direct route they would be able to beat them by several minutes, putting the explosives into place. Silently Joe watched as they slowed for the first time.

"They're at the first position," Joe said.

"How are our friends?" Captain Hall asked.

"They're maintaining speed behind us. For now they appear to be holding formation," he replied. The six assault dirigibles were in a V pattern behind the train, traveling quickly in pursuit. As long as the train kept their current velocity they would be unable to close the gap. Any minute now they would change that.

Shaking his head to clear a stray hair from his face, the zebra turned to the ram at the front of the engine. "All right, Noah, it's show time. You ready?"

"On your order, captain," he replied, turning his muzzle only slightly while keeping his focus on his controls.

Captain Hall looked ahead as they began the descent into the valley, dipping below the surface level and heading into the deep chasm through which stood the train's only chance for salvation. "Make it look good. We want them to think we're in real trouble."

"Yes, sir," he replied.

Pulling back on the throttle, the train slowed slightly at the ram's direction. Joe felt the deck shudder through his boots as their speed fell sharply, enough to make the timers jump forward, shifting the point of intercept. "Time to contact has just dropped to seven minutes."

"All according to plan," he said. "Status of the team?" Captain Hall stood behind Joe's chair, placing a hoof tipped hand on the headrest.

"Ellie and Lucas are at the third position." Joe watched the small indicators displaying their locations in front of the train. Placing the explosives, each one flashed a bright yellow indicating they were armed, with the detonators linked to Ellie's snowmobile. "Estimate time of completion, six minutes."

Captain Hall flicked his ears in a display of apprehension. "It's going to be close."

"It has to be," Joe remarked. "We can't give them any time to react if this is going to work."

"Remember, we have to be sure to take out at least three of the dirigibles or this will all have been for nothing." Captain Hall did not say anything further, knowing Joe was well aware of that fact as he monitored their pursuers getting ever closer. Zooming in on the display he could now see a faint white circle surrounding the enemy fleet. Carefully watching their approach, the indicator flashed once and shifted to red.

Joe looked over his shoulder. "We're now within their weapons range."

Noah held his left hand over the throttle. "Captain?"

"Steady as she goes, Mister Briggs. We need them a lot closer. They won't fire on us, not yet." He did his best to project strength to the three members of the current engine crew, but Joe knew they still might decide to fire warning shots, and if they did it could get complicated.

The polar bear looked up at the captain. "Ellie and Lucas are at position four." They had to set a total of twelve explosives on either side of the valley. Once the Coldhaven forces were in position, they would set them off and then hope the train was fast enough to outrun the aftereffects. Resting his paws on the console, his eyes darted to the left when a small indicator flashed red. They were being hailed.

Captain Hall joined him over on the left console. "All right, Mister Kennedy, time to draw them in. Keep them occupied as long as you can. We need them angry."

"Somehow I doubt that will be a problem," Joe replied. Extending his arm, he opened the channel to the lead dirigibles. Standing in the center of the visual pickup was Governor Natalie Cole, her glare cold and uncompromising. Dressed in a sharp wine colored jacket and matching skirt she seemed out of place among the rest of the crew and their dark uniforms. But no matter what she wore it was clear she was in charge of the rather impressive military forces of Coldhaven. She watched Joe and Captain Hall carefully as she took their measure, not revealing her own paw in the slightest.

Behind her, Valentine stood still like a sentinel guarding his mistress. The grizzly bear said nothing other than offering his imposing figure behind her as a backdrop.

At last she broke the silence, recognizing Joe with an unsettling smirk. *"Mister Kennedy."*

"Governor," he replied. Returning her stare, he stood his ground. "You're a long way from Coldhaven."

"*As are you.*" She remained cold and expressionless on the surface, but he knew underneath her calm exterior rested the cold determination of someone rapidly running out of options. While at some point he believed she had only desired her people's survival, the burden of knowing that Coldhaven was operating on borrowed time had driven her to harsher and harsher extremes. With time running out before her house of cards inevitably collapsed, she would stop at nothing to get what she needed. Doing all he could to show no weakness, he kept his eye on the timers. "*I must admit, I'm surprised to see you in one piece.*"

"No thanks to you," he replied.

She gave a conciliatory nod. "*I did what I had to do. You know that.*"

"So did I." He growled. "You were going to exile my son."

"*He broke our laws. I had no choice but to do as I would have for anyone else who would steal from our people,*" she said.

"He never would have survived out there on his own and you know that. Sending him outside the city was a death sentence." He gripped the chair tight enough to make marks with his claws.

"*And now you defy the very people who raised you, who protected your entire family for generations for this?*" she gestured at him dismissively. "*We offered you everything.*"

"I had a better offer," he said.

Governor Cole bitterly whipped her tail behind her. "*Then you stand with them.*"

Joe looked over his shoulder. "Gladly."

Leaning closer to the video feed, the captain gave Governor Cole a bold but firm stare. "Coldhaven forces, stand down and fall back to a distance of two thousand meters or you will be fired upon."

Joe looked up at him, but when the captain did not return his glance, he knew the statement had not been for her, but for him. The zebra had hoped to simultaneously provoke that exact reaction from him, but at the same time inform him that Lucas and Ellie had gotten to position six.

Six down, halfway there. Time to lure them in.

"*Who the hell are you?*" she asked, her ears flattening.

The zebra gave his best defiant nicker. "Captain Daniel Hall, commander of this train."

"*Well, Captain Hall, I should warn you, my dirigibles have their weapons locked on you and they have more than enough firepower to turn your train into twisted metal.*" She was bluffing. Joe knew that. So did the captain. She would never fire on the train, but both of them were buying time for something. Joe looked at the indicators. The dirigibles had begun descending from their cruising altitude.

"Captain," Joe said, but before he could continue, he was interrupted by Governor Cole.

"*Surrender to me and I guarantee your people will not be harmed.*" Valentine's protest was silenced by her paw. "*This offer expires the moment you take any aggressive action.*"

"I'm sorry, Governor, but I will destroy this train before I let a single one of your people on board." Captain Hall flared his nostrils.

"*So be it.*" She turned to Valentine. "*Begin your attack run.*" The screen went dark.

The assault dirigibles descended in pairs of two down into the valley. Chasing the train, they rapidly closed the distance between them. "Noah, hold your speed," Captain Hall ordered. The ram held his hand above the throttle, resisting the urge to kick in the train's acceleration while they approached the mouth of the tunnel at the far end.

Ensign Hague spoke over her shoulder. "Captain,

the dirigibles have dropped to within five hundred feet."

"What the hell are they doing?" Joe asked. In a surprising move, the lead dirigible launched something at the train with enough force it was felt throughout the frame, triggering numerous alarms.

"Report!" shouted Captain Hall.

"They've secured themselves to the train somehow!" Hague replied.

The zebra turned to the forward console. "Noah, can you shake them?"

Bleating in irritation, he turned to shout over his shoulder. "Trains aren't known for their evasive maneuvers!"

Another vibration and alarms indicated a second and soon a third dirigible had attached themselves to the top of the train. "We're being boarded!" Joe said. "Captain, I don't think I have to tell you what'll happen if we hit that tunnel while they're still attached."

"Then we'd better clear the train. You're with me." He pressed a control on Joe's console. "Attention all personnel, we are being boarded. Repel all intruders." The zebra opened a panel on the wall and tossed a rifle and an earpiece to Joe. "Let's go."

Emergency lights flashed along the length of the cars covering them in a shade of blue. Accompanied by an urgent sounding klaxon, it filled Joe with a sense of apprehension as they passed through the four command cars into the residential section of the train. Joe checked his weapon to be sure it was ready, doing his best to recall Ellie's lessons.

Captain Hall tapped the earpiece and spoke. "Hague, where are they?"

A moment later her reply came through. "*Sensors indicate the breach is in car seven.*"

"Understood." Pushing forward, he waved for Joe

to follow. The two men pushed forward through the crew quarters towards the source of the sensor reading. Most of the cars were empty when the crew was on duty, but as they entered the seventh car a body lay face down on the deck.

Joe moved down to check for a pulse and shook his head. "He's dead."

Captain Hall swore. Touching his earpiece again he looked towards the ceiling. "Hague, they're not here."

"*That's the source of the initial breach, captain,*" the painted dog replied.

"Where the hell are they?" the zebra asked no one in particular. Emerging from the other end, Laura stopped as the captain raised his weapon in anticipation. Upon seeing her, he relaxed and lowered the rifle. "Where did you come from?"

Laura looked at Joe and then back at the zebra. "The medical car. What's going on?"

"We've got intruders," Joe said. "Where's Emily?"

"She's with Doctor Thurgood."

"Have you seen anyone from Coldhaven?" the captain demanded.

Laura shook her head. "No, you're the first people I ran into."

Captain Hall marched to the far end of the car and gestured towards the open hatch. "They've gone down."

Joe looked at Laura. "Stay here." Descending the ladder after the captain, they arrived in the lower level of the train. The guts of the massive machine, it was here that most of her functional systems were kept. Vastly different in appearance from the sleek and streamlined upper level, it was clear this was where the engineers did most of their work.

The lighting in the lower level was much more subdued. It was at this particular moment Joe wished his fur was another color other than white. Looking down each end he saw no sign of the hostiles.

"Hague, they're down in the maintenance level. Where are they?" he asked.

"*I'm detecting a security breach in car four*," her reply stated.

"Acknowledged." Moving forward, the two men pushed towards the front of the train. Stopping before the entrance to car five, the striped equine opened it only to be greeted by gunfire. Taking cover beside the open door, Joe turned to the captain, who returned fire with some quick and expertly aimed shots. He gestured to Joe with five fingers. That meant there were at least that many hostile soldiers aboard.

Joe took a shot. The bullet missed by a few inches, striking the wall. The enemy soldiers fired back, forcing Joe to take cover once more. He calculated in his head the progress Ellie's team was making, along with how long they would have before the current situation became catastrophic. He held up four fingers, and then made an explosion gesture with his paws.

With a determined nod, the captain opened fire and advanced into the next available cover. Joe followed suit, feeling a bullet graze his left arm. A growl escaped his throat, blood dripping from the injury. He tested his arm, confirming the lack of serious damage, and then raised his rifle for another shot.

Two of the Coldhaven soldiers were already dead, having been killed by Captain Hall's advance. That left three. But they were holding position.

Why would they do that? Unless…

Joe cursed as he called out to the captain. "They're after something in car four."

Sparing a glance to the polar bear, he looked again at the enemy soldiers. "Damn."

"What's under car four?" he asked, knowing it was the situation room, from where they had planned their missions up to this point.

Captain Hall shook his head. "The main computer core."

"The coordinates," Joe said, understanding their plan. They didn't need the entire train, just the information contained in her main computer. If they got off with it the train itself would be irrelevant. They could return to Coldhaven and launch an attack whenever they were ready. Desperate, he cast a glance at the enemy soldiers.

"Hague, what's our status?" the zebra asked.

"*Three minutes until we hit the tunnel,*" she replied.

They were running out of time. Joe fired another shot, driving the remaining soldier at the door to retreat. Taking the advantage, they pushed forward towards the situation car's lower level. Following Captain Hall to the doorway, he glanced into the narrow gap to the next car. To his surprise, the car was empty.

"They're gone!" Joe shouted.

Hall stepped forward into the room. A glance upward revealed the hatch to the upper level hung open. "Damn it!"

Joe's eyes fell to the open panel on the main computer. Clearly they got what they had come for. The two turned their attention to the ladder, taking off in pursuit once more. Pulling himself up by his paws he emerged into the situation room where one of the crew lay injured on the floor, with Doctor Thurgood kneeling beside him. "Where did they go?"

The ebony furred wolfess met Joe's eyes. "They opened fire and ran towards the rear of the train."

"Take care of him," Hall ordered as he and Joe rushed down the train towards their initial access point. "We can't let them get off the train with that data."

Joe ran after them knowing their time was almost up. As they entered the sixth car he caught a glimpse of Valentine, who fired three shots in their direction. Joe returned the favor, but the Coldhaven soldier had already dashed around the corner and out of view. In pursuit, Joe arrived just in time to see Valentine disappear through the hatch. Cursing he climbed the ladder, peering out into the cold. Forced to squint from the wind and the snow he could only watch as the escaping soldiers ascended towards the dirigibles. Foiled, he ducked back inside, closing the hatch. "We've got to get back to the engine."

Captain Hall cast one more glance up at the hatch, one hand on the ladder. With a scowl, he turned on his hooves and followed.

Resuming his station, Joe looked forward. "Noah, full speed, now."

The ram turned towards his captain. "Sir?"

Joe locked eyes with him. "If we don't do this now they'll get away with the information."

"Do it," Hall ordered.

Noah reached forward and pushed the engine to full power. The train surged ahead, the strain evident as the vibration in the hull increased enough that Joe could feel it in his feet paws. Gripping the side of his console, the massive vehicle raced across the valley towards the tunnel opening and their theoretical salvation.

In response to her sudden surge in movement, the dirigibles found themselves pulled along with the train, each struggling to disengage the magnetic grapples that held them to their quarry. He cast his glance towards the front of the engine. "Noah, hold your speed until we're through the tunnel."

"I'll do my best."

Ellie's voice came through the intercom. *"Five of the dirigibles are starting to ascend."* Her report was confirmed a moment later by the sound of heavy cables releasing one by one.

"Report?" he asked Hague.

The painted dog shrugged. "Confirmed. They're starting to release from the train."

"Ellie, set it off," Joe said. He opened a channel to the lead dirigible. "I have to give you credit, Governor, I never thought you'd have the guts to pull off something like that."

Turning in response to the new signal, she smirked. *"Checkmate, Mister Kennedy."*

He glanced at the indicators. The first explosion had already gone off. "You have no idea how right you are."

With a derisive chuckle she rested one paw on the railing before her. *"So bold for a wrench turning traitor. We have what we need and there is nothing you can do to stop us."*

Joe smirked as the avalanche began. The dirigibles had risen to two hundred feet and climbing, but they would not escape this. He just hoped it was enough to catch all of them. He looked up at her one more time. "This is for Mike, you ivory furred bitch."

Whatever reply she was going to offer was drowned out by alarms sounding from all directions. Governor Cole cast one last look at Joe and swore. *"Pull up! All dirigibles pull—,"* her panicked voice ordered as the screen turned to static.

CHAPTER SIXTEEN
PREEMPTIVE STRIKE

For a few brief seconds it was as if time had stopped. Joe's heart skipped a beat as the sudden thunderous cry of the avalanche began to make its inexorable path down the valley's sides. Thousands of tons of snow and debris broke free from their positions on either side of the cliffs and cascaded down towards them all. The next few moments could only be described as pure chaos.

Captain Hall shouted for Noah to maintain speed, but most of his order was drowned out by the movement of the snow and ice falling towards them as they fled. It didn't matter, as Noah did not need to be told to push the engine to its maximum capacity, for without tremendous speed the train would suffer the same fate as those it sought to trap.

Silently Joe was grateful his son was off the train and in a place of relative safety. Now the only thing that mattered was outrunning the unstoppable force Joe had unleashed.

Two of the dirigibles collided immediately, their captains panicking and both ships falling to the earth in a screech of fire and twisted metal. With their balloons damaged they had no hope of escaping their imminent demise, and the weight of the snow would trap them if not outright crush their ships. Even if they survived there was no way they would be able to free themselves before the cold finished them off.

Falling debris pierced the third dirigible, sending it careening into the side of the valley. Panicked cries were soon silenced as the vehicle was crushed from above by the ever advancing snow.

Of the three remaining, only two managed to evade the force of the avalanche and rise to safety, being showered by snow but managing to avoid the catastrophic destruction of the other four. The avalanche weighted down the trailing craft and soon after, the sheer mass of the falling debris punctured the balloon sending the cabin down to join their fellows.

But there was no time to savor their victory. Alarms continued to wail as Joe watched the camera feeds become obscured by the sheer amount of snow and particulates filling the air and expanding ahead of the main field of debris. Biting at the rear of the train, they threatened to consume it in the icy hand of the frozen expanse.

With a surge of power, Noah poured everything into the train's desperate flight for safety, managing to pull ahead of the snowy behemoth seconds before the force of it slammed into the wall above the tunnel. Rocked by the force of the impact, Captain Hall was tossed off his hooves onto the deck. Joe held on to his chair, hearing the screech of metal and the sound of tremendous forces meeting an immoveable barrier. A few seconds later the train emerged from the opposite side in a burst of snow, steam rising from the wheels.

Slowly, Noah decreased the train's speed and

breathed heavily. With a hand on his shoulder, Captain Hall nodded his approval.

"Nice work, Noah." He turned to Joe. "Good plan."

Joe shrugged. "Hey, if it didn't work you wouldn't be around to yell at me," he replied, still stunned by the experience.

With a nod, the zebra glanced at Noah. "Full system diagnostic. I want a damage report and assessment as soon as possible."

"Aye, sir," both Noah and Ensign Hague responded.

"Mister Kennedy, report." The striped equine leaned over his shoulder to examine the readouts on the command console.

Several of the external camera feeds still reflected obscured views from the tremendous burst of snow that had dusted the train. Joe called up the readings from the last few moments and turned to the captain. "Four dirigibles destroyed."

"Not bad," the zebra replied, giving Joe a slap on the arm. "Where are the other two?"

"In one piece and ascending." Joe frowned.

Captain Hall leaned forward to examine Joe's display. "Hague, any idea on their current status?"

"I'm not getting anything beyond their current position, captain. Sensors are having trouble identifying anything due to the current conditions." The painted dog shrugged.

"It doesn't matter anyway," Joe stated, turning around. "They got what they needed. There's only one place they'll go."

"Coldhaven," Captain Hall finished for him.

"Exactly," Joe replied.

With a hoof tipped finger he tapped the intercom.

"Richard, what's our status?"

"I'm still conducting a damage assessment, but the short version is not good. I'll get back to you as soon as I've completed my analysis," the fennec replied.

"Make it quick. We don't have a lot of time." Captain Hall exhaled deep and slow. The train moved at one quarter speed as it pulled away from the tunnel now packed to capacity with snow and other debris. With no other choice but to go forward they would rendezvous with the snowmobiles further ahead at the far end of the valley. From there they would repair the damage to the train and take off in pursuit of the dirigibles.

The odds were not in their favor. Governor Cole had a head start, and even once they took off after what remained of the Coldhaven fleet they would have to find them before they reached radio range of the city. There was a narrow window in which they would have an opportunity to catch the dirigibles before they got close enough to relay their stolen information, and it was imperative that they do so. Should they be able to relay the coordinates of the Garden to the rest of Coldhaven, it would only be a matter of time before she managed to rebuild her forces. Once that happened, it would not be long before more assault craft would be headed their way.

It would take at least an hour before they had a complete assessment on the train's status, and probably about that long to recover the snowmobiles and determine a plan. The train had been fortunate enough to escape critical damage, but she was far from her full capacity. The repairs Richard had conducted had needed to be pushed much sooner than the engineer had desired and to a much greater degree than expected, not to mention any damage she had taken as a direct result of the avalanche.

No doubt he was occupied on the lower level with

his efforts to restore her systems. The train had been wounded, that much was certain, but with luck the injury would not be fatal. In his short time aboard the train he had seen its crew accomplish incredible things, and it was his genuine hope that together they would be able to pull off just one more miracle. Returning his focus to his console, he began doing what he could to assist the fennec engineer in his efforts.

Seventy five minutes later, the train slowed to allow the snowmobiles to board. Ten minutes after that, Joe, his wife and son, and the entire senior staff had gathered together to find out exactly what they were up against.

The mood in the situation car was solemn. Even without the slightest idea of the damage the train had taken, Joe did not have to ask to know how bad it was. With his own report to add to the matter, he knew the situation was grimmer still.

Captain Hall stood at his usual place at the far end of the table, with his hoof tipped fingers spread across the edge of the table display. He was more determined than Joe had ever seen him, his attention on the graphic of the train's current course and position.

Richard stood to the side of the table. His arms folded, it was clear he had been up to his elbows in train repairs. Tired, ragged, and pensive, he no doubt had his work cut out for him.

Noah looked disheveled, no doubt feeling some of the strain of the last few hours. The ram grumbled to himself as he entered some information into the computer.

The only person who looked anything close to normal was Doctor Thurgood. Still composed and graceful, the ebony wolfess kept her paws in the pockets of her white coat silently observing the crew around her.

Attempting to seize control of the moment, Captain

Hall addressed the group. "All right. As you're no doubt aware, our plan worked but not without complications. First, let's focus on the positive. Four of the airships are now disabled, leaving only two for us to contend with."

"That's still enough firepower to take us out if we're not careful," Richard said.

"Which is why we're not going to let that happen," the captain replied, cutting off further comments. "Richard, your report."

The display on the table's surface came to life with a status update on the train's current condition. Joe did not have to be familiar with the inner workings of it to know the damage was extensive. His large ears flattening as he spoke, the fennec began. "My team and I have conducted a full diagnostic of the train's systems and we have a problem." Highlighting the engine he gestured with a claw. "The train is powered by twin Pulse reactors. They were developed shortly before the disaster that froze the world though we don't know the exact nature of the technology's origin. They're designed to operate in tandem with one another to power all of our systems." Altering the display to show the two reactors, he continued. "Now, I had to shut down one of them to compensate for the temporary loss of the secondary command processor."

"But we replaced it," Joe pointed out.

"Yes, we did, but we didn't finish calibration before we had to increase speed beyond the recommended limits to pull off your little plan back there," Richard replied. "Under ideal circumstances I would've preferred another day or two to get the train back up to full capacity but when we pushed the engine to top speed it caused an imbalance in the reactors for which I am unable to compensate."

Captain Hall touched his muzzle in contemplation. "So what does it mean?"

"It means, captain, that we will be unable to reach more than half of our max speed until the imbalance is corrected," he said.

The group looked at each other in concern. The train's greatest asset was its speed, and without it they were vulnerable, to say nothing of being unable to catch the remaining dirigibles.

"Can you fix it?" Laura asked.

Richard exhaled. "Not while the train is running. To repair the imbalance and restart the engines we need to come to a full stop and shut the engines down completely."

"That's not an option," Captain Hall stated.

"Captain, I don't think you understand. This isn't a choice. If we keep operating the train like we have been we run the risk of damaging her systems beyond my capability to repair it. Now I can delay the work for a little while but if we hope to make it back to the Garden we need to find a repair facility, sooner rather than later." The fennec frowned.

"How long will the repairs take?" he asked.

"Assuming we find a suitable facility relatively quickly, eight to ten hours." He looked up at the zebra with an apologetic frown. "That's the best I can do."

"All right. Noah, find the closest location that will meet Mister Callahan's requirements and get us to it, best possible speed." He looked at the train's status diagram and frowned. "Richard, do what you can to shave that estimate."

"Aye, captain," the fennec replied.

"We've got a bigger problem," Joe stated. "The dirigibles have the coordinates for the Garden."

Ellie leaned forward. "What? How the hell did that happen?"

"How doesn't matter. The fact is they have it, and if we don't intercept them before they get within radio range of the city then we're done." Joe let the comment hang in the air for a moment while they all considered the situation.

Captain Hall folded his arms and looked at Joe. "How long until that happens?" he asked.

"Assuming the dirigibles take the shortest route back to Coldhaven, approximately thirty six hours." Joe zoomed out the display on the situation table and highlighted both the train's current position as well as the coordinates to the city. An estimated present location of the dirigibles sat near the valley coordinates with the countdown clock listed in the upper right corner in red numbers. "If we can't catch up to them by then, it won't matter."

Noah frowned. "That won't be easy. Even if the repairs take less time than expected it's still going to be a significant challenge beating them to the city. Now we know the tracks better than they know the ice but even still it's going to be tight."

"Not necessarily." Ellie pointed to the valley. "When the dirigibles were making their escape they took some damage on the way out. Now it wasn't enough to cripple them but it'll definitely slow them down, and unlike us they don't have the ability to stop and make repairs." She looked directly at Captain Hall. "They're also limited in their top speed, even in perfect condition they're not faster than we are, especially if we play our cards right."

"There's still the matter of what we do once we catch up to them," Joe said.

"One thing at a time, Mister Kennedy. Let's get the train battle ready, and then we'll catch up to Governor Cole."

"Yes, sir," Joe replied.

"Ellie, I want options. We cannot allow the dirigibles to make it back to the city," the zebra declared.

"You'll have them."

"Dismissed." With that, Captain Hall left for the

engine.

Remaining in the situation car, Joe let out a deep sigh. His wife placed a paw on his arm, resting her head on his chest. He met Ellie's glance. "What are our odds of stopping them in time?"

Ellie folded her arms. "If we complete the repairs quickly and find a good point for intercept, we have a shot. But it's going to be tight."

Joe nodded, accepting the meager hope her answer offered. He knew there was never a guarantee, but he had come so close to getting his family somewhere safe. He refused to let it slip away if he could prevent it. Staring at the display, he considered the situation carefully. "Where's the closest repair facility?" he asked.

Noah exhaled as he entered some commands in the panel on the table's surface. The display highlighted a location not far from their current position. "Here." He zoomed in on its location. "There's a potential maintenance substation about forty minutes from our present position. It's in the opposite direction, but it should have what we need."

"Should?" Lucas asked.

The ram sighed. "Most of the information we have on the train's network is over forty years old. Now the majority of the facilities have survived the time in between with relatively little damage, but we don't have the resources to monitor them beyond the remote sensors that tell us the status of most of the nearby assets. Now the computer says that the facility is intact but we won't know what kind of situation we're walking into until we get there."

"Lovely," Ellie quipped.

Attempting to redirect the mood, Laura looked at Noah. "But you think this place is our best option?"

"Yes. It's relatively isolated, and was intended to be

one of the regular maintenance facilities for the train before the Freeze. It should be intact and the odds are pretty good it'll have the equipment we need to bring the train back up to full capability." He restored the display to the default of the train's current position and course. "Beyond that, we won't know until we get there."

Richard gazed down at the representation of the train. "I'll get us back up and running. In the meantime, I'd suggest you three come up with some sort of a plan for how we're going to deal with your friends." He flattened his ears and then gave a half hearted sigh. "Now if you'll excuse me, I have some damage control to do."

"I'll be in the engine," Noah added, leaving in the opposite direction as the fennec engineer.

Traveling at its best speed, the train proceeded towards the repair facility. Once it arrived, they would have to work quickly if they were to stop the dirigibles from relaying their coordinates. One way or another they had to make sure the last two never made it back to Coldhaven. Though he knew that the city would suffer a significant hit with the loss of both the governor and the fleet, no price was too high if it kept his family safe.

As he looked around at the train and her crew, he considered the fact that they had taken him in on little more than Ellie's word. Such an event would never have happened if it had been the other way around. While it was true in the early days Coldhaven had taken in those it found out on the snow, years of isolation and desperation had made them cold and suspicious towards anyone that was not one of their own. Yet this hare he had found had agreed to help him even though he had been the one to capture her in the first place. True, he had been her only option, but a part of him wondered if she would have helped him regardless.

And then there was the fact of the train's mission.

Not only was she operating as both scout, salvage team, and cartographer, but she was on a mission of research to find the cause of the disaster that had turned the world into a ball of ice. Coldhaven had long since given up on searching for answers, instead only being interested in whatever could keep its population alive. Perhaps after enough time out in the cold you stopped feeling whatever it was that drove the train's crew to keep looking.

Perhaps it was fate or destiny that had brought him into their path, but whether it was something greater or simple dumb luck, Joe knew that he had to do everything in his power to help the train and her crew. In his desperate fight to protect his family and keep them together, he had been given a chance to make a difference. It was hard to believe that in the span of just a few weeks his world had gone from a small one of struggle and desperation to one of hope and shared purpose.

Standing beside them, he knew that he had been fortunate, and that he would do everything he could to repay their trust in him.

Returning his attention to the main status display, Joe considered the situation. Governor Cole would do everything in her power to take the train and the Garden if she could. To extend the life of her dying city she had been willing to walk into their trap knowing how dangerous it would be. She had been willing to risk all five dirigibles just for the chance to get the information she needed, and she would not stop now. With everything on the line for both sides, it was only a matter of which side was willing to sacrifice the most to protect that which was most precious to them.

He analyzed the situation along their entire route from the city, studying all possible routes they might take. Out of the corner of his eye, he noticed an alert the system had placed on the display, but before he could investigate a chime sounded followed by the voice of Doctor Thurgood.

"*Mister Kennedy, please report to the Infirmary*," she said. Her voice sounded calm but underneath he was almost certain he detected a note of concern. Abandoning his work for the moment, he set the display to standby and walked back through the train towards the medical car.

When he arrived, he stood outside the door to the waiting area for a moment, steeling himself for whatever was waiting for him inside. Steadying his paws and his facial features, he pressed the entry key and walked inside. Laura and Lucas sat waiting for him. Both of them rose as he came to embrace them. "Laura, what's going on?" he asked.

"I don't know," she said. "Doctor Thurgood summoned us all here a few minutes ago."

It wasn't hard to guess that this had something to do with Emily. Joe felt his breath catch in his throat as he looked at the door. "Is she all right?"

Before his wife could answer, the door opened and Doctor Thurgood emerged. "That's kind of what I wanted to talk to you about." She kept her paws in her white coat, her ebony fur sleek and shiny as she entered the room. "I thought you should all be here."

"How's our daughter?" Laura asked, her eyes pleading.

Lucas said nothing, but it was clear he was as concerned as his parents were about his sister's well being. He wrapped his arm around his mother while Joe clasped her paw in his.

Doctor Thurgood looked downward and then met Joe's glance. "Unfortunately I haven't been able to complete the cure just yet."

"Why not?" Joe asked, slightly baring his teeth.

She remained calm, her ears lowering slightly. "Some

of the files are missing."

"Missing?" Laura said loudly. "How can they be missing?"

Joe answered for her. "The data breach."

The wolfess nodded. "They got more than just the Garden's coordinates. They took a lot of medical files and other data including the rest of the information how to formulate the cure. Now I have enough that I can keep it stable for a little while, but if we don't recover that data before it degrades too much to be effective…"

It was not necessary for her to finish the sentence. Joe released his wife's paw and took a step closer. "How long do we have?"

"Not long enough," she replied. "The problem isn't keeping her stable. We've got enough meds on paw to do that for a while. The problem is potency. Every hour that goes by while this medicine is in a partially completed state it's losing its ability to do the job. We need the rest before the components start breaking down or we may not have time to formulate another batch. Some of the elements in this cure are so hard to find out there it might be years before we find another supply."

"And my little sister doesn't have that long," Lucas said.

Doctor Thurgood turned to Joe. "I know I don't have to tell you how important it is we retrieve that data."

Joe lowered his muzzle. "We'll get it, no matter what it takes." He glanced towards the door to the examination area. "May we see her?" he asked.

"Of course. She's been asking for you." Doctor Thurgood stepped side. "I'll be in my office if you need anything."

Joe thanked her once before following her into the examination area. His mood immediately brightened upon seeing his daughter. Her eyes widened, sitting up quickly upon their entrance with her arms outstretched. "Daddy!"

"Hey, sweetheart," he said, hurrying to greet her. His arms wrapped around his little girl, holding her against his chest. "How are you feeling?"

"Okay I guess. Doctor Thurgood has been giving me more of my medicine, but I'm still pretty tired," she said, looking up at him.

Joe smiled. "That's normal, but pretty soon we'll get you all fixed up and then you won't be so tired anymore."

"You hear that, kiddo? Then you might have to do some real work around here," Lucas said. "Like me!"

She wrinkled her muzzle and laughed. "Just point me in the right direction!" she said, sitting up slightly, but it was not long before she was overcome with fatigue and laid back against the bed.

Her mother gently lifted her forward and fluffed her pillows with her free paw. "Before you know it, you'll be a regular member of the crew!" Laura said, sitting by the window.

"All right, Emily, I'm going to go into my office and let you have some time alone with your family. I'll be right in there if you need me, okay?" she prompted, looking at the young ursine.

Emily nodded. "Thanks, Doctor Thurgood." And then she disappeared.

Joe smiled. "I'm sorry I haven't had a lot of time to spend with you, sweetheart."

"It's okay. I know you're busy. Andre has been keeping me company." She held up her doll from his usual place at her side. "Although…"

"What is it?" Laura asked.

"He was scared earlier, when there was all that noise and the train went really fast. I had to tell him we'd be okay, but he didn't believe me." She frowned.

Joe took his daughter's paw and squeezed it gently. "I know, sweetheart. We're being pursued by Governor Cole. She wants what we have and she won't stop until she gets it. I promise I'll keep you safe, but the scary part isn't over yet. Daddy has to do something and he doesn't know what'll happen when he does, but he's going to make sure you and your mother are safe. Your brother and I have a plan, and it involves you too."

Emily looked up at him, confused. Her ears flattened slightly and curved back. "How can I help?"

"By keeping Andre safe. I know that as long as he's safe, so are you, and then daddy and your brother can do what they need to do. We're going to be putting one last plan into action, and I know that as long as you're safe in here with Andre, that I can put all my energy into getting it done." He smiled as honestly as he could hoping it would convince his daughter everything was all right. Although there was much to do between now and when this was all over, it was a parent's job to make sure their child felt safe and protected, and he knew that mattered more to him than anything in the world. Every step he had taken from the moment he had started this journey had been for Emily, to make sure she had a home and a family no matter what.

Emily nodded, holding up her doll. "Andre says he's okay. He says you don't have to worry. He'll be brave and when you come back we can all sit and have pancakes together."

Joe smiled. "I'd like that."

"Is that a promise?" she asked, sitting up again and leaning towards his muzzle.

"I promise. We'll all sit down for pancakes when this is all over." He hugged her again, his arms wrapped around her in that all encompassing way that only ursines could do.

Full of all his love and strength he gave as much of it as he could to his daughter, smiling warmly when he pulled away.

"With raspberry sauce?" she asked, hopefully.

"You bet with raspberry sauce," he said, nodding affirmatively.

Emily squeezed Andre extra tight in celebration, and then looked at the rest of her family. "Mom, Dad… What's going to happen to us when we get to the Garden?" she asked.

Joe paused. Of course he had wondered the answer to that question himself but up until now he had not had the chance to actually ask it. Indeed, his focus had been on keeping Emily alive and his family safe, so much so that he had forgotten all about what was to happen after they arrived in what theoretically was to become their new home. Joe considered his answer, and ultimately settled for honesty.

"I don't know, sweetheart." He shrugged. "I suppose that will be up to our new friends. But whatever happens, I know we'll be together, and that's all that matters for right now."

Laura nodded her agreement. "Without a doubt."

Joe looked at Laura with a warm smile, touching her shoulder. His paw squeezed gently as he silently reassured her they would keep their family together no matter what. He knew that both he and Laura feared more for Emily's well being than she herself likely even suspected. They had spent so long fighting for her that Joe could not imagine any other way of being. She had been such a gift when she had entered their lives that the moment he held her he knew he could never let his precious cub go.

In this harsh world she should not have even survived her first few years. But luck, dedication, and her mixed blessing of being born to someone who served such an essential function within the city had resulted in her making it this far. All she needed was for her father to get her just a little bit further.

With her cure so close he could not allow the train's crew to fail. He would get the information Doctor Thurgood needed back from the dirigibles and he would keep their new home safe. There was no other option. Not if he wanted to give his little girl a future.

"I know you'll find a way to keep us safe. It's what you do." Emily smiled at him with that bright smile that always gave him strength.

He leaned in to kiss her forehead and nodded. "That's right, kiddo." He held up his wrench and gave her a salute with the tool, replacing it on his belt as the doctor returned to the room.

"All right, visiting hours are over. My patient needs some rest. As far as you two, Ellie says she needs you up front. We're getting close to the maintenance station."

Joe and Lucas nodded. "Laura, would you stay here and keep an eye on Emily?" he asked.

"Of course," she agreed. "If that's all right with you."

The ebony wolfess nodded. "As long as you don't mind giving me a paw around here."

"Whatever you need me to do," Laura replied.

"Be good for your mother, sweetheart," he said.

"I will." She smiled once more, and then the door closed behind him.

Ellie was waiting for the two of them just outside the situation room. "All right. I know you two don't know the train's systems as well as the rest of us, but let me give you a crash course in how this is going to work. Once we arrive at the maintenance station, we pull in and come to a complete stop. Richard will shut down the reactors and the doors will open. Once that happens we need to restock the train with as many parts and supplies as we can. You stick with me and don't fall behind."

"Yes, ma'am," Lucas said.

"Now this facility was one of countless such outposts originally intended to service the train on its trips around the globe, so it should have everything we need to repair the engine and keep us running. I've got a list on my tablet here for what we need and what'll come in handy later. When I give you orders, I need you to go to the section I tell you to and come back as quick as you can. For this to work we need to move fast. Got it?" she asked.

Joe nodded his agreement. A few seconds later, he heard the sound indicating the train was approaching an upcoming checkpoint. Two gentle beeps announced their approach, and the motion of the train slowed as it approached the platform. A loud hiss of air signified their coming to a complete stop, and the train's personnel went to work.

Operating as a team, the entire crew set their focus to the repair and restocking of the train. At Ellie's direction, Joe and Lucas carried spare parts from the repair facility to an empty car in the rear of the train designed to carry and store essential items for the train's journey.

At the same time, Richard worked to repair the train's twin reactors, his entire team running diagnostics and calibrating the system to restore it to full functionality. Though Joe desperately wanted to ask how it was going, he knew the fennec was working as quickly as possible. Yet he could still not stop himself silently urging the engineer to hurry. He knew such thoughts were pointless, though no matter how much he tried he could not banish them from his mind. Turning his energy towards his current task, he and his son carried most of the heavier items back to the train that the smaller members of the crew were unable to lift on their own.

The work progressed quickly thanks to the train's efficient crew. Yet every second that passed was another stretch of time that the dirigibles increased their lead. Somehow they would need to find a way to overtake them, retrieve the data from their computers, and make sure that they never made it back to Coldhaven. It was a daunting task, but one that Joe had to accomplish if he and his family were to find a place they could call home.

The dirigibles could take a more direct course than the train, but if there was one thing Joe had learned in his short time out here on the ice, it was that one had to be prepared for anything. Ellie and the others had more experience surviving out here than anyone from Coldhaven, himself included. And in the battle of us versus them, it might just be the element that tipped things in their favor.

Since Joe had met Ellie he had seen more things in a matter of weeks than he'd ever imagined living in the city. And from what he knew there was far more out there than he'd ever believed. Governor Cole had built eight dirigibles, and they had taken out six on their first mission. Now all they needed was to disable or destroy the last two.

Though he knew that the military commanders she had with her knew a great deal about combat operations they had never put their expertise into practice against an enemy like the train and her crew. So far their tactics had been effective, but costly. It had been a daring move to raid the train for the coordinates but the price had been a full fifty percent of Coldhaven's military forces, and now they only had two chances to get the information back to the city.

Governor Cole was getting reckless, and with her goal so close he knew she would make mistakes. All he had to do was capitalize on them. But he also remembered something else. Animals were most dangerous when they were threatened, and Governor Cole was nothing if not dangerous.

She would fight back with everything she had to survive, and so would the train. But at least this time they would be the ones doing the chasing. They also had the advantage of knowing exactly where the last two dirigibles were going. With only so many ways back to the city, they would have to remain within a certain area of the vast snowfields, and that would give the train the advantage.

The engineers worked tirelessly to repair the train's systems. Visible both inside and out, they had done everything they could to restore the massive vehicle to its peak capability. Though it would likely require much more time than they had to do a complete repair, it would have to do.

After seven hours, Ellie gave the order to wrap up any last minute tasks and prepare to return to the train. Whether it was good news or bad news Joe had no idea, but he suspected he would find out.

CHAPTER SEVENTEEN
CROSSROADS

Repairs continued at a rapid pace on all the train's systems. Working constantly from the moment they had arrived, the engineering crew continued their efforts to restore the train's full capability. They would need everything they could manage to catch up to the Coldhaven forces in time. Stepping over panels and equipment, Joe nodded to several of the crew on his way to the forward section of the train.

Not long after they had boarded an announcement had come over the speakers calling all of the command personnel to a last minute strategy session.

Joe inhaled deeply, knowing this would be their final confrontation. The next time the train encountered the dirigibles he would face Governor Cole and her military for the last time. If all went according to plan, they would disable or destroy what was left of the enemy forces and recover the information needed to cure Emily.

A part of him knew that it was necessary, though even so he wished for another way. But Governor Cole had made it clear there would be no middle ground. She would not settle for anything less than total victory. And neither would Joe.

Steeling himself for the events to come, Joe squeezed Lucas's shoulder, drawing strength from his child. Though Joe had always fought to protect them, their time on the train had taught him that Lucas was more than ready for anything, especially when it came to defending his family. The young polar bear had proven his courage long before he had gone out on the ice with Ellie, and they would need every single person at their best if they were to come through this intact.

Whatever their strategy they would need to approach the situation with caution. The dirigible commanders would not make it easy for the train to catch up to them, and they had proven before they were willing to take risks to achieve their goals. The situation was to their advantage which meant the train and her crew would have to proceed much more boldly to take them by surprise.

It was a high stakes situation for both sides, with everything on the table. There was no second place here, no consolation prize. It was winner take all, and neither side could afford to lose.

Arriving at the situation car, Joe and Lucas were the last to enter. Most of the senior staff were already gathered around the main display. With a nod to Ellie and the captain, he took his place at the end of the table. The polar bear attempted to read their expressions to gauge their situation but all of them appeared deeply focused on the tablet in Captain Hall's hand.

The zebra scanned the information one more time before returning it to Richard. "All right, people, let's call this meeting to order. You all know what's at stake, and you know what we have to do, so let's get to it. Richard?" he said, stepping aside to let the fennec provide his report.

"Thank you, captain," he said, giving everyone a momentary acknowledgement before sliding the data to one of the wall monitors. "The train is back up and running with partial main power online and all systems operational. As for the engine, it's currently initializing. Once it completes the process, I should be able to give you full speed, but it may not be what you expect."

"What does that mean?" Joe asked, louder than he had intended. He knew the engineer was doing all he could, but with his daughter's life in the balance it was difficult to control his emotions. He lowered his muzzle in silent apology.

The fennec looked at him with exhaustion in his features. "The engine has to be almost completely recalibrated from scratch. While I can give you limited bursts of full speed we can't maintain it due to the damage to the primary systems, until I can get the train to the Garden that's the best we can do."

"It's more than we had before, thank you, Richard." Captain Hall gave him a nod, and the fennec brightened slightly at the praise. "How long until we get underway?" he asked, turning to Ellie.

Her ears raised, she looked at the zebra with confidence. "Less than half an hour."

Captain Hall looked down at the display. "I'm going to hold you to that, Lieutenant." Bringing up the overview of the entire region, the screen shifted to show the train's current location all the way to Coldhaven. Their entire journey on display, it was now a race between the two factions, with the prize being survival itself. On the end where Joe stood, Coldhaven was represented by a small depiction of the city. The graphic even had smoke emanating from the center just like the real thing. Opposite the city was a small copy of the train, and in between, a massive spider web of the rail lines between them.

Marking a spot somewhere close to the city was a thin red line. The invisible barrier was meant to depict the point at which radio contact between the city and the enemy forces was possible. If the dirigibles reached this point before the train was able to stop them, it was all over.

Joe held his breath as the captain continued.

"Ellie, it's your show." He gestured towards the snowshoe hare. Stepping forward, she assumed a commanding posture as she addressed the group. "Based on our observations during our last encounter as well as an estimation of their likely course and capabilities from Mister Kennedy we believe the dirigibles are somewhere in this area." She entered a few keystrokes into the control panel and a rectangle appeared over a large swath of the frozen expanse between them.

"That's a pretty large area," Lucas remarked.

"It is, which is why you two are going to help me to narrow it down." Ellie entered a few more variables. "At the moment they're out of our sensor range, but once we get close enough, we should be able to pinpoint their location within a few kilometers or better." Moving to a different panel, Ellie entered additional information into the computer. "Provided we leave the moment we're ready, I expect us to intercept the dirigibles in a day and a half."

Joe frowned. "That doesn't give us much of a margin of error."

"Unfortunately, at our current capacity that's the best we can do," Richard said. "The cores are stable, but Captain

I cannot advise strongly enough against pushing the engines too hard."

"Noted," the zebra said, his eyes never leaving the display before him.

Ellie rested one paw on the table and addressed the group again. "Most likely we can shave that estimate the closer we get to the city. Once we know where they are, we can take a more direct path to intercept the enemy fleet." She paused. "Now we can make an educated guess as to their course, but if we're wrong we may lose more time than we can afford."

Captain Hall met Joe's glance. "I'm counting on your expertise to prevent that, Mister Kennedy. You know these people better than anyone else. What are they most likely to do?"

The question gave Joe a moment's pause. Before he had encountered the train he had never needed to think in terms of strategy, but now that he was on the other side, so to speak, things were considerably different. He knew that he had to consider his answers carefully as they might mean the difference between victory and defeat. "She'll head back to the city as quickly as possible, but she knows we'll be coming after her so more than likely she'll be prepared for an assault. If I had to guess, she'd position one dirigible a slight distance away from the other, just enough so that we can't board them both at once."

"Why not just split up?" Richard asked.

"She won't risk it, not with only two dirigibles left. She knows as well as we do that if the data doesn't make it back to the city it's game over for her. The best way to guarantee success is to try and make it as hard as possible for us to stop them before they reach the point of no return."

"So, you're saying that we may have to choose which dirigible to pursue?" Doctor Thurgood commented, her ears flattened and her face contorted into a scowl.

Noah gestured towards the interception area. "If we have to pick this could get complicated very quickly."

"Not to mention they may double their chances by duplicating the data. We can't risk either dirigible making it past the line," Ellie pointed out.

Richard shook his head. "If we can't cut down the intercept time, I just don't see any way we're going to be able to stop them both."

Joe looked down at the display. "So how do we do that?" the polar bear asked.

Richard stared at him blankly. "We don't. Without a more precise heading we're just making educated guesses. I can't improve the engine output without the Garden's resources."

"What are the criteria for calculating the point of intercept?" he asked Ellie.

The snowshoe hare shrugged. "Distance to Coldhaven, estimated maximum speed of the dirigibles, the train's engine capacity…"

"What if we don't take the entire train?" Joe asked. All eyes shifted to him as he posed the question. Continuing, he gestured at the display with a paw. "If we disconnect all the cars we don't absolutely need, that will reduce the drain on the engine, wouldn't it?" he asked.

Richard rubbed his muzzle carefully, his tail waving gently in thought. "It's possible."

Captain Hall turned to the engineer. "Can we do it?"

"Yeah, sure, we've got the ability to disconnect the cars, and each one is equipped with an independent life support system capable of functioning for however long we need it, but we'd need to decide right now which cars we can do without," he said.

Ellie brought up a display of the entire train on the

wall monitors. "As of this moment, we've got twenty eight cars. If we remove all of the cargo and passenger cars, all we need is the four command cars, the snowmobile car, and the medical car." She ran her calculations again. "Even with the reduced engine capacity we can reach them in a little over a day."

"How long will it take to reconfigure the train?" the zebra asked.

Richard wrinkled his muzzle as he worked out the numbers in his head. "If I start right now, I can have it done in an hour."

"Do it," Captain Hall ordered. The fennec nodded and once again disappeared to carry out his work. "Doctor Thurgood, I'm going to need your staff to make sure that the rest of the train's crew is prepared for a temporary stay here at the maintenance facility. See to it they're equipped with everything they need until we return."

"Yes, sir," the ebony wolfess replied. "Don't leave without me," she said to the striped equine.

Nodding, he turned back to the rest of the group. "All right. We need to determine who's coming with us and who's staying behind. I want everyone where they're supposed to be in forty-five minutes. We leave as soon as the train is reconfigured and we don't stop for anything. Understood?"

"Yes, sir!" Everyone called out in unison.

Captain Hall moved to block Joe and Lucas. "One more thing. If you're going to come with us, I want you in uniform."

Joe looked down at his jacket and work clothes. "Sir?"

"I'll admit I had my reservations about you when you first came on board, but since then you've proven yourself to be a reliable and trustworthy member of the crew. I figure if you're going to go into battle with the rest of us, you may as well dress the part, don't you agree?"

Joe gave a firm respectful nod. "Yes sir,"

"All right. Ellie will get you equipped, Mister Kennedy." Captain Hall moved to discuss a status report with one of the support crew, his attention now towards the battle ahead.

Ellie came to join the pair. "Nice work, the captain doesn't impress easily."

Joe nodded. "I'm just doing what I have to."

"No, it's more than that. You're really fitting in here. People like you are rare out there on the snow. Most folks won't think of anyone other than themselves and they'll put their own survival first, but not you. You've been fighting for your daughter her entire life, and when your family was in trouble you didn't hesitate before throwing everything away to keep them together and safe. That kind of selfless nobility is hard to find, and something I admire. If you're interested, after this is all over, I'd like you to consider becoming a permanent member of my team."

Joe paused, momentarily stunned by her offer. He had not even considered what he would do if he was allowed to stay in the Garden with his family. Certainly, he would have to find some way to earn his keep, but it had never occurred to him to remain on the train with Ellie and the others. The thought overwhelmed him with the realization that if he succeeded and Emily was cured, there would be no more reason for him to struggle so hard just to survive. He could actually decide on what he wanted for the first time ever. There would no longer be a mandatory work assignment or daily ration lines to keep him tethered to his responsibilities. He would have a choice.

Ellie looked at him, understanding the significance of her offer. She held up a paw gently. "You don't have to decide anything now." She paused. "Just think about it, okay?"

Joe nodded, as she left the two of them behind. Alone in the situation room, Joe looked at his son. Both ursines regarded each other silently for a moment debating which of them would speak first.

Lucas opened his muzzle and then closed it again. Appearing to lose his nerve, he took a few steps towards the door, then spun around. "I'm coming with you."

"Lucas," he began.

"Dad, let me finish. I know you probably want me to stay behind but I can't let you go without me, not after all we've been through to get here. If something happened to you or Emily and I wasn't there to stop it, I couldn't forgive myself. I intend to accompany you to take down the last two dirigibles and that's final."

Joe opened his muzzle again. "Son."

"I can't just wait here and be useless, dad. I can't help Emily here. I can if I go with you."

Once he was done, Joe smirked. "Can I talk now?"

Lucas shrugged. "Yeah."

"I'm proud of you, son. I think you should come with us. I know that you're my cub and you always will be, but I also know that you're old enough to understand the risks that come with being an adult. You showed a lot of courage out there in the valley, and you risked your freedom to protect your sister when you thought she was in danger. Do I wish this wasn't necessary? Absolutely. But if we have to do this there's no one I'd rather have at my back than you."

Speechless, he struggled to find the ability to speak again. Lucas sat down and rested his arms on the table. "I thought that would be more of an argument."

Joe chuckled and did the same, pulling a stool out

from the table. "It crossed my mind." He looked at his son with a gentle smile. "I know how dangerous life can be. Even in Coldhaven, a place I always thought was relatively safe, we lost people all the time. To the weather, to accidents, to other things. I know you're smart. It's why I wanted to keep you in classes as long as possible. But I also know that I can't protect you from the world, as much as I wish I could sometimes. All I ask is that you be sure you know what you're getting into if you come with us."

"I'm ready, dad," Lucas replied.

Joe nodded. "So far, you've been lucky. Ellie and I have been there to keep an eye on you through all this. I know you can handle yourself, but you've never been on your own before. No matter how prepared you try to be, things get complicated when you're out there."

Joe thought back to the first time he met Ellie, and having to watch Mike die as he left Coldhaven for the unknown. No matter how necessary his actions leading up to those things had been, he had not been ready for either. In an instant, his world had changed completely, and he had to start over with only his wits to keep him going. That, and of course his family. The journey had been long and difficult, but it had been his determination to keep them safe that had pushed him through even when he could not know where his actions would take him.

Such had definitely been the case in the valley, when it was perhaps little more than faith that had kept the train from being crushed under the very avalanche he had set in motion. He knew it had been a risky plan and perhaps it was not until now that he understood just how much of a gamble it had been. But one thing he had learned since leaving Coldhaven behind was that the only way to win was to trust the people at your back.

Ellie, Captain Hall, Richard, Noah, and Doctor

Thurgood. They had stood beside him from the moment he arrived, and it was at their side that he would face this last challenge.

Looking to his father, Lucas nodded. "I can handle it."

Joe extended a paw. "Then let's finish this together." He reached out his paw and shook his son's with a nod. With that settled their attention then turned to the next task, preparing the train for its upcoming mission.

The majority of the crew would be remaining with the passenger and cargo cars here at the maintenance facility. The backup systems would be enough to keep them heated and powered for several days. Once the non-essential crew had transferred to the stationary train, they would complete the reintegration sequence and from that moment on it would be a race to the finish.

Assigned a uniform from Ellie, Joe examined the garment in his quarters. Black with a patch of color on the left shoulder, the train's emblem stood in stark contrast to the rest of the uniform. The black shirt and pants fit over his frame, comfortable but light. Sliding the belt around his waist, it came complete with a holster for a handgun Ellie had given him. Equipped with extra ammunition, he examined it with satisfaction, admiring the utility and efficiency of it.

The vest had his last name embroidered on the patch over his left breast. Sliding it on, he admired his reflection in the mirror for a brief moment before he added the elbow and wrist pads that completed the outfit. Trading his old worn boots for some slick black military issue pawwear, he almost didn't recognize himself. With a flash of inspiration, he reached for his wrench, tucking it into the strap at his thigh.

Emerging from the bedroom, Laura smiled.

"Looking good, Mister Kennedy."

"Thank you, Mrs. Kennedy," he replied, giving her a lick on the cheek.

She smiled, but then looked into his eyes. "I wanted to be sure I saw you before you left." Laura sat on the arm of the couch. "Emily and I aren't going with you."

Joe nodded, having expected this conversation. Earlier they had been left with little choice but to barrel headfirst into danger. Now that they were leaving the majority of the train behind, it had made sense to leave as many personnel as possible with the rest of the cars. Though Joe disliked the idea of separating his family, however temporarily, he could not deny that it would make sense keeping their daughter with the others. "I understand," he said.

Laura embraced him, resting her head against his chest. "I know you do. All the same, you better both come back in one piece, clear?"

Joe smiled, nodding his agreement. "One hundred percent." He leaned in to kiss her. "I promise, we'll be together again soon. I didn't come this far to fail now." He offered a smile, hoping it was convincing. Whether it was or not, either way Laura did not react other than to do the same. Though they both knew they were nervous about the battle ahead, they had also known how much it mattered to focus on a positive outcome, especially for the sake of their children. This would work out. It had to. "How are the preparations going?"

Laura sighed slightly. "We're almost ready moving all of the personnel and equipment. In another fifteen minutes we'll be ready to disconnect the cars." She looked into his eyes. "We should be all right as long as…. When you come back," Laura said.

Joe squeezed her shoulder. "We'll make this work. I

promise." He gestured with his muzzle towards the bedroom. "Is Emily in there?"

"Yeah," she replied. "She's waiting to see her daddy in his shiny new uniform." Laura stepped out of the way. "I'll give you a moment."

Joe entered the bedroom where his daughter waited, her legs underneath the blankets. Propped up in the corner against some pillows, she stared out the window at the falling snow. "Hey, kiddo," he said, just loud enough for her to hear.

"Dad!" she shouted, practically leaping out of the bed to hug him.

Knocked off balance by her sudden embrace, the large polar bear smiled and placed a paw on her head. "I love you too, sweetie." He dropped to one knee. "I need to tell you something."

Emily's smile disappeared as he took on a more serious expression. "It has something to do with what's going on out there, doesn't it?" she asked, looking at the crew working outside in preparation for the reconfiguration of the train.

Joe nodded, holding her paws. "We're going to split the train into two parts. You and your mother are going to stay here, while Lucas and I are going after the governor."

"What?" she blurted out, surprised. "I thought we were going to stay together!" she shouted. "You can't go."

"I wish more than anything that I didn't have to, baby, but if we're going to make it to our new home, I don't have a choice," he said, knowing that no matter how true it was, it hurt him to contemplate being away from her for the first time since she was born.

"Someone else can go," she said. "They can send someone else." She sniffled.

Joe shook his head. "I'm afraid not, kiddo. No one

else knows Governor Cole like I do. They need me if this mission is going to succeed. We'll be back in a day or two."

"Why does it have to be you?" she asked. "Why does it always have to be you?" she repeated. "You always work so hard for us. I don't…" Emily paused. "I can't lose you."

And with that, Joe understood. He held her close. "And I can't lose you," he replied. "I promise, I will come back." He held up his paw, palm towards her. She pressed her own tiny paw against his, barely managing to cover the largest of his pads. With a nod, he looked into her eyes. "You know that I love you, don't you?"

She nodded. "More than anything."

"And you know I'd never lie to you," he added. "So believe me when I make you this promise. No matter how far apart we are or where we go, I will always be with you. Never doubt that you are my daughter and I would do anything to keep you safe." Their eyes met, and a tear formed on the edge of his vision. He wiped it away with the back of his paw and smiled. "Wait for me?"

"As long as it takes," she said.

He rose to leave, and paused at the doorway. "Take care of your mother while I'm gone." A nod from Emily, and he walked back into the main room. Laura and Lucas waited in the living area, the latter in a uniform similar to his. "We'd better get going."

Laura placed a paw on Joe's chest. "One more thing before you go." She kissed Joe on the muzzle, and her son on the cheek. "For luck."

With a salute, Joe stepped past her and stood at the door. "See you soon." The door slid open, and over the public address an announcement came in Captain Hall's voice.

"*Attention all train personnel. Please report to your designated cars. We will be separating the train for reconfiguration in five minutes. Captain Hall out.*" The speaker went silent once again.

"Time to go," Joe said, giving his wife one last look before the two walked towards the front of the train.

The situation room was a flurry of activity. Ellie stood over the situation table working on intercept scenarios while the two polar bears proceeded onward to the engine. Captain Hall sat at the left station coordinating the train's reconfiguration, while Joe took over the station normally occupied by Lieutenant Harper. Taking up a position at the rear of the engine, Lucas simply observed.

"All right, time to disconnect car twenty-six," Captain Hall declared.

A loud metallic clunk signified the connectors releasing as the first twenty-five cars pulled away from the rest of the train. Removing the snowmobile and medical cars from the original configuration of the train required careful positioning and could only be done while at a place like this facility with sections of track capable of storing them. Through a series of meticulously coordinated connections and disconnections the train went from twenty-eight cars long to a lean and sleek six.

Now less than a quarter of its original length it would be capable of sustaining maximum speed far longer than Richard's original estimates. Whether it would be enough remained to be seen.

"Reconfiguration complete," Noah reported from the engineer's station. The ram looked at his readouts. "Systems are online and functioning normally."

"And the rest of the train?" Captain Hall asked.

Joe nodded. "Secondary systems are functioning on the backup generators, sir. They should be operational for several days."

"All right. All personnel accounted for?"

"Yes, captain. All crew are at their designated locations." He looked over his shoulder at the zebra.

Captain Hall pressed the intercom. "Richard, status."

"We're in the green, captain. Ready to go when you are," he replied.

"Then let's not waste any more time. Take us out," he ordered the ram.

With a sudden surge of momentum, the small train pulled away from the maintenance facility, leaving it and the rest of her crew behind. Faster than he had thought possible the six cars sped towards the closest switching station. Once they arrived, they would swing around and pursue the last two dirigibles towards an inevitable confrontation.

Captain Hall waited until they were a few minutes away to reconfigure his display, no longer showing the maintenance facility but updated to show their current position and course. Turning towards Noah, he gestured towards the ram. "Maintain course and speed until we hit the switching station. Once we do, take the alternate track and direct us towards the city."

"Aye, captain," Noah replied.

"Mister Kennedy, join me in the situation room?" he asked. Noticing Lucas, he looked at the young polar bear. "I understand you're joining us on this mission?"

"Yes, sir," Lucas said, saluting with a level of rigidity clearly indicating both enthusiasm and unfamiliarity with the ins and outs of military protocol.

Captain Hall hid a smile, holding up a hand. "At ease." He sized the young ursine up. "I'm going to need to call you something other than Mister Kennedy, on account of your father. How about specialist?" he asked.

"Yes, sir," Lucas replied. "That'd be just fine."

"All right, specialist it is. Take your station." He

gestured at the spot his father had just vacated. Returning his attention to Joe, he motioned at the door. "With me." The two men walked into the fourth car where Ellie waited, her ears perking upward at their arrival. "Lieutenant Harper," he said.

"Captain," she replied. "Mister Kennedy." She acknowledged them both with a nod.

"What have you got for us, Ellie?" he asked.

The snowshoe hare highlighted the current position of the train. Traveling away from the maintenance facility, it was traveling along a track parallel to their previous course in the opposite direction. "We're proceeding at our maximum speed in pursuit of the two remaining enemy units. They're still out of our sensor range but given their destination and their last known heading we believe them to be somewhere in this area," Ellie said. The display on the screen highlighted a large rectangular section towards the middle of the massive region. "That's our current estimation as to the likely position of the dirigibles."

"It's reasonable to assume they'll take the fastest course to Coldhaven," Captain Hall said.

"Not necessarily. Governor Cole knows we're coming after her and she'll know our limitations. She may take a longer route if she thinks it'll cause us to waste time, but there are only so many ways to the city," Joe said.

Ellie nodded, bringing up some tactical data on the dirigibles on one of the side screens. "We know that the dirigibles have a crew complement of about twenty-five men, with each one powered by twin engines towards the rear of the craft. Now with the damage they've taken, their speed and altitude are reduced so they'll be forced to fly relatively low." She looked at the route map and tilted her head. "This means they'll have to contend with several natural hazards between us and the city."

Lucas raised his muzzle. "Such as?"

"There's a mountain range to the east blocking at least twenty five percent of the path to the city. If they were at peak capability, they could fly right over it but as it is they'd have to maneuver through the mountains and current weather analysis suggests significant winds."

Joe shook his head. "Unlikely. She'd stand as much chance losing the dirigibles to the mountains as she would to us."

"The second possibility is more or less the way we came. It's the longest, but it presents the least number of natural obstacles," she said.

"And the last option?" Joe folded his arms.

Ellie highlighted a third route. "This route is slightly shorter, but it travels through the remnants of a city, which means if they're able to get inside of it they can try to lose us in the skyscrapers." She paused. "Also, there's another problem." She overlaid the weather on top of the map. "Since we left Coldhaven behind a massive snowstorm has covered the entire area. Winds are at almost one hundred and twenty knots and visibility is practically zero."

Lucas touched his chin. "Could they go around it?"

A shake of her head. "Not without costing them more time than they have. Their supplies have to be limited given their size. With a crew that large they likely weren't prepared for more than two weeks at most."

Captain Hall turned towards Joe. "Well, Mister Kennedy?"

Joe considered all three options. None were particularly appealing, but each presented their own set of risks to a pair of damaged dirigibles. Governor Cole would choose the one she thought presented her the best option to leave the train behind and cross the line first. "The city."

"Are you certain?" Ellie asked.

Joe nodded. "Yes. Governor Cole won't risk the mountains, not with these conditions. All it would take is a single gust to destroy what's left of her fleet and she won't chance that. The path we took to get here is even more dangerous without some way to maintain direction. We have the tracks but if they get lost in there it wouldn't take them long to become hopelessly disoriented." He shrugged. "At least the city offers her some protection from the storm."

"It's also going to make intercepting them particularly complicated. Once they pass into the city, they're going to try to use it as cover which means they'll head for the city center as soon as possible." Ellie highlighted the long abandoned skyscrapers. "That'll be our best chance for intercept. Assuming you're right, that is."

"I am," Joe stated.

Captain Hall placed his hands on the surface of the table. "How long until we can narrow down their precise location?"

"Approximately sixteen hours," Ellie declared. "After that we should be able to ascertain their present coordinates and develop an intercept solution."

Lucas held up a claw. "I hate to be the one to ask, but what exactly is our plan when we do catch up to them?"

"We need to get underneath them," Ellie said. "Once we intercept the enemy fleet, we'll have a limited window when the dirigibles will pass close enough to the tracks to allow the team to board. The train will match their speed, giving us a brief opportunity to latch on and carry out our mission. Now the storm plus the damage to their engines does mean they'll have to stay as near to the ground as possible to maintain control but we're only going to have a few narrow windows to do it before they pull out of range."

"How narrow?" Joe asked.

"A few seconds at most." Ellie allowed her answer

to hang in the air.

"That's all?"

"I'm afraid so," she said. "I've prepared a series of grappling hooks for us to be able to climb aboard but we're only going to get one shot a piece at each intercept point. If you miss, you're going to have to move on to the next boarding location on top of the train."

"I think I hate this plan," Joe said.

Ellie threw up her paws. "Well, it's the best we've got." She rested her paws on the edges of the table. "This entire mission hinges on us being able to board them. We miss our shot we won't get another."

"We'll get aboard," Joe declared. "Count on it."

"They'll be expecting us so anticipate heavy resistance. This is their survival just as much as ours. There is no possibility of a cease fire, no peaceful resolution, it's us or them." Ellie brought up a diagram of the dirigibles. "Based on our observations so far and our sensor records from our last few encounters we've put together a tactical assessment of their capabilities." She gestured towards Joe to take over this part of the briefing.

The elder polar bear moved to the end of the table and brought up several images of the dirigibles in flight. "We know that the assault dirigibles are fast and maneuverable, but they do have limitations. Pound for pound we're faster than they are in open territory. In close quarters they have the advantage. If their captains are willing to take risks, they can outflank us but I'm betting they aren't willing to push their ships to the limits of their probable capabilities."

"Probable capabilities?" Lucas asked.

Joe shrugged. "Without getting a look at the inside I can't offer solid information about their exact specifications, but we can make fairly accurate guesses as to their likely potential." He looked up at the sensor scan, which indicated the dirigible's size, crew complement, and identifiable features dotting the outside of the craft. "Now she's armed with several small anti-personnel weapons on the underside along with two missile launchers on the forward hull. As long as we're behind and below them we'll be out of their firing arcs but with two of them there's a good chance one of the assault dirigibles will come at us while we're trying to board the other."

"Now the train's armor should be able to handle the small caliber weapons fire, but we cannot allow those missiles to strike the engine," Ellie said.

"With the limited size of the train we'll present a minimum target surface but all the same we cannot take too many missile hits so as soon as you're aboard we're pulling away to a safe distance," Captain Hall declared.

Lucas frowned. "In other words, once we're aboard, we're on our own."

"Pretty much," the zebra agreed. "Your objective once you make it on board is three-fold. You must find the medical data stolen from our computers. Retrieve or destroy the navigational data containing the Garden's coordinates. Finally, disable or destroy the dirigibles. They cannot make it back to the city."

Joe nodded his understanding of his orders. It was going to be complicated, but there was no allowance for failure. He was going to face Governor Cole for the last time, and the final remaining ties to his former life would be severed once and for all. He knew it was necessary, but as his memories turned to Mike, he wished more than ever that his friend was by his side for this. He thought once more of the years he spent within the city having no idea what waited just beyond its walls.

Yet now he was going to take on the entire Coldhaven expeditionary force armed with his son and Ellie, and together with the rest of the train's assault team they would ensure their collective future. It was a bold move, but neither side could accept anything less than victory.

Ellie concluded her briefing. "We believe their computer core to be on the lowest level of the three, near the engine room. The data we're looking for should be there. We retrieve what we need, destroy the rest, and then get off before the thing burns."

Joe nodded. "We'll get it done."

Captain Hall looked at the rest of the team. "We intercept in less than twenty hours. Get some rest. You may not get another chance. Dismissed."

And with that, Joe and the rest of the group began their preparations.

CHAPTER EIGHTEEN
NO SECOND CHANCES

Skyscrapers towered ahead of the train's course, standing like giant steel and glass sentinels above the swiftly moving vehicle. All that remained of the world before the Freeze, they stood as monuments to a civilization long past, now little more than cover for the pair of dirigibles that hid within their towering heights. The journey towards the city whose name had long been lost to history had been one of contemplation as Joe and the rest of the crew had prepared for what was going to be their final conflict with Coldhaven.

Far from home and a long way from backup, they were on their own against the last two dirigibles of the Coldhaven military. It was here that each side would make a play for their own group's survival, with their people's future in the balance.

Both had their own advantages going into this fight.

The dirigibles had the numbers, with two vessels remaining. Despite their damage and inexperience, they had the maneuverability and weapons that the train lacked. Capable of moving among the buildings, they could make attack runs on the train and dart away with minimal exposure. But it was this same strategy that would open them up to potential boarding actions, bringing them close enough to the train that they would be able to latch on with their grappling hooks and with luck, disable the engines rendering them useless.

For its part, the train was armored, with little more than a direct hit from one of the Coldhaven missiles being able to do any significant damage to her. With only six cars, she represented a much smaller and swifter target than she had during their last encounter, which would force the dirigibles to take their shot at a much closer distance if they hoped to hit their mark.

During their approach, Captain Hall had ordered the train to run silent, with her sensor profile reduced as much as possible to delay their eventual detection by the dirigibles. With power reduced to all non-essential systems she would blend in to the snowstorm around them, with little indicating their position other than the sound of the train rushing over the tracks.

Her running lights were disabled, with Noah requiring his instruments to navigate the train on her approach. They likely wouldn't do much good anyway in this snow and wind, with visibility being minimal at best. One of the worst snowstorms Joe had seen in years, it was limiting the train's scanning ability to within ten kilometers. Yet until it passed it was unlikely the dirigibles would be able to safely escape the city without risking being hopelessly lost in the white.

Dressed in a thick winter coat and the train's military

field uniform, Joe stood in the engine watching the crew prepare for their approach to the city. At the front, Captain Hall stood behind Noah, leaning on the wall as he monitored the train's status. Occupying Ellie's usual seat once again was Ensign Hague, her tricolor ears perked up as she monitored the sensors.

Standing beside Ellie he felt a certain anxiety as he considered what they were about to do. It was dangerous, but there was little choice, not if he was going to save Emily and the rest of his friends and family. Thinking of her, he summoned all of his courage and stood straighter. Ellie's paw squeezed his shoulder, wordlessly offering her support. Together they would face this latest crisis, and one way or another soon it would all be over.

The painted dog's ears shot up as she adjusted the sensitivity of her instruments. "Enemy sighting confirmed," she declared over her shoulder.

"It would seem your instincts were right on the money, Mister Kennedy," Captain Hall said.

Joe nodded. "Governor Cole knows what's at stake as much as we do. She's not going to take a chance this close to the finish line. Not on this. The city offers her the greatest possibility of victory, and the most resistance to us."

"We'll see about that," he said.

"I'm only detecting one dirigible," Hague stated.

Joe looked at the readouts. "The other one is out there, you can be sure of that. It won't make its move until we do."

Ellie looked at the display on the port side of the bridge. "The dirigible just altered course. They've seen us."

"Noah, take us in, three quarter speed." The zebra spread his hooves a bit wider on the metal deck, in preparation for the battle.

Closing in on the city, the skyscrapers started to take

up more and more of the view ahead. Once they passed the city limits, they would have no choice but to proceed until they reached the other side. Reversing was not an option as long as the assault dirigibles were in the air, and they could not afford to be caught unawares. With the sensors at maximum, they swept the city for signs of the second dirigible but for now, the first one appeared to maintain a steady course deeper into the forest of glass and metal.

"They don't appear to be in much of a hurry," Hague said.

"That's because they're not," Joe said. "Whatever their plan is, they know they've got the advantage. All they need to do is lure us in. Once they get close enough, they'll spring their trap and then we'll get a look at their endgame."

Ellie's ears perked up. "Any idea what that'll be?"

Joe shook his head. "She'll be counting on us to make a mistake. She knows we need to get close and slow down to grapple, so my guess is she'll let us do that and try to take us out while we're conducting boarding operations."

Captain Hall whinnied. "Risky."

"Not to her. She's certain she's got all the cards. She knows we're not going to let them go but she doesn't see us as a threat, not to the dirigibles." Joe straightened up behind Captain Hall.

"That'll be her first mistake." Captain Hall looked towards Ellie. "If they're going to give us an opening, we need to take it. Once we get into position don't wait for my order. Get aboard those dirigibles and carry out your mission."

"Aye, sir," Ellie said.

Hague spun around suddenly. "Captain, we're being hailed."

Captain Hall stared forward at the retreating dirigible hovering above and ahead of the train's forward view port.

Meeting Joe's glance, he nodded and gestured for Hague to put it on the speakers. "Let's hear what she has to say."

Governor Cole appeared on the monitor, her legs crossed, and her claws steeped together with Valentine on her left. Smiling just wide enough to show her teeth, the vixen regarded the train's captain before her. "*Captain Hall*," she intoned with mild derision.

"Governor Cole," he responded with equal disdain. "You're not getting out of here."

Amused, she smirked, resting her paws on the arms of her command chair. "*And here I was about to say the same thing.*" Sitting up, she looked slightly out of frame, no doubt reviewing information from a monitor. "*Your train seems a little shorter then when last we met.*"

Not taking the bait, Captain Hall nickered. "Missing a few dirigibles?" he shot back.

Governor Cole's face lost all of its superiority as she stared into the visual pickup, her gaze growing hard and her claws flexing. "*Cease your pursuit or I will turn that pretty little train of yours into a pile of twisted metal.*"

"You know I can't do that," Captain Hall said. "Let's face it, you know as well as I do neither one of us can let the other leave this city. So how about we don't play?"

"*Very well*," she replied. "*If that's the way you want it, then so be it.*" She leaned back in her chair. "*Increase speed to one half, ready all weapons.*" The screen went dark before returning to the default readout of the current weather conditions.

"The first dirigible is pulling away," Hague reported.

Captain Hall pointed ahead. "Noah, match their speed. Ellie, get going."

Nodding, the snowshoe hare turned and walked back through the train to the fifth car. Opening a hatch, she stepped into a small area with only a ladder and began to climb. Following her, Joe and Lucas were joined by three soldiers dressed in the same dark uniforms.

At the top Ellie paused for a moment to slide her goggles over her eyes and flip her hood to cover her ears. Doing the same, Joe pulled his eyewear over seconds before the blast of cold air struck his face. Snow immediately dusted his coat with a thin layer of white. Squinting from the effects of the wind, he gripped the ladder harder. Stepping out, Ellie kept low as she moved slowly towards the front of the train. Joe did the same, mimicking her movements. The six inched forward towards the engine, the wind buffeting the group making it difficult to hold position.

Joe glanced back to be certain Lucas was behind him getting only a glimpse of his son before the younger ursine's eyes were drawn to something above them. Turning to see their target, Joe swallowed. Outside of the protection of the train, the assault dirigible loomed menacing and deadly. Her weapons scanned the area below searching for targets. Without warning one of the forward turrets spun and faced the small group. "Look out!" Joe shouted, as the small gun opened fire. Ellie rolled to the edge of the train's roof, her boot hanging over the edge as she grabbed for purchase.

Joe dove to protect his son, hearing the sound of one of the others being shot and falling off the edge of the train among the hail of bullets. "We're too much of a target out here!" Drawing his first grappling gun, he took aim towards the edge of the dirigible as it moved off. He could not help but watch as it sailed towards its target, only to fall short and land uselessly below him. Dropping it as instructed, he cursed. From up ahead he heard two clinks of metal as a pair of their group latched on to the closest dirigible.

Pulling them upwards, Ellie and the fox that had hit their targets activated the switch to reel themselves up to the fleeing craft. Climbing over the railing, they disappeared as

Joe reached for his second grappling gun.

The first dirigible moved away from the train taking Ellie and the fox with them. Cursing, Joe spun around searching for the other in the mess of white snow and wind whirling all around them. Both polar bears and the wolf remaining moved forward along the length of the train. Despite his goggles, he could barely make out the buildings alongside them. The wind whipped across his face, covering his fur with a thin layer of ice. In addition to making it difficult to see, he found it harder to find purchase on the roof of the train, grateful that for now it remained straight in its course.

From the right the second dirigible approached on an attack vector. Firing a hail of bullets at the train, the metal projectiles bounced off the hull in all directions. Joe cursed as his son slipped, slamming chest first into the roof of the train. Suddenly the train shifted direction as the track curved on its path through the city. Thinking quickly, he shot his arm out, grabbing Lucas by the paw as he slid towards the edge.

His arms protested, but he pulled his son on top of him, clutching his body while the second dirigible opened fire once again. The bullets clanked against the hull making dents in the metal as the enemy craft sped towards the train. Turning, the wolf raised his grappling gun to try to board it. Joe opened his mouth to shout a warning, but it was too late. The metal hook latched onto the dirigible with a final clack. Unprepared for the change in direction, the wolf was pulled towards the rear of the train, letting go in surprise only to fall off the snowmobile car into the city below.

With only the two of them left, Joe pushed himself onto all fours. Staring up at the sky he raised his grappling gun and searched for his target. Lost in the snow, he looked around him for either craft. Out of the corner of his eye, he sensed movement as the assault dirigible emerged from the heavy snowfall over the train. Bullets flew all around towards the two polar bears while they dove for what limited safety there was on the roof. Swearing, he dropped his second grapple gun. Desperately trying to grab it, he could only watch as it slipped out of sight. He used his legs to push himself to his feet paws, taking advantage of the momentary calm while the dirigible attempted to get in position for another attack run.

Lucas clung to the roof to avoid the shots. His son slowly got up on his knees waiting for his father's instructions.

The air was eerily calm as he listened for the sounds of the propellers over the howling of the storm. Based on their pattern to date, they liked to come at the train from different directions. Turning towards the most likely possibilities, the assault dirigible sailed back into view and moved to perform a strafing run. Joe looked to Lucas and nodded, running towards the side of the train and jumping off. Clinging onto the access ladder, he grabbed Lucas as he did the same, narrowly avoiding the dirigible's weapons fire.

Opening his eyes, Joe saw hanging on the rung in front of him his second grapple gun. Caught on the ladder, it had hung on when he had dropped it from the roof. Taking it in his paws, he climbed the side of the train with his son close behind.

Back on the roof, he hauled Lucas up and searched for the dirigibles. Somewhere out there were the two deadly enemy craft and they were running out of time. Spotting the first, he saw it fire a missile at the train. Missing by several feet the weapon struck a building and exploded, sending fire and debris into the air. Moving closer for another shot, Joe knew this would be his last opportunity.

Raising his grapple gun, he fired.

With a satisfying clang, it locked onto the railing on the outside of the observation deck. Flipping the switch, the mechanism engaged, pulling him up towards the dirigible. Seconds behind, Lucas ascended after his father, the two polar bears hanging on tight as the enemy craft moved away. Once he reached the top of the railing, he pulled himself on board and swung his leg over the edge.

No sooner had he boarded than a pair of canine soldiers appeared. Grappling with the first, he grabbed his rifle, swinging him against the wall. The impact generated a significant thud as the German shepherd yelped from the impact. Pushing back, the canine bent Joe backwards over the railing. From his position he could see the other soldier approach his son's hook. Unable to intervene, he growled as he slammed the dog against the wall once more before using his full force to toss the canine over the edge. His yelp disappeared into the white below, leaving only the swirl of wind and endless snow.

Lucas rolled onto the deck just in time to avoid the setter's attack. Rushing forward, he tackled him at the midsection. The pair fell to the deck in a tumble as the younger polar bear fought for superiority.

Raising his weapon, Joe fired a shot at a soldier who'd emerged from the forward door. Pulling back inside, he knew they couldn't stay there much longer. Joe grabbed the canine by the collar and growled. "Get your paws off my son!" He slammed him into the wall, causing him to crumple uselessly to the deck.

"Thanks, dad." Lucas caught his breath, reaching behind him for his rifle.

Picking up his radio, Joe pressed the transmit button. "This is Joe. My son and I have made it onto one of the dirigibles. No sign of Ellie or Harrow."

"*This is Captain Hall. Confirmed, Mister Kennedy. We'll*

rendezvous with you on the other side of the city. Good luck." With that the radio went silent. Replacing it on his belt, Joe motioned for his son to follow him.

"Stay close. Watch my back and be careful." He stopped at the mid deck doorway. "When I say so, you pull it open and follow me in." Taking position on the left side of the door, Lucas gripped the wheel. Joe signaled him with a gesture of his paw, and seconds later Lucas pulled the door open.

Peering around the corner Joe fired two shots at the soldiers inside. Lucas spun around and fired at another. It was clear they were not in a good position. They needed to get inside the dirigible, and quick. Joe drew in his breath for a moment and pushed ahead, roaring at full volume. Shocked at the sudden appearance of the angry polar bear, the soldiers guarding the door were slow to react when Joe reached their position. He disarmed the first with a swing of his wrench. A swift strike to the gut dropped the second to the floor, heaving as he struggled for breath. A backhand strike with the wrench sent the other to join his companion on the deck, with Lucas entering a second later.

His questioning look as he sealed the external door was one of mild amusement. "We good?"

"Never mess with the maintenance team," Joe replied, replacing his wrench back on his belt. The assault dirigibles were much larger than the expeditionary units he had been assigned to for salvage operations. Unlike the civilian models these units were twice as long with an additional deck, and carried heavy armament on the lower level where most of the weapon systems were mounted.

"We need to find the command deck," Lucas declared, pulling his goggles off his eyes. Joe did the same as he attempted to catch his breath.

Turning towards the wall, Joe stopped and noticed

what appeared to be an internal map of the dirigible. "All right, I think I can use this to find our way around." Examining the layout, he nodded. "We're in the center mid deck. There should be access points at both the front and the rear of the dirigible. If Governor Cole is on board, she'll be on the bridge on the top level."

"They're not going to make it easy for us to get there," Lucas pointed out.

"I know. That's why we have to split up. Together we're too findable on a ship this size. We each make our way to the bridge, we double our chances." He checked his rifle. "You go forward, I'll go aft."

"All right. See you on the bridge," he replied.

"Good luck," Joe said, before heading towards the rear in the central corridor. He crept forward listening for any sounds of enemy soldiers. Wherever they were, they were being careful. No doubt after their initial assault it had driven them to adopt a defensive posture which meant taking them by surprise from here on in was going to be much more difficult. They had taken out several of their soldiers already, to say nothing of what Ellie and Harrow were doing.

Advancing carefully, Joe's ears caught movement behind him. Whirling around, he opened fire. The bullets ricocheted off the wall, hitting nothing. He dashed towards the aft of the dirigible where he encountered another three Coldhaven guards. Not slowing down, he charged them as they attempted to raise their rifles. The first one got off a shot, but Joe met his chest with the full force of his boot, sending him flying down the stairs.

With a growl that summoned his most primal instincts he thrust his paw into the throat of another, sending the seal choking on the floor. The third wrestled with Joe for his weapon, though years on the maintenance team had given Joe a significant strength advantage. Overpowering the much smaller weasel, he pulled the weapon out of his grasp, using it to knock him unconscious.

Gunfire from the upper level drew his attention towards the command deck. No doubt Lucas had encountered more of the soldiers. Hurrying to go after his son, he ascended the steps only to encounter more of them waiting at the top. He stopped, his weapon gripped in his paws.

Standing before him, Valentine held his son's arm behind his back, his claws inches away from his throat. "Stand down." To emphasize his point, he drew a drop of blood from Lucas, staining his fur pink around the wound. Wincing, Lucas bared his teeth as the grizzly bear held him in position. "Now."

"Don't do it, dad!" Lucas implored. "You can't let them win. Emily's depending on you!"

"So are you, son," Joe said. "And you know your mother would never forgive me if I came back without you."

Valentine squeezed the young polar bear's arm again. "Drop the weapon. I won't ask again."

Joe held his rifle looking at the chocolate furred ursine and knowing he wasn't bluffing. He would kill Lucas without hesitation unless he complied. Left with no choice, he dropped his rifle to the deck.

Flanked on either side by two guards, they moved in quickly. A rhinoceros and elephant grabbed Joe's arms and held him in place, while a small squirrel stepped forward hesitantly with a muzzle. Turning back towards his commanding officer, the grizzly bear gestured him forward with a nod.

Joe growled, as if daring the squirrel to make a move. He looked up as the grizzly bear lifted Lucas a couple of inches off the ground, his son trying not to cry out but left with little choice but to yelp reflexively from the sudden movement. Getting the message, Joe did not resist as the squirrel secured the muzzle around his face. Looking up, he received a nod as the large animals that held him secured him with heavy duty pawcuffs.

Bound and no longer a threat, it was only then that Valentine lightened the grip he had on his son. "There, that's better."

"You better hope I don't get free," Joe said.

"I think you're hardly in a position to make threats, Mister Kennedy. Now you have one opportunity to save your friends on the train, and that's cooperation." He tossed Lucas to two of his men and stepped closer to Joe. "I'll give you credit. I never expected you to make it this far." He placed his muzzle close enough to feel his breath on his own as if challenging him to make a move. When he did not, Valentine smirked. "Unfortunately, this is as far as you go."

"Are you going to kill us?" Lucas asked.

"That depends on your father," Valentine replied. "Hold the boy here. His father and I have an appointment to keep."

"Dad!"

"I'll be fine, Lucas! You just stay here and do what they say! I'll be back," he said. Staring ahead at the double doors, he knew Governor Cole awaited him. For what reason, he could only venture to guess. Perhaps she simply wanted to rub his failure in his face. Or maybe she wanted to make him watch as she took out the train once and for all. Whatever it was, he knew he was running out of time.

Valentine took the radio off Joe's belt and nodded once, gesturing for the two large animals holding him to march him forward. He lowered his muzzle in apparent defeat, searching desperately for another card to play.

He considered carefully what his options were. Even if he were able to free himself he would need to act fast enough to keep them from killing Lucas, and then there was the matter of retrieving the data he needed to save Emily and getting off the ship. To say it was a daunting challenge was a significant understatement.

The doors opened before him as he was pulled into the assault dirigible's bridge. Brought forward a few steps, Joe silently observed the scene around him. Along the perimeter of the command center were four stations manned by people he knew well. Members of the city guard, who had long ago sworn to protect the city of Coldhaven and who now sought to seize control of the Garden and plunder its resources.

The room was filled with a sense of foreboding, the length of the balloon cloaking the command deck in relative shadow. It was clear from the very sight of it that this room was designed for combat and little else.

Part of Joe could not believe they had built this entire fleet without anyone having the slightest clue, but then Joe recalled the supply trains. Witnessed during their escape from the city, they had moved top grade materials across the city out of sight from anyone who would ask questions. They had planned this for a long time, and now they were close to achieving their goal. All they had to do was cross the line and the train would lose.

From where he stood he could see the tactical readouts displayed on monitors built into the ceiling. The second dirigible was close by, and in the center of the indicator was a small graphic of the train. Still making its way through the city, they were counting on the expedition team to deal with the Coldhaven forces.

So motionless he had not even noticed her at first, Governor Cole sat in the command chair at the center of the bridge. On the main level, she watched the entire scenario unfold like pieces on a chess board. Calm and calculating, the arctic vixen silently observed as the dirigibles hunted the train in the snow and wind. It was just a question of which one of them would outmaneuver the other.

Turning to face him, she looked into his eyes. "Now, Mister Kennedy. I think it's time we had a little talk."

CHAPTER NINETEEN
ENDGAME

"I have nothing to say to you," Joe said, refusing to meet her gaze. The bridge was silent other than the sounds of the sensors searching the storm for the train. Joe tested his restraints, his eyes hard with fury as he refused to give her the satisfaction of seeing him at a disadvantage.

"On the contrary, I think we have a great deal to discuss," she said, noticing his efforts to test the cuffs integrity. "Oh, don't bother. I think you'll find it quite impossible to break free from those. They were designed with some of the strongest predators on the planet in mind." She uncrossed her legs, leaning on one arm of the command chair with her left hand in the air. "I must commend you and your new friends. You've led me on quite the chase."

"Glad we could accommodate you," Joe said.

"However, your efforts end here. I have enough weapons on these two dirigibles to destroy the train and everyone on it." She let that comment hang in the air for a long moment. Once she was certain she had Joe's attention, she continued. "But I'd rather not do that, not if I don't have to."

Joe shifted his glance to look at her for the first time since he'd entered the bridge. No doubt she knew that there were people he cared about on the train to say nothing of the cars they'd left behind. He kept his expression neutral, in an effort to avoid giving away any information though he suspected such an effort was only delaying the inevitable. He finally asked the next obvious question. "What do you want?" When she didn't answer, he continued. "You have everything you need. What more could you be after?"

She simply smirked, as if the answer was obvious. "Surely you've already worked that out yourself."

"You're still after the train." He flattened his ears, the aggressive move met with cautioning looks from his minders. Noticing their positions, he closed his eyes and lifted them back up. "Why?"

Governor Cole looked at him as if he was an idiot child. "I want its technology. You've seen what it can do. Compared to what we've been able to piece together it's more advanced than anything we have. I may have the coordinates but if I hope to stand any chance against what's out there I need something that can handle it. I'd prefer to take the train intact but I will kill everyone on it if I have to." She rose to stand. "Assembling this fleet took months, and you destroyed three quarters of it in a matter of days."

"And I feel just awful about it too," Joe said, earning him a punch across the jaw from the rhinoceros.

"Shut your muzzle, traitor!" the guard shouted.

Holding up a paw, the rhino refrained from offering another punch. Governor Cole leaned forward. "I'm going to find the train. That much is inevitable. How long this takes depends on you."

"I'm not telling you anything," Joe said.

She held up a paw and gestured for them to bring Lucas into the room. "We'll see about that."

"Dad!" Lucas called out.

Joe growled at her. "You leave my son out of this!" The polar bear paused as she drew a handgun and aimed at Lucas. "Don't hurt him."

"Give me what I want and I won't have to." The arctic vixen turned to Joe. "I'll give you credit. I never expected you to be quite so much trouble. Freeing the hare, escaping the city, burying half my fleet in the valley…"

"Thank you," Joe said, not certain how to respond.

"But the only thing keeping the two of you alive right now is that train and its secrets. Tell me how to find it and I will let you go." Aiming her weapon at his son's head, she stared at him. "Refuse and this conversation will end much sooner."

Joe considered his options. Even if he were free it was unlikely he could overpower the soldiers before one of them killed him or Lucas. He was not a soldier, not like Ellie. Yet even if he cooperated there was no guarantee she would keep her word, or that he would even know how to give her what she wanted, to say nothing of the fact that he could not betray the train. With few options open to him, he knew he needed to buy himself time. "All right,"

"Dad, you can't!" Lucas shouted.

The elephant backhanded Lucas across the face hard enough to knock him to the ground. Joe did his best to retain his composure, wanting nothing more than to rip them all apart. "But if I'm going to help you, I want something in exchange."

Governor Cole holstered her weapon. "Name it."

"The data you stole from the train. It has my daughter's cure on it. Give it to me and you can have whatever you want." He stared hard at her, hoping it was enough to convince her he was genuine.

She considered his request, rubbing her chin before finally offering a conciliatory nod. "Done." Snapping her fingers, one of the crew handed Joe a small device. "That's a portable hard drive. Everything we took from the train is on there."

Joe held it in his paws for a moment, overcome by the sheer reality that he held his daughter's literal future in his palms. "Thank you."

"Now it's your turn, Mister Kennedy," Governor Cole said.

With a nod, Joe walked towards the front of the bridge. The navigator, a stoat, paused and looked at her. "Ma'am?"

A simple nod and the stoat stepped aside.

Joe looked at the controls. They were a great deal more complicated than the civilian model he had served aboard, and he had only actually flown it once. Of course, for what he was planning skill was not a factor, but it did little to ease his nerves. Looking back at Lucas, he gave his son a nod. Grabbing the controls with both paws, Joe pushed forward hard. The balloon pitched violently, sending everyone on the bridge flying.

The rhinoceros slid along the floor banging his head into the console at Joe's feet. With a swift kick, he rendered him unconscious and began to search for the keys to the restraints. Feeling his paws close around them, he looked up in time to see the elephant and Valentine recovering from his impromptu maneuver. Slamming the controls to the right they fell off balance again, sending the entire crew to one side of the assault dirigible's command center.

Undoing his pawcuffs he wasted no time picking up one of the dropped weapons from the deck. With one claw he undid the strap on his muzzle, allowing the offending item to fall to the ground. He fired once at the elephant, dropping him to the floor before pointing it at Governor Cole. "Stand aside."

Unconcerned, she stared back. "No." With a gesture of her paw the door opened and Valentine entered with more soldiers. "You can't win this."

Joe looked at her and then at Valentine. "Lucas, come over here." He waited for his son to stand behind him, keeping the handgun aimed at Cole's head. "I just want to keep my family safe."

"Then you should have taken my offer." She gestured behind her as Valentine stepped forward and raised his weapon. Behind him, the rest of his men did the same. Faced with overwhelming odds, Joe knew that he was at a distinct disadvantage. His grip on the weapon wavered.

From the corner of his eye, several of the crew turned their heads behind Joe. Unable to suppress his curiosity he tilted his head to see what had caught their attention. Filling the window was the second assault dirigible. Its weapons were aimed forward as it climbed slightly above their altitude.

The radio Valentine had confiscated from Joe clicked to life. *"Joe, this is Ellie. Duck."*

Not wasting a moment, he grabbed Lucas and pushed him to the ground, shielding him with his body. A fraction of an instant later, bullets rained into the bridge of the assault dirigible, piercing Valentine and anyone left standing with holes. Jerking from the weapons fire the grizzly bear roared and grunted, collapsing to the deck in a pool of blood. The weapons fire continued for what seemed like forever until finally, it ceased. Joe kept his eyes shut until he was certain it was safe, then at last opened them.

What he beheld was a scene of violence and destruction. Everyone lay dead at their stations, the soldiers littering the deck with their corpses. The weapons fire that had peppered the bridge had effectively laid waste to the command center with holes in several of the controls rendering them useless. The fact that the balloon had somehow not been punctured stood out to Joe as somewhat of a minor miracle, but one he was certain would not last.

"*Sorry about the minimal warning, but it was the best I could do under the circumstances. You all right?*" Ellie asked.

Pressing the transmit button on the radio, Joe let out a sigh of relief. "You have no idea how good it is to hear your voice."

"*I've gained control of the second dirigible for the time being, but I wouldn't recommend we stick around much longer,*" she said.

Joe nodded, and turned towards the only living thing on the bridge besides he and his son. "Stand by." Aiming his handgun at Governor Cole once again, he looked into her eyes. "Give me one good reason I shouldn't kill you."

"I can't do that. You know that it's either us or them. We can't survive without the Garden's resources and I won't stop hunting you. It may take me time to rebuild my fleet but I will find you, and when I do I will make you pay for everything you've cost me." The white furred vixen bared her teeth, clearly unafraid.

Joe nodded. "Unfortunate." He turned the weapon on the navigation console and fired several shots into the circuitry.

Governor Cole stood up, her muzzle agape in shock. "What have you done??"

"I've destroyed the guidance system. Without it you

won't know which way you're pointed, never mind how to get back to Coldhaven."

In defiance, she bared her teeth at him. "You think this is enough to stop me? I'll get back to the city and when I do it's only a matter of time before the Garden is under my control."

"I don't think so." Joe lowered the weapon. "I think you'll be lucky to find shelter before you freeze to death out here. With that window broken this dirigible is effectively useless, and I doubt the other one will be much good either once my friend over there is done with it. If the storms don't get you, I'm sure the lack of heat will." He stood over her with his arms folded. "I offer you one chance to surrender. If you and your people stand down, we'll take you aboard the train and back to the Garden where we will hold you indefinitely until such time as we figure out what to do with you."

"And if we don't?" she asked.

"It's your choice, but we aren't coming back once we leave here, and you don't have enough time to make it back to the city without our help." He extended a paw. "Don't be a fool."

The arctic vixen looked around at her dead crew, the cold wind blowing into the bridge. The ship was effectively crippled, with no personnel to direct it and no way to determine their position. The snow began to accumulate on the consoles as the precipitation forced its way inside, building slowly towards its inevitable takeover of what would become just another frozen relic of the wastes.

"I'd rather die," she said.

"As you wish," Joe said. "Lucas, let's go." Activating his radio, Joe spoke into it. "Ellie, time to get out of here. Rendezvous on the ground and signal for pickup."

"*Will do. See you down there.*"

Governor Cole turned towards him. "You've murdered us all. You know that, don't you?"

"No," Joe replied. "You did that. I suppose I should kill you, but I don't murder unarmed people."

"What about everyone you left behind?" she asked, referring to the city.

Joe hesitated a moment. "They'll survive. Maybe what they needed is a change in leadership. I can't save them, not if they aren't willing to save themselves." He stopped at the doorway. "Maybe they'll become something different without you." He turned and left, leaving the vixen behind.

Twenty minutes later, the two dirigibles sat side by side just above the ground, their crews locked in the rear upper deck of both ships. Ellie and the fox stood not far from the snowmobiles, the train waiting a short distance away. The snowshoe hare extended her arms and embraced Joe, a warm smile on her face. "Glad to see you made it."

"I couldn't miss this, not after all we've been through to get here," he said.

Ellie looked at the pair of dirigibles. "Are you sure we should let them go?" she asked.

"No," Joe admitted. "But we have the coordinates and Emily's cure. I don't see any reason to go any further. The information has been purged from their computers. If they do manage to get back to the city, they'll have to start from scratch."

Ellie nodded. "Fair enough." She looked at the storm that continued to drop snow on top of them all. "How about we make our way back someplace warm, shall we?" she asked. "I know someone who's very eager to see you."

Joe nodded, eager to be reunited with Emily and Laura and leave all this behind.

Two hours later, the train was traveling back in the opposite direction with no indication of pursuit. It would be some time before they rendezvoused with the rest of the cars, as without the urgency of their departure it was decided that the engine could stand to get a little time to take it easy, a fact for which Richard was extremely appreciative. Joe sat in the situation car watching the train move across the virtual representation of the snowy landscape, eager to be reunited with his little girl.

Entering through the rear door, Doctor Thurgood placed a paw on his shoulder. The ebony wolfess offered a supportive smile, taking a seat beside him at one of the pull out stools. "I just thought you should know that everything is going smoothly for a change and we should have your daughter's cure ready by the time we reach the maintenance facility."

"Thank you," he said. "Truly."

"I didn't do much," she said. "Most of the hard work was already done. I just mixed the ingredients. You're the one who got her this far."

Joe smiled back. "Nevertheless, I owe you a great debt." He looked down at his paws. "All her life I wanted nothing more than to keep her safe and happy, but no matter what I tried I couldn't stop the thing that was killing her, a little bit at a time. The best I could do was delay the inevitable." He lowered his muzzle. "And then I met you all, and everything changed."

Doctor Thurgood placed her paw on his. "Well, for what it's worth I think you gave as much as you got. Life out here is complicated, and if we're ever going to find the answers we're looking for, we're going to need people like you." She removed her paw and stood, placing them in her pockets. "I'm told the captain has offered you a permanent position on board the train."

"He did," he confirmed, the offer having been validated upon his return to the train. Ellie had expressed her certainty of the value Joe would add to the team and insisted he consider it. Though Joe had never thought he would spend his life wandering the wastes in search of answers, he now had more to think about than simply surviving tomorrow. There was no longer a need to spend all of his time fearing for his daughter or wondering what part of the city would break down next. For the first time in his life, he had the opportunity to choose.

"And?" she asked.

"I haven't decided yet." He still wore the train's uniform from the mission. He looked down at it and shrugged.

"Well, I for one hope you choose to come with us. I've gotten used to having you around," she said.

Joe chuckled. "Thanks, doc."

"Anytime." She gestured behind her at the rear door. "I'll be in the medical car if you need me."

Joe looked over his shoulder and then became aware of the reason for the doctor's strategic retreat. Both Ellie and Captain Hall stood just inside the doorway. Entering the room the pair took up positions on either side of the situation table.

"I hope we're not interrupting anything," the zebra said.

"No," Joe replied. "Captain. Ellie." He acknowledged each of them with a respectful nod.

"I thought you'd like to know that we'll be rendezvousing with the rest of the cars in a little over a day and a half." He exhaled calmly. "It shouldn't take us long to return the train to its standard configuration before we set course for the Garden."

Joe stared down at the surface of the table, showing the train, Coldhaven, and the rest of their companions at the opposite end of the display. "And then what?" he asked no one in particular.

"Well, I suppose that depends on you," Ellie said. "Things aren't like they are in Coldhaven, Joe. No one will make you do anything you don't want to. If you like, you can build a home with your family in the Garden and never step out onto the ice again. But I do hope you'll consider my offer to join my team and see what else is out there." She looked up at the image of the USS Abraham Lincoln, the navy ship left trapped in a frozen sea, and the place where the two of them had first met. "There are a lot more places like that out there, with a lot more secrets to reveal. Maybe even the way to make the world like it used to be." She paused, reflecting perhaps on her own journey as they all considered that idea.

Joe struggled to comprehend a world not frozen in snow and ice. One where the sun shined and there wasn't a constant battle against the chill. Rumors had always persisted that the world had once been a paradise, but such ideas were always so far fetched in the face of a perpetual snowfall. Yet had it not been for this very idea Joe had taken his family away from the only home they had ever known in the hopes that they might find a place like this together?

The Garden was the closest thing to the world that was that remained on the surface of the planet. A small habitable zone isolated from any other untouched by the raging storms that constantly crossed the rest of the icy wastes. It was here that the train called home. And it was from this place that the captain and his crew launched their constant search for answers.

The idea was compelling, traveling the world with Ellie in search of the truth. With the ability to resupply at the Garden the train's range was practically limitless. Added to that the fact that the hard drive Ellie had retrieved from the Abraham Lincoln opened up paths they had never explored before and it was hard to pass up the chance to see where it led.

Yet one way or another he could not make any decisions without speaking to his family first. "I'd like to," he began.

Ellie, sensing where he was going, held up a paw. "The offer's open for as long as you want. You don't have to decide anything now. We'll get you back to your little girl and take you back to the Garden and when you're ready, you can give me your answer. Fair enough?"

Joe nodded. "Agreed." He extended his paw and shook hers in gratitude.

A little under two days later, the train returned to the maintenance facility. Waiting on the platform were the rest of the train's crew, including Laura and Emily. Joe and Lucas burst out of the train to embrace them, his arms wrapping around them as tightly as he could.

"Daddy, you're squishing me!" Emily protested.

The fur on his cheeks damp with tears of joy, Joe squeezed them one more time. "I missed you."

Laura kissed him, placing both paws on the sides of his face. "Welcome back." Turning to embrace her son, she smiled. "I'm glad you're both all right."

"Thanks to dad," he said.

"What happened?" Laura asked.

Joe hesitated. "We'll save that for another time."

"You should've seen him, mom. Dad was incredible." Lucas beamed proudly at his father.

Laura gave him a half smile. "I don't doubt it."

Joe smiled and picked up Emily in his arms. "It's time to go see Doctor Thurgood, sweetheart." He licked her face. "Time for you to be all better."

"Can Andre come?" she asked.

Laughing, he nodded. "Yes, Andre can come. Now

let's get you your medicine." Carrying her into the medical car, he was joined by his entire family as they walked through the waiting area into the treatment room.

Doctor Thurgood stood at the counter with her attention focused on the syringe as she measured out the dosage. "All right. It's ready."

Joe held her close as the wolf doctor rolled up her sleeve and gently injected the contents into her arm. "That's it?" he asked.

"That's it," she replied. "In a few days you should start to feel stronger, stronger than you've ever felt before." She smiled. "You've got a future now. I can't wait to see what you do with it."

Joe turned to the ebony furred lupine physician. "I'm grateful, doc. I can't thank you enough for giving my daughter a chance to live."

"Like I told you earlier, I just mixed the ingredients. You three are the ones that saved her." She squeezed his shoulder. "I'll leave you alone for a few moments." Walking out the door, soon the Kennedy family was by themselves.

Laura let out a deep breath. "I wonder what it'll be like up there in the Garden. Do you think it'll be like the stories?"

"No," Joe said. "I think it'll be better."

Emily wrapped her arms around her doll. "I want to see a tree."

"I'm sure you will, baby." He held her close, and then set her down on the counter.

"So what's going to happen to us?" Laura asked. "I mean, now that we're no longer being pursued?"

Joe paused for a moment and met his wife's glance. "For right now, the train is going to return to the Garden for some maintenance and much needed repairs. After that, who knows?" He paused. "We've been offered a place there. Captain Hall will need to clear it with their leaders of course, but he assures me it's just a formality. After all we've done we've earned a spot among them. Beyond that, I don't know. But as long as we're together, that's all that matters."

He knew that eventually he would need to discuss Ellie and Captain Hall's offer with her, but for the moment all he wanted was to enjoy this moment of peace with his family. It was hard earned and he had sacrificed a lot to get this far, but though he could not explain it, a certain calm came over him. At last he had found a way to keep his family together and safe. Whatever tomorrow held, it was enough for now.

His daughter would survive and the condition that had threatened her life was now a mere memory. Thanks to the medicine the doctor had found Emily would grow up strong and healthy, no longer under the perpetual threat of dying from the old world illness whose cure had been so far out of reach. She would live, which was the only thing Joe had ever wanted for her.

Lucas would no longer be condemned to a death sentence working on the burn team. He had proven himself to be a strong and capable young bear, something Joe had always known. Yet now that they were no longer living in Coldhaven, he would have the chance to choose his own destiny, as they all would.

Though he did not know whether he would continue with the train or not, at least for a while he would enjoy learning about his new home with his wife at his side. Before meeting Ellie, their future was never in question. Now, the possibilities were endless.

For the next hour or so, the train slowly returned to its previous configuration. It would soon begin the long journey back to the Garden where it was likely to spend at least the next couple of months receiving a full overhaul of its primary systems. Once complete, it would resume its perpetual mission to explore the distant ice for salvage and answers.

A part of Joe could not deny his interest in going with them. Indeed, his encounter with Ellie and the train had awakened something within him. Perhaps it was simple curiosity, or maybe he felt he owed it to Mike to make his sacrifice worth it. His friend had given his life so that they could escape the city, and now Joe had the opportunity to do so much more.

The things he had seen during the train's journey had fueled his desire to know what else was out there. No doubt Captain Hall and his crew had seen countless wonders searching for their answers to what had caused the world to freeze. A part of him yearned to be there when they found out.

Whatever his decision, he knew he would not have an answer anytime soon. The journey back to the Garden would take several weeks at half speed, and longer still to get settled in their new home.

Looking down at his young daughter, she yawned, attempting to suppress the exhaustion she obviously felt.

"Someone's sleepy," he said, leaning down towards her.

"I'm not tired," she protested, convincing no one.

Joe picked her up and smiled. "Let's get you to bed. You need your rest, sweetheart."

"Promise me you'll wake me up when we get there?" she asked.

Licking her cheek, he nodded. "I promise, you won't miss a single moment." In less than a minute, she had fallen fast asleep. Joe carried her gently to their cabin, setting her down in her bed. Pulling the covers over her, he watched her chest rise and fall as she dreamed of the world that awaited them. "Sweet dreams, kiddo."

Emerging from the sleeping area, Joe paused as he looked out the window to the snowy landscape beyond. Feeling his wife's arms around him, he rested his muzzle on her head, enjoying her scent against his own. "That feels so good."

"Is she asleep?" Laura asked.

"She is," Joe confirmed. He kissed her on the muzzle and smiled. "Some adventure, huh?"

"That's a bit of an understatement," Laura replied, pressing against him. "I'm just glad we're headed out of the cold."

Joe squeezed her close, their noses within an inch of each other. "I love you."

"I love you too," she answered.

"I'd give you two some privacy, but..." Lucas shrugged.

Joe was about to give his son a well deserved comment when the intercom activated, sparing him.

"Attention all personnel. Systems check in five minutes. Prepare for departure once final preparations are complete. All command crew to the engine," Captain Hall declared.

Joe smiled at his wife. "Duty calls."

Releasing him from her embrace, she gestured towards the doorway. Joe touched his paw to his chest, giving her a gentle bow before making his way forward to the command cars. The security officers at the door gave him a nod as he entered, arriving at the bridge where the others waited.

Captain Hall stood in the center, his hands behind his back. Noticing Joe's arrival, he nodded once at the polar bear. "Take your station, Mister Kennedy."

"Yes, sir," he replied, seating himself on the left

console.   To his right, Ellie flashed him a look of acknowledgment as the pair conducted their respective systems checks before their departure.

Returned to its original configuration, the train once again stood twenty eight cars long. Each one responded to his systems check with all of its systems showing in the green. The engine was not at full capacity, but it would get them home in one piece.

Home.

Joe smiled to himself at the choice of words. He had never thought of Coldhaven as home despite having lived there since he was born. It was not a place where you wanted to be, it was simply the only available option. Granted, it had kept him and his family alive for a long time, but home was not about simple survival. Home was about living, and finding a place where you could be happy.

Whether the Garden was that place remained to be seen, but it had more to offer than he had ever thought possible, to say nothing of giving his daughter a chance at a full life. And though he had not yet decided what the future held for him, he had begun to approach it for the first time with optimism, eager to see what tomorrow would bring.

For now, the train would begin its slow journey back to the Garden. Their course already determined by Noah, Joe would monitor the train's overall status while they traveled. Their course would take them along the coast for several days before turning inland towards their eventual destination.

Reviewing the train's condition, Captain Hall gave one last look around the engine before he turned his focus towards the forward view port. Stepping to the panel behind Noah, he pressed the intercom. "Richard, what's our status?"

"Green across the board. Engine is online and all

systems operational. We're ready when you are," the fennec's voice stated.

"Acknowledged." The zebra turned towards the rest of the crew. "I think we're all more than ready for this train to leave the station."

Richard chuckled. "She'll get us there, sir."

"I've no doubt." Releasing the button, he turned to Ellie. "Lieutenant Harper, report."

"Sensors are clear, no hostiles anywhere within range. Communications are fully functional." She paused a moment. "All crew accounted for and external hatches are sealed."

Captain Hall then turned to Joe. "Mister Kennedy?"

Joe reviewed his readouts and gave a confident nod to the captain. "We're ready to go."

Noah spoke over his shoulder with a slight smile. "Course prepared. We can depart on your order."

Stepping forward, his hooves making a gentle clack on the deck, he rested his arm on the wall. "Then by all means, Mister Briggs, take us home."

CHAPTER TWENTY
HOME

SIX WEEKS LATER

Awakening to the smell of eggs and bacon, Joe sat up with his eyes closed and allowed the aroma to drift into his nose. Sliding his legs over the edge of the bed, his foot paws touched the soft carpet on the floor of their home. Another warm and welcoming morning only served to emphasize why they called this place the Garden. After taking a few more moments to enjoy the sunrise, Joe walked down the hall towards the source of the delicious odors.

Already present was his wife and daughter, both of whom were dressed and in the middle of their morning routine. Noticing his arrival, his wife presented him with a cup of coffee. "There you are. I was starting to think you might hibernate all morning," she said.

Joe yawned before taking a sip of the coffee. "We had a long night."

"You've been having a lot of those, lately," she said.

"Repairing and calibrating the train's systems has been a much bigger job than we thought. Richard says it might be another three months before the train leaves the Garden again," he replied.

"Well, don't push yourself too hard," she advised. "There's plenty of time to complete the repairs. You know you don't have to work yourself until your claws dull any more."

"Yeah, yeah," he said, waving her away. "Why didn't you wake me up?"

Laura shrugged. "I know you've been working a lot lately. And anyway you looked like you needed the rest."

Joe conceded the point with a nod. "I'm just glad I didn't miss my little girl before she left for school."

"Who do you think you're married to?" she asked. "I'd never let that happen." Smiling, she presented a plate before both of them before returning to the counter to fix one for herself. "Now eat up. You both need the energy."

Seated at the table, he slid next to his daughter who smiled brightly at his presence. Gone were any signs of the illness that had kept her so weak for so long. Full of energy and eager for the new day, Emily beamed at her father with a wide grin. No doubt she was waiting for him to ask a question. He could tell that she wanted to talk about all the things she had seen and heard, but he pretended not to notice taking a long sip of his coffee as he held it in his paws.

Of course he was as eager to hear it as she was to tell

the tale, but he had to make her squirm just a little. "So what are you going to learn at school today?" he asked.

At last given an opening, the response arrived like water out of a floodgate. "Teacher says we're going to learn all about plants and the important role they play in keeping the Garden such a wonderful place. She says they produce oxygen and give us food and things to build with and everything!" Emily beamed proudly. "In fact, the word garden comes from the old world. She says it was a place where people used to grow things and it was the reason they named it that way." The young ursine held up her school book. "Plants can do all sorts of things like make your burns better and smell pretty and there even used to be ones that would eat bugs!"

"You don't say?" he replied, exaggerating his interest with a wide expression and a big smile. "Well, make sure you pay attention and listen to your teacher. She's got a lot of things to tell you."

"She's really smart," Emily agreed. "Next week Mrs. Kelly says we're going to learn about minerals."

"I look forward to it," Joe said.

"Papa, you're not going to be in class!" she replied.

Joe grinned. "I expect my little girl to tell me all about it!" He nuzzled her nose before taking another bite of his breakfast.

"After that she says she's going to teach us all about the train and its mission." Emily beamed. "I get to do a presentation since most of the kids have never been on it." She turned to face her father. "Mrs. Kelly says she might even ask some of the crew to come speak since it's such an important part of the Garden." She looked down at her plate, scooping a bite of egg into her muzzle.

Already suspecting he knew where this was going, Joe pretended not to have the slightest idea. "Well, good luck with that, sweetheart. I'm sure it'll be great. I bet the kids will love hearing all about it."

Emily looked at her father through the corner of her eyes. "You know, it'd be even better if you came to talk to my class."

"I don't know, I'm really busy these days," he said, gently teasing.

Laura elbowed him in the arm hard enough to make him wince. "Stop torturing her, already," she said, already knowing his answer.

Rubbing his sore muscle he nodded and held up his paws in surrender. "All right, all right! I'll be there."

"YAY!" she shouted. "Thank you so much, daddy."

"Anything for you," he said. Since coming to live in the Garden, Joe had seen how much the train inspired and united her people. Boldly exploring the frozen wasteland, their mission to uncover the cause of the Freeze had given them a purpose beyond mere survival. Driven by their search for the truth they had crossed the world for over four decades seeking their answers. And yet no matter how long it took, they kept trying. It was a quality Joe admired.

After spending all this time among them, he had come to realize that their very nature was one of selflessness. Coldhaven had been driven only by self interest. They had been willing to do whatever was necessary to prolong their own existence. But the people here sought not to benefit only their own, but all of the world's population with their efforts.

Whether or not he believed they would ever find the origin of the disaster, Joe could not argue the fact that the people here stood the best chance at being able to make use of the information. Perhaps it was simply wishful thinking, but hope was what had kept his family alive through their journey and hope was the very reason Emily was here now.

Although he could not say if he shared their faith in their mission, he could not deny his curiosity.

While he had still yet to make a decision on whether he would remain with the train, he had nevertheless enjoyed the opportunity to learn more about its systems. The time he had spent working on it during its long repair had gifted him with an appreciation of the advanced technology that had gone into its construction. Whatever its original purpose, it was clear that whoever had designed it had possessed a singular talent for engineering. And whether they knew it or not, its legacy stood to be much more than anyone had ever anticipated. It certainly had proven its value to Joe.

Smiling at his daughter, he gestured at the clock. "It's almost time for school. You'd better finish getting ready."

His own breakfast now eaten, his plate was quickly whisked away by Laura as his daughter rose from her chair. "I'll go get my books."

Joe watched her go and then turned to his wife. "It's so wonderful to see her happy and healthy."

Touching his arm, she smiled. "She was always happy. You saw to that." Conceding his point with a gentle squeeze, she let out a pleased sigh. "But I can't disagree. We spent so long praying she would see another tomorrow, and thanks to this place, she'll see a lot of them."

Joe held her tight. "That she will. I was thinking I'd take her to school today on my way to the train."

"You just want to spend more time with her," Laura smirked. "I know you too well, Joe Kennedy."

"That you do," he replied, thankful for her constant love and support.

A moment later, Emily returned from her room, backpack over her shoulders. "I'm ready!"

Joe gestured towards the front door. "Shall we?" he

asked.

Emily brightened and took his paw. "See you later, mom," she said.

"You keep your dad out of trouble," Laura said.

"Hey!" Joe protested. Emily giggled in response. "Traitor."

She covered her muzzle, though it was clear she was smiling. Pleased to see it, Joe motioned for them to continue.

Their home was towards the edge of what had proven to be a good sized population center, with much of the outer areas turned over to farmland to support the Garden and its people. A small residence just large enough for a family of four, it had been given to them as a reward for all Joe had done for Ellie and the train. It was not much, according to the person who had assigned it to them, but to Joe it was unbelievably generous.

In all his days in Coldhaven dreaming of what lay beyond he had never once considered such a wonderful home and a place for his family to live. For the first time beneath his paws there was not snow and ice, but grass and dirt. There were real roads, and people walked around without heavy coats to repel the endless wind. In a place they called the Garden, he had found paradise.

Emily smiled. "Daddy, can I ask you a question?"

"Of course, sweetheart. Always." He looked down into her eyes.

"Are you going to go with the train when it leaves?" she asked.

Joe tilted his head. "Who told you it was leaving?"

"A train is only a train if it has somewhere to go," she said. "Some of the kids said that when the engine is fixed, it's going on another mission."

Joe paused. He had expected to have this conversation with Laura, not with Emily. She had always been a smart child, and he supposed it was obvious to those closest to him that he would be considered. "Ellie has asked me, yes," he said, seeing no point in keeping it from her. "As for whether or not I'm going to go, I haven't decided yet," he admitted.

Emily looked down at her feet paws. "I think you should."

Surprised, Joe tilted his head. "You're the last person I expected to say that." He paused. "Don't you want me to stay?"

She shrugged. "Well, sure I do. But what they're doing is important. And they'd be a lot safer with you out there watching their back."

"I don't know about that," Joe said. "I've had some training, but I'm nowhere near as good as Ellie."

The younger polar bear stopped and looked up at him. "You kept us alive out there. Doctor Thurgood told me about how much you risked getting the train out of danger and keeping us safe. If they're going back out, they could use that kind of thinking."

"I'm not sure if they could survive more of that kind of thinking," Joe said, recalling the avalanche.

Emily looked at all the people passing by. Most of them waved politely to Joe and his daughter before continuing to go about their business. A few offered brief greetings but continued to give them space as they walked. "I want you to stay," she said. "But they'd be safer with you than without you."

"I'll think about it," he said, more torn than ever about which to choose. In truth, he knew that a part of him yearned to explore with the train and her crew. Whether they found the cause of the Freeze or not, there was so much out there just waiting to be discovered. Yet civilians were not allowed on the train, except in special circumstances, and certainly not families.

Joe understood why. It was dangerous out there. While Ellie and Captain Hall had insisted their missions were not usually quite as exciting as the one they had just concluded, one could not argue that there was a certain element of risk in searching the vast frozen landscape for salvage and answers. The environment of course offered its own dangers with the perpetual cold a constant reminder of the fragility of life. Snow, ice, and dangerously low temperatures made the likelihood of freezing to death a significant possibility, to say nothing of what else awaited them out there.

Though the world's population had decreased significantly after the disaster, there was more out there than just Coldhaven and the train. Indeed, the fiction that their city was the only survivable location in the world had been a significant understatement, with Ellie warning him of multiple threats to the train during previous voyages. Though some had proven more dangerous than others, there had never been anything capable of outrunning the train, so they continued to explore in search of their answers.

The train was most vulnerable any time they stopped, so such instances were always handled carefully, with the Expedition Team ready to go and prepared to rendezvous with the train elsewhere, should it be necessary. From what Ellie had told him, the train had been looking for someone to fill the gap in Ellie's team for some time, and he would be more than welcome.

A part of him was tempted to accept for the simple curiosity. Another wished to do whatever he could to pay them back for all their help. Yet signing up with the train would mean leaving his family behind, and while he knew they would be safe without him, he had never been apart from them in his entire life, and he was not certain he was ready for it.

His thoughts were interrupted by their arrival at Emily's school, where her teacher waited with a gentle wave. Joe returned it with a sheepish smile and then nodded. "Good morning," he said.

"Good morning, Mister Kennedy," she replied. "I see you're dropping off my favorite student today."

"I had to go to the train so I thought I'd walk her down," he said. "You take good care of her for me, all right?"

Mrs. Kelly nodded, the Border collie wagging her tail eagerly. "Oh, it'll be my pleasure. Emily is one of the sweetest kids in the entire school. And she's so smart to boot. I bet one of these days she's going to make some big waves."

Joe beamed a bit with parental pride, still overwhelmed with how far she had come in such a short time. "I'll pick you up when school's over, okay, honey?"

"Okay daddy!" She waved behind him as she saw some of her friends and rushed to greet them.

Mrs. Kelly smiled warmly. "She really is such a bright young girl. The other children are so excited to hear all about her adventures on the train and the city she came from. We don't often get new residents here, so it's a bit of an event when it happens."

"You don't say?" Joe asked.

She nodded. "You and your family are the biggest bit of news we've had in a while. Not to mention the hard drive."

"Isn't that supposed to be classified or something?" Joe asked.

The canine teacher shrugged. "Hard to keep a secret around here for long. I don't know what's on it, but most people know it's got some information that has the train crew very interested. I've heard rumors they're looking for a fairly long range excursion."

Joe shrugged. "No idea. But that does remind me. Emily said you're asking some of the train's crew to come speak to the kids."

"I did. It seemed like a good idea, give them a chance to see what you all do and how it matters." She perked up her ears. "Oh, that's the bell. I've got to get going."

Joe nodded. "Well, I promised Emily I'd come and speak so you can count on me."

"That's great news. I'll see you then," she said, before disappearing inside the building.

His parental duties discharged, he turned back towards the road and continued his journey towards his ultimate destination. The train, when not out in the frozen expanse that surrounded the small temperate area that was the Garden, was housed in a former train station that was converted for military use and operated by the Garden and its defense force. Officially at the disposal of the Garden leadership, in general it was under the discretion of the defense force with regards to its actual missions.

Still in its previous configuration, the train sat idle beside the platform, visible from the front of the building. Polished and sleek, she bore none of the marks of her latest adventure, the majority of her external damage having been repaired in the weeks since their return. The inside however, was another matter.

As promised, the captain had authorized a complete overhaul and repair of the entire length of the train. Though Richard and his team had been efficient in their work a number of longstanding issues had finally come to their attention, and the fennec intended to ensure the train was ship shape before she left port for what stood to be another long mission.

Cables lay everywhere as technicians and Garden staff maintained the various systems, with Richard standing over one of his people as they worked. Beside the fennec engineer, Captain Hall frowned. "I thought you said you had this system repaired."

"I did, in car five and six, but we've been having problems with the water pressure in seven and eight," he said.

Captain Hall looked at his data slate. "It seems like it's in acceptable levels."

"Not to me," Richard said, his large ears perking upwards. "This overhaul has been a long time coming, captain, and if we're going to go out there for another six months I want to make damn sure we've got everything set to go."

The zebra sighed in exasperation. "How long is it going to take to track down the problem?"

Richard sighed. "I have no idea, captain. I'm working on it along with the forty seven other problems I'm trying to fix today. You want to help, try and see if you can't get the display in the situation car working again."

"I thought this thing was supposed to be state of the art," Captain Hall griped.

The fennec stopped what he was doing and looked at him. "It was, forty six years ago. Now quit complaining and let me do my job."

Turning to the polar bear, the striped equine gestured to Joe. "Can I help you, Mister Kennedy?"

Joe looked at Richard and then back at the captain. "Having problems?"

"Only a million. It's good you're here. We could use your help repairing the primary systems," Richard said.

Joe nodded. "Whatever you need. Have you seen Ellie and my son?" he asked, scanning the car for them.

Richard shrugged. "Check the command cars. That's usually where she is these days."

The polar bear nodded his thanks and gave the captain a nod of acknowledgement as he made his way forward to the command cars. Entering the fourth car he found his son standing beside Ellie over the main display, which at the moment still appeared to be in diagnostic mode.

Ellie looked up at his arrival with a warm smile. "Joe. Good to see you. We could use the help."

"So it appears," he replied. "Lucas."

His son looked up from his work. "Ever since we brought the main computer back online we've been having trouble getting the navigation system to interface with the rest of the software."

"I assume you've already run a diagnostic?" he asked.

"Six times," Ellie said. "It keeps saying everything's fine."

Joe leaned over the display and pulled open one of the access panels. Flipping a switch, he was rewarded with the sound of the system powering up. "There."

"What did you do?" Lucas asked.

"The system just needed to be reinitialized. The shutdown must've reset the system to a startup mode," he said, rising to stand.

Ellie nodded her approval. "There we go." She looked down at the screen. "That was driving me nuts."

"Glad to be of service," Joe replied. "How are the repairs coming along?"

Lucas looked at his dad with a shrug. "Most of the systemsare on schedule but the train took a lot of punishment during its last tour. We keep finding issues that we couldn't detect until we started digging into her guts."

Joe nodded. The train was a remarkable piece of machinery, developed with some of the finest technology he had ever seen. Though it was clear she was designed for long term operation, even the finest machine would have been hard pressed to meet the demands needed of her out on the frozen wasteland. Yet she managed to pull through despite all the challenges and come out of it intact. Regardless of all the wonders he had seen the train pull off during their journey he would not be surprised if she had much more left to show them.

"Better to find them here than out there," Joe replied.

"Don't worry, dad, we'll get her ready," Lucas replied. "You can count on it.

Ellie nodded. "That we will. She's a tough old girl. There isn't anything the wastes can throw at her that she can't handle."

Joe smiled and then turned to his son. "Lucas, isn't it about time you got to class?"

"But I learn so much more here," he protested.

Joe held up a paw to forestall any further arguments. "It's important you learn everything you can from these people. Back in Coldhaven they were going to put you to work in the Candle, and I never wanted that for you. Here you can be whatever you want to be," Joe said.

"I want to stay here and help," Lucas argued.

Joe nodded. "I know. But you need to learn all the things they couldn't teach you in Coldhaven so that when you're ready you can face it head on." He patted him on the back. "You can help Ellie some more after class. Now get going."

"Fine," Lucas protested. "See you later, okay?"

Ellie waved in response. "I'll be here." Exchanging a brief smile with Lucas as he left, she looked at Joe with a grin. "He's a good kid. Smart. He'll make a great member of the crew some day," Ellie remarked.

"I've no doubt," he agreed. "What's our status?"

The snowshoe hare made a face before gesturing towards the master systems display on the wall. "Repairs are proceeding slower than expected but it's been a few years since the train has had a full overhaul so there are bound to be some delays, but the biggest problem at the moment appears to be the power regulation systems. Ever since we broke apart the train the systems have been popping in and out. Now we think it has something to do with the couplings connecting the cars but we're having trouble narrowing down the fault."

Joe nodded, knowing that the train was designed to be almost limitlessly expandable, capable of handling many more cars than it currently carried. Built to be interchangeable, with each of them able to be reconfigured in any order, it was notable due to its revolutionary power source which was believed to be able to operate for decades without refueling. No doubt that was why it had been chosen for its original purpose, whatever that may have been. Perhaps it had been meant for greater things than its current function, but if the train succeeded in its mission, what higher calling could there be?

In any event, it was clear that until the train was fully repaired, she would not be traveling anywhere. Examining the diagnostic readout, he gently rubbed his muzzle in thought.

"Well, the engine appears to be fine, so whatever the problem is it has to be something a little less obvious." Joe leaned back slightly as he considered the problem. "Does Richard have any ideas?"

"A few, but he's too busy with the systems integration tests. Captain Hall said to do whatever we can, but there's something else I want to show you first," Ellie told him.

Intrigued, Joe turned back towards the central display. "What've you got?" he asked.

"Remember the hard drive I retrieved from the Abraham Lincoln?" Ellie prompted, leaning over the display.

"Of course," Joe confirmed.

"Well, since we returned to the Garden I've been examining the contents in more detail and you're not going to believe this." Ellie's ears perked up as she entered several commands into the computer. The display changed to show the current network of the train's known routes. Crisscrossing the world, it showed every place the train had ever been.

Fascinated, Joe leaned inward to study the information. "That's incredible," he said.

Ellie nodded. "Forty years of missions. This is every place we've searched and every track the train has ever traveled."

Taking it in, Joe was awed by the vastness of the train's network. Before meeting Ellie he had never been outside of Coldhaven. He had never even known there was anyplace to go. Yet now he could see just how vast the frozen wasteland truly was, stretching on for miles in every direction. And yet even still it was clear that the train had only explored a fraction of the globe's total surface.

During the journey here Joe had never stopped to consider how far he was from the only home he had ever known, but it humbled him to realize that even that was a mere stone's throw when compared to the scope of the system's full scale. The level of engineering necessary to coordinate such a massive marvel only served to underscore the phenomenal capabilities of the world before the Freeze.

Even Coldhaven itself reflected the truly impressive knowledge required to manufacture such a complex system. And yet it was, at least in theory, this same power that had been turned against them either by accident or design. Something had turned the planet into an ice ball, condemning the rest of the world to a perpetual fight for survival. Many back in the city had long ago resigned themselves to the fate they had been dealt. Endless winter had stretched on for four and a half decades with no sign of lessening, and nothing the balloon teams had ever found had provided more than the barest hints of what caused it.

"That's impressive," he said.

Ellie entered another command. "And here are all the tracks in our database." The network expanded significantly, with veins and arteries crisscrossing the world, but even still large areas remained void of any signs of tracks being laid. "All of the information we have is what was present in the train's database when it made its way to the Garden but it was clear from the start there was intended to be much more. We don't know what they built it for but we do know that it started well before the disaster. The tracks were completed in sections, with each country being responsible for its own part of the network."

"This is all very fascinating but what does it mean?" Joe asked her.

Ellie folded her arms. "The train was modified to survive the conditions after the Freeze. Which means that they had to have seen it coming. Now we've always believed that the explanation for what happened was out there somewhere but we've never had access to the entire map of the tracks."

Joe gestured towards the display. "And that's what you think is on that hard drive?"

"Well, there's no way to be certain, but essentially yes." Ellie looked at the readout in the corner of the screen. "I've had the computer crunching away at it since we got back from Coldhaven trying to parse through all of the data we recovered and I think we may have found something."

The polar bear looked up at her. "I'm going to need you to be more specific than that," Joe replied.

Ellie nodded, her ears perked up in concentration as she waited for the system to complete its analysis. It was not simply the fact that the information had come from a military grade hard drive but also the reality that it had been sitting out there for forty years before it had been recovered. A gentle tone reported the information had finished processing, and with a gentle touch of her paw, the display changed once more, adding countless new regions to the train's maps.

Almost as if it had come alive, the new routes snaked through areas the train had never even known were accessible to them. The rail system had gone through every country, every region, across the entire globe. More and more seemed to appear as Joe watched it unfold, stunned into silence at the sheer vastness of the task before them. It had been the train's mission for all this time and yet they had only searched a fraction of a fraction of the total distance it had been capable of reaching.

When at last the process had finished, the maps covered every screen in the room. Information flowed from the hard drive like the vast contents of an ancient library. Searching the car he touched one of the displays with his paw and turned to Ellie. "And all this was in there?" he asked.

"From what we can tell," she replied. "We're still sifting through the information but it'll take us weeks to even begin to understand what we have here." Walking around the room, Ellie looked across the table at Joe. "One thing's for sure, we have our work cut out for us."

"I'll say," Joe agreed.

Ellie quietly stared at the data as the computer rotated through the displays, the maps changing and shifting as different areas appeared and others took prominence. The snowshoe hare lowered her ears and said, "Forty years of exploration and we haven't even scratched the surface of the rail network." The awe in her voice was unmistakable.

He once again considered their offer to go with them. For decades Joe had dreamed of a place like the Garden. The stories his mother had told of the world she had once known had filled his childhood with things he thought he would never see. And yet now that he was here he had no reason to want to leave, but he could not deny the curiosity within him to know the truth.

Joe had never thought of himself as an explorer. He had only left his home to find a way to save his daughter. Yet by that same token it was that very action that had given him a way to do just that. Without Ellie or people like her, Emily would not have made it and he would never have been able to forgive himself for being unable to protect her.

A part of him did not wish to leave his family behind. He knew that going with the train would mean it would be a long time before he would hold Laura in his arms again. But here he was not needed, not like he was in Coldhaven or on the train. Perhaps in time he would find a new role in the Garden, something that suited his talents. He was strong and knew his way around a tool, both valuable things no matter what he chose. Yet he kept finding his eyes drawn to the maps before them.

Ellie joined him on the other side of the table, staring at the endless railways and letting out a deep breath. "I know you're still deciding on whether to go with us or not, and I know it's a big decision. I remember how torn I was when I decided to join the train. My family wasn't exactly supportive of the idea."

"Then what made you decide to go?" he asked.

"I knew that if I stayed here, I'd never be satisfied

with just letting others do the searching. I had to be out there myself to see what was waiting for us," she said. "Besides, it's a hell of an adventure."

Joe looked at the central display and leaned forward. "I can't argue with that."

Ellie turned to face him. "There are things out there no one from the Garden has ever seen." She extended her paw. "So, what do you say? Don't you want to see what's out there?"

ABOUT THE AUTHOR

A trans woman originally from New York, Lauren is a fortysomething zebra with a penchant for hooved creatures, furry characters, and teddy bears. Her interests lean towards science fiction, post-apocalyptic settings, and transformation. Most of her writings usually include at least one of those things.

Known for being a passionate Star Trek fan, she lives with her partner and two cats.